PRAISE FOR CASTLE WITCH

HONORABLE MENTION AWARD WINNER
WRITER'S DIGEST

This book is exemplary in character appeal and development. Dangers and twists work to keep the story moving forward... world building is done well and the touch of romance should appeal to all readers.

—Judge, 32nd Annual Writer's Digest
Self-Published Book Awards

Castle Witch is one of those books I want to read again and again. With a magic system as lovely and fierce as the witch who wields it, author Madeleine Elizabeth has conjured a tale full of action and humor and swoon-worthy moments that will most definitely have you screaming, *"please, just kiss already!"* I fell in love with the cast of characters, most especially Etta and Aeson, the beating heart of this story. Theirs is a romance that feels true and earned; a partnership that resonates with every word on the page. A stunning debut—I will read anything Madeleine Elizabeth writes.

— Nicole Adair, author of *A Tangle of Dreams* &
Voted Most Likely

With a nature-focused magic system so well-drawn you can taste it, sharp and subtle characterization, and a story that feels both gentle and fierce, *Castle Witch* is your next comfort read. Settle in, get cozy, and be ready to gobble it up in a single sitting.

— Joanna Ruth Meyer, author of *Echo North* & *Into the Heartless Wood*

Castle Witch is a spell beautifully cast! It's the tale of a valley under threat, led by a young, benevolent bastard lord who depends heavily on the magic of the only surviving witch in the land. Author Madeleine Elizabeth has crafted a compelling and wholly original character in Etta, a witch who defies expectations in her world and in ours--clever always, compassionate to a fault, and fierce when occasion calls. Fans of medieval fantasy will appreciate the darkly alluring atmosphere of this debut novel, but it's the growing affection between Etta and Lord Aeson Crennly that will keep them turning pages late into the night. Expertly written and deeply felt, *Castle Witch* is sure to enchant readers, and leave them wondering what's coming next.

— Shannon Dittemore, author of *Winter, White and Wicked* & *Rebel, Brave and Brutal*

CASTLE WITCH

MADELEINE ELIZABETH

Hardcover ISBN: 979-8-9877268-6-0
Paperback ISBN: 979-8-9877268-9-1

Book design by Evenstar Books
Typeset in Walbaum MT Std
Titles in Old Dog, New Tricks Caps
Stock images from DepositPhotos.com

Published in 2023 by Extra Extra Publishing House.

This book has been rated

YELLOW

under the Extra Extra Publishing House
Scaled Content Ratings.

It has been determined by the publisher
this book contains a MODERATE amount
of content that may include, but is not
limited to:

Mature language or expletives
Sexual references or innuendos
Substance abuse or exposure
Graphic depiction of blood, bodily harm,
or injury; self-inflicted or otherwise

Extra Extra Publishing House encourages
all readers to practice autonomy in
consuming books suited to their comfort
and preference. This scale was developed
to aid navigation of ever maturing themes,
tones, subtext, and story elements.

For more information on our books please
visit our website at

ExtraExtraPublishing.com

For Jennifer,
My first fan. You're invaluable to this journey.
I'm so glad I haven't accidently killed you.
- ME

Iyl Raed

Gallo
Leohm
Bane
Graelands
Valley
Maer
Crennly
Wind Haven
Erron
Idyllands
N

Valley Maer

Aevic Stow
Maer Hill
Cote Crennly
Crennly Castle
Wind Haven
N

Prologue

H E WAS EMBARRASSING TO LOOK AT. A little lost cub with arms and legs full of muscle he hadn't grown into and eyes that shifted everywhere. He searched the litter of papers on his dead father's desk. His desk now. I was the very last thing on his list, and he looked wary of that fact. The castle alcove where he sat was draped with shadow, making his presence that much more hesitant. Truly too scared to emerge.

"You're meant to be my castle witch?" he finally asked.

I raised my brow and glanced out the arched window to my right. "I believe I'm meant to be dead."

He blew a burst of air through tight lips. "I know the feeling," he muttered, looking down and back up again. "Etaine?"

"It's Etta."

"My father was backing your studies here in the household?"

"To use my skills later." I folded my arms.

He left the chair and walked to the front of the desk. Old Jaeson used to take up the whole seat. His bastard son, Aeson

Crennly, barely left an imprint on the cushion. "I have the impression you don't want to be here."

I pulled my hair over one shoulder, and flicked it back again, hating how my cloud white waves stood out against the blue dress Old Jaeson had required as a uniform. I wasn't here to teach some bastard the politics of war. Our lands and the ones surrounding them had barely finished seceding from the greater kingdom, splitting one country into two. Those loyal to King Faelan had retreated to the south to form the Idyllands. It left us with the rebel king, Leohm, and his newly founded Graelands. Not without cost.

"Would you want to be here if your new ruler considered your kind better off dead or kept as slaves?" I asked.

"Slave? These records describe a well-paid asset."

I gave him a pointed look, something I'd never dared to do before his father. "All the same, the sooner I get out of this valley, the better."

"A twig of a girl traveling alone? You won't get far."

"Bold words for a boy who has only slept within these walls three nights."

He laughed and pushed his lips to one side, stitching a smile closed. "I realize I didn't know him, but I have a sense of why he favored you. The household however, seems less kind on the matter."

I looked at my feet. The staff tolerated me while Old Jaeson was alive, but they'd made their thoughts well known. Taking on a witch, even one without a necklace, was a foolish choice. My people had wreaked their own havoc in the skirmishes of Valley Maer before being burned into nothing. By the time I walked through the gates at Castle Crennly, they didn't even cheer in triumph.

"I wasn't his favorite," I said.

Witches were the first casualty as Idylland's King Faelan attempted to kill as many of us as possible before Leohm could gather us up and use our powers—as if we would've agreed. Leohm decided we were worth the sacrifice if it kept Faelan busy. Early battles were a hunt and a scramble to recruit or remove us as each King saw fit. But we weren't warriors, and fire claimed everyone else in my clan. I escaped, only to be discovered later.

It was my own fault, of course. Hunger made me stupid enough to steal from their traveling wagon. Old Jaeson caught me himself. He took one look at my carry bag of herbs and bones and knew what I was. At thirteen, I'd yet to even assist a birth. Regardless, he acted on an idea the rest of the household considered unwise.

Prilla in the kitchen wasn't so bad. She at least had the decency to look me in the eye, even when I asked for the feet off her slaughtered pigs. Riggs and his stable boys avoided me at all costs. It was stupid, really. If they knew anything about witches, they'd know I couldn't hurt them. Not yet.

Aeson tugged at the collar of his fine new coat and glanced over his shoulder. There was a pile of parchment and records detailing every working part of a castle that'd been thrust upon him a week ago. "You're welcome to read his notes. 'Keen eyes, quick mind, reportedly clever with her tongue, but she remains quiet in my presence.'"

I shifted my weight. I'd made a point not to be clever with the late Lord Crennly. He kept me alive even if he'd brought me here to the farthest corner of the map. He'd even provided what books he could so I might continue studying even if I wouldn't have the necklaces to prove it. It was enough to earn a sense of mourning from me when I heard of the ambush that killed him a month prior. He had been traveling home from the first gathering of Graeland Elder Lords. Everyone everywhere was still adjusting to King Leohm and plenty were still lashing out for wealth where they could find it. That's how Aeson ended up here.

I glanced at him as he paced, pushing unruly hair out of his face and stopping by the window to look out into the courtyard.

"I don't blame you," he said, pulling at his sleeves. "You're not sure you want to be here, and no one else is sure they want you here."

I stepped in his direction, and he nodded at the comings and goings down below.

"Later today," he said, "I have to go down there, and the head guard will hand me a sword expecting me to know how to swing it. As if every bastard is training to gain status under the next king."

No one with any sense of the world expects to be handed status. If Aeson's mother, a mora from nowhere of consequence, hadn't stupidly named him after his father, he wouldn't have been elevated. He wouldn't have been found. Bastards are killed quietly and quickly to remove any threat to true bloodlines. But Old Jaeson had stayed unmarried, and the intellect of Aeson's mother worked in her favor. Now, her son had a castle instead of a coffin.

He turned and offered a knobby hand that was wide and flat. He was only nineteen, but it was clear he'd grow into the same form as his father, with the strength of a wood bear and black hair to match. "I'd like you to stay on," he said. "Household opinions be heaped. I'll continue to fund your studies, but if you still want to leave in a year, I'll escort you myself. We can search for what's left of your people."

I regarded the courtyard first, then his hand. No one believed in either of us. We shared that unfortunate circumstance. Laying my narrow palm over his, we shook left hands and laid the other over our hearts. Keeping our palms flat at first with five fingers splayed, we turned them to fists with our index finger extended. It was the sign of the Innocents. Five siblings. One witch.

When he released my hand, I left the study without being dismissed. A castle cat startled as the door jerked closed and I thought about his proposition as I marched down the hallway.

I could wait a year.

SUMMER

SEVEN YEARS LATER

Chapter One

I WAS SALTING ALONG THE OUTER WALL when Emmaya found me. She emerged from the footpath so unexpectedly I might've taken her for another witch. But it'd been eight years since I'd seen any of my own people, and that was for the best.

Out of breath, sunset glaring behind her, she rested her hands on her knees. "It's Huritt." She named her four-year-old. "His cough will not let up."

Laying a hand on her shoulder, I took long breaths until her inhale and exhale was the same as mine. "I'll be right behind you."

She slunk away and I finished pouring the salt through the dirt, meeting the other end to encircle the castle. They would be home soon, and I didn't want them tracking the ugly wiles of court into the keep. Kneeling at the jointure, I crossed my arms, then lay them flat before the white line.

"Years, fears, and trials on breach; snap the shears, deny ill reach."

I patted the ground three times to seal the spell shut. With my eyes closed, the shiver of energy passed from my core and out through my nails, tingling like toes in cold water.

I could've told someone I was leaving, but when he was away I was hard pressed to care about any formalities. There were still diners in the main hall and Reeve, the castle keeper, might've been there, but I made him uncomfortable, and there was no point in pretending otherwise. All the more cause to slip away unnoticed.

Running to my rooms for my bag and the remedies I would need, I descended back down the stairs and followed the same path Emmaya had taken up the motte. It wound its way through the knotwood trees and came out at the first wheat field. The troughs were freshly planted so I skirted the edge until I came to the houses. Tote Crennly was our closest village, and it lay like a spider. Its eight legs bent away into different fields and the common well stood at its center.

On the east side of the circle was the bakery Emmaya and her husband ran. I slid between the buildings and knocked on their side door, which opened directly into their home rather than the shop itself. Roff swung the door open as the sun kissed the horizon and colored the village bronze. He cradled Huritt as carefully as he'd carry a plate of tarts to the window display.

"How is he?" I asked.

"Restless," his father answered.

Emmaya sat at their hearth, boiling water for tea.

I'd been there when she birthed the boy. His fist was by his head, ready to fight the world, and making his crowning that much worse for his mother.

"Bring him here," I said, pulling jars of sage and bay leaf

from my bag.

Laying him on a cot, I listened to his chest, then his back. Placing my palms flat so I was skin to skin on his ribs, I matched my breath to his and counted the ticks of his inhale. It hitched three times against my hand.

"Heavy congestion," I noted.

Huritt coughed in his sleep. His blonde hair was stuck to his forehead with sweat. "I'll make him a paste and we'll let it set between his shoulder blades for a quarter hour. You can keep the rest to use until he's better."

Together they thanked me and Roff disappeared to check on their older daughter. Emmaya watched him go, then fixed her eyes on Huritt with a line in her brow that said his discomfort was as much hers as it was his. "They'll be home tomorrow?" she asked.

I nodded, taking a bowl from her shelf and grinding the leaves to a powder.

"Bless the young master for taking to his role so diligently. A yearly court convening with all the rich lords of the Graelands? Sounds a nightmare."

"Torture, indeed." I looked up, eyes wide with horror. It was other lords that made me glad no other witches had been found. I hated to imagine what the Elder Lords would do if they had more of us at their fingertips. Some would be used to help them care for their lands and the people like I did. But far more would be paid to do things like souring the land of a neighboring lord or aborting the baby from a secret mistress. The petty and undignified things that only titles could breed.

Emmaya was right. Aeson took to his responsibilities with humility and devotion over the last seven years and the people adored him for it. Clearing her throat, she started again, "I know it's only Fair magic you give us, Etta, but I don't know what we would do without you."

I crimped on a polite smile, and we sat as the paste strengthened with the help of dandelion milk, then rolled Huritt over to his belly. He was a stout little thing but still floppy in his sleep. While the paste hardened on his back, Roff returned with a basket of left-over tarts from that morning.

"The very least we can offer," he said.

"Thank you." I forced the words out. They'd be delicious. They always were. It was the sentiment he delivered with them that made me squirm. I was only doing my job and it never made sense why that deserved extra acknowledgement.

After I'd washed the blending dish, I peeled the crust off Huritt's back and listened to his breathing again. Only one hitch. Smiling, I asked for ink and paper to write down a verse of Free magic.

Leaf for grief at tottering grin; stem relief from strength within.

Finished, I said goodbye and left them with instructions for the remainder of the mixture.

A full moon hung over the trees and the village had gone silver. With everyone abed, I kept to the main road and reveled in the peace of it. Emmaya and Roff were among the few villagers who would actually use my spell. Only a handful of other residents had taken to the idea over the years but in the twilight, I felt its effects.

Magic was so simple. It was everywhere. Humming through every strand of hair, pulsing in the tongues of people born high and low, glowing from the eyes of creatures in the dark. It may be only my kind could harness the Fair and the Fierce, but Free settled within every speck of dust. If I got one thing right, I hoped it was this little village and its people knowing their lives could be better if they just parted their lips and asked the world for help.

They simply needed to know their intentions and follow them honestly.

I was halfway back to the castle walls when my ears began playing tricks on me. Voices sounded on the road, and I squinted through the shadows. It was no trick. His entourage was passing through the village as quietly as they could, sneaking home in the dark. It wasn't like him to avoid the fanfare Tote Crennly would've offered for his return. The gathering, or as I thought of it "the blathering," must've been stupider than usual.

Dropping off the road, I dashed from tree to tree until they were too close, and I had no choice but to hide behind the trunk of an aged knotwood. Its bark was blacker than it was brown. I pulled my hood up to cover my white hair and pale face with the dark wool of my cloak. Most of the party passed without a second glance, but a set of hooves peeled off. It changed its cadence and came to a stop.

"My lord?" a guard called out. "Everything all right?"

"Yes. Just thought I saw something in the field," Aeson replied. His voice was like a river stone scraping over another. "The men are tired. Go on without me."

The rest moved on while his horse, Meadowgrass, snorted and stamped in the gravel at being held back. I rolled my eyes and held my position for another moment. When they didn't leave, I turned carefully on my tiptoes and scraped my cheek on the bark to peek around the far side. Meadowgrass saw me first, shifting her hindquarters around to face me. Aeson swiveled his gaze with Meadow's motion and scanned the shadows.

It was hard to tell if he saw me right away, but a breeze shook loose from the trees. My hood fell away and my hair went with it like the strands of the willow tree. He straightened in my direction, then turned towards the village. The moon lit up his profile. He smirked, the curl of it crinkling the corner of his eye. When he turned back, his irises caught mine for a split second before being taken by shadows again. Shaking his head, he lifted his reins and spun Meadowgrass around.

I watched them go. When their shape melded into the night, I ran back along the edge of the field through the copse of trees and in through the back gate. Stopping at the salt line, I made the sign of the Innocents and exhaled. It was a thank you to Iya, the First Witch and my patron. She'd kept everyone safe while they traveled and returned them with the same care.

Standing in the swell of its shadow, I thought of the time when I hated looking upon Castle Crennly. It seemed grotesque in design because it stood like a chicken's foot that was lopped off right where the feathers would begin. The central tower was four stories and Aeson's chambers were at the top. There was a wide landing where his stairs met the third floor, which housed the study and the rooms for the castle keeper. They rested over the main hall in the central toe. The two opposites were for household operations.

I entered on the northern end through the kitchen's side door. My rooms were directly above it, which helped keep my plants warm in the winter. Old Jaeson had set me there at the start since much of my work crossed paths with the herbs and spices they used. There was a spiral staircase in the closest corner of the kitchen that led almost precisely to the foot of my chamber door. It was meant for servants to reach the second floor with ease, but mostly it allowed me to come and go without notice. The kitchen maids were often too busy kneading dough at the long worktable or stirring something over the stone fire pit to notice anyone dashing from the door to the stairs.

The southern end of the castle held staff quarters on the bottom and guest rooms on top. We didn't receive visitors often. Aeson's bastardship excluded him from the circle of great parties or banquets. I imagined the Elder Lords kept this distance by way of their long noses but I had never suffered an encounter to know for sure. The only real visitor was Aeson's mother and that was never more than once a year.

Despite its location and small size, Castle Crennly had an inner and outer wall to encompass it. Unless war started again, there was little chance of attacks. It was too remote and too tucked away in the eastern region to be significant. Still, Old Jaeson had been militant that only two fortifications would do. Further proof that his original intent for me was far different than what Aeson had asked.

Somewhere between then and now, the stones ceased their imitation of an animal corpse and became a haven. I was alive and safe because of these walls, which was much preferred to the short life I led after my caravan burned and Old Jaeson began plotting strategic moves of his own.

With most everyone in the courtyard welcoming the men, it was easy to creep up the kitchen stairs, toss my bag in my room and carry on to the third floor. His study was the first door on the left. Since taking over, he'd rearranged a little. The left-hand wall still held all the accounts and histories for Castle Crennly but he'd pulled his desk out of the shadowy alcove to put in more shelves for my study books. With all the business conducted here, the room was generally overlooked by the household. There was little to entertain them unless one wanted to brush up on their knowledge of moss or the grain market.

The door brushed open and closed for me without a sound. Setting down the basket from Emmaya and Roff, I ran my hands over the book spines on my way to his desk. Someone had already made it up here to light the candles. Reeve must've seen the group approach from his rooms at the end of the tower and ordered it done. It was just like him to be on high alert. We were due for our annual infiltration of guests as it was.

In his second year, Aeson declared he didn't want the boys on his land to feel embarrassed should anyone ever hand them a weapon. So, when the spring planting was complete, we housed them for three days at the start of summer. They received basic lessons in sword fighting, archery, and horseback. This goodwill was one of the many things that earned him the cheer of a village welcome. Thus, his evening arrival was out of character. I could not imagine why he wanted to sneak home in the dark. Dropping into the chair, I tossed my legs over the arm and sat sideways, waiting.

Voices eventually rose up in the hall, echoing through the stairwell and making their way to the door. I heard him dismiss Reeve and send him off to his chambers. Then he shouldered the door open while holding a handful of letters and came to attention at the other side of the desk.

Lord Aeson Crennly was home.

Chapter Two

"You're in my seat."

"It's better than the others."

"It would be, wouldn't it?" He set his papers down, smirking.

"You've avoided the villagers," I said.

"And you didn't inform Reeve you were leaving." He loomed over the desk. A head taller than me now. "You're going to give him a true flight of panic one of these days."

"Reeve panics when his own hair falls in his face." I shook my head at him. "What happened?"

He rolled his shoulders back. Less of a stretch and more of an anxious tick. He'd long discarded the itchy hem of a wool coat for the simplicity of a linen shirt and closed leather vest but even so, he was uncomfortable as he replied, "My mother will be arriving soon. In addition to our other visitors."

"What?" I lay my hands on the desk, shifting forward. "Why?"

Mother Elma always had a scheme in tow. Something to move

Aeson along further. Something he'd politely act out for a month and immediately abandon when she stopped asking.

She was overjoyed when Aeson got carried off all those years ago, to run lands he'd never even seen. It meant her life as a mora was over. However, King Leohm was quick to inform mother and son that living together was not acceptable. Aeson's new status was not to be sullied by his common mother roaming the grounds. She was put up in a comfortable house near the town she'd worked in and over the years her meager frame became plump in a way that indicated thin bones and a life of recent comfort. No reason for strength when you no longer lift a finger.

I never could decide if allowing her to lord her new privileges over townsmen who used to buy her time was justice for moras everywhere or torture for well-paying men.

Aeson picked up a piece of paper from the pile he'd set down and offered it without meeting my eyes. Snatching it from his hand, I studied it while he walked around the desk and pushed me out of his way. He slumped into his chair with a sigh of defeat.

"This cannot be what I think it is." I hooked a footstool with my toe and dragged it over to flop down beside him.

"It is," he said.

I scanned the list of names. All of them, daughters. "They've changed their tactics? They want to marry you into submission. And your mother is coming to evaluate the candidates?"

He swallowed. "Some of the young ladies have even sent her gifts."

The grumble from my chest was as good as any of our hunting hounds. "Aeson."

He remained silent until I laid my hand over his and looked right at him. Running his other hand through his hair in a habit he'd developed over the years, he sufficiently ruined the part. "Half those women would try to talk me out of everything we've done for the villagers here. The other half are too expensive for me to keep. But I cannot argue with their fathers for another seven years, either."

I bit my lip. Our castle was small but successful since Aeson took over. He'd refused to tax his people any heavier than they already had been, relying on good will instead. Giving up the strategic priorities of his father, he stood firm in the belief that if he took care of his people, they'd take care of him. Every year, the Elder Lords called for levies. King Leohm would only allow it if it was unanimous, which meant they needed Aeson's vote. And he wouldn't budge.

I suppose it helped that I could bless every planting to bring about a better harvest than other lords. "What will you do?" I asked.

He looked away. "Lord Erron has requested a visit. He and his daughter, Calise, will be here shortly after the boys finish their training."

I stared in shock as he gave up his chair and paced the room. Taking a tart from Emmaya's basket, he bit into it as if this wasn't the most suspicious thing the Elder Lords had yet attempted. Gathering my hair to one side, I twisted and turned and twirled it into a haphazard coil beneath my ear. I let it go and stood in front of the desk, picking at my nails.

"It may not be so terrible. Some may even have pure intentions," he said, breaking off a bit of pastry and offering it to me. "These are good, did you want some?"

I ignored him.

"Calise Erron is said to be adventuresome," he tried again.

"They're even taking the way through Wind Haven."

I gaped. Wind Haven was the ravine at our southern border. Its road squeezed through the mountain range that cocooned us and was known for being cold, harsh, and not worth the trial. The only things that survived its narrow cliff faces were the odd goat and a handful of scarlet-scaled basilisks. They weren't terribly harmful. The goats scavenged about and the worst the lizards ever accomplished was slipping beneath one's blankets in the night. Still, that was enough to convince any maiden that making the longer journey to enter Valley Maer from the north was the better one.

"Why would Calise Erron put herself through that for a lord she's never met? Or his mother whom she's had no prior connection with?"

"Even if I had two cherry foxes to wager, I wouldn't presume to guess."

"Better for the foxes. It's insulting otherwise," I said, arms crossed. "This is so odd. You can't actually believe this bears good intentions."

He shrugged. "What if I do? What if they're just as tired of debating as I am and they're offering a peaceful way for us to work together at last?"

"And what if I seduce Garret and become a demure little soldier's wife?" I scoffed.

He picked up another tart and took a thoughtful bite. "Garret knows better than to ruffle your skirts. You're better off with someone who's never met you."

I huffed, snatching the tart from his hand and throwing it out the window.

He arched one eyebrow. "Allow me to apologize."

"Indeed."

"If you truly have your heart set on Garret, you have my—"

I picked up the closest candlestick and charged him. Ducking, he spun about and pulled a chair from the window table as a barricade. I threw the makeshift weapon, but he caught it before it broke against the wall. It was at the expense of his attention, and when he turned around I was there with a book off the table ready to ring his head with its leather binding.

"No, no, no. Not that one!" He jumped back.

I paused to glance at the title. *The Lore and Lure of the Cherry Fox.* It was one of his favorites. He'd been obsessed with learning about them since he first arrived, and he knew I wouldn't dare damage something so precious to him. As I hesitated, he grabbed my wrist and swung me around into his arms. With my back to his chest, he pinned my arms across my belly. I wriggled helplessly. Over the years he'd grown into his muscle, making our scuffles rather unfair.

"Truce." He heaved into my hair.

"No."

"Etta."

I elbowed him in the ribs. "Fine."

He winced and released me slowly, watching my hands for another attack. "To think, I made an effort to return in time for . . . *the season.*"

I crossed my arms. He called it a season, but what he meant was my birthday, which I'd successfully kept secret from the castle. He only knew because he'd made an effort to read every single account Old Jaeson left behind and found it on a forgotten page. "The young men are due in less than a week for their lessons," I said. "You return early for them."

"Of course. You've seen right through me." His head swung around in an exaggerated arc and glanced at me apprehensively. "I do have something for you though."

The glint in his eye caught me off guard, and I gave in to a smile. Rummaging in his coat, he pulled out three leather strands of different colors. Cords of Iya.

I stammered. "Wh—where did you get those?"

"I asked the royal scholar last year if he had any in his collection." He lifted the green and blue ones over my head and left the red on the table. "He's been looking on my behalf ever since."

They were too long, hanging almost all the way to my navel. Pinching them together, I tied them in a knot so they wouldn't be such a nuisance swinging from my neck. Aeson grabbed the silver plate from beneath the room's water pitcher and held it to catch my reflection. He glanced up and down between me and my tarnished image.

"How do they look?" I asked.

He cocked his head to one side. "Like they've always been there."

"What about the other one?"

We looked at it together. Red for Fierce magic. Something I'd never cast because Aeson abhorred the idea and I'd seen firsthand what it cost a witch. Under constant attack at the start of Leohm's war, Fierce magic rendered too many of my people powerless until there was no one left to protect us. The strongest power we possessed was also the one that broke us.

I had one book on the subject, and I'd been brave enough to open it only once. I tried to piece together another way to use it but the memory of my home cart burning to pieces overtook me.

I smelled nothing but charred witch grass for a week and I hadn't touched the tome since. Consequently, I studied enough to master Free and Fair magic but nothing more, which meant the green and blue cords respectively.

If I'd learned from my own people, it would've been a leading witch to give me these once I'd earned them. Because I was self-taught, it never occurred to me to ask for such a favor. Aeson deserved a thank you. I chewed my lip instead.

He shook his head and plucked the red cord from the table. "I'll store it away, for safe keeping."

I nodded with a sigh. "Huritt is sick. I went to see him."

"I trust he'll be better come morning. You wouldn't have returned otherwise, and our castle keeper would be packing his things with haste."

He was right. Had Huritt been any worse, I'd have spent all night with him. It was my job. The one thing he had trusted me with seven years ago when no one else trusted me with anything. I gathered the Baker's basket from the table and walked by him to the door. His hand sprang out and pulled at me. When I didn't fight him, he used his height to his advantage. I had to arch my back to look up at him.

"Aren't you going to welcome me home?" he asked. "It would be the proper thing."

"It would be." I grinned, loosening my hand from his. "Perhaps tomorrow."

I slipped out the door to return to my rooms, hiding in the shadows the whole way there.

Chapter Three

THREE DAYS LATER, on my exact birthday, I sat on the window seat of the study and watched as the farm boys trickled through the main gate and into the front bailey. The corner across from the main keep sheltered the barracks for our standard guardsmen. The stables joined it in the shape of an L but it was devoted solely to all our livestock. To accommodate the young men while they were with us, the great hall became extra barracks. Their voices echoed and shook the floor beneath me as they piled in, greeting each other with all the ego of adolescence. Their training would take place in the back bailey where the yard was long and narrow. This made it better for archery practice and running a horse.

I didn't mind that our young men had arrived the same day I should be celebrating, but when I saw Mother Elma's carriage lurch into the courtyard, I groaned. Holding my breath, I waited until Aeson had greeted her and led her inside. Then I left the study and took off towards my rooms, braiding my hair to the side as I went.

My chamber had three distinct spaces. The main room was rectangular excepting one corner, which offered a round bay of windows that looked out onto the fields. Benches of two different heights encircled the nook. They were filled with ferns, herbs, and flowers. More benches with more plants ran under slender windows along the length of the outer wall. They wanted for sunlight but not exposure.

The other half of the room met a different set of needs. Its innermost wall had shelves upon shelves of remedies, dried herbs, powders, oils, and other trinkets of nature I used most often in spells. There were two worktables as well, one tall and one low, with stools to match.

At the far end of the room was the door to my sleeping quarters, the smallest area of the whole spread. I needed little, so the room held no more than my bed, a side table, and my dressing chests. Rather than retreat to its privacy and avoid Mother Elma altogether, I went to the lower of my two desks and found a spool of thick red thread.

In my circle of windows, I faced the east and cut three equal strands using the knife from my belt. I pricked my finger next and wove them together in the warm summer air, muttering a familiar bit of Fair magic.

"Threaded breads, braided ties; ease the son from mother's sigh. Strand in hand and duty find; watchful bear, ever mind. Weave, cleave, ambition fit; string the knot, on blue respite."

Aeson didn't need much protection, but I knew from years prior how Mother Elma would wear him down over the course of her visit. Securing one end, I made a loop on the other and left my rooms again.

He was back in the training yards already. Arms crossed and shoulders hunched as he oversaw the organization of it. Reeve sat nearby, writing names and ages and occupations down as the boys introduced themselves. There was little change from year to year, but sometimes an absence indicated difficulty at home, and Aeson liked to know.

I stopped at his right shoulder and looked over the scene with him. The boys who knew each other from years past joked and jostled about. Some of them swung swords and tried to recall what they'd been taught.

Aeson cleared his throat with a soft tick. "How is your day?"

Rolling my eyes in his direction, I replied, "It is fine and uneventful."

"Just as you like it."

"Precisely." I turned and pulled his right hand into mine. Wrapping the thread around his wrist, I tied the ends together and laid his palm over his heart, covering it with both of mine and repeating the words I used upstairs. I finished by turning his hand over and tapping its center three times.

He was frowning when I looked up. "She is my mother, not a demon."

I begged to differ but held my tongue. "You say that every time she arrives. Then you are fatigued for a whole shift of the moon when she is gone. No doubt she has at least one complaint already."

His eyes wandered off and he fought a smile. "When you weren't in the courtyard at her arrival, she asked if I'd finally released you from your duties."

I shook my head. "She thinks I have too many freedoms."

"You do," he said.

Someone echoed his sentiment. Garret, our head guard, had joined Aeson on the other side and chimed into the conversation.

Making a face at them both, I wiggled my head at Aeson. "I don't see you proposing any restraints."

"And deal with your pranks for the rest of my life? I think not."

"Then send me away."

"You'd cause another war before sundown. I'm doing Leohm a favor by employing you."

Garret snorted and leaned around Aeson's frame. "He does his king a favor and punishes the rest of us."

I made a grandiose show of curtsying. "Let me beg your forgiveness."

"Stop that. Stand up." Aeson waved a hand at me. "No one believes you as it is."

"Well, I'd hate to give them the wrong impression," I said, jerking my head towards the crowd of boys.

Garret chuckled and walked off to correct a young man on his sword stance. When he was gone, Aeson moved closer. "Your general impression scares most of them as it is." He tugged on my braid. "Your mind is too quick."

"Then they show their insecurity. Only a little man fears an educated woman."

Aeson looked back at the farm boys. Most were younger than he was when he took over the castle. "Yes, they are little."

I tipped my head to the clouds and when I returned my gaze, he was smiling with his black bear eyes fixed on my reaction. Shaking my head, I turned to take my leave, not bothering to ask for it.

Aeson put a vice grip around my wrist, pulling me back to

face him. His lips pushed to one side, hiding his laughter. He flicked the end of my braid into my face. A few years ago, it would've tempted me to pick up a training sword and swing it in his direction but I had stopped sparring with him when even his lightest hits began to rattle my teeth.

"Reeve," I called. Our castle keeper was hunched over his papers, scribbling furiously. This was the only stance I ever saw him in. He could walk the halls that way without any difficulty, even while pushing his spectacles up the bridge of his nose. "Inform Lord Crennly I'll be leaving for the rest of the day. And welcome him home for me, as well," I said, glancing at Reeve. He studied us, deeply confused since I stood there shackled by Aeson himself.

"My lord?" Reeve asked. His voice was constricted like he was forever afraid to breathe too deeply.

"Ignore her," Aeson ordered. To me, he leaned closer. "I'll have a cake ordered for you when you return."

"I'll eat it atop your grave."

He broke first, laughter erupting from his belly. Turning me by the shoulders, he pushed me away before the first official training began. I passed through the undercroft that led from the back bailey to the front, our main courtyard, dragging my hands along the yellowed stones and over the pillars. The castle was at ease. It was always better when he was home. It made our world whole.

At the center of the courtyard was our black alba tree. I planted it five years ago as a grounding point for the castle. When called for, I would smudge and sweep everything out from inside and bring it to the alba roots for cleansing. And if anything called for cleansing, it was a visit from his mother.

Laying my right hand on the bark, I closed my eyes and asked its roots to come alive, and to seek strength from our grounds and keep everyone well-tended in the coming days. We would need it. Castle Crennly had never seen so many guests back-to-back, and the last thing I wanted was our home to be depleted of all that kept it steady.

With a heavy breath, I reached up and snapped off some weaker branches, in need of pruning regardless. I bundled them in a swatch and walked out the front gates.

Our outer grounds offered little in the front, but turning right, I followed the slope down towards the stream that ran through Valley Maer. At our walls, a snye broke off and wound around the east perimeter. I fanned the branches through the air as I passed by the back gate, the gardens, and the orchard. Across the tiny footbridge was the castle's wheat fields. There, I hugged the edge and walked south.

Reaching the end, I turned west and headed to the next corner. At the divide between wheat and barley, I heard bleating. I stopped and held a hand above my eyes, tucking the alba leaves in my apron pocket. Three lonely sheep were drinking at the water's edge. With no sign of their shepherd, I made my way to them. They greeted me happily by biting my skirt in search of grain.

"What are you up to wandering off this way?" I asked, crouching to pet their skinny snouts and kiss their heads. Scooting behind, I ushered them through the gap that separated crops and cut alongside the front of the castle to the road. With a pat on the butt each, I sent them down the hill towards the village and hopefully, their herd.

Back up in the courtyard, I entered the stables and found Riggs. He was the head hand now and the one who oversaw the castle's livestock. He was cleaning the harness from Mother Elma's carriage horse but looked up when he heard me.

"We're not keeping sheep this year, are we?" I asked.

He shook his head and put his work down, rubbing at one of his forearms. "Not since Lord Crennly decided he wants ducks on the winter tables instead."

I frowned. "I thought not. There were three wandering our back fields just now."

Riggs shrugged. "It happens. They're animals, not soldiers. The village shepherd will collect them."

"Very well." I stepped a little closer to examine his arm. "What's bothering you?"

"It's nothing," he said, going back to the leathers. I didn't argue but I spied a line of spider veins on his arm and shook my head. Riggs was not old enough to have his blood slowing in such a way. I walked off towards my rooms to make his remedy before it was too late for his request.

Stopping in the kitchen, I lifted some fresh blueberries from their stash. Mashing them with lavender oil and the greens of a carrot top, I let it set while I wrote a verse of Free magic specific to Riggs. I brought it back down with instructions on how to apply it with a fold of linen boiled in hot water. He took it and mumbled a thank you.

I returned to the back fields once more to finish fanning the air. I'd have to sweep the castle once all our guests were gone for good, but the alba branches would keep anything too dismal from settling right away. Satisfied, I dismissed myself from my duties and went back to my room to hide.

My door swung open after dinner. I was looking out the window, but I knew who it was. Only one person in the castle opened the door to my chambers without knocking. He was the only one who had a right to. It was probably the only lordly power he truly made use of.

"You know I can't let you skip dinner when House Erron arrives. It'll be seen as impolite," he said.

"What a terrible perception that would be." I kept my eyes fixed on the fields.

He came to rest where the curve of the alcove met the long wall, leaning against the joint. "Your hair's blue."

"Is it?" I looked down. "Oh. Blueberries. Riggs needed a fomentation."

"Just like you to fixate on work and not notice your own hair." Having barely settled, he kicked off the wall and dragged a stool over. Next, my water bucket for the plants. Once he was seated, he lifted a hand to my chin, inspecting my hair.

"How are the farm boys?" I asked.

"Still in good spirits. I suspect tomorrow will tire them out."

"And your mother?"

"Elated to have a proper young lady in the castle soon." He unbraided my hair and ran his fingers through it before retrieving a washcloth. Focusing on one small clump at a time, he wiped the blue out.

I recalled the first time he offered to dress my hair. It was shortly after I had changed my mind about leaving but the castle maids were still reticent to help me with anything. I was about to crop it off entirely when Aeson came across me at the stream, hovering over my reflection. Having been raised in a house of moras, he was familiar with the plaits and braids I hadn't mastered on my own. The maids eventually came around, but if not for him, my appearance would've become quite feral for a time.

"The castle will shift," I worried aloud. The thought spread across my mind and pushed against my ears. Energy shifts were as unpredictable as the people they followed. They could be good as easily as they could be bad. "It has never had a woman of status walking its halls."

He kept my hair in his hands, running it through his left and cleaning with his right.

"Aeson?"

He dumped the water out among the driest of my flowers and came back to my side. "We have you to keep us steady."

"And if the Lady Calise doesn't take to the idea of a castle witch?"

"Then we'll entertain the next young lady until we find one that does."

My ribcage shook. It had been years since the war. Years since witches were burned to ash in their home carts. Plenty of people had forgotten the fields we'd destroyed for the sake of strategy or protection. But a handful of others hadn't. Others included land-owning men like Lord Erron, and it was anyone's guess how they spoke to their daughters about a last surviving witch and the bastard who sheltered her.

Aeson was taking a risk on both our parts by playing a gracious host to someone who had probably cursed his name during last year's gathering. Despite my obstinance, Aeson ensured I had a safe and easy life. Not that I couldn't survive on my own. Certainly, it would be easier than when I was thirteen, but Castle Crennly had become more solid to me than my witches caravan had ever been.

"Nothing is decided yet," he said. "We will have to wait until they arrive."

Chapter Four

ARRIVE THEY DID. Ten days later, the tower trumpets sounded. From the southern tree line, a carriage drawn by four dapple greys emerged. It was flanked by two dozen riders. Aeson was wise to have them arrive after the farm boys departed. Otherwise, Castle Crennly would have overflowed, and we'd have had to slight some of them into staying at the village boarding house.

Ahead of the group rode a man with a straight back and a crooked front tooth. His heels pushed low in his stirrups and his chest puffed high, causing the grey in his hair to look as if it was falling off his head. He entered the front gate alone, followed by the Lady Calise's carriage. A pretty prize in tow.

The heads of staff lined up beside Aeson and Mother Elma to greet them. Lord Erron, Calise's widower father, introduced himself to Elma with all the courtesy a man of his status was trained to give. I couldn't help but notice the extra flutter Mother Elma gave as she dipped her curtsy, just like I couldn't help but notice the twitch of her eye when he informed Aeson he would only stay for a week before departing back home. For reasons unknown, he was happy to leave his daughter behind and let Elma chaperone.

I lingered only long enough to be introduced in the lineup and watch Calise sink before Aeson as he kissed her hand. He welcomed her to Castle Crennly while her eyes roamed his face instead of the grounds he described. She was sweet enough, with auburn hair pinned back for the journey and a simple green kirtle with white stitching.

"I hope Wind Haven didn't tire your party," Aeson told her, releasing her hand.

"Not at all my lord." Her voice barely carried across the breeze. "It was wonderous to see the wilderness in its grand state."

Mother Elma cleared her throat. "We're delighted you made the journey. We hope the north fulfills every whim of your heart. Our castle is honored to host such a beautiful young woman."

We. Ours. I dropped a curtsy as a means of slinking behind the crowd and spun on my heel to march off in search of fresh ginger. I needed a solid chunk wedged in my cheek to keep the nausea of what I'd witnessed at bay. Under the shadow of the kitchen's side door, I glanced back to look them over as a match while a stable cat rubbed against my legs.

Calise was a bit shorter than Aeson. She was faint in the chest but wide in the hips. It would give her easy births, but nursing could prove difficult, especially for a girl unaccustomed to the harsh weathers of the north. I shooed off the cat and my thoughts and slipped away.

Not long after I returned to my workroom there was a knock at my door. A guard from the Erron party. He had stood over

Calise's left shoulder. Up close I saw he wore green trim along his cape, distinguishing him as a personal guard assigned to Calise and not Lord Erron.

"You're Lord Crennly's castle witch?" he asked.

I swallowed. The title grated on me even if it was informal. Aeson would never claim it himself. "I am."

"Lady Calise asks if you have any peppermint to freshen her room."

Against all intentions, my brow furrowed. It was a strange errand to send a guard for and surely our maids had placed flowers in her rooms to scent it for her stay. Mother Elma would've harangued Reeve over the gesture. When I didn't move right away the guard rolled his shoulders back and started again. "She's not fond of sweet florals."

"She prefers the good herbs?" I folded my arms. He nodded, and I rummaged along my window shelves, digging for the pot of glossy green leaves. "Not the delicate request I'd expect from a young woman, but she can keep this for her stay."

He bristled. "You'd be mistaken to carry such a judgement. Lady Calise is more resilient than she appears."

Passing the peppermint plant to him carefully, I nodded. "Please, take my apology. You surely know better than I could. How long have you been her personal guard?"

"Since the lady was fifteen."

If memory served me and Reeve's histories were correct, that was when her mother passed away and Calise became the only heir to their lands. Lord Erron was still young enough to impose himself on another wife, but he hadn't. Anyone Calise married would inherit the Erron lands upon her father's death, so why bring her to a lord of low birth?

It was equally unusual to assign someone so young to a lady's personal guard, but it wasn't unheard of. He must've been barely twenty when he took the assignment. I looked back at him and shook the hair out of my face. "And what is your name?"

"Berrin."

"I'm glad to make your acquaintance, guard Berrin. Do not hesitate if there's anything else Lady Calise needs during her stay."

He bowed, and I took the opportunity to study him as his gaze was averted. There was not a speck of grey in his hair, and the skin along his neck was still taut with youth. He might've been closer in age to Calise than I first thought.

"You must be well esteemed by Lord Erron for him to trust you with the protection of his only child. A daughter, no less," I said, watching his reaction for subtle flickers of anything suspicious.

Berrin swallowed hard, unsure of the compliment. To that, I could commiserate. It was less than one moon ago I sidestepped Emmaya's accolades myself. Anyone born outside noble approval was not expected to earn it.

I offered a smile. "I didn't mean to make you uncomfortable, guard Berrin."

Berrin shook his head. "You didn't, ma'am." And with nothing else, he swept out the doorway and down the hall. I stared after him, wondering after his demeanor as Aeson came up the back stairwell.

"Are you going to ask me for peppermint too?"

"No. Why?"

I shook my head, deciding against any jest that he might be looking to please Calise or her elegant neckline. "Nothing. What are you here for?"

"I was checking on tonight's banquet. Laken burned herself putting pies in the oven." He explained, naming our most senior and most clumsy kitchen maid. Taking a deep breath, I nodded and reached for my burn kit. Moving by him, he stopped me with a pull at my apron strings. "Where were you when House Erron arrived?"

"I was there."

His face came together. "I didn't see you."

Of course, he didn't. Ever since her first visit, I laid it down as a personal rule that any time we assembled I placed myself as far away from his mother as possible. I yanked the apron strings from his hand and flicked the ends at his fingertips.

I lifted my shoulders and gave him an innocent smirk. "I was there."

The banquet meant I had to dress nice for dinner. A punishment imposed only when Mother Elma haunted the halls. After changing into a smoke grey shift and a black kirtle to contrast my eyes, I called for a maid. The stitching of the over dress was plain, but if my hair was braided to match, it would appear as if I put in real effort. Work smarter, I say.

"You carry your knife to banquet even with guests?" Layla asked, bustling about my waist. It seemed imperative to her that the string at my back lay in a perfect knot. She was six months new, but I preferred her to the other castle maids. Stringy brown curls framed a narrow face over an even more narrow body. From a distance she could be mistaken for meek, but her gaze demanded otherwise and that made it easy to be myself in front of her. She lacked the caution other girls in the castle wore about themselves like oils behind their ear.

"Certainly," I said. "This way they'll talk to others and not to me. That's the goal."

She shook her head and finished her fussing. "There. Fine enough for even Mother Elma to be pleased."

I whinged. "Maybe we should rip it off and start anew."

Layla folded her arms, as stubborn as her curls of hair. She flapped her hands at me as if cooling a hot loaf from the ovens. "You're forever prickly, Miss Etta."

"It's just Etta," I corrected.

"With respect"—she dropped into a low curtsy—"you're Miss Etta to me."

I quirked an eyebrow at her and walked to the wooden seat in front of my mirror. "You don't mind a prickly disposition?"

Layla laid her ribbons aside and stood behind me, draping my hair across my back. "I've met real evil. And no offense, Miss Etta, but you're not it."

The distinction made my heart warm. Most people are spared true encounters with malice or wickedness. It said much about their character if they truly saw me as dangersome. As she began to braid, I cleared my throat. "And where have you met this evil, Layla?"

She stuck a clump of hair in her teeth and started a second braid using the whole of the first braid as the center of the next, weaving separate sections above my left ear. Speaking slow, she explained. "I held a different station before this. Do you recall the laundress next to the boarding house?"

I nodded. The building was recently abandoned. Its roof had sunk in, and its cloudy glass windows had been reclaimed by the villagers.

"The laundress herself was a lovely woman. But she was

rather worked to the bone because her dear husband—Brothers and Sisters watch over him—couldn't work. He had an injury from the war and couldn't stand or sit comfortably to stir the waters anymore."

The drop of her voice and the silly shake of her head told me the launderer was perfectly capable of sitting and standing, just not stirring.

"Laundress took me on to help in his place and as it turned out, her husband was just fine so long as a girl would consent to her knees for his discomfort."

I lowered my jaw and ran my tongue over the sharp bumps of my back molars. "You don't strike me as a consenting young woman, Layla."

She betrayed a tight-lipped smile and focused on blending the second braid into a third. "It doesn't stop some men from trying, does it?"

"No. Not always."

"On about it," she sighed. "He needed something off the top shelf in their cupboard one day and asked me to fetch a ladder." She lifted her shoulders high and dropped them again. "I'm no carpenter, though. I thought those saw marks on the top rung were supposed to be there. Poor man fell and snapped his neck instantly. I came here to look for work and ma'am Waters remarried a farmer in the west fields. She looked happy when we parted ways."

With a firm nod of her chin, she approved of my hair and stepped back. I turned to take her in after hearing her story and we shared a keen look. Her green eyes glimmered like the scales of a river trout, the slim ones that are hard to catch. Furthermore, when she smiled, her lips parted to reveal a set of fishlike teeth, small and pearly and a bit razor edged on top.

"Is your hair to your liking? Patterns are good for a witch, right? It mirrors the spells you write, or something." She twisted her face up with uncertainty.

"Yes," I said, surprised at her knowledge. "Life and nature are well balanced, so a spell must be the same. It is the reason for rhyming couplets."

"I see," she said. "Then surely Mother Elma will hate it."

Mother Elma, in fact, had been given free rein to style the event, and that meant every fireplace was ablaze and the Crennly Crest hung in every corner. Elma would never risk the guests forgetting who hosted them. Our shield was caelle in style. Its border was green with a blue horse on one side, red bear on the other, both facing a green tower in the center.

Upon entry, I noted the servants pouring wine wore squares of cloth with the crest stenciled in charcoal. Laken appeared and offered me a drink. She had been reassigned to keep her from any more ovens until her hand healed.

"What rotten pox is this?" I asked, poking at the symbol on her shoulder.

"Oh, she marked up as many of us as she could to make the staff seem more extensive. She even instructed us how to pour the wine in just so a manner."

My drink steadied with my stony reaction. She couldn't be serious.

"She'll be lucky if I don't accidentally pour it straight down her skirt," Laken added.

I turned away to hide my laughter as Garret approached. Laken offered to refill his cup but when he refused, she wandered away to find a more enthusiastic drinker.

"Witch," Garret said by way of greeting.

"Guard."

"What do you make of our guests?"

I sipped my wine and tilted my head one way, then the other. "Odd, I'd say. For a group that took the harder path, they don't seem wanting."

Garret bobbed his head. "I've asked why they chose to rush in such a way, and I've yet to hear the same answer twice."

My eyes found his face. He was five years senior to Aeson and had even fought in a few of the last battles before Leohm's War ended. He made it out with only a scar on his left forearm and had taken over when the previous head guard passed from his own battle wounds. It was the same year Aeson arrived, and they'd found their footing together like brothers.

Trust was hard earned with Garret, so I trusted him as Aeson did. Peaceful and patient, he wouldn't utter an accusation without good reason, but he wouldn't assume innocence either. In that moment, the peace in his eyes was dim. He scanned the room over and over, checking for details amiss. His thin lips disappeared completely when he pressed them together at anything deemed suspect.

"Might I share with you an oddity of my own?"

Garret flexed his ear, but kept his face trained on the crowd, which was overflowing with noise and nonsense. Cheers went up as Aeson finally entered. He was followed by his mother who received no cheers but plenty of clinks and gulps as people downed their cups "in her honor." If the hall hadn't been enough,

Mother Elma had obviously set her decorating eye on Aeson too. Dressed in Crennly red, he looked terrifically self-aggrandizing.

I told Garret of my encounter with Calise's guard. He squinted one eye but said nothing.

"What title bred lady doesn't want flowers in her room?" I finished off.

"That is hardly anything. But still something."

The room quieted as Calise entered next, escorted by her father. She looked exactly as prized chattel ought to. Wisps of hair were coiled atop her head and gemstones were pinned amongst the tresses. She had changed her kirtle as well, from green to red, bright enough to match Aeson. The neck swooped from one shoulder to the other over a cream shift.

Stopping at Aeson's feet, Calise lowered herself so far to the floor I worried she might get stepped on when the party started again. Reeve appeared at Aeson's right and offered him the finest goblet the kitchen possessed. He took it graciously and drank before offering Calise the next swell. I leaned over to Garret.

"Could I borrow your hood? I feel an urge to vomit."

"Find your own. I'll be needing this one myself."

Sniggering, I looked back to watch Calise lift the goblet to her mouth. She paused right before her lips graced the rim. Her eyes found Aeson's, and she crinkled her cheeks with an impish grin, then flicked her gaze to someone else and took her sip of wine.

As everyone else raised their glasses and bowed their heads, Garret and I kept our eyes straight and followed her line of sight. Guard Berrin stood across the room completely upright until he noticed us. He dropped his head down at the last second.

Everyone stood once more and I leaned towards Garret again, another question on my mind. But I stopped as one of Calise's maids walked by with a sprig of fresh peppermint in her hair. Looking around at the others, my first question was quickly replaced by another.

"Enjoy yourself, Garret. If anyone asks, someone got sick."

I breezed out the closest door and hurried down the servants' hall up the stairs to the third floor where the guest rooms were. At the door to Calise's room I listened, then knocked. The scrape of a chair came through and an exasperated red-haired maid yanked the door open, keeping the partition narrow. She greeted me politely, but her eyes wandered to the side.

"Excuse me, I'm Lord Crennly's castle witch." Hearing the term twice in one day made me wish for an entirely different position to introduce myself with.

"What d'you need?" Her shoulder jerked as if pushing something away.

Feigning ignorance, I touched my forehead like a featherbrain. "I'm afraid I need a trimming off the plant I gave Lady Calise this afternoon."

While she debated this, I took a breath and touched the wall with my right hand. There was another body behind the door, another spot of life. And no matter how they struggled, the redhead was not letting them into sight.

In my chambers, I sat by the window and rolled the twig of peppermint in my hand, thinking. As Garret had expressed, there was enough of nothing to be something. Something amiss and something unique about House Erron and their arrival. The behavior of their maids only bolstered that observation, but I set that aside and focused on what I could address on my own.

Rolling my neck in a circle, I locked my door and popped the window open with a fist. Filling a small jar with water and placing it on the window ledge, I dropped the trimming inside. Then I adjusted my seat to face the night.

The peppermint quivered in the breeze and moonlight shone off each curl of a leaf. I took a slow breath and focused my eyes on the tiny stalk. Lifting my gaze, I found the moon next and stretched my arms towards it, palms flat and forward.

"Green and gleam the moonish bud; coddle root, till sunny stud. New to brew a minted bone; spark as stars, though light unshown. Stalk from mine, a witch's health; waters lush, share its wealth."

I closed my eyes and took another breath, then flipped my right palm up and grasped the energy glossing in through the window. Splaying my fingers next, I cast clockwise through the air over the jar.

Lastly, I pulled the knife from my belt and cut into the meat between my left palm and the lowest knuckle on my archer's finger. Squeezing out three drops into the water, I sat back and smiled at the little plant. I waited for the energy shift between the sky and the peppermint to complete before I patted my heart three times and carried the jar to a trio of potted love lilies for the night.

From the lower work desk, I took a strip of linen and bound my finger before grabbing a shawl for my shoulders and falling into bed. It'd only been a day but I was well weary of the guests who'd invaded our walls.

Chapter Five

MY DOOR KICKED IN shortly after breakfast was served. I hadn't attended, but I heard the commotion and the laughter as everyone recounted their joys and jokes.

His face was pale, and his eyes a bit too dark. It was clear he hadn't slept enough. I was mid reach for a jar of fermented garlic when he strode in and threw his arms up.

"Did you even attend last night?"

I rolled my eyes. "Of course, I did."

"Did you eat?"

"Mm." I averted my gaze. "I drank."

He crossed his arms and raised his chest while I stepped down from my stool and strolled past him. At my desk, I set down the garlic and reached for eggshells I had swiped from the kitchen at daybreak. Toothaches were common during the cold weather festivities. Too many sweets on too many teeth. A solid supply of garlic would ward off infection, and eggshells would offer strength. Both were a necessary preventative and I liked to be prepared long before they began to crop up.

As I reached for a mortar, Aeson grabbed my wrist and pulled me across the width of my desk. He turned it and selected my bandaged finger specifically. "What is this?" he asked, black eyes hunting my skin for other injuries.

Wrenching my hand away, I pointed to the sprig of peppermint, which had awoken with two fully formed buds. That's what Fair magic does. There's plenty of energy to go around, and the world speeds up for fair trades of it.

"I did not realize our guests liked to be enlivened at every moment of the day," I explained. "I need to grow more if they are going to use it up so quickly."

"What do they want it for?"

I shrugged. "It seems Lady Calise enjoys a sharper aroma over a sweet one."

He didn't even hear me. Instead, his eyes stayed dark, glancing from my hand to my face.

"It's only Fair magic. I promise." I walked to the pot and showed him more closely. "Two little leaves. Cease your worries."

He joined me by the window and examined the little bit of greenery that had pushed forth in the night. "You do not like House Erron."

"I don't care about them." I scrunched my shoulder to my ear but thought better of what I said. "At least, not beyond what hospitality calls for."

Aeson frowned and leaned against the wall. "She's nice. If you chance to talk with her."

"I do not doubt she is." I eyed him. Other than fatigue he was comfortable, so I ventured on. "But there is something curious about their house, and the way they keep their maids."

Straightening against the stones, he asked, "What do you mean?"

I recanted my interaction with the red-haired maid, how after I had explained my request she insisted on locking the door shut to cut a bit off the plant herself. Then stuck only her arm through and slammed it once again after I'd taken hold of the item.

"Perhaps she had a lover with her," he suggested. "If it were one of our men, he probably feared you'd get him in trouble."

"Everyone from our household was at the banquet."

"Perhaps her and whomever else were merely annoyed at being left behind."

"But why were they left behind? To guard their things?"

Aeson balked at this, and his mouth turned down. "Should I be insulted? They don't trust our servants?"

I stepped closer to the window, looking down into the fields. "Lesser men would certainly be offended." When he didn't say anything, I glanced back at him.

He bore a broad grin. "Lesser men? So, you think of me as a great man?"

"That's not what I said, Aeson." I pushed by him and walked back to my desk.

"But it was implied." He followed at my heels.

"Get out of my rooms." No sooner had I breathed the words than shrieking started from deeper in the castle.

"You're the castle keeper, he's your *lord* and *master!* It's your job to know his whereabouts! Find my son!" Mother Elma's voice ricocheted down the hall. I pictured Reeve stammering out a reply under her horrid eye.

"Get out of my rooms," I repeated. "I do not want her in here."

"Say I'm a great man again."

"I never said it in the first place." I grabbed his overcoat and tried to pull him to the hall. "My plants will die if her breath so much as broaches my door."

He squared his shoulders and flattened his boots to the floor, unmoving.

"Aeson!?" his mother screeched.

I shifted towards him, stepping as if the whole floor was riddled with eggshells. When my toes were nearly kissing his, I dripped my voice out like pear syrup. "You are a great man, Lord Crennly."

He pulled away, lashes fluttering. I never addressed him so properly.

"You are undoubtedly blessed with great purpose." I paused to drop my tone. "Like a fertility cycle. Purpose, yes, but generally unbearable. And I never seem to be rid of you."

Turning his head away, he crossed his arms to ward me off and backed up towards the door. "That's nothing I need to know of."

I grabbed his elbow, the framework of his cowering, and shoved it around. It spun him right out the door, which I locked immediately. Right away came a whomp through the wood, shaking the panels in their iron braces. "Iya. You are a witch," he said.

I pictured him slumped on the other side. He was smiling. I could tell by the whisper that protected the word witch. It only sounded when the corner of his mouth was snagged by amusement. After a moment, he sighed, and his footsteps tapped away.

Once my morning work was completed, I wandered down the spiral staircase and checked on Laken's burn. After, I helped stir a pot of ground corn for a mush to be served at dinner. With nothing else to do, the back yards called to me. I found Garret there alone. He was hunched over a bench, inspecting the fletching on a batch of arrows.

He faced away but turned his head as my shadow crept up on his side. "We need to tell Smithwik to find a new fletcher. His work remains steady on the head, but these feathers are ghastly. With the Brothers' grace, Lord Crennly will never set his eyes upon these."

I craned my neck to see, although I knew little about fletching arrows.

Garret dumped the load unceremoniously to the side and turned to face me. "That lot is better off as quills."

"Where is everyone?" I asked.

"Oh, haven't you heard? The whole of the house is taking a tour of the village. Mother Elma wants House Erron to see all the goodwill her son puts towards his people."

"Sisters, she's insufferable." A growl set loose in my chest. "I'm not sure what's worse, hosting a fleet of guests or hosting her."

"Lord Erron remains reluctant to be hosted. He's declined the outing entirely."

"He dared insult Mother Elma in *her own* castle?" I made a face, still embittered over her false authorities from the day before.

Garret chuckled. A raspy sound born from late nights and ale driven singalongs. Sitting beside him, I shared the same curious story about the hidden maid of House Erron.

"That explains why I couldn't count them all last night."

"You knew there were maids missing?"

He nodded and I straightened, laying my palms flat on my knees. I waited for a breeze to swirl by and when it tugged at my hair, I conjured a quick wish. Free magic.

"Whispers, tricks, and maiden hints; wind unwind the peppermint."

"You think you'll get anything?" Garret asked.

"It is too provoking not to try."

A commotion arose from the courtyard, and we turned towards the undercroft. There was a tinkling laughter and the crooning tenor of Mother Elma. Aeson's voice shouted to a stable hand to bring his horse. I wondered if Calise would ride with him to show off her fine upbringing. Mother Elma would surely be in the carriage. Despite her social arrogance, she couldn't ride a horse. I wished she'd try. The old hag could've used a new sort of tumble. Something to knock sense into her.

I scampered away from the bench, whispering through my teeth. "I'm afield and you don't know when I'll be back."

At the top end of the back bailey was a short passage to the galley way between the inner and outer wall, and the field door I liked best to sneak out of. If I reached it fast enough, I could disappear in the tall grasses near the creek. But I had to make it from one wall to the other without being seen. The distance was that of three wagon widths. I stopped behind a stack of grain bags, eyes on the access door. Behind me, there was no scrape of a boot to be heard, only the muffled stomps in the front yard as the group prepared itself.

Glancing one last time, I ran fast and lifted the hem of my dress with one hand. Dipping my head under the archway, I trotted a few more paces before stopping to rest against the cold wall, and a shiver ran through me. Triumph.

"Where are you off to?"

"Poxes," I snarled.

Aeson stood at the door. His elbow rested against it at ear's height, and he had one knee bent as the other braced his position on the slope. The very picture of a casual inquiry. My thoughts bubbled about like the stream at the bottom of the path.

"I need to gather some pears," I said.

"Has the kitchen run out?"

I parted my lips, hoping a lie would reveal itself but it took a moment too long. "Laken," I said. "She had a rash on her cheeks this morning and I need to make her a salve."

"Hmm." He dropped his arm and took a single stride towards me. "That's odd, because Laken just brought out a basket of pastries for us to share with the children below and"—he paused to shake his head and stare me down—"I saw no rash."

"Really?" My voice pitched. "It must've healed itself. Wondrous. I'll just cast a bit of Fair magic to the trees in case it happens again."

Pivoting, I traipsed through the shrubbery and rejoined an established path, heading away from him as fast as possible. Halfway to the creek, he slung me back by my apron straps. His boots were rooted firmly atop a boulder in the ground and one hand clung to the knot at my back.

I slumped forward, dropping my head and shoulders and the whole of my weight into the fabric until I was a show puppet. It was a tactic that worked well when we were younger, and he wasn't strong enough to hold me up that long. I could almost always escape him this way. It left him to carry or cut the strings as he pleased.

Fighting to keep me upright, he elaborated. "Your presence alongside our outing"—he grunted again as I hung heavy like a scared goat—"has been requested by our guests."

I scoffed. "Sisters scorch your tongue if you think I'm going to believe that." Even if it were true, I'd rather fall on my face than face a day with his mother and House Erron's social pleasantries.

"It was me." A frail voice echoed beneath the tree branches.

Stiffening, I reached around and took hold of Aeson's forearm to pull myself up and steady my feet. Above us at the door in the wall, stood Calise. She radiated the serenity of a summer sky in a blue kirtle. Another gratuitous nod to Castle Crennly.

Aeson and I stared at her in surprise, although the left side of his face wasn't turned up in a grimace like mine was. After my shock passed, I pushed Aeson down the hill so I might fold my arms at the damsel of House Erron.

"My lady?" I asked.

"No one else has a castle witch." She pulled a lock of auburn waves over her shoulder and fussed it with both hands. "I would be delighted to see what you do. They claim Castle Crennly only spins because of your spell work."

My brow arched so high my hairline itched. Lowering into an awkward curtsy I turned and gritted my teeth at Aeson. "This is a rich approach, even for you."

Having recovered his footing, he smiled at Calise, then bowed just as low to speak without his words floating too far. "She is telling the truth. Whatever you do, do not speak of fertility cycles again. She's a *lady*."

I fell over with laughter, having already forgotten my ploy to remove him that morning. Cupping my hands to cover the noise,

I snorted through the gaps in my fingers all the same. Aeson took the opportunity to square my shoulders and turn me towards the path again. His hand stayed at my lower back all the way up the hill, passing Calise without uttering a word. With one last shove, I was through the back door and on the way to the carriage.

"There you are," Mother Elma called from her seat, although her face soured when she saw me in tow.

I reached the steps and curtsied to her. "I apologize ma'am, the fault is mine. One of the stable cats died, and I had to harvest the organs before they lost their potency. They're terrific for women wanting to conceive an heir for their husbands." I waited to see her face unfold from horror to hope to doubt over whether or not I was telling the truth. Pleased, I climbed up and sat in the seat farthest from her.

Following one surprise with another, Calise settled beside me. As she adjusted her skirts, she angled her head just so to utter a question. "Is that true?"

I hesitated. Aeson had only just admonished me on the point that Lady Calise was, in fact, a lady. She was the heir to House Erron even if I held deep distrust over their rush to arrive and their hidden maid. But when I caught her eye, it was brimming with curiosity. So, I cranked my jaw about and adjusted my own skirts.

"Not at all." I flicked my sight from Calise to Elma and back to Calise. "I just like to watch her face turn red."

Lady Calise pressed her lips tight against a laugh, and her cheeks puffed like a mouse with a morsel of cheese to hide. Just as I thought the day might not be so dreadful, I was rapt on the head with a set of reins. Aeson glowered at me from his steed and saddle. I ignored him. His mother was already looking elsewhere, unsuspecting of the joke I'd made of her.

Looking to the sky with barely a cloud to offer shade, I exhaled and closed my eyes to the sun's warmth. "I can't believe Garret betrayed me."

The carriage lurched forward, and Meadowgrass clopped slowly beside my ear. "Garret said you were long gone afield," Aeson admitted.

I reopened my eyes to study his face. It appeared truthful. Although, I was not alone in my studies. Calise looked between us.

I shut my eyes once more. "Good man, Garret."

Over the turn of the carriage wheels, Aeson exhaled in exasperation. "Does everyone in the household lie for you?"

A bump in the road rocked our seats, and I smiled. "I believe so."

Chapter Six

A SWARM OF CHILDREN met us in the village. The throng of servants and workers behind us bore the brunt of it as they carried the pastries, spare firewood, and extra blankets from the castle. If I'm being honest, I hadn't made a trip to check on our people since before the farmers' sons had stayed with us.

While Aeson and Calise distributed the treats among chattering mops of hair and Elma oversaw the scene from the carriage, I slunk away to Emmaya's door.

She greeted me with a smile and offered a braid of milk bread with poppy seeds. "Not as good as eating the flower itself but perhaps it'll take the edge off your afternoon?" She said it with a wink. Everyone was well aware of Mother Elma and her wiles.

"How's Huritt?"

She nodded in the direction of the children. Huritt was at the front of the line where Aeson was telling him off from a second meat pie.

"Is there anything else you need?" I asked.

Emmaya shook her head but cast her eyes around the village circle and towards the shepherd's home. "No, but you might take your time with the herder's wife." Her brows leveled out in a dark line across her forehead.

"What is it?"

She shrugged one shoulder. Her simmered gaze fixed across the way. "There's been some talk, and she's been blotchy in the face more than once the past few weeks."

"I see," I said, searching for the shepherd and seeing only his wife, Ellara. She stood in the shadow of their door. On her shoulder slept a nursling, and below that her belly was starting to swell again. I ground my teeth and nodded thanks to Emmaya. "I'll see to it, thoroughly."

I didn't go right away. I took my time moving from each home and shop and checking every resident for ailments, scratches, or bruises. There was a cabbage compress for a new mother, some thyme tea for the boot maker's aging father, and a cinnamon and honey spread for the butcher's son whose joints were too swollen for a boy his age.

"You may eat it with toast but nothing else." I pressed his chin between my thumb and forefinger until he met my eyes. "I'll tell the baker as well, so she knows not to spoil you with many more cakes."

His lips pouted but he acquiesced. As he darted off, I looked to my last stop. I had hoped that taking my time would give the shepherd a chance to appear because most everyone else had come to greet their lord, but there was no sign of him.

"Ma'am Shepherd. How are you?" I asked, poking my head around the threshold of their doorway.

"Oh, Etta. Hello." She sunk into a wooden chair near the door to latch her baby on.

I knelt before her, quietly folding my legs up so as not to distract the flailing daughter in her arms, Kella. I'd attended her birth. Once the girl had drifted to sleep, her chunky arms slumped against the shepherdess's chest. "She's still nursing well, with the next growing already?" I asked.

Ellara put on a smile. "Very well. My milk is nowhere near ready to shift. There will be food for her for some time."

"That's happy news." I glanced around the room, inspecting their shelves and finding them sparser than they ought to be.

Since Aeson gained his bearings over Valley Maer, he'd instructed me to check on Tote Crennly as often as they'd welcome me. I'd taken it upon myself to leave certain things behind like jars of clove pods and handfuls of turmeric. Aeson had also ordered the almoner to send on old dishes as they became too worn for the castle's tables. This way, everyone had the very basics for living. As we came to care for them, they began caring for each other, swapping tools and treatments as needed. But there was near to nothing on these shelves.

Ellara caught my wandering eyes and looked away, smoothing the hair on her daughter's head. "We lost some sheep to hill foxes last month. Nothing to bring to the butcher, so we made do by selling some items."

All their items from the look of it. I nodded with a face of understanding as the other children dashed back from their turn at the carriage. At least they had full bellies that day. One of the middle boys who'd been born before I was any help collided with Ellara's knees and she winced.

When she stretched her arm down to fix her dress and redirect his attention, I glimpsed a bruise over her forearm. Four finger shaped dots, spread evenly. I looked away and cleared my throat. "I'll see if our lord can do anything to mediate this setback for you."

Ellara squeezed out a smile but said nothing. I shifted my seat on the ground to obscure my hand. The show in the village circle was beginning to dwindle, but I had just enough time to unwind the bandage on my finger and break open the slice of flesh I'd made the previous night.

I squeezed out seven drops for Ellara and her children. The shepherd would have to find his blessings elsewhere. Especially once Aeson heard my report. It took three deep breaths for me to find words good enough to protect Ellara without cursing her husband at the same time.

Moving my lips as fast as I could before one of the kids broke into my thoughts, I swept through the couplets.

"*Soiled knees and hunted fleece; wanting needs, recover peace. By mother's ear, herd the time; child patient, youthful shine. Tend the ones with mild look; let wools protect their master crook.*"

I stood and bid Ellara goodbye, tapping my finger three times on the door latch. I headed back to the carriage and stopped at the well for a ladle of water to wash my hand. Aeson's eyes hooked on the action as I rejoined them, but he wasn't about to say anything in front of Calise. It would disrespect his people to air their troubles before strangers.

He sent the servants who'd accompanied us back to the castle and then turned to the driver. Mother Elma had requested a ride through the fields, to see his property. Before we could reseat ourselves in the carriage, Calise swept her gaze over the village. She had sent her guard, Berrin, away with our staff. This left her to be doe-eyed before Aeson without an audience.

"You must have an Altar House somewhere, right?" she asked.

Aeson glanced my way and nodded at Calise's curiosity.

"May I see it?" She flattened the front of her dress. "We have one on Erron lands, of course, but we have no reason to use it. Or even care for it."

Waiting for my approval, Aeson turned his gaze on the eastern leg of road where the Altar House lay in a grove of knotwood trees. I didn't know what to make of Calise's request, but I had no reason to deny her, so I dipped my chin and led the way. Aeson suggested his mother stay behind and thankfully she agreed. She was as uninterested in seeing the place meant for my people as I was uninterested in having her in it.

Despite its significance, I rarely entered the building. It felt separate from me even though this might've been a stop for my caravan before they were burnt to the ground. My elders might have used the statues inside to ground themselves before moving on to the next town. But I was all that was left, and it felt wrong to be here alone.

Still, it was clean and the six round windows were polished regularly. I suspected Aeson was behind that gesture, although I'd never asked him. The doors gave way and with the sun still near midday, nothing shone through the windows. Shadows lay on the walls like moths in rest. I grinned.

Calise coughed beside me, squinting to make out the interior. The statues spread out like a hex. Six fair points, with no leading power. Each Brother and Sister faced one another across an open floor stone mosaic. Moss filled the gaps and wildflowers encircled it all. The farthest to our left was Inger. She was the eldest Sister and the most righteous. According to witches, her anger and rage was the ember that started the world. Across from her stood Aeo, his face carved to be plump with the joy and curiosity he held. At his left shoulder was the Brother Aeden, whose long face mourned everything that came and went. His counterpoint was Iigus, the Sister with the most penetrating brow. She was full of revolt and responsible for transforming the rot of death into new life. Aelus sat in the corner to our right. He was the Brother who feared everything. Time, death, loss, and even hope with all its inherent despair.

Closest to the door was Iya. Her siblings may have created the world, but they had neglected to communicate its ways to the people that lived in it. She was born as a conduit to connect humans to the earth. The First Witch. Or, as my people called her, The First One.

"How does it work?" Calise whispered to me over the bump of her shoulder.

She would have been taught the history lessons. She would know how we traveled from place to place in clans, never settling anywhere. There was no reason to. Nature was more than capable of caring for itself. It was humans that needed help. And that's what we did. Travel, tend, teach, and travel again. In my hesitation, Aeson swept by us and began to speak, starting at Iigus and stepping clockwise around the six points.

"Magic is merely intention. Free is free. That's why anyone can use it." He glanced back at us. "But only a witch can cast Fair and Fierce. Only they are capable of accessing the other layers of power beneath an intent."

"What happens if an ordinary person tries to cast above Free magic?"

I snorted. "Nothing." Glancing her way, I lowered myself in

a half curtsy and explained further. "You can make all the same sacrifices and use all the same tools, but you can't carry the energy the way we can."

Calise frowned and stepped into the circle, trailing Aeson's path. "So, you're like a river, or the current within it."

"I'm a pitcher, at best." I made my way to the center of the room following the patterns in the floor, which were an elaborate labyrinth design that gave each Brother and Sister a path to its center in case they ever lurched to life one day. Not likely. "I can be filled and used to pass life from one place to another. But I can be emptied as well."

Aeson stopped before Aeo, arms folded, and looked to me, then Calise. She cleared her throat. "Emptied?" she asked. "Forever?"

I shrugged. "I don't know for sure. I've never cast in Fierce."

"We don't need it here," Aeson said.

Calise looked between us but seemed to make nothing of our statements. "What is the difference?"

My lips quirked. "Intention, again. Free only needs a little bit of prompting. A simple string of words, or a whisper over one's shoulder. Fair needs more, and Fierce calls for a lengthy spell. The spell must be clear, and the intention honest."

Standing by Inger, Calise turned on her heel and looked at me. "Honest?"

"I can't cast a spell for good wishes if it's driven only by polite cordiality. If you secretly wish for someone's death, no kind spell will ever overtake it. It simply won't work."

"Magic can tell the difference?" Calise went wide eyed. "How do you make any of it work?"

Aeson laughed, the clarity of it reaching the top of the domed ceiling. "The witch writes the spell. And the spell is only as good as the witch who wrote it."

I dropped my gaze to my feet and worried at the cut on my finger until a trickle of blood ran into my palm, but I didn't add to what Aeson said.

Calise was halfway to Aeo's statue when she stopped again, giggling under her breath. "I've heard you are exceedingly clever. You must be very good at writing a spell."

Again, I stayed silent. There was nothing special about what I did. I only considered the person I was writing for and tried to capture their essence with the words I used. Calling a bully of a boy a bit rambunctious served no purpose if, in truth, he was filled with reckless craving.

"I've heard some texts refer to them as Innocents. Why?" Calise asked. "They are responsible for all things good and bad are they not?"

"They are children of power, but children nonetheless," I said. "And we don't admonish children for their natural impulses, do we? They are innocent. It is the grown men and women who are less so."

She smoothed her hair and turned away. "Yes. I see. And you are right. Children are certainly innocent."

The pair of them finished the circuit and exited the door without me, heading back to the carriage. I focused on Iigus first and moved over them one by one with blessings until I got to Iya. For her, I dropped to the floor and made the sign for five and one, then bent in a child's pose and waited for the chill to travel down my spine. In the threshold, I used his favorite expression. "Iya. You are a witch. Thank you."

Chapter Seven

FROM HER SEAT ALONE on the other carriage bench, Elma made talk of the singular beauty of the landscape. But after she misidentified the corn for wheat, Calise stepped in and began asking questions of Aeson such as how to tell a harvest was done and the best way to gather it.

I tuned them out, thinking instead of Ellara again. If her milk shifted too soon and her baby didn't take to the oily premilk that would arrive before its next sibling did, Ellara would need help in the winter months to keep the little girl healthy. If no one else in the castle or village was nursing at that time, we'd have to search out a wetnurse. Not a terrible solution, but not always a time efficient one either.

While we trotted by open pasture, clouds gathered above. Elma predicted weather by the end of the day, but if she knew anything, she'd know the wind was blowing east and would take the clouds away in a matter of hours. I looked across the distance and caught a blob of figures in the field. Straightening, I squinted in the hazy sun and leaned forward.

"Stop the horses," I told the driver.

"What's that?" He turned to hear me better and I shook my head. Standing, I braced myself on the frame and jumped out, eliciting a gasp from Elma and a wide-eyed look from Calise. Aeson knew better. Walking around the back wheels, I crawled through the fence and tromped into the grass, sighting in at the figures one more time. Their voices were indiscernible.

"Go on without me," I called over my shoulder. But again, Aeson knew better. I fell to my knees and placed my hands on the ground. With eyes shut, I asked the blades to tell me what they felt.

The voices that shook them were agitated, and the bodies heavy upon their roots. I sat up again and rolled my shoulders back. I loved speaking to the wind, but I hated calling it. Crossing my arms and placing a hand over the curve of my ribs, as close to my lungs as possible, I pointed my nose towards the faraway scene and inhaled.

Drawing the air to me was a delicate balance. Breathe, hold, turn my chin, release, repeat. The goal was to create a new current strong enough to bring the voices to me, but that meant redirecting it as well.

Once I got a strand running through me, I let go of my torso and lifted an arm in each direction, stretching my fingertips and opening my hands until the air pushed against my palm as a cat would bump their head into it. With a twist of my wrist, I pulled a stronger gust of wind to me on the right side, bending my elbow all the way past my ear like an archer.

I looped the current around my head so it could play with my hair before it slipped down my other arm and back out into the field. Wind always listened better when I gave it something to show off with. Sure enough, it whipped my hair from its braids and shook my lashes as it spiraled around on its way by. Leaves and twigs cocooned me in a cyclone, and I gave it a smile.

"Thank you," I whispered as it gained momentum, the sounds growing in volume.

". . . heaping sun. Good for the grass but . . . Should we move her?"

I cocked my head and tried to piece everything together.

"Calf a'crowning . . . waters too . . . no bucket."

Twisting my arms until they were palm down, I cradled the gust of wind to my chest and patted three times over a lung. With a heavy exhale I returned everything to the pasture and slumped back, resting my hands on my head.

"What is it?" Aeson's voice was low.

Turning around, I saw he had dismounted and removed some of the fencing so he and Calise could join me in the grass. I had to admit, they looked quite noble together. You'd never know only one of them was raised that way. Mother Elma stood in the carriage, blocking the sun with her hand but watching us all.

"One of the milk cows. She is delivering, but she's not well. She needs water or neither will survive."

His eyes danced between me and the carriage, then to Calise. We both knew what we'd do if there weren't guests to attend to. Calise pieced it together on her own.

"We have water in the carriage. Will that be enough?" she asked.

I twisted my bottom lip between my fingers. "Anything would help at this point."

"Well?" She stuck a fist on her hip and looked at us.

"Calving is a messy sight my lady, if you truly don't mind, I'll assist Etta and I'll return quickly."

But Calise had already turned and lifted her skirt to get over the fence. I stood to take a flask from her before lowering myself to Aeson with forced decorum. "I'll run ahead," I said.

He glanced at Calise and offered his arm. "We'll be along."

I didn't wait for him to finish. I took off. Using the last bit of breeze that still sung through my hair, behind my ears, I reached the cow and her attendants in no time. She was barely breathing when I plopped down by her head. The farmer and his son wiped sweat from their brows.

"I saw you as we passed by. What's wrong?" I asked them.

The son answered. He was a stick of a thing, and his trousers were patched at the knees. "She didn't come in when we called them for feeding last night, mum. Thought she might be at the gate for the morning, calf on the teat, but it was none such luck. We come to look and found her like this."

It was too sunny a day for an animal to labor without food or water, especially after spending the night in the same condition. I blew a rush of air out of my lips and waved my hand at her hindquarters. "You worry about the calf. I'll get the water into her."

They set to work as I cupped her grey mouth in one hand and dribbled water along her lips with the other. I pulled her head into my lap to lean over her ear and inspire whatever energy was tucked away beneath her heart.

Her eyes fluttered at my voice. I set the flask down as Aeson and Calise arrived. I acknowledged them quickly and returned to the laboring mother. Eyes closed, I promised the grass I'd return with skins of blood water if they would send their health up through the mother's hide. There was a tickle at my fingers as it grew the tiniest bit to reach her coat and find its way to help.

With a moan, her belly ballooned up and her muscles convulsed. As it settled, her back legs twitched. I offered another pour of water to her, and her body gave another contraction. And another. And another. Upon the fourth time, a gush came from her hind end as the calf spilled out and the sac popped all at once.

Together, the farmer and his son dragged the baby closer to its mother so she could bathe him. I looked up to Aeson whose hand clenched at his side. He was unable to help for the sake of appearances. The calf let loose his first little mewling bellow, and Calise's lips quirked in a smile. She looked from the mother and babe to all of us resting on a blanket of fresh grown greens.

"If anyone deserves a banquet in their honor, it is you, not me," she said.

I thought she was joking but she wouldn't be talked out of it. By the time we returned to the castle she was shaking with ideas and exhausting me with questions over my likes and dislikes. Lord Erron unknowingly came to my rescue when he met us in the courtyard and announced he was leaving a day earlier than intended. Calise's excitement deflated with that one sentence.

"Your banquet design will be lovely. I'll be sorry to miss it," he said, holding her shoulders in each hand. He kissed her forehead and strode off. Calise twisted her neck and set her jaw. Clearing her throat with a delicate tune, she marched off towards her room. Berrin tried to address her, but she waved a hand and kept her head down.

I watched everything from the trough as I rinsed my hands again. When the tumult had subsided and servants from both houses filtered away, I shook off the urge to follow Calise and eavesdrop and opted for Aeson's study instead.

He was already there. His back was to the door as he looked out the window. Between two fingers, he rolled an ebony bristle of hair. A fox whisker. He kept a skinny vial of them in his desk. The collection had taken years to gather. Anytime he went to the fields, his eye wandered to the grasses underfoot. While the hill foxes of the valley also had black whiskers, theirs were short and thick like an embroidery needle. His beloved cherry foxes on the other hand had long wisps that brushed against everything they passed. It is said that's how they gather the wisdom of the lands they live on. The whiskers were the only proof Aeson found that any lived in Valley Maer.

As the lock clicked shut, I thought about opening it again for the sake of etiquette. If Elma knew how often he and I were locked away in this room together in the course of a year, she'd surely faint. Haggard old woman be cursed though, and the opinion of House Erron certainly weighed nothing on my mind.

"The shepherdess?" he asked as I crawled up on the window seat and pulled my knees to my chest.

"I don't know what's at play, but their house is sold empty of wares, and she has bruises on her body."

His shoulders fell and a great whoosh of air left his chest. As I could have predicted, his hand ran through his hair, ruining its part. "We'll send Garret with some fresh wares, and he can inquire softly at the rest of it."

"We might need a wetnurse too if the nursling goes off her milk come snowfall."

He dipped his chin and glanced at me from beneath black lashes. "How's your hand?"

I rolled my head around and looked at him indignantly.

"You used it for them too, didn't you?"

"Yes." I sighed.

"Why the left? Your dominant side is stronger."

Turning up my palm, I used my right index finger to trace the line of broken skin. "The left side aids the mothers."

Setting his precious totem down, Aeson stepped forward and took my hands in his, brushing his thumb over the same line. "Are you excited for your party?"

I glowered at him and slid off the window seat, but he wouldn't release my hands.

"You could talk her out of it. At least delay it. She likes you well enough. And you her, I think." I tilted my head to one side, trying to find his eyes.

"She is hardly fussy in any way," he confessed.

I shook my head. "She is not. She might fit in quite nicely."

He drew in a long breath and looked back out the window. I pulled away, dragging my hands through his. I needed to visit the stables if I was going to bring blood water back to the field as promised. Aeson pressed his thumbs into the center of my palms, as a means of stopping me once more. He pinched at my wounded finger. "This is why I let them lie for you."

Chapter Eight

THE GRASS SANG when I returned the next day. Removing the same fence posts Aeson had, I led my horse, Sparrow, through the pasture to where the milk cow delivered. I walked in a circle around the imprint we'd made and poured the skins out. I thanked the grass and the soil and the wind for sharing its power.

Once the water had sunk deep enough to reach the roots and the worms, I tied the skins back onto my saddle and made to mount up when the thought of Calise's many questions came to me. The more time I spent in the castle, the more time she had to ask about my favorite ear oils or something equally unimportant. I patted Sparrow's neck and told him, "We'll walk."

Pulling the reins over his head, we strolled through the field, rejoining the road which ran central through the whole valley. The stream gurgled beside it most of the way. Sometimes it rushed and sometimes it flowed as gentle as a butterfly's wings. As we passed the white willow, the landmark for Tote Crennly and a favorite spot of the villagers, Sparrow tossed his head and blew air from his nostrils. Following the turn of his nose, I saw Ellara's husband asleep beneath the willow wisps. A shadow among shadows.

Tying Sparrow to the closest fence, I parted the leaves and stood over the shepherd. He was long gone in a dream. His crook was nowhere to be seen nor were his sheep. Again. There was no bottle nearby and when I bent to sniff at him, there was no hint of ale either. I put my hands on my hips and looked about, deciding whether to wake him myself or call a hill of ants to do it for me. Not wanting to disturb their industry, I left the ants alone and kicked the shepherd's boot. He started with a cough and scrambled into a sitting position.

"Your flock seems to be missing," I said. "Or are you no longer a shepherd?"

He took me in. I saw the recognition on his face. "Ah. Castle witch. What should I help you with?"

"How abouts your lord and master? You could help him by returning to work."

"Eh." He twitched half his nose and mouth at the same time and waved me away.

"We visited your wife and children yesterday. Your home appears in dire need of replenishing. We'll be by again soon to bring aid, but if you don't find your flock, you'll lose the one under your roof. Consider it a warning."

"Very well." He slumped back to the ground and lay an arm over his eyes. "You've delivered your threat, castle wife. Be gone and leave a man to his well-earned rest."

"Well-earned, is it?"

"*'Tis.* Like that little bastard lord on his hill. Do you help him with his rest? Does he earn that or pay extra for it?"

I rolled my eyes. It was not the first time I was accused of being Aeson's pet by men who couldn't comprehend how to unify towards a singular goal like the success of our lands. In the shepherd's case, marriage.

Glancing at our surroundings, I pondered how much energy it would sap from me and the tree to have the strands of willow leaves hang him upside down for a spell. But I settled for the road, leaving him to his nap and his grave digging. His consequences would be more fun to watch if I kept my hand off the spade.

Mounting Sparrow, I pointed his nose to the castle. Behind me, the shepherd called out again. "Oy, castle wife. Tell the bastard I swore allegiance to his lonely father and not to him. If he wants to quit me for a new shepherd, he'll have to dig up Old Jaeson and hope the man can still speak."

Nudging with my heels, I asked Sparrow to gallop the rest of the road. We swerved around the back of the village and straight up the hill into the courtyard. I needed to do something with my hands before I galloped back and wrung out the lazy sop. Dismounting inside the stables, I pushed my hair back, exhaling with a growl and pacing around the barn.

"Ah! Witch Etta. Just who I wanted to see," said a voice.

"Lord Erron?" I turned, surprised to see him dirtying his boots as he sauntered down the alleyway between stalls, paying the muck no mind.

"I'm leaving in three days' time, I'm sure you've heard."

I dipped a curtsy. "Yes, my lord."

"Might I trouble you for a draught? Something to ease the aches of traveling through harsh territory at my age?"

Distracted by thoughts of the shepherd, I stared at him

stupidly for a moment, lowering and lifting my jaw until I came back to the moment. "Of course. Nothing too strong, I presume. We can't have a lord tumbling off his horse in the day, right?"

"Oh no, no. You misunderstand me, my dear. Something to comfort my sleep. I can no longer bear the hard stone floor as I did when I was Lord Crennly's age."

The request was odd. Lord Erron must have surely had piles of furs and cushions for the first journey through Wind Haven. There was no reason not to bring them along on his return home. But the desire to have one less stranger within our walls urged me on.

"Yes. I see," I said, bending in a curtsy to signify my departure. "I shall have it for you the morning you depart."

"I'll need it tomorrow."

My knees popped as I stood up again. "My lord?"

He straightened the sleeves of his shirt and cleared his throat. "No offense, witch. I hear tremendous things about your abilities. But if the strength isn't to my liking, I'd like time to have you brew it again."

"Of course." I dropped another curtsy and rushed away before he could ask me anything more. I didn't want anyone else to approach me. There were already enough questions and curiosities and requests in my head and there was only one place I could plant them.

My garden was east of the outer wall, down the slope, and close to the creek. Everything else belonged to the castle kitchen. But this square of soil and earth was solitary to me. The plants I couldn't grow in my windows grew here. Flowers, weeds, herbs, roots, and a handful of spell-ridden parchment all lay in these grounds.

Pushing the tiny gate open, I collapsed in the center. Bent, belly over knees, I folded my arms beneath my head to make a pillow of my forearms, leaving a gap to breathe the cool air straight off the earth.

Mother Elma. Peppermint in hair. Secret maids in rooms. Hurried arrivals and hurried departures. Sleeping draughts. And worst of all, a banquet in my honor. If only I'd a fertility cycle due to be indisposed with.

Inhaling and exhaling on a rhythm, I imagined myself sinking beneath it all. My flesh and cold skin would shred to pieces for worms to devour. My energy would thread through their stringy bodies and return to the soil. Garden roots would snap my bones in half to suck the marrow out and run it up into the lilies. Pretty soon, the tickle of plant tendrils reached me, creeping through my hair and slipping along my ankle.

"Take it," I muttered. "I want to be done for the day."

With that, my shoulders pulled to the ground and my spirit stretched in all directions. The sensation was that of ants marching from a hill if the hill was my spine. My hair was tugged into the green stalks and a thorn cut into my calf as the briar circled up my leg. Fair magic was a fair trade. Some of these plants would be consumed in powder or drink, and it was only right that I let them drink from me when I could spare it.

"Miss Etta?"

I gasped and wriggled free, hooking my chin over my shoulder to see Layla at the gate.

"I'm sorry. I was sent to call you in," she said, rubbing the cracked wood with a thumb.

"Of course. What now?"

"Lady Calise wants to know what you think of table settings."

"I think they're better suited to her eye, not mine." I shook my head, catching a pair of sparkling black orbs behind the leaves of a potato plant. "I'm sorry, Layla. I'll be right there."

She nodded but watched on as I reached out and waited for the garden snake to coil around my fingers. A female. Young and not ready for snakelets. Steady in my palm, she lifted her head to mine.

"Make sure the stable cats don't see you," I said, tapping her nose with my pinky finger and setting her back down.

Layla held the gate open and latched it before trailing me back up to the wall. "In the great hall," she said, peeling off to help in the kitchen.

I made my way alone, eyes droopy, heaving a sigh before pushing the doors open. Aeson had managed to put the event off for a week, but Calise wouldn't waver any more than that. In the echo of the high ceiling, a table had been laid with three different settings. Calise was bent over them, switching her head from side to side. Berrin stood by the wall, silent as ever.

"There you are. Please, tell me how best to celebrate your talents."

Stifling a yawn, I perused the options and selected the simplest one. "Celebrate the food for me, Lady Calise. The finery is just a prop, and the staff will take more pleasure if they don't have to polish anything."

She thought for a moment, running her long hair through her clean fingertips. "I suppose you are right."

I hid another yawn and gestured towards the end of the house. "If you encourage our cook to make something she loves best, it's all the celebration I need. It honors the castle and the village and all the peoples who take part in it."

Calise turned to face me. The corners of her mouth turned down with her thoughts. Her eyes scanned me from top to bottom to top again. "They say your ways are unusual, but I've only heard sense from you and Lord Crennly since I arrived."

"They?"

She heaved and flipped her hair back over her shoulder. "The lords and ladies of Leohm's court. He does not keep it the way they do in the Idyllands. But we take and send letters all the same. I've heard how Aeson denies their calls for new taxes and levies. He is known as a bit of a renegade at their gatherings."

It was the first time I'd truly spoken to someone on the other side of the argument. Everything at Castle Crennly made sense to me because it followed the natural order of the world. I fed the garden so the garden would feed me and my spells when I needed it to. Aeson fed and clothed his people so they were strong enough to work when the fields called. He may not have been raised to carry a title, but he knew well how to carry responsibility.

It occurred to me that Calise had more insight to the courtly world than either Aeson or me. She was raised in it. She saw the war start and end and watched a whole new kingdomhood take hold. She knew what men were like on both sides of a regime. It was only because her father was part of the yearly gathering that we were entertaining them at all.

If Lord Erron was one who agreed Aeson was a renegade, there was even less reason to rush up through Wind Haven for a visit. And no reason at all to trust a young, unmarried lord with his only daughter alone.

"Will that be all, my lady?" I asked.

She took her time answering but said yes all the same.

As I departed, the kitchen maids blocked the doors open

to begin setting up for dinner. Sidling by them, I climbed the stairs to my doors and slid the lock shut once I was inside. Then I stumbled to my bedroom and ripped off as much of my clothes as I could before falling into my pillows.

It was a click, click, clicking that woke me up that night. Accompanying it was the scrape of a claw on glass. Rubbing my eyes clean of sleep, I fumbled out from beneath my furs and yanked the door open from my bedchamber to the workroom. The noise led me to my casting window.

An owl swooped in when I opened it. It was barred and tiny and precise as it flew to my tallest desk and landed in the middle. His talons tapped quietly as he shuffled around the parchment, turning to me in the dark. I walked forward and bowed my head. "You should be hunting, sir."

He turned his head all the way around as if confirming we were alone. When his beady eyes, encircled by plume spectacles, focused on me again, he ruffled his feathers and wrestled with something at his feet.

Squinting through the night's blue glow, I plucked the object up with no opposition from him. It was a dead mouse. An infant. Pink and plump and not one tuft of fur. I knew better than to expect an explanation from Free magic. With the message received, I offered the sign of five and one and gave back the cold lump of skin. "Thank you."

He leapt to my arm and shimmied up to my elbow, taking the time to inspect my face before turning and whisking away with the mouselet gripped in his talons. I watched his silhouette against the sky until he dropped back into the trees and blended away with the shadows.

Chapter Nine

WHEN THE CASTLE ECHOED WITH MORNING VOICES, I slipped a robe over my shoulders and padded down the stairs to the kitchen.

"Prilla?" I asked. Our head cook looked up from the long work bench that ran down the center. She stood with a bowl viced between her hip and her left hand while her right fist kneaded a dough in circles against the smooth pottery. "I'm keeping to my room this morning. Will you send up whatever's left after the household eats?"

Prilla flashed her tired blue eyes and went back to her task, nodding at the instructions and not waiting for anything more. I snuck back and shut my door again with a heavy push. Turning to the shelves, I shook the hair from my face and set to work.

Chamomile, turmeric, cinnamon, poppy, celery seed, and the roots of a wild yam. I still wasn't sure what to make of Lord Erron's request, but at that moment I was grateful for the occupation. It would fill my morning and keep me away from the great hall. Even though days away still, I dreaded what might be starting in preparation for my doomed night.

It was hours past sunrise before anyone knocked on my door and even then I was slow to respond. My hands were stained blood orange from the turmeric meat and more than a few poppy seeds fell from my robe as I stood to answer.

It was Aeson with Lady Calise at his side. It was her presence and her presence alone that kept me from groaning at the interruption. Instead, I swept into a curtsy, something I hadn't genuinely done for Aeson in years. Additionally, I was not dressed for the day and though it was not unusual for him to see me so disheveled, Calise blinked more than once at my state.

"You weren't at breakfast, or dinner for that matter," said Aeson.

"I ate all the same," I snipped. I glanced at Calise and added, "my lord." Gesturing to the tray next to the mortars on my desk, I winced. It was rather untouched, but at least I had drunk my tea and bitten into a honey biscuit.

His jaw shifted to one side, and he turned to offer Calise entry. She walked in with a look of wonder, eyes sparkling in the window light. I watched as she admired the two worlds my chamber encompassed, the greenhouse along one side and workshop along the other.

The ferns danced, elated to have someone new in their midst. Their magic buzzed in my ear and whispers shook through them as Calise passed along their little green tendrils.

Inching the door closed, another hand reached out from the hall and pushed it open again. Guard Berrin. It was in that moment I concluded three people was far too many to have in my space. Hospitality called for behavior, so I lowered myself and welcomed him in. He took no more than a few steps before planting his feet and erecting himself in the corner like a statue.

"Beg pardon, my lady." I looked to Calise. "Was there something you hoped to have my assistance with? Or have you come to check on the brew for Lord Erron?"

She faltered in her steps and looked from me to Aeson to Berrin. "Oh, no. I was unaware he had asked for a favor. I came on my own behalf."

"I see." I glanced at Aeson who was heavily invested in an empty vial on my table. Clearly this was against his intentions as well. "What service might I be today?"

"Flowers," she stated. Her face was clear and pure, and she looked at me straight on as if that was a perfectly good explanation.

"In addition to the peppermint?"

"For your banquet."

"Ah." I threw another look at Aeson whose back was to me now, as invisible as he could get without leaving the room. "Well . . ." I had never thought about flowers in my life unless I was calling out the magic within them.

As if knowing I needed a stalemate that morning, something slithered beneath my door past guard Berrin's feet. Streaks of green and brown rushed over the floor. Calise gasped and Berrin jolted alert, reaching for a dagger at his waist. Aeson spun at the commotion just in time to see me drop a hand to the floor, offering refuge to the garden snake. At the same time, I held my palm out to Berrin.

"Stay that blade or find it through your ear," I said, grinding my teeth.

He hesitated, dagger gripped in the air, eyes flicking between the snake and Calise. "It may be venomous to my lady."

Before I could stop myself, I felled my shoulders and flopped my head in his direction. "It is venomous to *nothing*. It is a harmless garden creature who heeds no warnings." I turned my gaze to the loopy thing in my hand. "When I said don't be seen by the stable cats, this is not what I meant."

"It's all right Berrin." Calise cleared her throat but her lips stayed tight. "Surely a castle witch knows what she is talking about."

I glanced across the room at Aeson. His eyes were stuck on Berrin's squarish head with a hand on his belt. Few knew of it, but along the back was a thin strip of leather stitched over the base. It created a narrow sheath for a palm blade to hide in. It was obscured by the cut of his vest but always within reach.

"To that point," Aeson started, "I would never allow your lady a visit to Etta's workshop if there was any danger to be found. I hope House Erron has comfort in that by now."

"Precisely." Calise straightened and pushed her shoulders back, smiling. "Although, I must ask, is this common behavior for the creatures on your land?"

Aeson looked to me but neither of us had a sound answer. Taking it upon herself, the snake coiled higher along my arm, then wriggled her way to my neck where the chill of her scales caused me to shiver. She must not have found safe hiding in the night and been stuck on cold cobblestones instead.

I gave a small giggle as she slithered behind my ear to my hair. She draped herself around my neck, pulling her tail into an S shape at the hollow of my throat. Calise's jaw dropped lower and lower. Catching herself, she drew a long breath and turned about the room.

"Flowers, then."

Avoiding Aeson's gaze, I sat down on the window stool and looked out at the yard. "I would have you instruct the village children to gather wildflowers and bring them to the castle, whichever ones they love best. Give them a quarter coin each and the day will be as memorable for them as it will be for me."

Calise nodded and looked at Berrin who had resumed his role as statue in the corner. She brushed by Aeson and barely gave her guard enough time to open the door. The two disappeared down the hall while Aeson lingered. He stepped my way, unbothered by my companion.

"You look awful."

"Thank you, my lord." I rolled my eyes.

Careful not to bother the snake as she rested, he slipped a finger under my chin and tilted it up to meet him. "Your spirit is half gone. What did you do?"

"I fed the garden yesterday."

His head rose up in understanding, then dropped to one side. "Don't forget to feed yourself."

He let me go and left without any other remark. And he was right. I was a mess of loose hair and stained clothes. Reaching tentatively, I found the narrow string of scales around me and brushed down the back of her head. There was not enough warmth coming from my body to soothe either of us, which left only one option.

It wasn't an easy walk to the creek pool but after I finished blending everything for Lord Erron's sleeping draught, the castle still held too much commotion. And all of it was just inches from my door. Rather than call for a tub, I left with a clean shift, a pale green kirtle, and nothing on my feet. Walking barefoot afforded the chance to soak up any magic lingering along the path, sending itchy tremors along the soles of my feet.

In a few weeks' time, the heat of summer would break, and the lower currents would go cold as the world below slowed down for autumn. Tree roots would cease their reaching and voles would make good with whatever hole they'd built for themselves. It would be good to visit before I had to start retreating as well.

By the time we reached the pool I was rejuvenated enough to strip my clothes and dive straight to the deepest pocket. Under the water, I pushed and kicked with my legs, spiraling back up through the blades of sunlight. Surfacing, I looked for the snake and found her on a log. She was stretched out long and skinny in one of the hot beams breaking through the trees.

"What do you make of a mouselet? Other than a meal?" I asked, laying my arms over the log and resting my head on my hands. Her eyes remained closed.

While she sunbathed, I scrubbed at my skin and tugged at my hair until the knots came free. Then I climbed out and pulled the linen shift over my head. Settling in the tall grass, I listened to the swirl of air around me. It hummed in the branches and bent the water reeds to and fro.

Closing my eyes, I put my hands over my belly to think. What would a baby bring to Castle Crennly? It would bring security to Aeson, and that alone was enough to wish good will towards him and Calise. But if Lord Erron held the same views of Castle Crennly as the other Elder Lords, it made no sense to hope for marriage between Calise and a bastard lord who would never bend to the greed of their gathering. Unless it was the aspect of death I should be looking at and Aeson was in danger.

I finished dressing and looked at my friend on the log. "Are you returning with me?"

She pulled her tail up to resettle herself and I took that as her answer. With no more clarity than I'd brought with me, I started the way home to Aeson.

It hadn't been a complete lie when I said the pear trees needed blessing, so I stopped among their trunks before reentering the castle walls. There were eight of them, four in each row, and the farthest grew only a few paces from where the creek bent around and encompassed the far end of the kitchen gardens. It was the very spot where I had decided to stay at Castle Crennly.

It was less than a month before my agreed upon year was ending. I'd been counting the days and planning what I would pack when I left to find my people, if there were any left. To avoid raising doubt or suspicion, I was still studying each day. Before Aeson had the desks built for my workspace, I had no choice but to open my books on the table in his study and hang over the pages as I memorized plant remedies and how to use the power in each seed.

I had come across an idea for speeding up a harvest if weather caused damage or a season fell short. It required six freshly picked seeds of the land. For me, that meant pears. It was a tedious task, but I brought the book and a small fern to test my spell and set out for the orchard.

Climbing the tree was easy. As was the scooping out of seeds. But in my curiosity, I hadn't thought about climbing back down. I was amidst the branches with fresh seeds in my fist and only one arm left to scale the trunk.

My foot slipped on the smooth grey bark, and I fell, hitting my chin on a branch with a yelp, then landing flat on my back. My breath froze in my chest and the sky slowed above me while I wheezed and waited for my heart to steady.

Sitting up, blood dripped from my chin onto my waist apron. My eyes stung from stupid embarrassment as I looked around, hoping I was alone. But Aeson was there, hurrying up from the direction of the creek.

"Are you all right?" he asked.

I looked away, wiping my eyes.

It didn't stop him from sitting in the grass next to me and bending to see better. "Let me look," he said.

"It's fine. It will heal quickly enough." I held my palm to my chin, but blood kept spilling over the web of skin between my thumb and index finger. I scooted away and he followed, crawling through the dirt. "The castle laundress will shout when she sees your clothes so dirty." I tried to put him off.

"Let her shout. It's my coin that goes into her pocket every month."

I sharpened my gaze at him.

"I . . . I don't mean it like that," he sputtered and hung his head. "It's not my coin. Not any of it. But it's in my care now. Which is absurd because all I need is a warm bed at night and some hard crust to gnaw on when I get hungry."

My heart had calmed itself by then and I took a deep breath. Aeson looked up at me, his hair long enough to fall into his face and hide the hope in his eyes. A few more beats and I conceded to shimmy my way closer. He pulled the knife from his belt and cut a strip of fabric from his own shirt.

I opened my mouth, full of opinions, but he held a hand up. His black eyes met my grey ones with nothing but sweet pear scenting the space between.

"Let her shout," he said, staring at me until I swallowed down my thoughts. Then he carried on. "My lands will only be as good as my people, and my people will only be as good as I treat them."

Relenting, I lowered my hand and let his replace it. He held tight with the cloth along my jaw, applying pressure to stave off the bleeding while his other hand cupped my ear and supported my head. He watched the water while I watched him and when he dared to remove the fabric from my skin, he leaned even closer to check the wound.

"Better?" His breath was filled with lemon cider, his favorite drink before he ventured into the world of ale. "Is there something you can make to help it along?"

"There is."

He stood and offered his hands to help me up. Satisfied that I was okay, he wandered off towards the creek again and left me alone. I grabbed the book and marched straight back to my rooms. From then on, I carried my own knife under my apron, and I didn't test my spell until the next spring. Nor did I bother treating the cut of my chin. Rather, I wore the scar as a reminder never to be so stupid again.

Ever since that day, I gave the pears the same blessing each time. I hadn't written it though. He did. In the middle of them I turned with my left hand over my heart, right hand casting outward into the trees. My eyes swept over the keep behind the two walls, over our fields, then returned to the creek.

"Grow your leaves as good as we; only as good as what we seed. Balance thus, trading treat; honored roots, fairness sweet. Take sun, air, water and dew; take from us what we take from you."

I tapped the scar on my chin three times, smiling. When the pull of power dissipated from my joints, I waited until the roots creaked and the pear trees shifted in the earth, stretching with renewed comfort. Then I turned for the castle and everything in it, wishing that lies carved free as easily as seeds.

Chapter Ten

ISCRAPED THE BREWED INGREDIENTS out of their dish into a wide mouth vial and filled the rest with a clove tea to mask the uglier flavors. Swirling it carefully and counterclockwise, I made my way to Lord Erron's room. Passing Lady Calise's room, I paused. There were voices inside, low and rumbling.

I thought about pulling a gust of wind from under the door, but the voices came closer on their own, coupled with footsteps. With no time to risk, I tiptoed down the hall and waited with my eyes fixed ahead.

When the door to Lady Calise's room groaned and swung open, I lifted a hand and feigned a knock to her father's chamber. But it was Lord Erron himself who left her room, and with his head still tucked behind the door he spoke violently. "I expect news within a fortnight."

Clasping the vial in both hands, I tried to look earnestly at his door as if I was unaware he wasn't inside.

"Oh, witch Etta, looking for me?"

I turned towards his voice and put on my best look of surprise. "Lord Erron, indeed. I have the brew you requested."

"Excellent," he exclaimed. "Most excellent. I shall sample it tonight and report back to you in the morning."

"Very good, sir." I curtsied away and didn't look back. Instead, I hurried down the stairs and into the bailey yards, searching for Garret. He wasn't in the front or the back or the stables. I found him in between the inner and outer wall helping Smithwik with a broken wagon wheel.

They muttered and mumbled for a short while before Smithwik nodded his head and turned towards the forge. Garret brought his attention to me, at last. "What is it?"

"What sort of mischief could an unchaperoned lady get into in a fortnight's time?"

"How do you mean?"

I shook my head and ran my hands over my hair. I detailed what I'd heard and added in Lord Erron's request and everything else that had happened in the last few days, including my encounter with the shepherd. Garret listened as he rubbed one shoulder. I made note to "accidentally" make too much liniment and give the excess to him as soon as I could.

"It'll take Lord Erron nearly a fortnight to ride home down the southern road. Whatever he wants accomplished he wants it done immediately."

Behind us there came laughter and a high-pitched squeal, which was Mother Elma's attempt at an infectious giggle. Garret and I turned towards the noise to see Elma, Calise, and Aeson strolling through the front gates. Calise had a purse of coins slung about her waist. Her consideration of my request didn't go unnoticed, but the mystery of everything clung to my thoughts.

Aeson lifted his head before they reached the second gate, glancing around at the yard. He was forever checking that no one went without help if they needed it. I stepped around Garret to hide in case Aeson looked our way. Garret pivoted. "He'll know I'm talking to someone, and he'll know it's you," he said.

"Nonsense."

"You're the only one that hides from him."

I opened my mouth for a sharp retort, but Layla trotted up at the same time.

"Yes?" I asked.

"Prilla has a half dozen rotten eggs that got lost in the back of the larder. She wants to know if you want them in your rooms. Something about cleansing foul spirits," Layla explained, all the while her gaze drifted from me to Garret.

I nodded. "Please. And tell her thank you."

Her eyes hung on Garret for half a moment too long. She caught herself, flashed a smile and said goodbye.

"This is unexpected," I said as Garret's eyes followed Layla all the way back to the door. "Is this something that has struck in the moment or have you noticed her before?"

"Neither of us have noticed anything. We've barely spoken since the day she arrived and I led her to Reeve's accounting chambers."

"You should speak to her again. Immediately."

Garret went back to the wagon wheel and made a show of knocking on the wood, checking for more weak spots. "Has your witch wind brought anything back to you?"

"A dead mouselet."

His eyes jerked up at me from over his shoulder and his mouth wrinkled like it had touched curdled milk. "A dead mouselet?"

I nodded and wandered over to the wall to rest against it.

"Which part is more important? The death or the baby?"

"Free magic isn't that accommodating."

Garret grumped and heaved a sigh before straightening my way again. "I'll tell the guards to watch House Erron's comings and goings more closely through the lord's departure, and we'll continue even after."

"Thank you." I left him with the wagon and climbed the spiral steps back up to my room. Layla was setting down a basket of horrific smelling eggs as I opened the door.

She turned at my entrance. "Foul spirits?" she asked.

I softened my gaze and closed the door. "Like energy attracts like energy. If someone is feeling particularly cross or defeated or saddened for any reason, a rotten egg swept from their heart outward along each limb in repetition will lift the bruise from their spirit and gather it within the shell."

"Then what?"

"I bury them beneath the mushrooms. Fungus delights in taking the horrid and making it whimsical," I explained. Layla giggled. The dimple of her cheek made me think of Garret again and I averted my eyes. "Is the kitchen expecting you to return right away or could you help me with something?"

When the sun had shifted well past midday, I sent Layla off to find Garret with a jar of liniment. She disappeared down the hall and I stood in the dark damp with my eyes shut. Pressing my fingertips into the mortar between the castle stones, I dragged in a long breath, searching for any stress or worry or panic.

Everyone was at ease. I attributed a majority of that to the fact Mother Elma was gone to the village with Aeson and Calise. Locking my door, I snuck along the corridors to the study and planted myself in front of the back shelves.

One by one I pulled my books out and sifted through the pages, searching for anything that put to use a dead mouse—infant or not. But nothing in Free or Fair called for dead or dying bodies, which left Fierce magic. I was positive House Erron was not that sort of threat.

The pile around me grew as pages opened and overlapped. Each new book I pulled down was used to shove the other books out of the way until I was a frog of a witch surrounded by lily pads of parchment, eyes floating across waves of text, nowhere close to solid ground.

Shadows grew tall against the walls, and I looked at the window. The sun retreated behind the trees and gave the room over to grey. Reluctantly I dragged my books back together, closing and stacking them beside me. When it was tall enough, I folded my arms on top and rested my head on the tower of knowledge.

I dozed and drifted away through the fields and in and out of the village homes, thinking of the shepherdess with her invalid husband and her children at her feet. One on her breast and another in her womb. I drifted through the hall in front of House Erron's guest chambers and in and out of my own windows and along every potted plant in my room.

There was something very obvious before me. I could sense it. Without using heavier magic, I couldn't see the pattern in the strings. Each one connected to another but there were only loose ends. A web with no center. A spider might have helped me but

I knew from experience, they gave only silent lessons. They held better, after all.

The light stomp of a boot gathered outside the door before it swung open. I didn't bother looking his way since it could only be him, but I fluttered my lashes so he'd know I was awake. Barely. He stepped between the books and slid to the floor beside me.

"You missed another meal," he said. "Were you even listening when I said it wouldn't be allowed during House Erron's stay?"

"I was listening. It's not been intentional."

"If only I could believe that."

I peered at him over the crook of my elbow. "Believe it this time."

He looked around the books. "All right. This time. What kept you here?"

"I asked Free magic for help with the hidden maids, and it brought me an owl who brought me a dead mouselet."

"Charming."

I sat up straight and rubbed my face. "Only Fierce magic wants a death in its midst. Death or the semblance of it."

"You're not doing Fierce magic for anything."

My chest filled and hardened. "I have no plans to."

"Then what do you make of it?"

I tossed my hands out over the books. "I make nothing of it. Perhaps it was simply the exchange of helping the calf to life. One bundle of energy for another." It was the only sensical explanation I could come up with. "Otherwise, there's no sense of death surrounding House Erron."

Aeson tilted his head to the ceiling and puttered his lips.

"Did you check on the shepherdess while you were in the village?" I changed the topic.

"I did," he groaned. "And I saw what you saw. I have already instructed Garret and Reeve to call on them with anything more the cupboards can spare. Then we shall see."

"Give the shepherd a fortnight," I said. It would give Aeson something to worry about while Garret looked into House Erron's plots.

"Anything else?"

"No." I sat forward and gathered the books to replace them on the shelf. "How is Lady Calise today?"

Aeson turned his eyes from me. "She's . . . very gentle towards the children. You would have been glad to see how they smiled for her."

I swallowed and focused on sliding the books back into their rightful places. "They deserve every smile we can bring to them."

He nodded and turned back to me. "A messenger arrived while we were there."

"Another lord preparing to send his only daughter your way?"

"This one promises an even bigger banquet for you. One you'll be unable to scheme your way out of." He reached across the distance and flicked my earlobe. "No. Lord Faeler Bane in the west wants to send us a horse."

"Whatever for?"

"He is aging and he has no heir of his own. His letter would imply he doesn't trust the nephew that stands in line to care for his favorite mare and wishes to deliver her to us for the remainder of her days."

"How odd."

Aeson shrugged. "Castle Bane is well known for their horses, and I met the nephew once at the court gathering. He's a right rotten potato. Smells like one too."

I covered a snort, and Aeson smiled at me. "Then we can't blame him, can we?"

He shook his head. "If the mare is as splendid as the letter would have me believe, we should give her to Garret."

"Garret," I said, shimmying up to my knees. I leaned closer with my secret. "Speaking of your favorite head guard. You'll never guess what I saw today."

"Do tell." He grinned.

Describing it all to him, I finished off by stating, "There was so much magic passing between them I could've brought a dried daisy back to blooming with half a spell. And I wouldn't even need rhyming couplets."

"You seem well adjusted to this given your own interest in Garret." Aeson smirked and I sat up straighter to swat at his head. He caught my wrist easily and turned my palm over. "How's your hand?"

Tugging it away, I told him, "It will be closed by tomorrow. A good dinner will help. I should go see what the kitchen has left." I stood to take my leave.

"Must you always be running away? Or hiding?" He leered. "You're as guarded as the foxes."

Pausing by the door, my hair lit up in the growing moonbeams. I bit my lip. "I'm sure I don't know what you're talking about."

Chapter Eleven

L ORD ERRON WAS EAGER TO DEPART when the day arrived. By the time I was dressed suitably to see anyone off, his horses were tacked, and his men were all mounted. Horseshoes clicked about the courtyard as the hot summer breeze brought the smell of clover to their noses.

When he saw me, he hurried over and offered a cordial bow. "Witch Etta, your brew making skills are exceptional. Such a draught will soothe me the whole journey."

I wanted to remark on his obscurity the day before. I'd kept my eye out for him in case my brew hadn't worked. It was his own concern to start with. But he and Calise had spent the day together in his rooms and took no visitors. Thinking better of it, I curtsied back. It was more important to me that he be gone for good.

"Thank you, Lord Erron. Be sure to keep it from the sun to preserve its potency."

He nodded and his eyes caught Calise's near the doorway with

Mother Elma. I stepped away and folded in behind other servants where she wouldn't see me.

Aeson appeared last and bent over in the grandest bow I'd ever seen him make. I wasn't sure if it was out of respect for Lord Erron or for Calise. But he seemed set on reassuring Lord Erron that Lady Calise's care would be of the utmost importance to him, and Mother Elma would be ever present to preserve Calise's reputation.

Lord Erron smiled generously but gave minimal thanks. He mounted his horse and took the lead through our front gates, shaking his hair out like he had when he arrived. As soon as the last foot and hoof had stepped beyond our walls, Calise clapped her hands and searched me out in the crowd.

"Our celebration is near." She beamed from ear to ear.

The household staff knew me well enough not to turn in my direction. Frankly, none cared that we were serving another banquet. The only bit they cared for was good meat and an excuse to open a few extra barrels of honey ale. The banquet might have had my name at the center, but any cause for a bawdy night of mischief was enough to make the staff step to preparations easily.

Garret appeared on my left with his horse in hand and Aeson's next to it. "Our lord has sent me to deliver new wares to the shepherdess and her children. Should I have them fetch your horse as well?"

I folded my arms and studied everyone milling about the courtyard. They were debating if it would be acceptable to open a barrel for good cheer as they cleaned the hall and hung banners.

"No," I said, glancing at Calise and guard Berrin. "No, I will stay and help Lady Calise with her decorations."

"You want to help plan a party?" Garret raised a brow.

Rightfully so.

Lifting my shoulder to my ear, I tipped my chin and explained. "I want to be sure Lady Calise has everything she needs for the day and if there's anything amiss with House Erron, I shall assist in unraveling it."

Garret chortled and shook his head, offering Aeson his reins as he stepped closer.

"You're not joining us?" Aeson must've heard bits and pieces of the exchange.

Interjecting before I could offer a different answer, Garret made every word crawl from the back of his throat. He let the secret breathe a bit of air before slipping it back inside his chest. "The witch wants to be sure she's nearby to help Lady Calise if any trouble arises."

Aeson regarded me with a tight jaw, then dashed a look at Garret and sighed. "Be *nice*."

"I thought Reeve was going to the village."

"He must stay with Prilla to keep track of the menu. And do not deflect," he growled from atop his horse, glancing back at Calise. "Promise you won't scare her off?"

"Are you planning something the castle should be aware of?"

He didn't reply. Instead, he pointed Meadowgrass beyond the gate and Garret followed with a shrug. In their absence, I turned to find Calise, and sadly, Mother Elma. Meandering, I took my time approaching and dropped into a light curtsy for both of them. Elma pointed her nose to the sky and departed without acknowledging me. So much for a dedicated chaperone. Calise smiled and faced me directly.

"Will you be staying at my side today? I want to be sure everything is just right for your dinner."

I forced a smile and spoke through the crease of my lips. "It'll be perfect. I'm positive. I look forward to it very much."

Calise clapped five little claps with her delicate fingers and spun towards the castle. I allowed Berrin to follow first and trailed by two paces to observe them. In the great hall, it became apparent that Calise without a chaperone was different from the Calise I'd seen so far. Her movements became looser and more pronounced. A hip jutted out this way and her head tilted that way as she examined the placement of banners. In her fine dress she even crouched to her knees to level out a table runner.

Berrin was at her heels the whole way. Less of a statue and more of a shadow to her every movement. When Calise dragged a chair to the center of the room so she might examine her design from a bird's height, Berrin nearly tripped trying to help her step up. He stood stock still with his arms spread wide in case she fell.

"That's not necessary, Berrin. I'm quite balanced."

"But if you lose that balance, my lady."

Calise turned and looked down at him with both hands on her hips. Her mouth ticked with a smile before she remembered me sitting near the head table and licked her lips to disguise the act. "The absence of my father is no excuse to forget one's place."

Berrin's arms listed a bit, then dropped fully. He gave half a bow. "Forgive me, my lady."

She didn't accept him. Rather, she simply turned back to her task and left him berated on the ground beneath her. Satisfied, she nodded a firm nod and hopped down, away from Berrin. "My maids and I will spend the afternoon arranging the flower vases." She looked my way. "Will you join us? Or does the castle require your attention?"

Despite all my suspicions, I allowed a smile. Calise knew

perfectly well by then I had no interest in flowers, and she had given me an avenue of refusal. Aptly done for a young lady with no practice running her own home.

"The castle requires my attention now. I will excuse myself." I backed away and strode out the front door but not before I saw Berrin approach Calise again only to be brushed aside and left alone as she found the stairs to her room.

I went to the front gate. It was past midday and Aeson would surely be returning with Garret soon. Outside in the shadow of the outer wall, I placed both palms on the stones and asked the tremors if anything was wrong in the castle or if anything needed tending while I waited. There was nothing, of course.

The disease of House Erron grated on me. With Lord Erron gone, I might've expected Calise to act differently, but it was Berrin's behavior that made me stumble. His fretting and worrying seemed out of character from the stoic man I had first met. Perhaps Lord Erron had threatened him prior to departure. After all, Aeson and Calise had grown closer the last few days and Elma was not the pinnacle of moral guardians by any means.

Their horses clopped up the motte road as I paced back and forth, ripping hangnails from my cuticles until they bled. Garret was leading at a light trot while Aeson followed behind. Meadowgrass tossed her head. Her hindquarters bounced and flinched in a way that told me her rider was agitated. When Aeson saw me, he slowed and dismounted at a walk, tossing his reins in the air and expecting Garret to catch them.

My spine stiffened and I stole a look at Garret, who shook his head. When Aeson was directly before me he stopped, rigid and unspeaking.

"Lady Calise and her maids are arranging flowers, they no

longer needed me," I said.

He nodded and studied the archway behind me. "And you were well spoken, I trust?"

"I was unspoken." I dropped my head. "She didn't need any input from me."

Aeson nodded again and heaved a great breath but stood on in silence.

"The shepherdess?" I asked, looking up between them. "Was the shepherd there?"

"Yes." Aeson's teeth didn't even part to answer. He reached for my hands next and held them both up for scrutiny. "You've been fretting. What for?"

I waited for him to look up into my eyes before using his title honestly. "Caring for your castle, my lord."

The wire that held his brow tight seemed to snap and he rocked backwards, dropping his shoulders and lowering our hands. "Yes. Yes, as you always are."

It was clear Aeson was not going to inform me as I hoped, so I cleared my throat and took my hands away from his. "Your mother has been in her chambers since you left. Perhaps you should check on her. If she's unwell she'll certainly not tell me. I imagine Calise and her maids would love a visit from you too. It'll give them something to chitter about."

He straightened his vest and looked up, sliding his gaze along the turrets and towers. "I'll see to them now. And Etta?"

"Mm?"

"It's a banquet for you, do not forget. Be sure to dress for the occasion."

"Is that a command?"

But he'd already walked away, and his voice swept over his

shoulders. "Only if you hear such things."

"What the poxes was that about?" I asked Garret as soon as we were alone.

"There was nothing amiss at the shepherd's house," Garret said.

I balked. "I don't understand."

He shrugged. "Their shelves were stocked, items returned, and to my eyes, the children were wearing fresh clothes."

My brow sunk so low that my nose wrinkled alongside it. "How could that be possible? They were destitute barely a week ago."

"Shepherd said he was able to recover from his losses on his own."

"That's a pile of rot."

"Speaking of rot, he had some words for our lord as well." He dismounted and whistled for a stable boy to jog out and take the horses. "He was sure to remind our young master of his parentage."

"I hope he dies of the blue plague, the heap." I glowered down the road, hoping a chill would run over the shepherd's back from this distance. "What do you think happened?"

Garret shook his head. "Perhaps he truly managed on his own. Or the townspeople helped. After all, you're always encouraging them to foster one another."

"Why would Emmaya alert me to Shepherd's difficulty if others were ready to help?" I huffed. "And it doesn't fix the bruises I saw on Ellara."

Throwing his hands up in surrender, Garret licked his lips. "There are too many possibilities, witch. I will keep watch and wait for something else to reveal itself."

Against better behavior, I lifted a hand and rooted for another hangnail to persecute. "How were the children? And the shepherdess, her belly?"

"We left the children full and the mother comfortable."

I nodded, pondering whether it would be better for her baby to arrive ahead of the cold weather or later so he or she could strengthen in the womb before joining us earthside. "I think I will go find Laken, see if she has any pressing injuries to tend to."

"Hoping for an excuse to leave your banquet early? I doubt he'll appreciate that."

"I leave all the banquets early. He is not bothered half as much as he claims to be."

"He is bothered. I promise," Garret said, turning away.

I made a face at the back of his head, jogging to catch up. "Oy! I forgot to mention, Layla was looking for you."

His eyes brightened for a mere moment, betraying him. "Was sh—Oh, you witch." He kicked a clod of dirt at me as I ran by cackling.

Chapter Twelve

S EXPECTED, THE BANQUET DAY was a source of joy for everyone in the castle. One unexpected delight was turning away everyone who came to my door. Since the event was for me, I claimed the whole day to get ready and look my best. Mostly I worked and chatted with my plants, but I also allowed myself a cat's nap in the afternoon.

When I had no more time left to abuse, I took the longest route possible to the great hall. Knowing me all too well, the staff raised their drinks in lieu of applause. It was an act which gave me true gratitude. After all her hard work, I made sure to walk the perimeter and admire Calise's design. The flowers certainly looked decadent but none of the vases contained any peppermint. If Calise truly preferred the sharper scent, I saw no reason to hide the fact, especially since her maids continued to wear sprigs in their hair.

Prilla had outdone herself and it would not have surprised me if Aeson had snuck word to her about all my missed birthdays.

There was roast pig with cinnamon apples, baked pears with crisp sugar, and pots of pie in two different stacks. One pile was filled with savory vegetable fillings and the others were stuffed with summer berries.

I cast my gaze wide and smiled and curtsied and thanked Calise. When she demanded I stand at the center of the room so she might toast me and my talents, I obliged quickly so Aeson would keep his reprimands to himself and everyone else could get back to their drinks. Seeing him in the crowd, I was at least cheered by the fact he wore blue that night. I'm sure his mother was relieved since she thought it the lesser Crennly color on him. In truth, it was the one that complimented his hair best. Elma herself was nowhere to be seen, thankfully.

After the cheering, Calise pulled me close and stuck her nose into my hair. Her lips practically married the top of my ear. "Has your Lord Crennly ever had a lover?"

I thought she must be drunk but there was only lemon cider on her breath. "I'm sorry, my lady. If he has, I am unaware."

"Is that so? But you're so close. Everyone in the castle says, 'if you can't find one, find the other.'"

My eyebrows stitched together in a square knot. Surely no one said such a thing. "Is there a particular concern you are looking to answer, my lady?"

She pondered this a moment, sipping her drink and running a finger around the rim. "Is he a goodly man? Kind? He's not gentle in the yard only to be cruel once the pomp has disappeared, is he?"

I assumed she was asking in anticipation of a proposal, engagement, and marriage. I couldn't blame her. Lord Erron left her to fend for herself with a man she hardly knew and a potential mother-in-law whom no one wanted to know.

"Aeson is . . ." I'd never truly praised him to his face, let alone in someone else's confidence. "He's the hope that cruel men try their best to extinguish."

This didn't reassure her. Her lips pouted and her eyes fell, struggling to lift again and find him in the crowd. She took another drink from her cup and nodded. "Thank you, Etta."

I bobbed a quick curtsy and left the conversation as fast as I could, lest Garret should find me next and ask after Layla's affairs. He'd be in for a true shock. When no one was looking, I swiped a cheeseboard off the end of one table and ran down the darkest hallway, up to my rooms.

Locking the door, I sat in the curve of my tower window. Nibbling the cheese with one hand, I pulled a lily down with the other, then a crocus, a stalk of lavender, and a variety of ferns. We sat together, the greens and I, whispering among ourselves. And none of them asked me any questions.

Chapter Thirteen

T HE MORNING WAS RESPLENDENT WITH SILENCE. I had no idea how long the celebration lasted but it was enough that no one was quick to rise or fast to speak when dawn unfolded across our fields and warmed the uppermost castle walls.

I crept from my bed and down to the kitchen, nodding to Prilla but saying nothing as I stole a leftover raspberry tart and small pitcher of cream. In my rooms, I put the flowers from last night back in their place and checked on the peppermint. It had grown into a solid bit of shrub with three extra arms and leaves budding all over. If House Erron exhausted their unexplained foliage whims, it would do nicely as a replacement.

Opening all the windows to let in the late summer air, I dragged my stool to the wall and collected herbs for the shepherdess. Arm extended, I nearly dropped a jar of dried blue cohosh when my door banged open and Aeson spun into the room.

Closing it quickly, he flattened his back against the boards and slid to the ground, head hung between his knees and hands clasped at the back of his hair. I regarded him quietly until it was clear he wasn't going to speak first.

"You look wretched."

"The appearance matches the inner discord."

I rolled my eyes and stepped down carefully, arms full of ingredients. When they were safely set upon my desk I walked over and stood above him with arms folded. "Aeson." I nudged his foot with mine and waited for him to look up. "What's wrong?"

His face was pale and his hair was matted. "I think I did something, but I don't know what I did."

"Well, there's no blood on your hands or your clothes, so I'd say that's a good bit of news." I lowered myself to the floor. "Although, these are the same clothes you wore for the banquet."

His shoulders straightened and he pulled at his garments, wide eyed. "Are they?"

I slipped onto my bottom to take him in. "Aeson, what's wrong?"

"I can't remember." He shook his head and shifted upward, trying to gather himself and his thoughts all at once. His index finger found a dried smear of food on his overcoat and scratched it away. "I woke up this way, in my bed, but I don't . . . I don't think I was alone the whole night."

My throat constricted. "What do you mean?"

Pulling his knees tighter, he mumbled into his lap. "I think someone was with me. My blankets don't smell right. They smell different."

"Like what?" I swallowed.

"Peppermint."

I exhaled long and slow and two times over, then laid my hands flat on my knees. Behind me the ferns were gossiping already, trembling with curiosity at Aeson's state. "It's not terrible," I said. "It's just not ideal. Can you recall which maid it might've been?"

"Maid?" He whipped his eyes up and met mine in earnest. "You think it was her maid?"

"It has to have been. She doesn't wear it herself." I tweaked my neck. "And isn't that better? You're certainly not the first lord to lift the skirts of a lover's maid before the lover."

Aeson kicked his legs out flat on the floor and leaned forward. "Don't say it like that. She's not my lover. But it's clear, isn't it? It's clear that my mother, Lord Erron, even perhaps Calise, they hold an implication to everything. This visit is more than an introduction."

"A trothplight was clear before they arrived, yes."

"If it was a maid, it would be disrespectful to her if I've done something untoward."

I brought my chin to my chest and took a deep breath, asking the breeze from the window to sweep over Aeson and settle his nerves. "It would be, indeed. Yet Lady Calise would be smart to still consider a man who cared in such a way. Most lords would see it as their right and property."

As the breeze ruffled his hair, the energy sung by me and after another moment, he blew a gust of air from his chest and shook his head. When his eyes landed on mine, they were clear. The frenzy had left him.

"You look lovely," he said. "Why do you look lovely? It was your banquet, didn't you celebrate?"

I shrugged.

"You snuck away, didn't you? As always." He rubbed both hands down his face. "And I didn't notice? Why didn't I notice? I always notice."

I made a face and took him by the hand, pulling him up and over to the window stool among the plants. "Sit," I ordered.

He did as instructed and I handed him a stone mortar. Dragging a pot of violets out from behind some gardenia, I placed it next to his right foot. Beneath his left, I lay a curl of peeled birch. Its edges arched into the floor to get rid of whatever madness he suffered.

In the bowl, I dropped the meat of one walnut, a sprig of rosemary, and the dry leaves of a celery plant. Handing him the pestle, I told him, "Grind it together, and every time you exhale ask the blackness in your head to leave."

He nodded and set to his work. I watched from my desk as I scribbled a simple spell just for him, then withdrew my knife from beneath my work apron. Taking it to the water bucket, I made sure the tip was clean and returned to his side.

Aeson rarely asked me to cast upon him. Everyone else came before his own needs, like I had under the pear trees. I turned the knife in my hand, frowning. "It's not like you to drink so heavily."

"I didn't think I had," he said.

Running a thumb along the blade I asked, "Do you remember ordering me to make myself pretty the days before?"

He scowled. "Yes. Choice starting point."

"And you remember through to the start of the banquet?"

"Yes."

It was my turn to wipe at my face and shake my head. "Let's expel this, whatever it may be, then we'll know for sure what else needs doing."

With his consent, I tilted his head and made a thin slice along his right temple. A scant trickle of red appeared and once a single drop had clustered, I lifted it on the tip of the knife and dropped it in the bowl.

"Valley streams, veils over blue; banquet schemes made truth untrue. Erron heir, lord and maid; slumbers end, deception spade. Serve the host with minds own meal; turn the bowl and lower the seal."

The wind shifted again, pulling a draft from under my door and dragging it through the room out the window. As it kicked up, I found one last ingredient—mustard seed. Dropping three into my left palm, I pressed my thumb to the blood on Aeson's head. Coated in red, I made a bloody print in my palm until the seeds stuck to my skin.

"Open," I said. He blinked a few times but obeyed, lowering his jaw so I could hold the mustard seeds to his tongue. "Let them melt," I ordered, focusing on the wind next and the clarity of his eyes. I didn't notice my fingers had cupped his jawline until Aeson laid his hand over mine. Our eyes caught for a moment, but I looked away, finding a cloud in the great distance. I aimed the wind towards it and repeated the couplets two more times.

The air current slowed as the seeds disintegrated. Dragging my thumb over his lower lip, I used both hands to tap three times on either side of his temple. Finally, nudging my little stool closer with a foot, I sat before him. "Give it a moment and try to recall the rest of the banquet."

He wiped his mouth, hung his head and tugged at his hair. After three very long breaths, he looked up with a wince. "Still nothing."

I scoffed. "Nothing?"

He shifted in his seat and handed the bowl back to me. "You know I'd never ask if it wasn't dire, but you didn't forget something did you? Miss a step?"

I smoothed my hair out and ran through what we did. "No. The only way it wouldn't have worked is if I had—" I froze.

"What?" Aeson's head lifted, and his jaw went slack.

Shaking my head, I put the bowl down and stepped away. "That doesn't make sense."

"Etta. What doesn't make sense?" He stood and followed as I zigzagged across the room. When I didn't answer he blocked my way and gripped my hands, his eyes pleading with me. "Speak. Please."

I grimaced. "Did you share a drink with Calise? Did she serve you herself last night? Or perhaps one of her maids poured your cup for you?"

"Maybe." He pinched the bridge of his nose. "Did she speak to you? I have a flash of a memory. She was walking towards me and away from you."

Taking my hands back, I cringed and shook my arms out. "She wanted to know if you ever had a lover. If you might be kind or cruel behind a closed door."

He pushed his hair back, the mystery picking at his mind.

"Lord Erron asked me for a brew before he left. To help him sleep. He wanted it quite heavy. If you were served that, something of my making, I can't undo it."

Aeson groaned and let out all the air from his lungs. "If she served me your draught last night, you mean."

I nodded. "Magic demands intention. You know that. I can't change my mind. I can't reverse something I did first. I can offer something new, an amends, but in this case, what's done is done."

He didn't lift his head or even bother to reply. Instead, he reached for me, pulling me closer to slump against my shoulder. "I need an explanation for this ploy," he said.

I raked my hands up through his hair and pulled his attention forward. "Go. Wash your face. Bathe and change into fresh clothes. You'll feel better and we can summon Lady Calise to explain herself. It is my draught they misused under your roof."

He looked on for a long while until his gaze hardened and his hands inched up my wrists, covering my fingers with his. His knuckles twitched against mine. Bearish as he was, I hadn't seen him cower since his first week in the castle. I didn't like it. When he straightened, it was to his full height, shoulders pushed back and chest full. But when he spoke next, he barely used any breath.

"What am I to you, Etta?"

I steadied myself and gave him the same honesty I'd give my magic. "You are Aeson Crennly. Appointed lord of this castle and the luckiest thing to ever happen to these people."

He heard me well, letting the words gather inside him as his eyes fixed on the next course of action. Pulling our hands down together into one big fist, he kissed the glassy tops of my nails, nodded, and left.

Chapter Fourteen

FTER LAYLA BRAIDED MY HAIR BACK and I put on my grey dress, I locked the door to my room and climbed the stairs to the study. Aeson was already there. His face held better color and his clean coat was a much-needed improvement.

"I have already called for them," he said, sitting behind his desk. For the time being, the part in his hair was still straight.

"Do you know what you'll say?" I asked, moving to his right shoulder.

He shrugged.

"Calise seems to be generally innocent in her other interactions. I suspect a similar tactic may work."

"Thank you," he said, glancing up with a wounded smile.

Footsteps echoed in the hall and Calise entered in the simplest day dress I'd ever seen her select. It must have been a mark of the surprise we'd caught her in. Guard Berrin was with her, of course. His charge looked at ease for a woman who may or may not have drugged a lord in his own castle the night before. She smiled brightly and dropped low to Aeson.

"Good morning, my lord."

Aeson waved his fingers from where they rested on the arm of his father's old chair, but he didn't speak.

"To what do I owe this beckoning so soon in the day?" Calise tried again.

His chair creaked as he sat up and pulled his arms across his chest. "Did you enjoy the festivities last night, my lady?"

A practiced liar might have been unbothered, but Calise was new to whatever game she was playing, and it showed when the corner of her mouth twitched at the mention of the banquet. "Surely, I did. I hope you did as well, my lord. And you, Etta." She glanced my way. "You most of all."

I was eager to quash her hopes with my escape from last night, but Aeson came to and I watched his lead from the corner of my eye instead. "It's the strangest thing," he said. "I can't remember if I enjoyed it or not. I can't remember anything. It's as if my sleep was not natural, as if it swept all my memories away in the night."

"Strange indeed." Calise pressed her smile even tighter and from across the room I wondered if she was trying to swallow her teeth before they made way for her confession.

"Etta informed me she brewed a sleeping draught for your father to ease his travels along the way home. On his request, of course."

"It's true. My father is a man of his comforts."

"And did he take it with him as he intended?" I asked, stepping forward from my place behind Aeson. Formalities were nuisance enough and this scraped much deeper on my nerves. "He asked for it to be rather strong. Strong enough for a man in his prime.

Enough for even my own lord."

"Etta."

I ignored the warning. "If one of my own brews was misused against this castle's lord and master, I want a sound understanding of why."

Guard Berrin stepped forward next, a hand flexed around the hilt of his sword. "If your castle witch thinks she can insult the integrity of my lady, be aware it won't be tolerated."

"I'm not *his* castle witch. I'm *the* castle witch and I served House Erron with duty and hospitality. If my integrity has been twisted for ill purpose, I will not tolerate it, and you'll find I don't require a man to defend it for me."

Aeson stood up, shifting his weight towards me. "Etta."

I glanced at him, then away, gritting my teeth in the direction of my study books. At the very least I hoped he would demand a search of their rooms for the drink that Lord Erron claimed to take home.

"As my *not* castle witch has made known, though she might've shown more tact, we suspect foul play with the draught she made for Lord Erron. If Lady Calise would be willing to share what she knows, perhaps we can piece together the peculiar night I have arisen from."

Aeson stared down guard Berrin, neither one breaking to look back at Calise. She was beginning to sway on her feet. "Is there something wrong, my lady?" I asked, stepping around the desk to see her better. We'd be in a separate mess if she had accidentally ingested some brew in the course of her schemes.

"Might we open a window?" she asked. "I'm sorry. This commotion has unsettled me."

I frowned but did as she requested. It made no sense, yet

again. The same lady who marched across a hot field to bring water to a birthing cow should not be so easily disturbed by a mere argument. When the air in the room gave way to a fresh gale, Calise took a deep breath and smoothed her skirts.

"I doubt I can evade the pair of you together, so I'll tell you." She stepped towards the desk. "I did keep a portion of my father's draught. And I did serve it to you last night. And we were alone in your chambers for some time."

Guard Berrin's feet shifted towards Calise and right back again. Aeson's jaw fell so far I thought I would need to call a stable boy with a shovel to pick it up again. "What in the name of every Brother and Sister for?" he asked.

Calise fluttered her lashes and dipped her chin in modesty before she elaborated. "I wanted to be close to you."

"She's lying," I said.

"How dare you!" Berrin shouted.

"Berrin!" Calise yelped.

"Stop!" Aeson bellowed. He rocked back and fell into his chair, pounding his fist on the desk. "You don't wear peppermint in your hair, my lady. And peppermint is all that scents my pillows. Etta is right. You are lying."

All eyes fell to Calise. Mine and Aeson's were full of speculation and Berrin was looking for a command, a cue, or a directive. She looked across us all and turned back to the window, pulling in as much air as she could at the same time as the wind shifted. The stench of horses and manure blew up into our faces.

Calise turned her nose away, but the effects were already settled. She clutched her chest and belly, dropping down to throw up on the dusty floor. Aeson jerked upright from behind his desk, standing with both hands planted on top. Berrin started towards

Calise and stopped, looking between us and twitching every which way in conflict.

With her back arched that way, bent over her regurgitation, I saw the owl clear in my mind's eye. "You're pregnant," I realized aloud. "The peppermint is to alleviate the smells around you, isn't it?"

She nodded from the floor, dry heaving and wiping her fine lips.

I looked to Berrin. "It's yours then? This is the cause for your incessant attention?" I dug a kerchief from my pocket and handed it to him. "Help her."

Berrin slid to his knees at Calise's side and his hands caressed her back. Every string of observation knotted at the center. Each thread and every weave. His devotion, her distance, and the aroma Calise made sure would follow everywhere without planting the evidence on herself.

Behind me, Aeson cleared his throat. "I was meant to be the security? Was that it? Lord Erron doesn't want his only heir and daughter tarnishing the family name with this scandal?"

"My father doesn't know," Calise replied. "He had his own designs for this. I simply saw an opportunity to sidestep his wrath."

Aeson slumped back down into his chair. "Who took me to my chambers? You couldn't have borne my weight in your condition, and this doesn't explain why my pillows smell of peppermint."

Sitting up and resting in Berrin's arms, Calise looked more at ease than she had in her entire visit. In turn, Berrin wiped her brow and brushed the hair from her face. His thumb swept around the curve of her ear in a tenderness that looked odd from such a statue of a man.

"Send someone to my room. Ask for Merla," Calise said.

"I'll go," I told Aeson. "And I'll find someone to clean this up." He nodded and I turned on my heel. Marching straight down to the kitchen, I found Layla and pulled her aside. "Lord Crennly's study requires cleaning. Make sure to bring lemon and thyme for the mess and tell no one who or what you see in there. Use any lie you wish, it doesn't matter. Understand?"

"Yes, Miss Etta."

"Good." I left her to carry on by herself and climbed up to the guest tower. At Calise's door I hammered my fist against the wood so hard I risked splinters. I didn't stop until a bleary-eyed maid yanked it open. "Merla. Now."

Her eyes startled and she nodded vehemently, leaving the door open as she left to find Merla in the sleeping chambers that adjoined the main room. The minute Merla appeared before me I knew why she was kept hidden. She had the same color hair and delicate features as Calise. Not identical by any means, but under a drugged drink no man would be able to tell the difference.

"It's time you introduce yourself to my lord properly," I told her, leaving for the study.

She trotted along as best she could and when we were all safely in the room, I locked the door and checked it three times. Merla cast her eyes about and flared her nostrils at Calise's mess. Layla was wiping diligently and only glanced up to give me a complicit nod.

"Poxes," Aeson said, looking between Calise and Merla.

"You see it?" I asked.

Merla chuckled. "Well, the lady wasn't sure how much comfort you might require once we got you in your chambers. She didn't want you hoping for a brunette only to bed a blonde. I must say I was disappointed at how quickly you fell to slumber." She ran her eyes over him, and I briefly considered shoving her face into Layla's bucket of suds and vomit.

Pointing a finger, Aeson ordered, "Keep your disappointments to yourself."

"You're not a maid at all. You're a mora." I looked at her more closely. It was her complexion, her shape, and the way her maids dress fit too snugly in some areas and too loose in others.

She shimmied her chest and puckered her lips. "Not everyone can afford to be virtuous. Although"—she glanced at Calise— "virtue seems to be in short supply here."

"*You wench*," Berrin started up, but Calise pulled him back to her side, glowering.

"You were well paid for your services and discretion."

"You have my discretion, but seeing as my services are complete, I see no reason to play pretty and polite now. Unless someone else likes the act and has the coin for it." Merla looked again at Aeson and popped her lips at him.

He fumed, nodding his head at the door. "Get rid of her."

I moved to push her from the room, gladly, but Layla stood up at the same time. The bucket in her hand swung a bit and sloshed dangerously in Merla's direction, causing Merla to back up a step. "Allow me, Miss Etta," said Layla. "I'm all finished and must dispose of this waste as it is."

"Thank you, Layla," I conceded and held the door for them. When their footsteps faded away and the door was safely locked again, I whipped around to face Berrin and Calise. They moved towards a more comfortable chair at the window table. Seeing the paleness on Calise's face gave me pause. Grumbling, I turned back to the door and knelt. Sucking in a long breath, I called a current of air from the hall and under the door, wrapping it around me like I had in the farmer's field before I pushed it out the window.

"There," I said, returning to my place behind Aeson at the desk. "No more foul smells for you, and our voices won't be heard."

"She's being generous," Aeson informed them. "Now tell us what designs your father has for me."

Chapter Fifteen

"THE ELDER LORDS don't like what you're doing here. You know this," Calise said plainly, relaxed in the chair. Berrin, at ease now that his secret was out, sat beside her with his hand twined with hers. Calise continued, "Your people are thriving and the villages in your care have only grown in the last few years. Your crops are better and stronger and when your farmers go to market, they outsell everyone else."

"Jealousy? Your father ordered you to seduce me because he and others are jealous." Aeson leaned back in his chair.

"Simply put—yes."

"Add some complications."

Calise adjusted her seat, lifting a hand to play with Berrin's hair absentmindedly as she explained. "If I could secure a marriage with you, your profits could be negotiated as my profits."

"You mean your father's profits," I sneered.

"Precisely," she said. "And if that weren't enough for him, he wants Wind Haven."

Aeson's face scrunched at this. "Wants Wind Haven?"

"Our lands begin where the passage road ends, and yours are the same on the other side of the mountains are they not?" She didn't wait for anyone to answer. "If my father could claim power over both parcels, then he would hold sway over the passage. He could chip it away and tax travelers for their use of it."

I folded my arms. "Did he truly think that marrying Aeson would ensure compliance to such an idea? Furthermore, it would give Aeson a hold on Erron lands upon your father's death."

Calise withdrew her hands and wrung them in her lap. "I'm not sure. Knowing my father and the company he keeps it wouldn't be farfetched to imagine something darker was to be ordered once I settled here."

I swallowed and looked back at Aeson, simmering at his reflection in the silver drawer hooks of the desk. After pulling his hand through his hair, he cleared his throat. "The two of you may leave now."

Calise and Berrin looked at each other and stood slowly. I opened the door for them and as they passed, I laid a hand on Calise's arm. "If you need anything, send Berrin to find me. I can provide more than just peppermint for your comforts."

She nodded and released Berrin's support as they slipped out the door, stepping back into their roles of innocent lady and diligent guard. I shut the door tightly but asked the wind to keep its current flowing out the window. Then I found my way across the room and sat back against Aeson's side of the desk.

I stayed silent, listening to the sounds of stable hands and workers in the yard below. The castle was fully awake now and the staff were doing their best to find their chores amongst a widespread hangover.

"If that draught had been any weaker," Aeson began, "if that mora had not been disappointed, she might've ended up the same as Calise."

I dropped my chin, unwilling to acknowledge his meaning aloud.

"Another woman paid and puffing with a child but no father."

Taking his hand, I told him, "If Lord Erron had asked for anything stronger, you might not have woken up."

The corner of his mouth ticked. "Is that concern for your lord and master I'm hearing?"

I shrugged innocently. "Who else would pay so nicely for my indignation?"

The words barely left my tongue when Aeson reached for my side braid and tried to pull me over. "Awful," he said, although his smirk betrayed amusement. Laughing with him, I pushed away and straightened. He stood and strode towards the window, running both hands through his hair. "I need to think." He looked over his shoulder. "Keep an eye on everyone for me? I'll be off for a ride."

"Of course," I agreed and watched him leave without another word. In his absence I released my favor of the wind and whispered a thank you. Then I turned to the books. I had a new spell to write.

With most everyone still tired from the night before, there was little to tend and I was able to stay in the study most of the day jotting down notes on House Erron into the late afternoon. When I finally returned to my rooms, Berrin was just about to knock on the door. He saw me down the hallway and waited until we were inside before he spoke.

"The excitement of the morning has not subsided. She wants a tea to settle her stomach."

"I'll make it now," I said, laying my papers aside and sending him down to the kitchen for hot water. In truth, the kitchen had all the same ingredients for this concoction, but it went without saying that Calise needed secrecy from us.

Berrin returned quickly enough and watched as I stirred in fresh slices of ginger, ample honey, and two drops of sharp vinegar. I whispered a quick spell into the cup and sent him on his way. Alone again, I pulled the next mixture together.

Weaving the long stalks of a green onion into an anklet, I laid it to soak with a mash of walnut, witch hazel, amaranth, and barley. At dinner time, only half the household appeared in the great hall. Calise stayed in her room, and Aeson had yet to return from his ride so the small lot of us ate in silence and cleared our own plates.

In the dark of the staircase, I smiled to myself. Few in the castle would notice what they did not feel anymore. Invigoration. With Calise's plan exposed, there was no need to play coquette with Aeson. The energy in the towers had shifted at last. Intentions had been made. I would've bet both my necklaces that everyone naturally knew House Erron would be departing soon, although they had no explanation as to why.

With the anklet good and sopping, I lifted it from the bowl and laid it on a crystal plate in the casting window. I watered the plants as the sun crept away behind the hills, tired from the long day above. The moon replaced it, coursing a slow silver path into the sky, turning the treetops into blue shadows. Then I sat on the window stool and waited.

When the castle was quiet and nearly everyone was asleep, my door brushed open and shut. He approached the window but stayed out of sight. "You're casting?"

"Yes."

"Shall I leave?"

I shook my head, turning to him. He leaned against the stones where the alcove met the wall. His eyes were at peace. Whatever turmoil he carried out of the study in the morning was left in the fields or discarded in the dirt along the road.

"Protection for Calise and Berrin," I said.

He pressed a smile to one corner of his mouth. "A kindness they barely deserve."

"Perhaps. But I think we all know what it is like to be oppressed by the odds we are given."

He hung his head and nodded, his black hair shimmering like creek water in the night. Bending at the knees, he slid down against the wall and stretched his legs out. Once he had settled, I stood and found the love lily.

"Here," I told him. "She'll make you feel better."

He laughed lightly and took it from my hands. I grabbed my stool and went back to the window. The moonlight was bold by now and ready for me to work with. Palms forward and flat, I twisted my wrists and pulled again and again until my forearms tingled like a swarm of bees were crawling along my skin. Satisfied with what I'd gathered, I lowered my hands over my pelvis and squeezed.

"*Errant on love, the Erron white dove. When blood applied, let life run shy. Dry what is red and leave the shell dead.*"

I splayed my fingers over the anklet as the pull came from

behind my elbows and ran along my skin. It burned through my knuckles and beneath my nails like a blade slicing along their beds. As soon as the sensation subsided, I stiffened my fingers and patted my hips three times to cut off the spell. Pulling my hands back, I shook them out, shuddering.

"What?" Aeson stood and came closer.

"I just always forget what the sting of the moon feels like with that one."

"Is it that way every time you do this?"

I straightened and rolled my shoulders back. "I don't do it that often."

Aeson squared his feet and crossed his arms over his chest. "None of our maids have had a baby in four years. Forgive me if I do not believe you."

I disregarded him and took the love lily off the floor, returning it to its companions.

"You think your work under my roof goes unnoticed, but it doesn't. Neither do you."

"I'm flattered," I muttered over my shoulder. Checking the plants and closing the window, I spun around and nearly smacked into him. I hadn't realized how close he was standing.

"Fair magic is supposed to cost you something more. You look unbothered already."

"This particular spell costs only the woman who wears it. Each moon, a blood anointing." I raised a brow at him and when I saw his face contort with curiosity but no conclusion, I elaborated, "You instructed me not to speak about fertility cycles anymore."

He rolled his neck to the side and stepped away. "Why do I even come in here?"

Stifling the laughter in my chest, I walked to the lower desk and sat down. "I'm not sure. It's not as if I invite you."

"By all means"—he swept an arm out wide, which made a magnificent shadow in the moonlight—"go forth and find another lord to pay for your daily indignation."

I couldn't stifle my laugh any longer. Instead, I pulled my knees up and bit into my skirts, muffling the sound from traveling through the walls.

Aeson shook his head and grinned, pulling the stool over to sit in front of me. "I presume nothing notable happened while I was gone."

"You presume correctly. Everyone was too haggard to cause any trouble."

He sighed. "And we don't need to worry about Layla? You seem to trust her completely."

I nodded and smiled from the back of my chair, upright again. "Layla removed her previous employer, and no one has discovered her yet."

Aeson's gaze went wide. "As her present employer, might you see how that offers little comfort?"

Belly shaking with laughter again, I turned my head back to the windows. "Unless you plan on dragging her to your chambers against her will, you have naught to worry about."

"As of this morning, I've no plans to drag anyone to my chambers ever. Willing or not."

"Yes, well. By Merla's account your chambers are rather unexciting."

He reached up to flick my cheek, but I batted him away and he gave up easily, opting for another weighted breath.

"What conclusions did you find on your ride?"

"Lord Bane," he said.

I looked at him lopsided. "The dying old man with a fancy mare?"

"Yes." He set his elbows on his knees and clasped his hands together in the space between. "If you recall, he also has a miserable nephew set to inherit his lands when he passes."

I bit back a smile and drummed my fingers along the edge of my desk. "He does. It would be better if he had an heir, wouldn't it?"

Chapter Sixteen

ESON CALLED CALISE AND BERRIN to his study the next morning. I arrived a moment later with the anklet in hand, wiped clean and charged by the moon. Taking Calise to the window, I gave her instructions to keep the casting potent each cycle after her baby arrived. Satisfied she had a full understanding, I turned her back to Berrin who took her in an embrace, softening seamlessly from statue to clay when she lay her head on his chest.

Aeson blinked at their affection and cleared his throat. "What I am proposing is less than ideal, and I cannot guarantee its success."

Calise nodded, willing to listen even without an absolute promise.

Aeson lifted the letter he had received in the village. "Faeler Bane in the west. You know him?"

"I met him at a solstice three years back."

"He is worried he will not live out the fullness of another

year. I know because he wishes to send me a prized mare to keep her safe from his deplorable nephew."

"Haefwit?" Calise asked.

"The same," Aeson replied.

"How does this help us?"

"How does it help *you*," I corrected. "If Faeler were to suddenly find happiness in matrimony and produce an heir, Haefwit would have no claim over anything, and Faeler's soon to be widow would find herself in a very powerful position. With more lands than even your own father."

Calise laid a hand over her belly, piecing together our meaning and looking up to Berrin's face. "The plan holds some hope, I suppose. We will have to act immediately. My father expects word from me soon and this secret will not stay small much longer."

Berrin nodded. "Can we be sure Lord Bane won't find suspicion in Calise's arrival?"

Aeson stood and folded his arms over his chest. "Faeler is worried he has no time left. My advice is don't waste it. Be obscure, but do not lie. If you show him you are the safest hope for his lands and his people, he will spout whatever tale you want him to. This is my belief."

Calise rubbed a hand from one hip to the other, then turned towards me. "Men feel safer when their heir is certain. Is there a way to ensure a boy?"

"Yes." I met her gaze directly and held a hand up to Aeson at the same time. He would know that such a casting would surely be Fierce magic. "But it will not help you here."

"Why not?" Her fingers found Berrin's and squeezed until her knuckles went pale.

"It would've been one whole moon before you knew what had

happened." I gestured between her and Berrin. "I don't know how much time passed between your discovery and Lord Erron's plot being shared with you. I know it was nearly two weeks to travel here, and you have been here for another fortnight still. The Innocents have already chosen your baby. Boy or girl. It is done."

Calise's face fell, and she rubbed a cheek with her free hand.

"I might be able to sense it, however."

"Really?" Her face lifted.

I took a breath, roaming my eyes over the bookshelves. Aeson walked around from his seat and blocked my view. "It's a Fair spell," I said, ignoring Aeson and addressing Calise again. "That means the price is yours to pay. Like the anklet I have just given you."

Berrin tightened his grip around Calise. "What kind of price?"

Walking to the shelves, I pushed Aeson out of my way, just barely. He was staunch in his frame and gave me no more room than I needed. Finding the book I wanted, I laid it open on the table and flipped through its pages.

"Simple things. A lock of hair. A drop of blood. Do not be alarmed guard Berrin, and feel free to keep that dagger stowed," I said, running a hand over the list of ingredients. "It will take me most of the day to gather and prepare the fresh ingredients. I will fetch you when I am ready."

Calise and Berrin turned to leave. I followed but Aeson held a hand up. "If Calise is to depart so suddenly, we must provide a reason for her discontent."

"That is easily done, I would say." Calise lifted her shoulders and dropped them quickly as if the task was truly that easy to carry.

I looked between them all. "I shall leave it to your hands."

"I will go with you," Aeson said.

"No." I crumpled my face at him.

"Yes," Calise confirmed. Beside her, Berrin nodded.

"We need to slight Lady Calise," Aeson said. "There is only one person the castle will believe could offend a guest that greatly. To further that point, I must favor the offender over the recipient, in public eye."

The three of them nodded and exchanged one continuous look, but it was Berrin who spoke the horrid phrase I'd recently learned. "If you can't find one, find the other."

I scowled at the lot of them, then jerked the door open and stomped off. Aeson was quick to follow, projecting his voice. "Etta, get back here."

"I hope you catch the blue plague for this."

"That is no way to talk to your lord and master," he hollered.

"I shall find another!" I lifted my skirts and tried to run. Aeson had the benefit of men's clothing though and chasing me down was easy. He caught up as I reached the bottom step of the stairs, delivering me to the second floor. Grabbing my arm, he spun me about and blocked the way. I wrestled out of his grasp and glowered at him.

"My Lord Crennly, please, stay with me. I swear I will not speak anything of it." Calise came down the stairs next, spouting nonsense. Berrin's footsteps fell behind her.

"I did not agree to any of this." I ground my teeth at Aeson who made no efforts to conceal his amusement.

Chest shuddering with laughter withheld, he started again, "I order you, witch. Face the Lady Calise and apologize. Now."

"No." I grabbed the nearest candle from the wall and threw

it at him. The flame extinguished in the air, and wax fell to the stone floor with four perfect plips, cooling instantly. While Aeson's attention was distracted, I scurried down the stairs, to the great hall where I could use the servants' door to access the kitchen, then back up the other flight of stairs to my chambers.

To my horror and surely to the others' delight, the great hall was buzzing with servants cleaning up the last of the banquet decorations and scrubbing the floor. I stopped in the entryway to stare on in panic. Everyone paused in their work and looked at me, Aeson, Calise, and Berrin stumbling along behind. Whipping my head between the room and Aeson, I shrieked at him. No words, just fury.

"Brothers and Sisters, Aeson, what is this?" Elma's voice came from the other end of the hall. Excellent for Aeson and Calise's plan, but the very last human I wanted to be subjected to.

Before Aeson could conjure up an excuse, I marched across the room and stuck my face under Elma's bulging eyeballs. "The time for your departure has long since passed. If you had any sense, you would know that and be gone and the happenings of the castle would not be yours to overhear or stick that wicked nose into, you vile, vile woman!"

"*Etta.*" Aeson's voice echoed off the walls now.

"No." I turned once more, waving my arms at the three of them. "I will not take part in your stupid plans. The whole lot of you are horrid this morning. *Horrid!*"

Making my way unchallenged out the door and down the servants' hall through the kitchen, I heard the commotion rise behind me. Calise's voice soared above it all. "I promise, my lord. It is no big offense. Stay with me. Let us enjoy this day together."

"What has the witch done now, Aeson? Tell me." Elma made

sure her voice was heard, shouting to the high ceiling so her opinion would ricochet off the beams. "I've always said you give her too much sway in this household."

Ignoring it all, I ran, kicked my door open, then slammed it behind me. In my bedchamber, I grabbed a cloak to keep me warm in the breeze and slung my gathering bag across my chest. Pulling my hair out from beneath the strap, I twirled it around into a knot and secured it with a length of leather cord.

Back in the main room, I stopped short. Aeson had snuck in and was waiting quietly near the window. "I told you. I do not want you with me," I said, moving to the shelf for a handful of clover.

"And we told you, for this to appear believable I must offend Calise in a way that would make her feel unwelcome."

"Lock her in a room with your mother and you will accomplish the same goal." I shook my chin at him and cinched my belt tighter, making sure my knife was secure.

"Speaking of my mother, I will have to pay for that later."

"Pay for it now and leave me alone." I grabbed my stool and practically flung it over to the wall beneath my highest shelves, which were stocked with extra bottles, jars, vials, and squares of parchment for packaging up whatever I foraged. Filling my bag, I hopped down and headed towards the door. "Get out. I want to lock this while I'm away."

"You are truly angry at this?" he asked, crestfallen amongst my plants.

"Yes. Get out."

"Not until you admit there was sense here."

"Then lock the door behind you." I left and slammed the door a second time. Rushing down the stairs, my chest burned. Irritation did not adequately describe the energy pulsing through every muscle and every strip of sinew that connected my bones to my body. Calise and Aeson may have had their desired outcome, but it was at the expense of my tempestuous standing in everyone's minds. It was unlike Aeson to overlook that fact.

Down in the courtyard, I sucked in a bundle of air. I was ready to bark at a stable hand for my horse. But I changed my mind. I'd had enough people for one morning. Instead, I slipped through the wheelbarrows and pitchforks and did it all myself. Tethering Sparrow to a post in the barn, I brushed him down with care. I wouldn't allow Aeson's stupidity to cause my poor manners on an innocent beast.

Tightening the girth on my saddle and pulling the bridal up over Sparrow's head, I led him to the front bailey and turned him around the black alba tree. As we came about, Aeson's horse was led out from the other end of the stable, and I groaned.

"I told you." He appeared beside me with riding boots on his feet. "I'm going with you." He straightened and cleared his throat noisily. "And if it takes all day, I will bend your ear until you bend that wretched will of yours and apologize to Lady Calise."

I shook my head and said nothing. Aeson's horse was not yet ready for him to mount up, but mine was. I swung my leg over and didn't wait for my feet to touch the stirrups. Kissing my lips, Sparrow took off through the gate, and I left Aeson in a cloud of dust.

Chapter Seventeen

B Y THE TIME SPARROW AND I crossed over the tree line, Aeson and Meadowgrass were on our tail. I reined Sparrow in and let him breathe under the shade of oak and knotwood trees. Slowing down beside us, Aeson loosened the reins on his mare and lifted a hand to push the matted hair from his face. He'd worked nearly as hard as Meadowgrass to catch us. She was a good horse and faster than most could keep their seat on. Her speed demanded every ounce of focus her rider could muster. Frankly, Aeson deserved the exertion after such a gleeful performance in the castle.

We walked in silence until the perimeter walls were long distorted by branches. Leaves were beginning to brown at their edges. Summer was drying up. Within two more full moons, the ground would be coated and crusted with fallen leaves and autumn frosts.

"Should I apologize or just let you push me off my horse?" Aeson finally asked.

I kept my eyes straight ahead. "What if I want both?"

"You shall have both."

Twisting my neck to look at him, I huffed and bit my tongue. In response, he trotted ahead and cut off the path. "I mean it," he said, kicking his feet out of the stirrups and dropping his reins completely. Holding his arms out, he gestured with his hands. "Come on, one good shove to fix whatever's wrong."

My face warmed and my lips burned with emotions I didn't have time for. "Nothing is wrong." I steered Sparrow around Meadowgrass and walked on ahead, casting my eyes out into the forest.

In a minute, when Aeson was riding beside me again, he started once more. "Will you at least share what you are seeking out here?"

I heaved a long sigh, putting off my reply. "I need the eggshells of a rock dove, a tuft of fur from the wood rabbits, and fresh spring water from its source."

"All that in addition to blood and hair from Calise and Berrin both?"

I gave a dip of my chin and carried on the search with my eyes.

"The doves have long since hatched. How will we find eggshells this late in the year?"

"I believe I said it would take most of the day. Just as I said you didn't need to join me."

"And miss out on all your righteous company?"

I shook my head, denying the smile that wanted to stretch over my lips. Clicking my tongue at Sparrow, I led him off the trail and towards the creek. Aeson followed and we tracked the water for another mile until it began to dwindle and narrow. I dismounted, tying Sparrow to a grey oak. Meadowgrass went beside him, and Aeson waited with them both as I walked up to find the trickle of water from a cliff face ahead.

With two vials full, I returned and helped Aeson water the horses. We tied them back to their trees and I scanned the forest floor, chewing my lower lip and sweeping my gaze from side to side.

"Wood rabbits?" he asked.

"Yes," I said, meandering away. When I found the dugout edges of a burrow, I sunk to the forest floor. Behind me, Aeson crouched into the leaves without a sound. I ran a hand over each ear, tapped both sides of my nose, and flattened my palms on my knees.

"Jumping skips, and burrow tricks. Whisker twitch, and whisper itch. Share from claws with padded paws."

Slipping my fingers into the floor debris, I connected my magic to the cold earth and the dim lit burrow beneath. A smile creased my cheeks, and I gave three pats to the ground, inching forward each time like a hop. Calling animals was a lot more fun than calling the weather.

When I opened my eyes, five of them had emerged, sitting on their haunches before us. "I do not need all of you. Silly things," I said. One hopped forward and stretched his front end, arching to sniff at my nose. "May I?" I asked.

With a quick kick, he bounced into my lap. I combed down his back with my fingers, gathering as much fur as I could. With a scratch between his ears, I set him down and reached for my bag. I folded the parcel of fur away first then pulled the clover out. Laying out the entire bunch, the other rabbits bounded forward. They devoured it in half a minute and hopped back to their burrow without a backwards look. I stood without dusting myself off, turning back to Aeson who looked at me quizzically.

"Do you ever think about anything except your work?" he asked.

I was already rummaging in my gathering bag again. A bottle would be best for transporting the eggshells once we found them. "What else is there to think of?" I frowned at him and went back to my search.

"Anything. It's just, you're always so singular in your thoughts," he said. I shook my head at the remark and when I was certain everything was in order, I moved to pass by, but he stopped me. Wrapping his hand around the strap of my bag he pulled me close and searched my face. "Tell me what I did wrong this morning."

I blinked, surprised he was still so bothered by it.

His voice pitched when he spoke again. "Tell me how to make it right."

"There is nothing wrong and nothing to right."

"Your sudden lack of indignation tells me otherwise."

My shoulders slumped and I used both hands to push all the loose hairs out of my face. "It is nothing. It is just a mere difference between you and me."

"What difference?"

We returned to the horses, and I took my time untying Sparrow. Rather than mount up, I walked through the trees with Aeson and Meadowgrass in step beside us. He held his words back but not his gaze. That was fixed on me.

"It's different for you, Aeson. You united these lands in a way your father never quite accomplished. As Calise said, everything you've done here has succeeded. They prosper because of you. Because you tend to their needs before your own and they show their gratitude tenfold over when they go to the fields."

"But what is this difference you speak of?"

I pulled down on Sparrow's reins, halting us in the middle of the trail to face Aeson. "You're not some forgotten piece of history that was wiped out. You've earned your place in your father's chair and no one even remembers the gangly bear cub that arrived here seven years ago. You're just, Aeson Crennly. Lord and master."

His brow furrowed and he stepped closer. "And what do you think you are?"

Scoffing, I walked on, nearly to the dry part of the cliff face. "I'm the castle witch of course. The tumultuous little girl that everyone tolerates because she can stitch a wound and soothe a burn. What were the notes? Sharp with her tongue but kept from his presence."

He gave an exaggerated moan. "If only that quality had stuck."

Finding a new tree to tie Sparrow to, I took the bag off my shoulders and looked up at the rocks. Focused on the task at hand, I told Aeson, "I will climb up and find what I can. Just, catch me if I fall."

He looked between me and the rock face. "I don't recall agreeing to this plan."

"I'll be fine."

"No. I'll climb."

"Aeson, stop it." I walked on and set my hands on the lowest ledge.

Wrapping his arms around my waist, he lifted me easily and stepped back, dragging my hands from the stones. I twisted until he set me down, but he wouldn't let me out of his arms. Instead, he pinned my own behind me. "Ask me who you are."

"What? No. Unhand me, you heap."

"No," he laughed. "You reminded me who I am, who I have become. Now let me do the same for you."

"I just told you who I am. Were you not listening?" I stomped on his foot and dashed a few paces away.

"I listened as well as you ever do," he panted, chasing after. "And you're wrong."

I folded my arms and turned my head skyward.

"Etaine, witch of Castle Crennly. Loved and trusted by everyone within the walls, in Tote Crennly, and all the lands of Valley Maer alike."

Shaking my head, I found a break in the trees. Dodging his reach, I ran past him and threw myself at the rocks again. Aeson was not deterred. Grabbing once more, he held me tight, chest snug against my back and his mouth to my ear. His voice slipped through the mess of my hair, coming undone in my struggle, but it was clear all the same.

"Huritt," he said, naming off the baker's boy.

"What's he got to do with anything?"

He didn't explain. Just carried on with another name. "Laken. Prilla. Riggs. Garret. Layla, I imagine. The shepherdess and all her children. That cow in the field and her farmers. Calise and Berrin. Every maid in the castle it seems."

I saw his point and tried to elbow him away, but it only served as a chance for him to turn me around and rope us together like celery stalks grown tight against one another.

"Let's not forget the garden snake. The garden itself. The pears. The coughing elder in the village right now. And that's just the last few weeks. What about Smithwik two years back when he hurt his leg? Even my mother during summer solstice that one time."

"You tricked me into that."

"You didn't leave me a choice. She needed that remedy." He chuckled, leaning in closer as I slid my hands up his arms to push off of a stronger foundation. "You spend every waking breath tending my people and my lands. If you agree with Calise then you agree with this. It is your doing as much as mine. Whatever air of tumult you think still follows you is long gone. I promise."

I averted my gaze, straining my neck towards the forest. If I could avoid his expression, I might be able to avoid his accolades too. "No longer tumultuous but still a little girl. That is the knowledge you reassure me with?"

"I would acknowledge you as a woman were I not fearful of being slit from neck to navel in the middle of the night." He tightened his grip.

"You think I'd wait for you to sleep?" I dug my fingers into his arm but found my strength waning. It slipped out beneath me like an unseen patch of mud.

"You cannot bury yourself in the shadows and whimper when no one finds you," he retorted. "If you believe this is the account people hold of you, it's only because that is all you've allowed them to carry."

His hand finally relaxed and his palm flattened against my lower back. A tremor crept up my spine. And it felt like magic. The surprise of it stopped me and we stood for a long moment, breath caught between us, exchanging air but not words.

My mouth was dry but I managed to swallow and felt my fingertips again. "You have made your point. Thank you, my lord."

He wilted, shaking his head. "Formalities. I might have guessed."

Stalking away through the trees, he left me still and breathless. He climbed the cliff face as he demanded, and all I could do was stand as solid as the grey oaks. I stood for so long the creeping thyme, with its bright purple flowers, twined around my feet and my ankles. Wiping my face free of whatever Aeson had possessed me with, I glanced down at the glossy leaves and wiggled my toes.

"I can't," I whispered. "I have work to do."

The creeper paused for a minute and considered this before retreating and spreading out across its kingdom floor again. Pebbles showered the earth from above and Aeson jumped from the last ledge, landing steady and strong. He came to me with one hand crinkled and awkwardly shaped. I barely got the jar out of my bag in time.

"I didn't think to take that with me," he mumbled. "I hope this is enough."

Turning his palm over the lip of the jar, he deposited a pile of broken eggshells. The crisp curves were riddled with black and grey freckles. "It's perfect."

He nodded and walked away. I watched him go and watched his steps falter before he turned back. "I'm sorry I scolded you."

Clutching the jar and my gathering bag as tightly as I could, I shook my head so hard the rest of my hair came loose and fell around my face, dancing with the breeze. "It is nothing I didn't deserve."

He worked his jaw around, holding something back. Probably another pile of wrath. Well deserved. "I gave you grief earlier about attacking my mother. I shouldn't have. In truth, it's best that she leaves as well. Then we can get back to the life we lead here, without any other disruptions, or visitors for that matter."

Chapter Eighteen

WE RODE BACK THROUGH THE TREES IN SILENCE, but before we emerged onto the fields, Aeson tugged on his reins and brought Meadowgrass to a halt. I stayed in my place behind him, but after a moment, he turned his head to the side and instructed me, "Come here."

I guided Sparrow up alongside him but left space between us. He regarded the distance with a smirk. Nudging the far side of Meadowgrass's belly, he used his inside rein to pull her in a sidestep all the way until our knees bumped. I watched from the corner of my eye, fussing with my hair and gathering it over one side.

Exhaling the weight of our conversation in one long collapse of his ribs, he slumped in his saddle and plunked his forehead on the knot of my shoulder. "Are we all right, Etta?"

"Yes."

"I didn't think it would matter. Surely by now you'd know how indebted everyone is to you. Every baby born, every fever burned, every ache and ailment are tended by your hand. There is little that happens here that doesn't have your mark on it."

"And what happens if one day the baby can't be coaxed? Or the fever won't break. What happens if I can't cure them with a spell, or something burns in my name?"

He shifted to find my face more clearly. "This is your worry? Etta, it has been years since anything burned in the name of witches. You don't use Fierce magic. They know you differently."

I buried a growl in my chest. "Perhaps."

He narrowed his eyes, evaluating the word.

"I'll work on it, all right?"

"You'd better," he said, glancing across the open fields at the castle. "Do you think it's better to arrive separate or together?"

"Separate." I sharpened my gaze at the outer wall. "I'll sneak in the back door like I would if I was truly trying to avoid you."

"When are you not?" He righted himself in his saddle and threw me a grin. "I shall return to the study and draft a letter for Calise to carry to Lord Bane."

I nodded and held Sparrow back until Aeson was far enough to convince the castle we wanted nothing to do with each other. Then I loosened my reins and let Sparrow pick the pace, chomping at the tall grass along the way. As we neared the outer wall, I turned him and trotted around to the back access door.

Dismounting, we passed under the arch and through the alley, entering the courtyard from the side. I kept my head down as I ordered a stable hand to unsaddle and brush Sparrow before putting him away. Holding my bag snug against me, I crept in the kitchen door and up to my rooms. Just one more spell to cast before I could be rid of this mess.

Writing spells for people I didn't know well was harder than I anticipated. After reviewing House Erron's location and history, checking their shield again, and considering everything I had learned of Calise, I still struggled. She had, after all, stolen one of my brews, drugged Aeson, and let a mora accompany him to bed.

As ink stained my fingers and my quill scratched over paper, I dug deep for honest purpose. Send Calise safely on her way, with success in her wake, and keep Valley Maer safe from her father.

Keeping that intention clear as I wrote a spell to reveal her growing child was a task that took me most of the evening. As I finished, the sloshing of pots and pans started in the kitchen below. I flung my window open and stretched, gulping the air. The night's wind blew so confidently I was tempted to flip over and tilt myself out of the sill. Let the breeze carry me away from my worries.

Shaking off the thought, I left to find Aeson in the hall. He saw me through the crowd and took his cue. Back upstairs, I left the door ajar for everyone to slip in easily. When they arrived, I sat Calise in the middle of the plants with a fern at her feet. Berrin hovered like a falcon on the wind.

"Left palm," I said. Calise lifted her hand to me, and I placed an onion and a snipping of calendula upon it. Walking to the desk, I retrieved a bowl filled with the day's gathering. Spring water, muddled with the fine powder of crushed eggshells, and rabbit fur. Each piece had been chopped in half save for one. There was only one whole to be found from all the others. Back in front of Calise, I offered it to her. "It'll taste wretched, but you don't need to swallow it. Simply swirl it around your tongue and spit it back into the bowl."

She froze for a moment before taking it from my hands. Her expression curdled as the mixture hit her lips, and I couldn't say I blamed her. While she did as I asked, I turned to Berrin with a cup.

"What do I do?" he asked.

"Hair first, blood second. And it must come from a split in your lip, so you may use your beloved dagger at last."

"My lip?"

"Yes," I said, walking back to Calise. "Yours too. All this started with a kiss, did it not?"

Calise spit out the brew and I traded her the bowl for a cup. Berrin crouched beside her, trimming the tips of her hair and pausing before he pierced her lip with the fine point in his hand.

Once he'd stepped aside, I sat before Calise and the fern and took their cups. Turning the fern pot until I had three clear fronds to work with, I placed the bowl center and the two cups on either side with the other leaf tips dripping down past the rims.

Then I found Calise's eyes. "You might feel some aching in your womb. I promise the baby is safe. It's just the magic feeling for who it might be."

She nodded too many times for it to be a sense of confidence or comfort. I wagged my fingers and shook my hands, running through the words in my mind. Honesty. Intention. I had to hold on to that. No matter what. The spell would get distracted and turn fruitless if I lost sight of my truest aim.

Starting on the left, I swept my hand from the front frond and off into the cup. Three times. All the while, reciting the corresponding couplets.

"Amber swirls from sweet sea air; tresses in curls from dove

hearts fair. Mother, lover, girlish silly; Cal is her, the heiress lily. Drips, drops, along the frond; mirror the one and fill the pond."

I moved to the right.

"Stoic, proud; no ruckus or rowd. A chin so stern, guarding a heart; kissed the hand at station start. Drips, drops, along the frond; mirror the one and fill the pond."

I flattened my left palm towards Calise and the other to me. Once the magic curled around us both, I snapped my fingers three times over each cup. Done.

The shadows grew tall around us but I didn't dare disturb the spell. Just as a caterpillar might, the water from the bowl inched up its fern leaf, swirled at the base and selected its cup. I waited until every last drop had made its decision before grinning openly. "Aeson," I broke the silence. "Would you light a candle, please?"

He shuffled through the dark and brought one to light. As the flame grew, I reached for the cup that held Berrin's blood and all the water. Offering it to Calise, it took a moment for her eyes to focus. After discerning which cup had been filled, she gave a sob of relief.

Berrin fell apart next, and I barely crawled out of the way in time as he came to hug Calise's legs and lay his head in her lap. Stepping back in the dark, Aeson found me and pulled us as far into the corner as we could go.

"This is a strange moment to be privy to." He shook his head. "It is not for us."

"I know. But I am happy to give her this relief."

"You are better than I can be the last few days."

I found his hands and held them tight. "No more banquets in my honor. For your sake."

Pinching my pinky in retaliation, he leaned closer. "I don't think I'd want to know."

I looked up in the dark, barely making out his face.

"If it were a boy or girl," he explained.

"Would you hope for one or the other?" I asked, fully realizing that one day I might serve more than just Aeson as head of the household.

"I think it would depend." The shadow of his eyes found mine in the dark, then clipped back to Calise and Berrin.

Before I could ask him on what, someone cleared their throat. Calise stood and stepped closer. "Thank you, Etta, for doing this. I feel better in our departure knowing I have something certain to hint at with Lord Bane when we get there."

"Aye," Berrin said. "Me as well. This gives her safety where I couldn't provide it."

I wanted to say something about being more discreet in their affair moving forward, but she already had her anklet, so I withheld my comments. "You're welcome."

"This will require another bit of performance in the morning," Aeson reminded us.

"I respectfully request to be left out of it this time," I said.

The three of them laughed but I didn't lower my glare until Aeson agreed and committed to it. "We'll manage without you, I promise."

"May I have a moment with Etta?" Calise asked, gesturing towards the door and looking between Berrin and Aeson. "She does need to apologize to me, after all."

Berrin left immediately. Half his actions still tethered to his duty as a guard. Aeson on the other hand, lingered, dragging his feet and eyeing us over his shoulder. When the door finally latched, Calise took my hands in hers, and my spine went as rigid as the trunk of our black alba.

"Yes, my lady?" I asked, angling my head away.

"He is lucky to have you in his service," she said. On the heels of Aeson's own praising, I fought back an eye roll. I knew who and what I was, and I didn't need another person claiming that I was anything else. "You are just as lucky to have him."

One of my eyebrows lifted.

She laughed. "You two may delight in your goading and badgering but he will protect you. Not just as a witch, but as a . . . friend," she said, looking strange. "You may not need it now, but you are right about him. That air of hope is difficult to find in this world."

I licked my lips and tried to pull my hands from hers. She wouldn't release me. Instead, she held tighter and pulled closer.

"If my father has shared his intentions with anyone else, you should know that more will test you. They will poke and prod at your triumphs here until they can prove the world is as they want it."

"As they *make* it, you mean."

"Yes." She squeezed my hands tighter still. "He will need your protecting as much as you will his. Do not lose your friendship for anything."

I scanned her face for signs of jest, but her mouth was sure and solid. Her eyes were trained directly at me. The word hit heavy on my ears, but she was right. Aeson had become my friend since he arrived. The care he bestowed on his subjects was not exclusive of me despite my regular disobedience. "I won't," I told her.

She looked down, dropping our hands to rub her belly. It was still flat, but like she said, it would reveal itself soon enough. "I wish you could be there when this boy makes his entrance.

Everyone should have a castle witch, even if they're not half as good as you."

"Thank you." The words tasted sour.

"Will you forgive my poor attempt at espionage before I leave?"

I shook my head. "There is nothing to forgive. You are a woman playing as well as you can in a world made for men."

"And what world does a witch belong to?" she asked. There was no answer. My world was destroyed. By men. She eyed the door with moonlight glinting in her eye, and the candle glowing across her cheeks. "If there is anything I can ever do to make amends for tiptoeing a plot through your halls, please write to me."

I reassured her that I would and she dipped a curtsy of respect, sweeping out the door. Her and Berrin disappeared, and Aeson entered once they were well and gone. "Did you apologize?"

I folded my arms and leaned my hip against the desk. "She issued a warning is all. To be on our guard if other lord's make their presence known."

"Ah." He tilted his head to the ceiling. Outside the window, an owl hooted, and the chirps of castle bats filled the air. The night hunters were waking, which meant it was time for the sun dwellers to sleep.

"If the castle is to empty tomorrow, I should pay a visit to the bees."

Aeson smiled out the window, light catching his eyes. "What will you bring them?"

"Only the pears. It is too late to ask Prilla for a cake." A yawn overtook me. "I'll leave before the castle stirs."

He bowed his chin to his chest, humming in agreement. "Give

the queen my regards."

"I will." I made sure to step on his toes as I walked to my sleeping chamber, gripping the door with one final sentiment. "Goodnight, Aeson."

Chapter Nineteen

A S PROMISED, I left before the kitchen even had bread in the ovens. Saddling Sparrow, I guided him out of the courtyard with my carry bag full of pears from the orchard. We walked the whole way, clopping through the village just as the shops were opening their doors and babies cried for morning milk.

The bees were still rousing for the day when I arrived. Leaving Sparrow a good distance from their tree, I removed my shoes and walked the rest of the way quietly. The few gatherers that were awake hummed around me, crawling through my hair, and folding themselves up in the pleats of my skirt. I sank to my knees before their hive and laid my forehead to the roots, thanking them, blessing them, informing them our guests were leaving and we appreciated their devotion to keeping our lands fertile and welcoming.

Sitting up again, I pulled out my knife and sliced the pears into small pieces, spreading the feast across my skirts. As the sugar struck the air, more workers emerged from above and swept down to feed. I hummed a lullaby for them, the only one I could recall from childhood. Although I couldn't remember all the words, I was fairly certain it was a story about the winds of the world. It seemed to soothe the bees, so I reserved it for their presence only.

I lay with them for a long while as the most curious hive members cleaned my hands of sticky pear flesh. It was all I could do to breathe steady against the tickle of them in my palms.

Their honey supply for the winter was nearly complete. They'd made enough to provide the castle with all that was needed for winter coughs, with plenty left for them to survive the season. It would be a good addition to what we'd gather at Lummis alongside the first grains.

By the time the sun hung almost directly above, they had finished my offering, and I sat up carefully. With one last blessing, I mounted Sparrow and cut through an empty field. To the east, a small train of horses and carriages emerged from the village. They would head north out of our valley and then west, to Castle Bane.

I stopped and called up a wind, holding my breath so long I risked falling out of the saddle. When I felt sure it understood my meaning, I sent it towards House Erron's convoy. The wind would be at their backs all the way to their stop tonight. It would speed their travels for everyone's benefit.

Taking the back path behind the village homes, I tied Sparrow outside the shepherd's house. Their smaller kids ran amuck in the village center with the eldest daughter on their threshold, watching. She looked seventeen or so. Her face was mostly clear of skin marks, but her body no longer fit the dress of a younger girl. Begrudgingly, I was grateful for whatever it was that supplied them the new clothes Garret had noticed on his visit.

"Good day," I greeted her.

"Good day," she replied, her voice raspy but clear around each sound. A bit like a queen bee herself. It suited her brown eyes and honey skin. "Ma's laying the baby to sleep if you're looking for her."

"And your father?" I asked. She shrugged and I took the liberty of sitting down beside her. "Is he afield?"

"He could be. Da doesn't talk to us any much more these days."

"He's been unhappy."

She didn't comment.

"What's your name?" I knew very little about the older Shepherd children. Only that there were two sisters, one dark, one fair, and three brothers. I hadn't been here when they were born. Only Kella, the nursling. If I started with a name, perhaps I could soften the darker one's edges and gain a new perspective on her father.

"Saana."

"Beautiful," I said. "Like your mother's name."

As if summoned, Ellara emerged from the back of the house, startling when she saw me. Her belly had grown some, but her gait was still easy. "Etta. You're back."

"I am." I stood and shook out my skirt, stealing an extra step inside the house. "Garret said you'd had a stroke of good luck and regathered your wares. I wanted to be absolutely sure there was nothing you still wanted."

"No. Everything is back as it was."

"Good," I said, squinting past her in the dusty light. Her statement was questionable. They had wares, yes, but some already seemed to be missing. Again. "And the baby is strong?"

She found the nearest chair and collapsed with a sigh. "Yes. He kicks all night it seems. Spun around just yesterday. Saana and I felt his form in the afternoon and he'd put himself the wrong way for a spell. He's back where he should be now."

"That's good." I exhaled in relief. It was not unheard of for some babies to make their way feet first, but it was harder on the mothers than a proper crowning, and the thought made me pick at my nails.

Ellara closed her eyes, enjoying a moment of stillness in her belly. I used the chance to scan her kitchen more thoroughly. I was positive they did not have what they should. Not enough to manage the number of mouths they fed every day.

There was a thump at the door and the shepherd himself stumbled in. He wavered a bit until his eyes adjusted from the sunlight. Gaining his bearings, his eyes fell to me. "Castle wife," he snarled. "What are you here for?"

"Checking on your unborn child, sir." I tipped my chin up at him. "But I'll be on my way, I'm sure you're anxious to be with your family."

He glanced between Ellara and me as if there was a secret in the air he might glimpse. In response, Ellara tightened her arms over her belly and turned away from me. I nodded to her nonetheless and stepped around Shepherd's frame. Passing over their threshold, I whispered the same spell to keep the kids healthy and safe until their father could be brought to his consequences.

Untying Sparrow, my thoughts swung back and forth trying to make sense of cabinets that could empty and fill and empty again as fast as the shepherds were. I disliked knowing something was rotting but being unable to sniff it out.

"I'll ask you to stop checking on my family, witch wife."

Of course he had followed me. I turned back to face him. With his thumbs hooked on his belt, he leaned a shoulder against the outside wall.

"Your family are wards of Castle Crennly," I said. "It's my job to check on them as it is Lord Crennly's job to care for them."

"We don't need his care. We need no help from him at all." He snapped his teeth at me, and I saw flecks of white on his tongue. Red colored the corners of his mouth. My heart dropped. Sweet water. Odorless and distilled by the pressed petals of the sweet wood blooms. It looked like a bean paste in its cruelest form but could be watered down for easier consumption. Worse than ale and not found anywhere near our valley. At least, not naturally.

I dropped my reins to point at him, stepping closer and breathing the wet straw stink of him. "How did you come by those sores, master shepherd?"

He fixed his eyes on me. "It's none of your business, is it? Errand girl."

Shuddering, I gathered my skirts and climbed back into my saddle. I needed to find Garret and Aeson. Sweet wood or its water was not something I used in my workshop, so I had never bothered with its whereabouts or origins. The addictive side effects were too risky. Everyone was entitled to their choices but choosing stupidity confounded me. Shepherd was playing a terrible game.

I looked him over one last time. From the drape of his clothes, there was nothing in his pockets, which combined with their shelves to make nothing at all. No answers and no starting points.

Sparrow and I galloped the whole way uphill.

A better sight met my eyes in the courtyard. Elma's trunks were being loaded onto a carriage and the horses tacked up. The wretch herself was nowhere to be seen but that was preferred. I led Sparrow straight into the barn and dismounted there. While I combed him down, stewing over what I'd just seen, Garret found me.

"You missed a good show."

"Did I?" I asked, still breathing short and shallow.

He nodded. "Mother Elma broke half the pottery at breakfast this morning."

"She what?"

Garret drew in a long breath. "Mm. Lady Calise ordered her things to be packed and readied and our young lord's mother threw a better tantrum than any of the village children could produce."

I muttered an insult under my breath as I pushed the straw down Sparrow's back. "What did Aeson do?"

"He was calm as ever. As if House Erron's departure was no surprise to him."

"Mm." I was too busy grinding my teeth to really hear the question that lurked beneath Garret's observation.

"What's wrong?" he asked. "You're lacking your charming demeanor."

Spine stiff as a board, I tossed the straw back in a pile and laid both hands on Sparrows back to collect my worries. "Shepherd has sweet water on his lips."

"What did you say?"

I turned and wrapped an arm around my middle, digging

through my hair with my other hand. "White spots. Red mouth. It could only be sweet water."

"What wretched Sister would give him that?"

"I don't know." I swallowed, eyes darting all over the stables as if the problem were before me and I would spot the solution among manure piles.

"We have to inform Lord Crennly."

"Yes," I said, dreading the thought. Breathing normal again, I painted on a smile. "How's Layla faring this morning?"

"I imagine she is well." He adjusted his belt. "The shepherdess? And the kids?"

I lifted one shoulder. "Mostly at ease. Running wild in the town center."

Garret sputtered with his lips next, rolling his shoulders back. "I'll select half a dozen guards to search any obvious hiding spots. And I'll set two more to follow Shepherd."

"Somebody gave it to him. I'm sure of it," I twisted my hair around my fingers. "He was adamant he didn't want us to keep checking on his family. Said they needed no help from Aeson."

"Who would give a lowly shepherd a dose of sweet water? It's not cheap."

I threw a hand up. "According to Lady Calise, any of the Elder Lords."

Garret stiffened at this and arched an eyebrow. "Perchance someone else bought back their household goods and left that in the mix."

I nodded.

He kicked at a loose stone in the floor, muttering to himself. "To what end though?"

"Sir." A stable hand had snuck up beside us. He shifted his

weight back and forth, trying to keep his gaze on Garret but slipping my way every few moments.

"What is it?" Garret asked.

"Smithwik asked me to tell you that Henrick is missing again."

"Who's Henrick?" I asked.

"The new smith apprentice. He arrived last season. Decent lad," Garret said. "Except this is twice now he's not even been on the grounds when he's supposed to be at the fires."

I examined the boy's face, freckles painted across his nose and blonde hair stuck in every direction. "Is that all?" I asked. He wobbled a step away.

"Stop it, witch." Garret patted the boy's shoulder. "Ignore her, she thinks herself dangerous. Thank you for the message."

The boy nodded and ducked back out to the yard. We watched him go but neither of us moved. "Is this something to be concerned about?" I asked.

"Just lads being lads," Garret said. "More than likely, Henrick has a girl in the village or in the fields somewhere."

Untying Sparrow and leading him to his stall, I nodded. "Then I'll not worry. Leastways, not about that."

Garret frowned. "If you want, I'll inform master Aeson of what you've learned when he turns up again."

"No, that's not—" I looked back at Garret. "Turns up?"

He shrugged. "No one has seen him since Lady Calise said her goodbyes and Mother Elma smashed the breakfast dishes."

Chapter Twenty

MY FEET LED ME TO HIM WITHOUT GUIDANCE. I walked past both gardens, over the first curve of the water, through the orchard of pears and to the left. There was a pocket of earth that had been shaped over recent years to fit a single person, sometimes two. It was close to the water and blocked from view by the last pear tree. Unless someone was to walk all this way, a person can hide from every window in the castle.

Scooting down next to him, I left the babbling to the brook, and he was content to do the same. I thought of the sweet water and the next closest lands and which lord might have the moral flexibility to provide a once decent shepherd with enough drink for him to disregard his duties and become obstinate. A few names came to mind, but I couldn't be sure of any of them. Lords and ladies were Aeson's responsibility, not mine.

"Do you think she's gone yet?" Aeson spoke at last.

"No," I said with my legs drawn up to my chest and my head

resting on my knees. "She'll want you to see her off like the ambitious social climber you've become." His eyelashes fluttered and his eyes rolled off to the side. I couldn't tell him about the shepherd. Not when he was so close to being free of his hosting obligations. He needed rest.

"I heard I missed a riveting performance at breakfast," I said.

"I am sure you missed nothing." He glanced at me slantways. "She cursed your name at least three times, and I suspect a dozen more once she left the room."

I lifted both shoulders in an exaggerated sigh. "Dear me."

"She says your impertinence will scare off every woman in the Graelands and unless I cast you out, I hold no hope of finding a good wife to manage the castle for me."

"Manage the castle for you?" I raised a brow. "Your fictitious bride is impressive."

He grinned but didn't laugh. "I keep thinking," he started. "What if it'd been a girl? And if Faeler does indeed die this winter? Those lands could still end up in the hands of someone awful in years to come."

"But they won't."

He plucked a pebble from the ground and flicked it into the water. "It's something to worry about. Something *I* should be worried about. Plots aside, the Elder Lords are right."

I saw where his thoughts were going and looked away. "Aeson, you're twenty and six. You have plenty of time to find a wife and burden her with as many children as will make you feel better."

His scowl wouldn't lift. "If something unfortunate were to happen, promise me you won't let Haefwit come sniffing around."

"I'll poison him at the first chance," I joked, but his expression stayed solemn. "Poxes. If you're so fretful about it, I could send a rider after Merla. Give your chambers a chance at redemption."

His eyes jumped, boring into mine. Slowly, the amusement slipped from his irises to the corner of his mouth. I had almost broken through his melancholy. "Honestly," he said. "Do you prepare these abuses in your free time?"

"Why would I need to? You give the best fodder."

A small huff escaped his lips. It was a bit of laughter with no real target. "Do you think they'll be okay? Lady Calise and guard Berrin."

"I do," I said, pulling the corner of my mouth up into a smile.

"Me too," he said. "They have each other. Calise knows how to appeal to Lord Bane, and Berrin is smart enough to see where he must stand in order to secure her title."

"Indeed." I reached across the distance and lifted a spider off Aeson's boot. It was long legged with a body the size of a pea. "You're too close to the water, little one. Head back to the trees where the flies are easy to catch, and you have branches to weave in."

Aeson watched as I turned towards the orchard, setting my hand down on the grass and pointing the spider off in a better direction. When his eyes caught mine, he cleared his throat. "Calise expressed once more how indebted she feels to you," he said. "And requested that you might help her again come springtime when Castle Bane's fields are ready to plough and plant. Assuming everything succeeds."

"What could I possibly do from here?" I asked, readjusting to face him better.

"Might your enchantments last over a longer journey? Castle to castle, rather than castle to field?"

I saw exactly what Calise was after. If she could bring about a similar harvest as what we delivered here, it might satisfy her father's ill intentions. She'd have married well, produced an heir, and gained power over more land than we offered here. All within the space of a year. "She is resourceful. We must give her that."

"We must." He nodded. "Are you willing? They will have to be ready and delivered in time for spring, before winter's true end."

As a surprise to even myself, I bowed my head to the idea. It was a good plan, especially if it could turn Lord Erron and others from sabotage to something more sustainable.

Aeson slid closer and brushed his hand along my neck, startling me. Fingers swooped under my chin and pulled my gaze to his. His thumb ran along the length of my scar.

"I never thanked you." I slipped my hand under his to imitate the motion, pushing through the swell of skin until I felt bone. Looking past him, I found the tree it happened under.

His smile grew and died in the same breath. "Probably the first and last time you ever let someone help you."

I frowned, positive he was wrong, but I couldn't think of an example to argue with.

Withdrawing, he raked his hair into a mess and huffed. "I will go see my mother off. We have more important things to look after." He stood and walked away towards the courtyard, trusting me alone in his favorite spot.

Visiting my chambers, I grabbed my broom and gathered lavender, rosemary, and white sage. I made a fan with the first two and a number of bundles with the third. I started with the rooms

House Erron had occupied, opening every window and setting a burning bit of sage in every corner. Then I lifted my broom to the ceiling and swept. Casting lines across the beams and stones, rounding each corner, and dragging the bristles down the wall, I swept out everything House Erron had brought with them. Good wishes and ill.

Stopping at the threshold, I went to Mother Elma's rooms next. Once more I burned sage in the corners. Before I took my broom above my head, I used my fan of herbs. Chanting over and over, I cast her presence out and asked the wind to put her ambitions at ease. She may have disliked me, but I understood she only wanted Aeson to have an easy life. If the wind would follow her carriage, it could whisk away some of her fears.

I swept her walls next and took it with me down the corridor to join House Erron's leftovers. I swept everything right down the stairs through the great hall and out into the courtyard to the circle of dirt that surrounded the alba tree.

Finished, I returned to my rooms with the door locked and encircled myself on the floor with as many plants as could fit. In the center I breathed in a rhythm. Three beats in, three beats held, three beats out. The leaves moved cautiously, shushing themselves and taking turns drawing from me as I sunk deeper and deeper into the peace that had finally settled in the castle. Free of visitors, everyone could go back to their accustomed roles.

I drank in the remaining fluster and exhaled to the roots around me. They would make better use of the tainted energy. They could churn it with their soil, break it apart, separate the good from the rot and suck it back into order where it would serve a better purpose.

Chapter Twenty One

THE NEXT MORNING, I stood at my desk thinking of Garret's plan. Sweet water was easily hidden. It might be smeared inside a fold of leather to be licked off later or soaked into thick parchment and chewed upon. And it could be drunk if the distiller thinned it out enough.

I needed a way to help if the guards didn't find anything as they trailed the shepherd. In the renewed quiet of the castle, I passed no one on my way to the study to consult my books. Just like before, I folded my knees beneath me and pulled the books down one at a time. The pages turned and fluttered and shuffled and flapped under my hands as I searched for the best shrubs or grasses to commune with. Ones that might distinguish between the earth's fresh water and the sharpness I imagined sweet water would offer.

I was pondering the options with my back against the bookshelf, one book overlapping another in my lap, when the door creaked open. Aeson heaved a breath, and I thought his whole body might deflate with the burden of so many visitors dismissed. Finally, a day without social performances.

"What are you searching for?" he asked.

"Ways to help Garret. Ways to have the land tell me if something tastes strange." I looked up and challenged my gaze to stay with him. It wouldn't. "Our shepherd has gotten ahold of sweet water," I said at last.

His mouth parted at this, and he turned to look away, then came right back, wetting his lips. "You're sure?" he asked.

"Yes. I wanted to tell you yesterday. I promised Garret. But you had so much on your mind already." My heart was weak beneath the words. "I should have noticed sooner had I not been so fixated on House Erron."

"It seems Calise was more correct than we thought. Something unfriendly is crawling towards us." He shut the door tightly and walked halfway to me. "Is your idea possible?"

I shrugged, toying with the necklaces at my throat. The green and blue. Free and Fair. Striding the rest of the way to his desk, he found his chair and crumpled upon it, setting his elbow on the arm and his chin on his palm.

"It's strategy. Let Garret devise the best way to search, and you can select the best way to cast. You will need his knowledge as much as he will need your support."

I nodded absentmindedly, looking up and out the windows. The question tugged at my mind so much I wished to tip my head and shake out the contents so I might see it all more clearly. I was apprehensive about casting this way. My harvest spells only encouraged and strengthened what would occur naturally. I had never asked the land to spy for me. That sort of deceit was left to the world of men. And I would've liked to leave it that way.

AUTUMN

Chapter Twenty Two

W HEN THE CASTLE WAS GOOD and resettled in its ways, Garret knocked on my door after breakfast one day and led me to the study. He laid our valley maps on Aeson's table near the window and the two of them stood side by side like eaglets at the edge of their nest, eyeing the landscape.

"Where do we start?" Aeson asked.

Garret came to attention. "I thought we might herd him into a corner."

"Herd him?" I asked. "You don't think he'll recognize that approach?"

"Shepherd already believes he's safe in his schemes. If we start at Tote Crennly, it'll make him aware we are looking, and he will have to report to someone or make a move."

"And if he moves his supply?"

"I've sent guards out of uniform to the farther villages. In a week's time we may begin. They're to notify me if the shepherd is in a place he doesn't belong or with a person who doesn't belong."

Aeson nodded. "We encourage a reaction and see where the reaction takes place."

I folded my arms. "And if he does nothing? Or moves the supply somewhere where no guard is hidden to see?"

"That's where you should focus, witch," Garret said. "I've marked the next likely hiding spots. We found nothing at the first lot." He glanced at Aeson before addressing me again. "If you've found a way to search the land, this is where to start. If the shepherd makes no move within a few days, we will move to the outermost boundary by Aevic Stow, then back again. We will hedge him into the middle."

I chewed my lip. Garret's plan made sense. If the shepherd wanted to move his stash away from chance discovery, he'd move quickly, but he'd be unable to get it off the lands in one day. He'd have no choice but to stop in Maer Hill, the village between us and Aevic Stow. It would expose him to the guards. And for now, that's all we needed.

"I will work at a spell and let you know if I'm successful."

We shared a look, nodded in agreement, and cleaned up the table. Garret departed and I was right behind him when Aeson spoke up.

"Etta," he said, waiting for me to turn back. "Are you sure about this?"

I stared at him, then looked to the window, trying to find an answer. He wasn't one to doubt me. After all, it was he who told Calise about spells being as good as the witch.

"It's okay if it doesn't work," he continued.

"No, it's not."

"It is," he said. "There are more important things."

"More important than saving a mother and her children

from the hands of their languid father? Keeping them safe on our lands? Providing them with a warm home? Keeping a wicked drink out of our villages?"

"Not at the expense of yourself is all I mean."

I blinked. "My whole purpose is the expense of myself."

He stepped forward. "Yes. But it is equally important that you remain healthy and safe as well. Try not to lose yourself to this or at least, don't turn your hair blue."

I crossed my arms. The severity of his gaze folded and the muscles at his jaw flexed.

"Go on," he relented.

And I did, shaking my head before he thought of any more nonsense to bestow.

Chapter Twenty Three

Aftere writing and rewriting until my fingers were sore, I sat in my chambers the next day to practice. I still wasn't sure about the wording, or the elements I was using. For that matter, no one was. Prilla had given me a long look when I asked for a sample of every vinegar she had in our pantry along with extra salt, sugar, and her sharpest wine.

Nonetheless, I took two ferns to the floor and fed them in kind. After each flavor was administered, I'd meditate and ask them to unfurl or wilt according to how the "food" tasted in their veins. When that part of the spell seemed sound, I shifted my tactic to mixing flavors and studying which one caused wilting. The ferns were tickled either way regardless of the differences.

Against wiser thinking, I changed my plan again. I gave one fern everything sweet and the other everything tart. This elicited a difference, but the wilted fern also went quiet and unspeaking, which wouldn't be reliable in the fields. I had to believe not every drop of sweet water would make it to Shepherd's lips. Some would fall and I would need to identify where.

By dinnertime, I had a headache. Layla had slipped a plate of food onto my desk, but it had gone untouched. I was very near to throwing the plate and the desk out through the largest window.

At my left, one fern bounced, full and shining. To my right, the other fern wilted beyond comprehension. The ends recoiled as though pleading with me for relief. On the floor lay a handful of dried fronds that had suffered under my failures. I moved a little energy between the two just to keep it from giving up entirely.

Placing them back in their respective spots, I gripped the edge of the window and swallowed my frustration. Then I swept up the dead buds and laid them into the soil of the afflicted fern, pouring over it with fresh water.

The door kicked in and Aeson stood at attention, taking in the sight of me, my disastrous work desk, my untouched plate, and the drooping fern. I waited for admonishment, but he only sighed and walked to the desk to collect my food.

"You didn't call for breakfast and you didn't even attempt dinner," he said. I opened my mouth to lie but he held up a hand. "Don't bother. I've already asked the kitchen."

I was relieved. The power to think quickly for anything, even a lie, would've eluded me. I sank to the floor and leaned against the wall. He placed the cold plate of food in my lap.

"What should I do?"

I managed a laugh. "The peppermint. If you would." When the pot was between us on the floor, I instructed further. "Just one leaf will do. Ask it nicely for help, crush it in your palm, and lay it on my forehead."

He did everything with precision, switching hands with me so I could press the oils into my skin, then he asked, "What else?"

My shoulders bowed. "Apologize to the fern for me." I reached for a crust of bread on my plate. The tension in my head had begun to unravel and the thought of chewing didn't seem so awful anymore.

"What am I apologizing for?"

"For my disgraceful abuse. It didn't deserve such torture today."

He frowned and crouched near the leaves. "Well, hello." The longest frond stretched towards his greeting, and he lifted it with an index finger. "I don't normally speak to any of you, which seems unjust since you are kinder than the main occupant of this room." He glanced my way, and I flicked a button mushroom at him. "Please trust and believe me when I say she didn't mean whatever she put you through today. We're seeking something and someone very bad on our lands. Your help has great purpose, and you have our thanks."

A weak smile tugged on my lips. "You could kiss it for good measure."

"You're making a fool of me now."

"I am not. Ferns love to flirt."

He glanced between me and the fern about a dozen times before twisting forward and lifting the same leaf to his lips. It bounced in his hand and caught him off guard. "Ouch!? It . . . bit me."

I sniggered, exhausted by the action and tempted to fall sideways onto the floor. "I guess your blood was necessary to the apology."

Aeson pressed a finger to his mouth and came away with a spot of red. "Did you know that before you ordered me?"

Shaking my head, I held a hand over my heart for sincerity.

"Plants are not animals. They are pliable but that doesn't make them amiable. It's why they're so quiet. If no one truly knows they can speak, they don't have to listen."

"Perhaps you should ask for help from something more talkative." He dabbed his lip.

Our eyes snapped to one another's. He was right. I worked through the idea as he did the same. "It has to be the right animal. Something that will identify with the mischief at hand."

"Otters," Aeson suggested, then shook his head. "No, they don't travel far enough on land. And the waters will freeze soon."

"I would say starlings, but they're not mischievous *enough*. But perhaps they can help another way." I forced the last bite of a seasoned tomato down and pushed up. My headache was clearing faster as the food settled in my belly. Aeson stood as well and steadied me although I tried to push him off. "I need to visit the garden."

"Water first."

I thought he was speaking of the plants, but realized it was me he was trying to take care of. To appease and remove him from my immediate thinking, I gulped down an entire cup from where it sat on the table still, also courtesy of Layla. I nodded, grabbed a pinch of seeds from a jar and left my door open, making my way down the stairs without him.

In my garden with the gate closed, I fell to my knees, quiet and still, thinking long about how to ask for what I needed. It wasn't lost on me how quick I was to ask the land for help. I trusted nature because it acted naturally. It was people I was unwilling to approach. They were full of unnatural acts. All in pursuit of good manners and polite behavior.

I shook the awareness from my head and tsked the air,

catching the slither of the garden snake beneath the shriveling potato leaves. First, I whistled slow, allowing the sound to grow as I moved my palms to my chest and brushed outward, smoothing imaginary feathers.

"Delicate talon and sharpest mind; feathers to fly the farthest find. Clearest eye and deepest ear; align the mischief, truest fear. Offering chirps for those in wind; heeding seed, for song on spin."

I closed the spell with three fingers held before my lips, then divided the seeds between each hand and waited. My palms fell flat and open in the air beside me, my head tilted back. It was a moment before I felt anything, but eventually, the prickle of claws landed on the joints of my fingers with two on one side and three on the other. All of them starlings or sparrows except for one jay, of course. As thieves of the trees, it wouldn't have felt right if at least one hadn't turned up. They were always ready for free food. I frowned at him, but he ate without shame.

Clearing my throat again, I explained to them with another verse.

"A job to be done, and safety to won. I ask the eyes to rake, and ears that make. As plots devise, the nose must thrive."

Upon hearing the words, the jay took off. Of course. The others remained and one from my right side hopped along my arm, piercing my skin through the sleeve and coming to rest on my shoulder. He shifted from side to side and finally plucked at my hair.

"Oh, I see." I let my arms fall and they scattered to the walls and fences, waiting. Pulling my knife out, I parted my hair and lay it on the front of each shoulder. Doing my best to keep the cut even, I sliced through one and then the other and held the pale strands out with both hands. "I suppose the frost is nearly here.

You'll need the warmth."

Taking turns, each bird removed a tuft of hair and departed.

It was dark when I made it back to the access door and considered the cold more seriously. Garret could carry out most of his plans in the snow easy enough, but I had limited options. I turned on my heel and stepped back down the path, calling in the darkness.

"Tell them to be here before too long."

Chapter Twenty Four

FOR THREE WEEKS I paced between the courtyard and the third-floor hall each afternoon, watching as people came and went. The Maeben harvest passed and our fruit stores filled up, as did our barrels of spiced ciders. Guards and field hands and messengers and stable cats passed through the front gate and none of them brought Garret news of the shepherd. It appeared his plan did not alarm our languisher in the slightest.

I slept with my windows open every night, even as it got cold, and the oak leaves embraced their new colors. From my window, I watched the world shift every evening. When House Erron had departed, sunset was still a rainbow of greens and blues and yellows. As autumn consumed the valley, the rainbow gave way to earth tones. The bright colors of summer faded until they were every shade of brown and gold.

It was akin to the spring calves piling on top of one another to sleep. Russet lay next to auburn lay next to red lay next to ginger. When the frosts began to kiss them each night, I'd wake to see it all shimmering in the distance until finally the leaves began to float away from their mother limbs and find new purpose on the ground.

Through all this, I left the castle every other morning to search Garret's suggested spots with the spell I'd honed with the ferns. But there was nothing. And I was still waiting for my animal recruits to turn up. I couldn't imagine what the birds had made of my request and had an even harder time trying to guess who would answer the call.

Making sure to pass through the village after each search, sometimes I saw the shepherd and sometimes I didn't. Ellara's belly grew but I watched from a distance. I was happy to see Saana watching the smaller children more and more. Her blonde-haired sister, a year behind in age, showed herself more often as well. At her own expense. The boys played far more tricks on her, singing her name as they chased her with half frozen mud clods. "Mello, Mello, Mello!" went their chorus.

When, perchance, the shepherd was there, his lips stayed red and his tongue white, but I never saw signs on anyone else. The shepherd was selfish with his vices, and I supposed I should be appreciative of that.

Between the days I searched, I tended the castle as I always did in the cold seasons. I was grateful I had enough supply to treat each ailment. At that point in the year, I kept my gathering bag on me at all times with the remedies I needed most often. That way, I didn't have to return to my chambers every time someone coughed.

While I was walking back from the study one day, Aeson caught me on the third-floor landing. Stopping me with a hand to my belly, he declared, "If you become any more disheartened about this ploy, you'll invite the first snowfall before any of us are ready."

I frowned, folding my arms at him. "The longer his stash stays in this valley, the more chance someone else has of discovering it. Someone who shouldn't. Like a child."

"Would it cheer you to know, the guards in Aevic Stow have noted a few extra visitors from over the border?"

"Perhaps." I brightened. "But visitors could just be visitors. Were they unseemly?"

"The guard who noted them has been ordered to keep further watch on their business, to determine just that."

I chewed my lip. Aevic Stow was our northernmost village close to Valley Maer's entrance and a common stop for travelers. I'd only seen it a few times. It boasted a longhouse at its center and a large boarding house at the boundary between us and Lord Gallo.

"Fine," I said. "Consider me cheered. Although you hardly appear the same."

He screwed up his face and looked away at first. "I've received a letter from a southern Elder, near the Idyll border. It is more urgent and more plain in its message. He has four daughters. He has asked I pick whichever name sounds best to my ears and he too will deny any calls for tax levies at the next gathering."

My stomach went sour. "And what family is this? It sounds as though you would do the daughter a favor by removing her from those walls."

"It doesn't matter."

"It might matter," I said.

"Did you not hear me? They are settled beside the Idylland border. Lands that have yet to forgive witches for the war wounds they cast. I do not care how adequate his daughters are if they are apt to abuse you or our ways upon arrival."

"I will guard myself if it means you having an ally."

His gaze swiveled to mine and glared. "You held more concern over House Erron."

"That was before we had evidence someone was trying to sneak under our doors. Any support is better than none, is it not?"

He growled and folded his arms. I glared back and did the same. Neither of us budged, but his eyes eventually wandered, taking note of my hair. He made no remark, but his gaze softened, which bothered me more.

"If you're going to lecture me again about how I must keep my own health and safety, allow us to descend the stairs so we can find a crowd who wants your suggestions. I can watch myself."

He rolled his eyes and opened his mouth to retort but a door slammed from the floor below and cut him off. Somebody shouted, "Another fever! Tell her to come quickly."

Chapter Twenty Five

AS SOME SORT OF REPLY TO MY WORRIES, I passed Reeve the next day in the great hall. I'd finished my morning scout and returned early to check on Laken, who'd managed to chip a tooth while falling upstairs. As usual, Reeve had his arm desk cradled on the left like it was a precious bag of coins while his right hand pushed the hair from his face and nearly knocked his glasses off.

I was shaking my head and hiding my endearment from him when I caught the smell of peppermint. "Reeve," I said. "Are those today's letters?"

He looked over his right shoulder and spun all the way to the left in order to face me and I hid my amusement once more.

"Well, are they?"

"I . . . um . . . Yes, they are. I was on my way to seek Lord Crennly's rep—"

I grabbed the stack of papers off his person, flipping through them and tossing them back into his arms faster than he could manage. Near the bottom was a letter with the seal of Castle Bane on it. I exhaled with a grin.

"Those are Lord Crennly's personal letters," Reeve said.

I flapped a hand at him, breaking the wax. "He won't care about this one."

Inside, the script was clear and pretty with minimal swirls. It was just like Calise to be dignified in her writing without being overdone. She and Berrin had arrived at Castle Bane with no difficulty. To Haefwit's dismay, Calise was immediately well liked by the entire household. Faeler had found her obscure proposition to be a promising one and was even delighted to hear of the friendships she'd made with us at Castle Crennly.

I grabbed Reeve by the shoulders and shook him. "Thank you, Reeve."

Running upstairs and down the third-floor hall, I burst through the study door and skidded to a stop in the middle of the room. Behind the desk, Aeson looked up from his work and scowled. "Barbs yesterday. Smiles today," he said. "Who has perished? The shepherd, I imagine."

Shaking my head, I walked forward with more composure and stuck the letter under his nose.

"This is addressed to me," he observed. Reeve rushed in through the door behind me, spouting apologies to Aeson and hesitant insults in my direction.

"In addition, my lord, there came an extra horse with the messenger. He said you'd know what to do with it?"

Aeson held a hand up to settle him and sent him off to find Garret, then set a stern look in my direction. "This is bold, even for you."

"Rot and poxes. There is only one bit of news we've been

waiting to hear from her about. What else could it have been?"

"Plenty of things that do not involve you."

I sneered. "You're bluffing. What secrets do you have that I don't know?"

He reclined against the back of the chair and looked me up and down. None of his normal tells flickered across his face. There was no corner smirk, no lowered lashes, not even a glance to the left. Checking over my shoulder to be sure Reeve had disappeared entirely, I stepped closer, looming over Aeson's show of innocence. He let a grin slip and after a long minute had passed, I leaned back, arms folded.

"Am I intruding?" Garret's gravelly voice came from the door.

"No." I crossed my arms and glared at Aeson. "Lord Crennly was just being smug."

Garret looked between us and shook his head. "I'm afraid I have a poor report."

I spun and stood alert. Aeson came around to join me. "What is it?" he asked.

"The guards I had stationed at Aevic Stow have fallen ill. They're traveling home to recover."

My posture slumped and I rubbed a hand down my face. "What have they fallen ill with?" I asked.

"One has swelling behind the ears and cannot speak. The other injured his leg trying to follow the charges they'd seen the other day."

I very nearly chewed a hole through my lip, but nodded all the same and told Garret I would watch for their arrival and prepare what I could for them.

"Thank you for the report, Garret," Aeson said, gripping our head guard's shoulder in camaraderie. "Take heart. There is a gift for you in the courtyard. Do not argue."

Garret bowed, eyeing us both with curiosity, but left with more hurry than he normally would have. Alone again, Aeson pulled me around to face him.

"Your smile has disappeared," he said.

I shook my head, deciding I didn't want to argue with him that day. "I suppose there is still time before the snows. My Fair magic will surely bring something before then."

"Say that again with more conviction."

Rolling my eyes, I walked away without complying. Nearly half the season had passed, and we had nothing to show for it.

Back in my room, I stood at my casting window and toyed with the cords at my throat. Breathing by threes, I repeated my spell for the sparrows with all the conviction I had.

Chapter Twenty Six

AFTER RECEIVING HER LETTER, I spent the next few days looking through history records for the size of the fields at Castle Bane and allotting seeds for Calise. The two guards Garret had mentioned returned and with that I forwent my excursions from the castle to keep a constant watch on them. In truth, it all served as a good distraction until my Fair magic replied.

Four more mornings passed and I woke to something scratching at the bottom of my bedchamber door. Opening one eye, the faintest of shadows appeared at the gap of the threshold. It disappeared, returned, then disappeared for good. As I sat up, rubbing sleep from my eyes, there came the sound of papers shifting. Glass scraped over wood and crashed to the floor with one clear pop. There was a soft whirring as the cork surely went rolling away.

I yanked my door open and saw the shuffling must've been going on for some time already. My papers and notes were in disarray, everything with a cork had been chewed on, the soil of nearly every plant was dug up and scattered across the floor, and in five places of their own choosing sat the culprits.

"Ugh." I shook my head. "I should have guessed." Barrow squirrels, tall ears and muddy red fur, their bodies were smaller and more akin to a munk. Two sat on the tall and short worktables respectively while two hid in the leaves near the window, and one sat plainly before me on the stone floor. "How would you like it if I came to your nest and shook everything up?"

The one on the floor rested peacefully on his haunches, cleaning his whiskers and looking about as if he had no idea what I was speaking of. I tugged a robe on and ventured down to the kitchen. Spotting Layla, I asked her to assemble as many extra nuts, fruits, and berries as they could possibly spare, then returned and began sweeping up the dirt.

As I returned the soil to the pots, I apologized to every leaf, stalk, and stem. And I promised fresh compost before the day was done. The corks were easier, only two were truly unusable, and my papers needed reorganizing as it was. While I cleaned, the five barrows scampered up to the tallest shelf and watched me from behind the bottles, their little faces magnified by the glass and recolored in shades of blue, green, and amber.

Just as I was coiling my hair on top of my head, Layla swept in and set down a bowl filled with food. With no hesitation, all five squirrels leapt from behind the jars and descended upon her. Layla squealed and I laid a hand on her shoulder. "It's all right. They're no danger to anyone but themselves. They just have very little manners and even less respect."

"What are they doing here?"

I regarded them over one shoulder. "They're helping me with

something. So, if you see any cats headed towards my rooms, shoo them off."

Footsteps echoed up the stairs and Garret appeared next. His mouth twitched a smile at Layla before his gaze shifted to me and his whole face went smooth. "Sorry, I did not intend to interrupt."

"Come in. We're just eating breakfast." I flung a hand at the bowl full of squirrels. The food was half gone, their bellies half full.

Garret eyed them and I saw the questions rise and fall in his mind before shaking his head and deeming it unimportant. "It's a private matter, Miss Layla."

"Of course." Layla curtsied and made her way by him, passing too close and using the proximity to lay a hand on his arm as she went. "Beg pardon," she said.

When the door closed, I smirked at Garret. "How is your shoulder? Did you need any more liniment?"

He huffed. "I suspected as much."

I walked around my desk and found a new bottle to replace the one that shattered, picking up the dried blooms of purple toadflax from among the broken glass. The leader of the barrows hopped down to investigate my doings and when he found I held no entertainment, he scampered across the floor and sniffed at the door to the hall.

"What is it?" I asked, standing once more.

"Lord Crennly has decided not to wait until I can replace the guards in Aevic Stow. We will visit the shepherd again tomorrow evening. Perhaps if we apply more pressure, he will give way."

"That's good." I picked at the hem of my robe and looked at the bowl. Its fillings had been replaced with four sleeping squirrels.

Garret raised an eyebrow. "Can they be trusted?"

"They're overconfident. They like to chitter about things that don't concern them. And they excel at slipping about unnoticed." I folded my arms. "I think they're perfect."

Garret jutted his chin, biting back his skepticism. I couldn't blame him. Barrow squirrels were a nuisance for the farmers, not by destroying crops, but simply going through everything and slowing the work down each time a task had to be redone or swept up. They were nosier than even Mother Elma.

"You'd better go." I flicked my gaze to the door. The fifth barrow still had his nose wedged between the wood and the wall. "Layla is waiting for you."

Rolling his shoulders back at my hint, he tossed his hair out of his face and turned without saying goodbye. In his absence, the fifth barrow jumped to the desk and rested his front paws on my sleeve.

"And you?" I asked. "What price will you and your brothers be asking of me in exchange for your help?"

He sneezed and went back to the bowl, tipping it to one side as he crawled in and curled up on top of the others.

I nodded in understanding. "I shall inform the kitchen. You may stuff yourselves for two days and then you must set to work."

Chapter Twenty Seven

T HE FOLLOWING AFTERNOON, I gathered my prepared jars of red raspberry leaf, cramp bark, haw, yarrow, and motherwort. At the commotion, the leader of the barrow squirrels jumped up with interest and sat on my shoulder, tucking himself beneath my hair. I pulled a cloak over us both and padded down through the kitchen. I took the longer way through the back access door and down the side path into the fields.

Cutting across the brown grass, I watched the sky and hoped the other guards would have some news to report before the snow trapped everyone in and slowed our comings and goings. If Shepherd wanted to, he could hide his stash and leave us grasping at nothing until the warm weather returned. The idea of another entire season being useless did not appeal to me.

In the village, winds had blown everyone inside and demanded they close their shops early. There were no children to be seen, not even outside the shepherd's house. I knocked lightly, then loudly when there was no answer. Eventually the door squeaked open, and Saana peeked around the wood.

"Is your mother home?" I asked.

"Yes. I'll fetch her." Saana opened the door the rest of the way and pushed it snug shut once I was inside. Her youngest brothers and sisters were spread on the floor, entranced by a blob of salt dough that was rolled flat so they could press different objects into it and copy the shape. Between them were a pile of snail shells, sticks, oddly shaped rocks, and a fork missing one tine.

"Miss Etta." Ellara came around the corner, holding her back with one hand as if she was trying to push the babe out through her belly button. I was right to come early with the herbs she would need.

"I brought you tea to steep before and after your delivery," I said, taking out the jars and laying them on her table. At the same time, I glanced along their shelves. Everything looked in order. And Saana's dress was surely new, fitting her even better than the last one I'd seen.

"Ahh, thank you." Ellara's face flooded with gratitude, and she sank into a kitchen chair right as her husband appeared from the back of the house. He stopped short when he saw me. The whole of him looking a few stones lighter. A fact that told me his body must need a regular dose of sweet water to keep from trembling.

"Good day, sir," I offered, as politely as I could bear.

"Good day, castle wi—witch."

"You're not afield with your flock?" I asked.

He glanced back to the room he'd emerged from and shook his head. "The weather has gone too cold for them. They're penned."

"I see." I slid my gaze across his face. He'd washed the red from his mouth, but the white dots along his tongue were undeniable. I tried to study his hands to see what he might have been working with last, but a gasp turned me back towards Saana.

"What is *that?*" Her eyes bore straight into my neck.

"Oh." I swept my hair back farther. "A barrow squirrel. He found his way to my workroom," I explained, excluding the fact that four more still slept there. I didn't want the shepherd to be greatly familiar with their presence, but the situation offered me an idea. As casually as I could, I held my hand for the squirrel to crawl onto. Glancing at Saana, then meeting the barrow's eyes firmly, I suggested, "Why don't you get to know him better?"

The barrow crept off my hand and onto the table, making his way to Saana. She offered a scratch to his head before the rest of the children noticed what was happening. They screamed unanimously and scuffled over one another to get to the table.

In response, the barrow leapt from the table to the shelves, down again, over a chair and back into the other rooms of the house. Following as a herd, the children disappeared, and I cleared my throat. "I hope there is nothing too dangerous for him to make trouble with."

Shepherd widened his stance and puffed his chest a bit. "Nah. The kids do more harm than that little beast ever could."

"Good, that reassures me," I said, although the shepherd was dead wrong. Had he been a crops man and not spent his trade tending to livestock, he'd know better. Children might be inquisitive, but they simply didn't possess the nose of a barrow squirrel nor the memory.

I shifted my attention to Ellara and explained when and how to brew her teas. Right as I finished up, the little barrow came slinking along the wall back into the kitchen. Having successfully escaped the children without notice, he snuck up behind the shepherd and took a long sniff of his boot. I made sure to keep my sights trained on the family as I stood and said my goodbyes. Seemingly from nowhere, the squirrel popped up onto the closest chair and continued to my shoulder.

Saana let me out the door and just as I was stepping down, Aeson and Garret swung round the corner on their horses. They saw me before I could duck away, leaving me no choice but to greet them in passing.

"Etta?" Aeson's expression twisted up. "What were you doing here?"

I stepped back as he dismounted. "Herbs for the shepherdess. For when the baby arrives."

"I see, and was your visit productive?"

Lifting my hair to reveal my companion, I grinned. "With some help, yes."

His head tilted and he smiled, coming closer. I shifted to keep the distance between us wide and safe. "What is it?" he asked.

"Do not approach like that in front of the shepherd," I said. "He does not need any more weapons to goad you with."

"Sir?" Garret's voice floated past my ear, but Aeson held a hand up. He focused on me instead, which was just as bad.

"He thinks our behavior is entirely too intimate." I didn't want to use the colored language the shepherd had offered in the past.

"He is a ward of *my* lands. Let him stoke his rumors and see where it brings him," Aeson grumbled.

I clenched my teeth. "Perhaps that is fine for you, but *I* don't want anyone on any lands thinking I'm paid to pleasure your whims—any of them."

He fell back a step, lifting his jaw up and down but producing no sound at first. "You're right," he managed. "Sorry. That would be . . . unsuitable." His neck flushed red, shaded even more by the black cloak that draped around him.

I shook my head at his stupidity and glanced at the squirrel on my shoulder. "I have something that may lead us onward. So don't worry Garret too much while you're here."

Aeson swallowed, looking to our head guard and presumably the shepherd. We had stood together far too long for my comforts. Nonetheless, I waited for Aeson to nod in understanding before giving him a wide berth and heading back to the castle.

Chapter Twenty Eight

CLIMBING THE STAIRS TO MY ROOM, I reached up and pulled the little barrow from his roost, cradling him to my cheek. "When you see your brothers, you must tell them everything you can about that man. His scent, the rhythm of his heart, the timbre of his voice, anything that will identify him."

He wiped his face clean with frail paws, the nails no bigger than a needlepoint. When I set him down inside, he hopped right to the bowl and chirped relentlessly. I put my cloak away and left my rooms again, heading towards the study.

Pulling the maps out, I lay them side by side to create as accurate a spread as I could and assessed them. Marking the points Garret had suggested, I looked about the rest of the landscape and picked five new spots. The barrows could cover a decent amount of ground from each location, which gave me confidence their aid would yield some direction.

"Sorted it all out?" Aeson asked, standing in the half open doorway.

I blinked. "You've returned quickly."

"You told me you had a lead and not to let Garret worry."

I frowned, rolling up the maps and returning them to their places. "I have something like a lead. It's not the same thing."

He walked to the window and leaned against the ledge. "It will come. I am sure."

"What is this sudden serenity?" I asked. He looked at me but offered nothing beyond a shrug, which stirred my chest even more. "I tell you that one of the worst and ugliest substances is in the hands of an errant ward and all you say is 'it's not important' and 'don't worry.' Where is the Aeson that holds urgency over problems that will impact the tables of everyone in the village come springtime?"

He twisted against the wall and crossed his ankles, relaxed as ever. "The snows will be here in no time, and the shepherdess will have a babe in her arms, and there will be very little we can do until the land begins to thaw. The season is against us."

I crossed the room and planted my feet before him, searching his face for something that made sense. All he did was raise a smart eyebrow and crack half of a smile. When no more criticisms came to mind, I dragged a hand down my face, ready to concede if only to avoid my own distemper.

Aeson pushed off the wall and stepped closer, still smirking. He swept my hair up behind me, over my shoulder, knotting it into one hand. "It's still so short. How do I steer you away from trouble?"

My hand slipped along his wrist and under his palm, following the crevices of hair his fingers had sculpted. Forcing his release, I glared and petted the strands smooth. "It will grow back," I said. "And it appears it has a whole season to do so."

Chapter Twenty Nine

TWO DAYS LATER, I had five small bundles tied full of food for five small creatures. Donning my cloak, I placed all the parcels in my bag and slung it over my shoulder, then held up the feeding bowl. The barrows had spent the better part of yesterday feasting again and sleeping in a heap when they were finished. The bowl seemed the simplest way to transport them all.

Down in the courtyard, I decided on the more time-consuming course of action. I left Sparrow and opted to walk to each destination. It meant I'd be gone all day from the castle and, more importantly, away from Aeson. We hadn't spoken since the other afternoon, and I was in no rush to alter that arrangement.

His sudden indifference confounded me. It wasn't like him not to barrel headlong into aiding a crisis. Perhaps he was trying not to get his expectations up by forcing the reality of time to be considered.

Either way, the long walk would put my energy to better

use and give me a chance to leave some Free magic in my wake. Cutting across fields and half frozen creek crossings, I wandered from stop to stop, speaking to the air at every mile.

"While ground does rest, and less the tread; pull fruit to chest with acts embed."

I hummed it over and over and over, thinking of Iya and her communion between men and the natural world. I wanted to be sure the lands felt my intention. I would settle for anything, any scrap of news or whisper of malice.

As I walked from the largest oak in our southern woods to the crags of the cliff to a hollow in the ferns where one could lay flat and completely disappear, I conjured up the image of a wave in water. Picturing the castle from a bird's eye, I asked the waves to return to its walls like a home shore.

"Bring it back to me. To us. Please," I whispered into the wind.

My last stop was a knotwood tree near the valley stream. The oldest I knew of on all our lands. It was rooted along the road a mile north of the white willow where I had found the shepherd sleeping that day in summer. It grew as high as my own windows, expanding to allow a clear view of its surroundings. If I were the shepherd, I wouldn't return to the white willow for any reason, but the knotwood tree offered just as much shelter from prying eyes, so it made for a good alternative while allowing both trees to be watched.

The leader of the barrows was last in the bowl and when we were close enough to the tree's ragged bark, he sprang out and ran up the trunk. Nimble as a breeze.

Tossing his sack of food up after him, I called out, "I'll return as often as I can with whatever sustenance I can steal from the kitchen."

I stood back and slumped among the tree roots. I hadn't meant to acquiesce to Aeson's plan but somewhere in the previous days, I had resolved myself to no immediate progress. The realization churned my belly and a mouthful of dirt sounded more appealing than meeting his face and confessing that he was right.

Huffing, I stomped my heel into the soil and turned home. As I had hoped, the sun was beginning to set. The farmers from Tote Crennly were returning as well, carting in the last of the squashes and root vegetables from the fields. With luck, dinner would be over by the time I was behind the castle walls again.

Passing through the village, someone called my name and I turned to see Saana rushing out her door with a wake of children behind. Mello's plump figure stayed on the threshold and let Saana do the talking.

"What is it?" I asked when Saana was close enough. "Is your mother well? The baby?"

"Yes." She nodded and her gaze flicked about like a cat's tail. "It is only . . ."

I pulled my cloak tighter and urged her on. "Yes?"

"Da has gone."

My neck pulled back, stiffening at the top of my spine. "Gone where?"

Saana lifted both shoulders and kept them high, crossing her arms over her chest. There was more to say but it was clear she wasn't sure if it was safe. "Da has been up to something, hasn't he? 'Tis the reason you and the castle lord and guard Garret have been visiting us."

The question trembled in her chin and curiosity gleamed in her eyes. She was nearly a woman but wasn't sure how to stand her ground or when, let alone whom to trust. I decided on honesty.

She needed to feel equal to someone even if that meant me. "It is."

She nodded and swallowed, lowering her shoulders a little. "He left yesterday morning and never returned. Mello and I can care for the sheep through the cold, but my mother . . ."

I set a hand on her forearm. "Your mother will be fine. I will see to it. When the baby begins to make his way, call for me at the castle. In fact, call for me at the castle with anything you might need, you or your brothers and sisters."

She smiled meekly and shifted her weight. Over her shoulder, her siblings had loosed a chicken and were chasing it round the well. "There's something else."

I let my hand slide down to clasp hers. "Whatever it is Saana, trust that you are not betraying anyone. Aes—Lord Crennly knows men are not perfect. But we suspect your father of some dangerous indiscretions. It is that curiosity we are trying to unriddle for the wellbeing of your family *and* your father. He is at risk otherwise."

Her exhale fogged in the cold. She let her shoulders fall. "He's been meeting with someone in the pens at night. I don't know who though and I never saw his face."

"What did they talk about?"

"Just the comings and goings. Deliveries, harvests, that Lady Calise, his lord's mother."

I frowned. "Was your father paying for this information?"

"Not exactly." Her face fell like she had failed at the task I hadn't set her too. "He promised the man something. I could tell by their way of talk. But there's no coin to pay with."

This caught my attention. "Your shelves, they are well stocked."

She shivered in an evening breeze and pulled her arms tighter. "He wasn't buying it from the village. It just appeared."

"Saana?" Ellara called from the door. Mello had disappeared. "What are you doing? Gather the children and bring them back in. I need your help with the serving."

"Go," I said. "And thank you."

Saana dropped a mild curtsy and steered back towards the little kids. Worrying my hands together against my cloak, I turned back to the castle with Saana's information tucked under my ribs. Someone outside our lands was doing their best to pry their way in and understand our happenings. I hated to think what they were aiming to change once they did.

I had barely closed my door when he swung it open again. "You've been gone all day," he said, staring me down while I hung my cloak on its hook and pulled my hair to one side.

"I have."

"And what were you doing?"

I waved my hands at my bag, the empty bowl, and the reborn quiet of my rooms. "I was placing my charges in position . . . for the season," I sneered.

"Why did you go on foot? You did not think to tell anyone?"

Shielding my gaze from him, I turned to check on the plants. They were happier now that my window was closed.

"You are avoiding me," he said.

"Yet there you stand. In my doorway." I nearly cursed at him but didn't want contempt so close to the plants.

As if to provoke me, he strode across the room and settled a footstep behind. He waited, tolerantly, as I finished my rounds before turning to face him. With his eyes boring into mine, at least a dozen remarks blinked across his lashes before he dropped his gaze. "Was there anything to note in your passages today?"

I tucked some stray hair behind my ear and submitted to civility. "No. But I was stopped in the village, by Saana, one of the shepherd's daughters."

Aeson folded his arms and squinted, searching his memory. "Is that the pretty one?"

Something in me went rigid, and I was tempted to smash a flowerpot over his head. Of course the only way he could remember a girl would be either pretty or plain. Grating my teeth, I nodded. "Yes. The pretty one."

He blinked rapidly but listened well as I shared the information. When I finished, he stepped away and paced the width of the room, muttering how he ought to inform Garret and pondering if it might be one of our household acting untrustworthy.

Rolling my neck and shoulders back to stare at my ceiling, I grunted and told him, "It will come. Don't worry."

His footsteps faltered, then hurried and halted in front of me. I lowered my chin carefully, avoiding his expression until I couldn't any longer. He was smug. "What did you say?" he asked.

I shook my head, puzzled. "I do not recall."

He tutted his tongue at the back of his front teeth and tilted his head as if listening to an echo. "It sounded like you agreed with me."

"You are mistaken." I found his eyes and held them with my own, resisting every tremor of amusement that danced behind my lips. A part of me loathed how impossible it was to stay annoyed at him, but our verbal derisions were far too fun.

"A dream, I suppose. Fantasy." His amusement gave way and both his cheeks dimpled. He stood, gazing at me for too long until one hand lifted and twirled the ends of my hair. "She is not *that* pretty."

I snatched my hair and all the rest of me away, pulling my elbows tight with the opposite palms like I were cinching a buckle into place.

"Yes, she is." I dropped one ear to my shoulder and looked slantways. He wasn't doing anyone favors by denying what the eye could see. Saana was pretty. I imagined her at the Simhaen fires that would burn soon, surrounded by admirers as they fought to offer her cups of pear cider. Forbid it if she ever went out into the world, kings would fall at her feet.

Aeson was still looking at me and for longer than made sense, I looked back. It was a prickle along my neck that finally tore my gaze from him to the window. Outside of the mottled glass, snow had begun to fall.

Chapter Thirty

THE SNOW DIDN'T STICK RIGHT AWAY. It fell all night and melted by the next afternoon. It tried again the day after and melted still. On the third day, nothing fell but when I cracked my window to peek at the purple blue clouds, the weight of intent stretched my ribs with power.

I shut my eyes and wished and hoped the land was ready because it was time to close in. Shuddering into the cold air, I spun towards my sleeping chamber. It might be my only chance to check on the barrow squirrels for some time. Autumn might have a couple weeks left, but winter wanted to remind everyone of her place before she arrived in full. She was a cantankerous spirit.

Rushing, I dressed warmly and secured my belt and knife around my waist. I pulled my bag over my shoulders next and ran down the stairs to the kitchen. Prilla saw me and lifted her brow.

"You here for the little fiends?"

"Yes." I laughed. "Anything will be better than nothing."

But Prilla was generous, and she portioned out some of every berry she had in store. She did the same with the nuts and seeds. Lastly, she folded up squares of old cheesecloth, which were too worn to be used anymore but perfect for warming a nest.

"You are splendid indeed." I thanked her and went on my way.

As I waited beside the black alba tree for Sparrow to be saddled and brought out, Garret and Aeson emerged from the undercroft. Their heads were bent together, and words churned between them. Aeson saw me first, leading over until they were both beside me.

"Where you off to?" he asked.

"The heavy snow will be here tomorrow. I'm going to check the trees before I am stuck for another week or more."

He nodded but his eyes were held in the distance.

"You might inform Reeve. He should let the house and town know so everyone can make last preparations," I told him. He nodded, sinking his chin lower each time and wandered off without any other word. I looked to Garret. "What sort of plague is that about?"

"That boy Henrick was missing again this morning. He's found now but our young lord was just there to speak with him. I observed, but either the boy is a simple idiot or a very adept liar. I have a hard time believing it's the latter."

I twisted my face up. "Did Aeson tell you what the shepherd's daughter shared with me?"

"He did." Garret smoothed the scruff on his chin. "And if the boy could form a proper sentence, I'd be more inclined to suspect him."

I snorted, covering my mouth too late, and drawing the attention of the stable hands around us. I waved them off and turned towards the barn door. Sparrow was ready. Taking the reins, I climbed up and noticed Layla meandering through the yard. Winking, I shoved Garret's shoulder with my toe. "Good luck."

He looked towards Layla and turned back to curse me, but I was already out the gate.

I worked backwards, starting with the leader of the scurry at the knotwood tree. He emerged pleasantly enough and took the items I offered, but with only three days having passed he had nothing to chitter about and nowhere to lead me.

The others were the same. All I could do was leave them with food and cloth and Free magic blessings to keep them warm and safe until the snows eased up. As I headed back, Sparrow's hooves clopped on the cold ground, echoing off every stone. Gradually, I felt relief at the coming snow. Much of my work in the warm seasons meant travel. Growing, tending, visiting. When everything was alive and blooming, it required my attention everywhere outside the castle.

Winter meant I could rest as well, even if this winter would be spent waiting for news of the shepherd. A flurry in the back of my mind.

Sparrow and I trotted back under the walls to a much quieter courtyard. Morning chores were done, and everyone had retreated inside, away from the cold. After I handed the reins to a lone stable boy among the stalls, I followed the trend and returned to my rooms.

I attempted to clean, but so much of it had been done after

the barrows first arrived that there was little left. Dragging my stool to the center of the tower windows and using the same bowl I had for Calise, I filled it with water and laid it in my lap with my knife.

My winter spell was easy enough, but it took time. Lifting my right hand, I cut a line across the back of my wrist and pricked the base of my index finger where the skin went from palm to knuckle. Hanging my hand limp above the water, I recited the words first before stirring my fingertips counterclockwise against the movement of time and growth.

"Cold the Hill, wind and ground; greet the chill, Stow sleep in mound. Coat in fur, den the Maer; just as every lordly bear. Should stem too soon presume to grow; return root and toe to soil below."

I stopped stirring and held my hand flat upon the surface, letting the blood trickle along my skin and mix like cheap ink. It swirled thin and wispy with the motion of the water until at last everything stilled. The draw of energy started at the creak of my elbow. It shivered out the wounds I'd sliced and along my upper arm, tickling into my right ear like the purr of a cat.

Satisfied it had taken enough from me, I stood and walked to the far end, working backwards again. Dipping my fingers and splashing across every leaf and petal, the act would bid my plants good slumber for the time being.

I dumped the remainder of the water onto the fern from my spell practice weeks ago. It was alive but a bit dreary still. It needed the blessing more than anything else.

I slipped the bowl back onto a shelf and found a bandage, pinning the end in place when I couldn't tie it tight enough. If Layla had been around, I might've asked her, but the silence was comforting, and the thought of people was less so.

Opening my door, I listened to the commotion downstairs in the kitchen with a good idea of what was beginning to take place. Other than winter solstice, it was the only spot of cheer the castle got to celebrate while we all huddled inside for the coming months.

Creeping barefoot up the stairs, I stuck to the shadows and slipped into the study as quietly as I could. To my relief, it was empty. No doubt Aeson was already sitting in his seat in the great hall below, slouching with his head on one fist and rattling off answers to Prilla and the rest of the kitchen staff.

Smiling at his torment, I ran my hands over my spell books until I found the dustiest one alone in the bottom corner with not one crease on its spine. *The Wiles, Whims, and Passions of Fierce Magic.*

It was brought with others that Aeson had sought out for me in our second year together. He'd discovered a scholar with a wide collection of books concerning Free and Fair, and this had been in the pile. There was no use for any of it, and the man wanted the whole stack gone from his library.

Sitting in his chair, I reclined and set the book to rest between my lap and the edge of the desk. I hadn't glossed through the pages since that day. I'd barely mastered Free magic at the time, and Aeson had already made it clear he didn't want Fierce castings to shadow any corner of my room.

Consequently, all I knew about Fierce magic was that I shouldn't—not that I couldn't. With a tinny squeak that could've fooled a mouse in the wall, the spine bent back on itself as I lifted the cover. The pages shifted and resettled with a gasp like they'd been holding their breath all these years. My throat closed against an urge to apologize.

One at a time, I scanned the pages, searching for guidance I could rework to make weaker. Or cheaper. Or power sources that didn't call for quite so much. But everything called for either a clear sacrifice or an exchange that would render me useless for days after. Most of them called for both.

Pouring myself empty of every current connected to magic would cost time apart. On the surface it didn't appear terrible, but I'd seen how it left other needs unmet. Loved ones could literally die. In our case crops could be struck with fire, or a blizzard could freeze one of our villages and there would be nothing to do for it.

Fierce magic amputated everything that gave me a purpose.

I sat like Reeve, hunched closely over the pages and sunk so deep in the implications that I didn't hear the door open or the footsteps that followed. It wasn't until he stood on the other side of the desk and pushed a breath of air through his throat in two rasping tics that I realized I was no longer alone. Sucking in a sharp breath, I sat up, pulling the book to my belly and slipping my hands over the cover.

"You think that will work?" He arched one eyebrow.

"It might work to keep you from assumption."

He exhaled and loosened his shoulders. "I will not assume anything."

I looked at him a while longer before glancing back at the book. Running my tongue over my teeth and trying to even out the thoughts in my head, I rubbed the corner of one page between my thumb and forefinger.

"Some of them are silly to look at, calling for strange contraptions to keep the power of a spell running through—" I almost said *me* but swallowed the word before it choked either of us. "Some of them do good. Some of them ask for sacrifices I would never want to make."

"But all of them collectively?" he asked.

"You know the answer to that. They sacrifice me. My connection to Iya. The lines that run between me and the natural world are severed for so long that it risks the everyday harmony I am meant to offer."

A crease formed at the center of his brow creating a distinct line between his eyes.

I took a breath and straightened in the chair. "Look here"—I let the book fall open again, pointing—"I could call on the land to locate the shepherd but accounting for time renders that spell useless. By the time we got there, he'd be gone, and I'd be unable to cast again." My breath caught, and emotion burned along the rim of my eyes. "This is why . . ."

Aeson came around and slid the book from my hand, closing it and setting it as far away on the desk as he could. "Why what?" He sat down on the footstool, eyeing me intently.

"This is why we are supposed to be together, me and my people. Fierce magic would be different if there were more of me. Our family caravans would have allowed one to locate and one to track." I looked away. "I am alone."

When he didn't speak, I dragged my gaze back to see him wounded. Eyes cast down and shoulders slumped. I realized what I said and gathered a fresh wave of air.

"I did not mean—" I began, but he reached across the distance and grabbed the edge of my chair, scraping the feet over the floor and pulling me until our legs touched. Then he took my right hand and unwound the bandage I'd hastily secured on my own.

"I know you didn't," he said, meeting my eyes while his fingertips ran across my skin and kept working. "Just like I know you know it's a lie."

I folded my lips into one another to hide a smile, but he saw it all the same. What he said in front of the cliffs that day had seeped further and further into my mind. Perhaps I was unacknowledged by my own doing, which brought with it an inherent isolation. "I'm sorry I invited such a somber moment."

His face lifted. "I'm surprised you know that word. Does it feel foreign on your tongue?"

I swatted at him with my other hand, but he dipped his head like an obstinate colt and knocked me away easily. "I only meant to make amends considering the festivities that will soon be upon us."

He shook his head, ignoring the thought.

"Come now. Of the two of us, you like your birthday."

"I did," he started. "I do. And I will be happy to see everyone at ease and in good spirits for a few days. We haven't had that since Lady Calise was here. But I feel selfish this year."

"How so?" I asked.

He still had my hand, turning it from side to side, inspecting the skin that had been broken by my knife. Satisfied it did not need any closer attention, he went to rewrapping the bandage tighter and tying the ends together so it might stay longer than the pin could have ever held it. Finished, he looked up and around but not at me. "I find myself more invested in what I want this year rather than what the castle needs."

I sat relaxed, resting my chin in my palm, elbow on the arm of the chair. "And what do you want, Aeson?"

"From you? Indignation." He laughed and stood up, collecting the book and putting it back in its forgotten corner.

"The same as every year?" I grinned and pushed out of my

seat, passing around the other side of the desk, adding floor space between us and heading to the door. "There is a certain excellence in that sort of consistency. You're welcome."

"Yes," he said, catching up before I could grasp the door handle. His arm looped my waist and pulled me around, pressing us tighter than the study had ever witnessed before. "I want you to tell me that you like me."

I sputtered, blinking and fighting back laughter. My eyes darted everywhere, searching for something sturdy and sound. Anything to stop his request ringing in my ears. "You want me to what?"

"I just, I can't always tell. You tolerate me more than anyone else. I know that much." A smile lifted on his cheeks, kissing the corners of his mouth. "But do you like me? As a person? As a friend? As a . . . man? Or is this all . . ." He turned his gaze to the windows, the walls, the whole castle. "Is it just an occupation?"

My tongue ran dry, and I licked my lips once, twice. Bit them even. But the longer I looked at him the more I felt how serious he was. I shifted in his arms, and he pulled me closer still, raising my right hand to run his thumb down the divot of my tendon, that soft crevice on the white of my arm.

The same ache that slithered up my spine under the trees grew once more from the press of his thumb to the knot of my elbow. Magic. Again. As if everything I'd given to the water that morning was being returned.

"Tell me," he urged. "You give me so many allowances, so many glimpses into your work, and you take every jape like a mere pinch on your skin but does any of that mean—"

"I like you," I blurted out. "You are . . . good. You are a good person and a good man and if you were not I would have never stayed to help. These people, this place, you, it matters. Everything matters."

When his fingers closed around my wrist, I realized I was shaking. I didn't like what I had just put between us. His eyes roamed my face and his chin jolted to one side, expression narrowing as if he hadn't understood what I said. But he shook his head and returned to his normal demeanor.

"I can replace a shepherd, but the same cannot be said about you, Etta." He glanced over his shoulder at the bookshelf. "You are not to sacrifice yourself for any reason over this inquiry."

"I had no intention." I pulled out of his grasp, nodded, and with my head tucked down, I spun and wrenched the door open. When the latch clicked back into place, I ran.

Chapter Thirty One

THE NEXT MORNING, I emptied out my bag and began walking to and fro between my rooms and the staff quarters. With the snow settled across our fields, the air turned dry and lifeless in the walls. Colds and coughs increased everywhere, and I spent a great deal of time delivering teas, fermented garlic, clove oil, and the crushed eggshells to the servants who'd sampled too much custard.

Restless and annoyed, I took a different path every time trying to distract myself from not being able to check on the barrows. It was better that way. Should the shepherd have seen me out and about engaging with a squirrel that resembled the one I'd brought to his house, I'd have been in trouble. But the not knowing clung to me like a lost bee, constantly buzzing in my ear.

When Aeson's birthday finally arrived, I couldn't stay hidden anymore. I had Layla braid my hair again but I waited until the last possible moment before heading to the great hall. Dressed in my grey shift, I wore my plum kirtle instead of the black.

It was the only celebration in the year that truly demanded my best dress. Aeson was, despite his modesty, the lord of our castle and our lands and if anything truly called for regard to my appearance, it was this.

The hall was crowded by the time I crept in the back. Everyone in the castle had pushed in and even some of the braver village folk had trekked up the hill in the snow. The sour scent of too much ale in too many beards burned my nostrils as I made my way to the end of one table near a vase of rosemary and other herbs. It stifled the odor enough to breathe comfortably and hid me from view.

A cheer went up as the main course was wheeled into the room. It was a tower of roasted ducks under onion sauce anointed with sour cherries. They brought it to the head table where Aeson dutifully sat in his seat with a smile painted on. Reeve, Garret, and even Prilla took turns giving toasts and admirations about Aeson's devotion to the land. After each one, mugs were slammed on tables and fists shook in the air.

No one could possibly disagree. Calise said it herself in her confession. Our lands thrived in direct correlation with Aeson's commitment to everyone's well-being.

When the whooping and hollering stopped, Prilla handed Aeson a goblet of honey ale to pour over a suckling pig stuffed with pears and charred asparagus. There was a long pause, and I peeked out from behind the rosemary stalks. By the time I could see his face clearly, he was dropping his attention to the meal before him. No one else could eat until he began.

He rushed through the performance and tossed a welcoming hand in the air with a grin I could tell was forced. Aeson never used the angle of his chin to smile. He used his eyes, his cheeks, the quirk of his mouth if it was leading to laughter, or the lift of his ears when the smile caught him off guard. The clench of his jaw was an act.

Once his plate was full and he'd chewed his first bite, chaos erupted. Knives clanged against plates, wine plopped into cups, chairs scraped along the floor and laughter burst like flames finding air in a chop of wood.

I wove through the bodies near the food tables and swiped a freshly filled plate when its owner set it down to pour their drink. Pushing my way to the back as fast as I could, I came upon Garret and Layla sitting closer than the crowd really demanded. Flopping down on the bench across from them, I held both hands up in a plea. "I promise I'm only here to eat quickly, then I will be out of your way."

"He's looking for you," Garret said, one brow arched.

"No, he's not," I said.

"How would you know? You've been flitting about the corridors like a trapped bat for weeks and taking the long way every time you visit the servants' wing."

I ripped into a roasted duck leg with my teeth bared and shook my head.

"It is true," said Layla, leaning against Garret and rubbing her cheek along his shoulder. "Normally, if the staff needs to find our lord master, we look for you first. But lately, that hasn't worked. It's thrown the whole household off as if you're a broken compass. You're spinning the wrong ways."

I liked Layla enormously, but her bravery in front of Garret was uninvited. "And what of it? People are allowed to spin any which way they want."

She shrugged and took a sauced carrot from Garret's plate.

"I'm only saying it's strange. And you know what the castle always says, if you can't find one, find—" She stopped at my glance.

Garret took a swig of his drink but not before letting a chortle slip out from his chest. The two of them clearly shared a like mind about the topic. I rolled my eyes and pushed up from the table, but he snapped his fingers at me. "No. While you're here, gander your eyes that way."

I followed his direction to a circle of hobbledehoys, stable hands and farm boys from the castle and village alike. One of them had flat black hair clinging to a round head. His back was bent a little too much for a boy his age. A sign he was already familiar with the stance of a smith. His hands stretched long and knobby like a frog's as they were used to controlling a hammer and anvil. "Henrick?" I asked.

Garret nodded. "The snow has kept him from disappearing like he was, but he's been bothering the other workers and asking about different jobs and better positions."

"You said he could barely form a sentence. What makes him presume a better position?"

Garret lifted a free hand, palm open and up as he used the other to gulp his drink. Beside him, Layla cleared her throat. "He's bothered the maids too," she said. "Asking what it's like to work inside the castle and what everyone does and when."

"Perhaps not so simple?" I asked, meeting Garret's eyes.

"Simple minds in the hands of smarter ones can accomplish a lot," he said.

"What's your plan?"

"He's had a follower assigned to him since Layla mentioned it to me, a week ago. Nothing yet, but as I said, the snows have kept everyone in."

"And nothing from the guards at Maer Hill? No sight of the shepherd?"

He shook his head. Layla squeezed his arm and even leaned over to kiss his temple right in front of me. It was clear she'd made herself his confidant as well as his comfort.

"Did the shepherd ever go to the willow tree at the road?" I asked.

Garret shook his head. "My guards said it was part of his daily path, but he only shooed the ewes off from settling under the branches. No more than that."

I grunted and looked back at Henrick, cocking my head. "Well. Let's see if there's anything worth squeezing from this one's ears, shall we?"

"Witch. No. Stop it." Garret tried to stand but Layla pulled him back, laughing and shaking her head at him. This allowed me to make my way unbothered. Whether it was her own desire to keep Garret close or an understanding that I needed a chance at Henrick myself, I considered forgiving her comments about Aeson and me.

For a few moments, I stood directly behind the boy and listened. He and the rest of the circle were prattling about winter and how nice it would be when spring returned and brought the girls from their homes to bathe in the stream again. Eventually, one of them saw me, and his notice rippled around the ring of them.

Henrick turned at last, stumbling back a bit when he recognized me. I stood quietly with my hands clasped in a V against the skirt of my dress. I stared, unspeaking, waiting him out. Some of the other boys in his party sank away in the crowd, but a few stayed.

One finally coughed to clear his throat. "Apologies ma'am. We meant no offense."

"Why would you offend me? It's not as if you were conspiring indecency towards my body. Were you?"

Their faces turned a collective shade of scarlet as I stepped closer, meeting Henrick's eyes directly. He swallowed at last and realized that speaking was his only escape. "You're the castle witch."

I lifted one hand to my chest. "Are you sure?"

This caught him off guard and he stammered, looking away, like there might be a sign to confirm what he thought he knew. "Yea . . . Yes. Yes."

"Good." I moved my hand from my chest to his, tapping one finger on his sternum and watching the thrum of his pulse quicken through the skin of his neck. "It's important to be sure of oneself, Henrick."

"Yes mum."

"Especially if you want to raise yourself in the esteem of those around you." I wanted to give him all the room in the world to find his footing, so I might see where he chose to stand.

He glanced away, already losing his comprehension of the conversation.

"I heard you want a higher station at the castle, a place of more significance?" I inched my hand to one side of his collar. He lifted his free shoulder, perhaps too scared to move the other under my touch. "Were you hoping to serve someone in particular?" I asked.

He scowled at this. Not liking the implication or insult to his ambitions.

Cupping his face with both hands next, I let my eyes swerve over the contours of his face. There was barely a spot on his skin.

He was only a bit older than the shepherd girls. "You could serve me." I smiled, wishing the garden snake was here to slither down my arm and whisper in his ear. "Do you know what sort of magic I could weave with your fine hair? Your clear skin?"

He froze as I ran a hand over his head and traced the blade of my finger along his brow then lifted a hand for inspection. "I've no wish to serve you, mum," he said, trying to set his jaw and puffing his chest up when it didn't work. "No offense."

"You consider me unworthy?" I pulled back and clasped my hands before me again, just as I had when we began. He didn't disagree with my deprecation, not even out of polite manners. "I shouldn't have offered."

He was unsure what to make of the exchange. It was clear to me, however, that his beliefs were not his own. Someone was working to influence them. It might have been Henrick meeting Shepherd in the night, but it could just as easily have been a messenger from the Elder Lords. I'd have to leave that piece to Garret. Dropping a cordial curtsy to the lot of them, I swept out the closest door and back to my quarters.

Pushing my door open and shut by way of slumping my back against it, I shut my eyes and exhaled. Parties were exhausting. No matter the purpose.

"I must admit, I always thought you were faster with your escapes."

Popping my eyes back open, his shadow stood across the room, silhouetted in the moonlight. I clutched the door handle, wondering where I could hide if I slipped out before he strode his way here. I sighed instead. "You should be downstairs with the revelry."

He shook his head. There was enough light to catch his profile from the side and reveal he was looking straight at me. "I don't want to be downstairs."

I folded my arms. "What do you need?"

"You have been avoiding me. Again."

"I have been working. People are sick. As it goes with the winter."

"Yet every time they tell me you are one place, you are gone by the time I arrive."

"What do you need?" I repeated, trying not to think about what Layla said. We were not compasses, and we were not spinning falsely. It was just an oddness of time like how some petals unfurl a day late for the sun. Nature might have a perfect design, but it doesn't mean it's followed perfectly. The same was true of people.

He stepped forward, halfway to me. "I put you on the spot, last time we were . . . and I'm sorry. I know it's not a place you like to be. I knew better and I shouldn't have coerced you into sharing yourself that way."

An apology was the last thing I expected. All I could do was stare through the darkness, barely making out the jut of his chin or the curve of his lips. "Ap —Apology accepted," I exhaled.

He offered his hand through the grey space that separated us. And despite my smarter impulses, I rocked forward off the door, giving him my hand in return. He took the other once I was closer and we turned in a solitary dance until we had switched places. One step at a time, he nudged me backwards.

"There is something else." He sighed. "I've had another letter. No daughters this time. Only negotiation."

"Negotiation?" I asked.

"There is a lord who asks that you serve him for a year, and he will support all my causes in exchange."

I gulped. Leaving Valley Maer would be a punishment for me, but if it meant a solution for Aeson, there could be worse things. "Would that help?"

"Perhaps, but his castle is well known for his inhospitable wife and the curious way maids arrive in one season only to depart in the next with a babe in their belly."

My breath stopped and my steps faltered. "There are so many people in need. They seem to be everywhere."

Aeson nodded. "There are. But I'm not entertaining this. Neither should you. There are other ways to fight. Better ways."

"What other ways?" I asked. "Is this why you have been so attentive to my whereabouts?"

He didn't answer, just nudged me the last few steps until we stood in the moonlight together. I had a better view of him. And he held a real smile, although it was guarded by his eyes and didn't fully spread over his face. Letting my hands go, he plucked at the pleats of my skirt, squinting in the silver light. "You're always in purple for my birthday," he said, glancing up to confirm. "Just like Iya."

Running a hand over my braids, I tilted my gaze away and nodded.

"I suppose you are to stay hidden up here for the rest of the night?" he asked.

I gritted my teeth. He could order me back if he wanted. "I had intended on it, yes."

He took a long breath and gave it an equally long release. "Goodnight, Etta."

"Goodnight, Aeson," I replied but he left swiftly, latching the door before he heard me whisper the rest. "Happy birthday."

WINTER

Chapter Thirty Two

THE MERRIMENT OF AESON'S BIRTHDAY rolled right into winter solstice two weeks later. It was a convenient bit of timing that made the season easier for everyone to bear. On the morning after, I woke to the pounding of fists on my door. Stumbling from my bed and through my workroom, I yanked the door open to see Saana beside one of the stable hands.

"My mother," she heaved, before turning and running off down the stairs.

I glanced at the stable hand and shook my head. "Get my horse ready, and one for her if she hasn't already disappeared."

He knew as well as I did there was no need to have escorted her all the way other than wanting to keep her in sight a bit longer. The least he could do was be helpful. Shutting the door in his face, I rushed back to my sleeping chamber and dressed, tugging on my apron and tying my hair up with no close attention. With my bag slung over my shoulder, I filled it with everything I might possibly need and slipped my warmest boots on.

Outside, they were trotting Sparrow out with a piebald at his side. I found Saana and nodded. "You know how to ride?"

She shrugged. "I keep one leg on each side and my head in the middle, yes?"

"Yes." I smiled, watching as she got seated. Then I swung up into my saddle and led the way.

It'd been a few days since the last snowfall. The road down to the village had already been tamped down and returning to her home was not so difficult. At her door, we slid off our horses, and Saana nodded at the front steps.

"Let yourself in. I'll put the horses in our pens for now."

Admiring her authority over the situation, I did as I was told and found Ellara inside near the fire. Her next oldest children were doing their best to soothe her, but it couldn't replace a proper doula or midwife. One of the boys was running a comb through her hair, and Mello was in the kitchen already boiling water. She glanced my way, blonde curls shaking with the motion.

"I don't know how hot to make the water," she stated, staring at her feet, "and the blood frightens me."

The boy nearest Ellara, with the comb, chimed in, "I've tried to fill the tub but the rim's too high."

I smiled at them both and offered to shake the boy's hand. "You've done well. Your other sister will be in soon. She and I will take over, but I thank you for your assistance."

Saana entered just as he was backing up. "Thank you, Mello. Keltin, perhaps you can stoke the fire for us? We'll need to heat even more water."

Mello slunk away to the back rooms and Keltin stood at attention with a nod. Turning, he began to pick through the logs for a few solid pieces. He glanced back at Saana, checking for approval, then carried on with his task.

I went to Ellara and crouched before her. She smiled, which cheered me. It was good that she was still breathing easily and calmly. The rumbling had not yet begun inside her belly.

"It always feels the same and it always feels different, don't it?" she asked.

I shrugged. I had no idea. I didn't plan on ever being in her position. Birthing a child would mean I'd found a man tolerable enough to set one in me. And since most men were children themselves, I saw little chance of that happening.

Ellara shifted on her stool, ankles crossed and knees open. She had her elbows propped behind her on a chair to rest against the base. I remembered this position well from Kella's birth. It was her starting point, before baby slipped lower.

"May I?" I asked, gesturing towards her belly. When she nodded, I scooted forward and splayed my fingers wide, feeling the babe's position. "He stayed head down, good."

"He will be easy. I feel it," Ellara said, rubbing her hands along the top of her belly. "I would sense it already if something were going to be amiss."

Grinning, I left her side and went to the table, laying out my supplies and helping Saana fill the pots and move them to the fire. Just as we set the last one on the grate, Ellara moaned. It was a long exhale with a narrow whisper at the tail end. Like wind at a cracked window. Too much momentum and not enough room to squeak through. When it was over, she hummed and rocked her hips from one side of the stool to the other.

Resettled, she glanced up and caught my eye. She knew what I'd heard. It was the same sound she and every other mother made when the next leg of the journey began. I reached out and touched Saana's arm. "Get the blankets."

She disappeared into the back of the house, and I poured the first pots of water into the tub that someone must've dragged in earlier that morning. I couldn't picture Saana doing it all herself, but with Mello's help and some from the boys, I suppose they could have managed it. With or without their father, this family was more than capable, and the thought offered relief. Ellara and the new baby would be more than safe for the remainder of the season.

By the time Saana returned, Ellara had shifted her weight twice more, moaned again, and uncrossed her ankles to squat. I took the pile of cloth from Saana and instructed, "Get behind her to start. Support her under the shoulders until her labor is more active. When we get her in the tub, you can sit in front of her."

If this delivery was like the last one, Ellara would transition through each stage with nothing in front of her until it was time to push. Then she'd need someone to ground her. Someone to hold while her baby uncoiled himself from her waters to ours.

While Saana took a seat behind her mother, running her hands through Ellara's hair in place of the brush, I sat off to the side, replacing Keltin at the fire and pouring the pots out as needed.

The smaller children lined up on the stairs much like they had done when Kella arrived. But as the sun turned bright yellow through the windows, and the town stirred outside, I dug through my bag and scraped up enough loose coins for each of them.

I made them form a row at the door and asked them to swear on their plump little chests before I let them go. "Find something for breakfast. You must stick together and do not dare return with anything too sweet for the morning. Your mother has a bit more to go before your next sibling arrives, and I'd hate for you to buy something fancy but unfilling."

Like a clutch of goslings, they wobbled their little heads and scurried out the door, scattering into the crowd. I waited for Mello to reappear, but she stayed hidden away from the mess of childbirth.

Ellara was struggling to breathe through her contractions and needed the time in between to rest. Her grunts and groans were minimal. We still had some time. She waved a hand at me as I returned to my little post by the fire.

"We do not deserve you," she said.

I gave a light chuckle. "You are people on these lands, you are entitled to this care."

"Maybe," she said. "But my husband, wherever he is, has not fulfilled his duties upon these fields. It would be within Lord Crennly's right to disregard us now."

"Ma, I think by now you know Lord Crennly is not the same as other lords, and neither is Miss Etta," Saana said, offering me a smile and readjusting beneath her mother. I watched as her gaze ran over Ellara's arms, tracing the remnants of her mother's bruises with her eyes and setting her jaw tight.

"Your daughter is right," I said. "The way he sees it, your children will grow up to serve these lands, so it's only right we serve them first. That means serving you."

Ellara tried to nod but pitched forward instead, vocalizing through the next contraction as it rippled across her belly and over her hips. "Oof. Very well," she breathed.

"Save your energy, ma'am. It appears the next stage is upon us."

Guiding Saana through the steps, we lifted Ellara and supported her to the tub, easing her into the water one leg at a time. From here I pointed Saana to the frontside, so she might hold her mother's hands as the next waves crested inside and swelled out through Ellara's muscles. In less than a few hours, Ellara would have one more child to feed and Saana would have another brother to stoke the fire in years to come.

The children were ecstatic. They swooned and swarmed and stuck their hands out as if reaching for sweets to touch their fingertips to their newest brother, Grennly. They berated Ellara with questions about how babies feed and why they have no hair. Mello cringed at the answers. Ellara pushed the hair back from her own face. She had sweat a bit harder after Grennly crowned, his chest wider than his head, a doughty boy in the making.

I watched them from the kitchen. Ellara was reclined in their best chair near the fire again, and Saana was teaching the younger kids how to caress the infant without startling him. An idea came to me that was more presumptuous than I'd ever thought before and I approached them slowly, wringing my hands behind my back. "Ellara, Saana?"

"Yes?" Ellara replied, head dipping low to kiss her nose against Grennly's.

"You'll need to be on bed rest for the first week. Saana is more than fit to attend to you, but I'm concerned about the younger children. They will be underfoot and in need of attention themselves. I believe that will be too much, even for you, Saana." I smiled her way, and she nodded in understanding.

"Where shall you take them?" Ellara asked, sharing a look with Saana then meeting my face with great interest. "Surely not the castle?"

Chapter Thirty Three

THE ELDEST BOY, KELTIN, elected to stay behind. Mello too. As it was, I sensed the commotion of a castle would've overwhelmed her.

Overseeing the move, Saana rode alongside the cart on the horse from our stables. Dusk had fallen when the wheels slugged through the snow into the castle gates. They turned around the black alba and stopped at the main door. I dismounted and helped the three little ones hop down one by one as Prilla emerged from the kitchen door with Layla behind her. They looked upon the brood with well-founded skepticism. Saana gathered her brothers and sister who were already running circles around the tree. She shook her finger at them with firm instructions.

"The youngest is only recently off her mother's milk, and has just a few teeth," I told Prilla. "We will have to be mindful of what we feed her. The boys, I suspect, will be pleased with anything that comes from the castle kitchen. They're rather delighted to be here."

Garret appeared from the main door and strode over, giving the kids a wide berth. "I heard we were to be invaded. I suppose I should be glad they're no real threat yet."

"Speak for yourself," Layla chimed. She lifted Kella and snuggled cheek to cheek with her, flushed with sweetness. "They are too precious."

Grunting, Garret eyed the scene before him and crossed his arms. "And where are we housing these rascals?"

"Yes. Indeed," Prilla joined in. "That's my question as well."

"It's only for a short while. They can have my rooms," Layla said, glancing at Garret. "It's not as if I've slept there much in recent weeks."

Her amorous guard turned dark red and grumbled, stepping closer to me to whisper. "And what did Lord Crennly say to this?"

I shrugged. "When I speak to him, I'll be sure to give you a full account."

Garret looked down his nose, tightening the lids of his eyes as if aiming to loose an arrow. "He doesn't know."

"I'm sure he's heard. You did, after all." I tossed one hand in the air, indifferent. "Besides, not six moons ago he was bleating about filling the castle with a wife and children."

"So, you've given him the children but no wife?" Garret's gaze was cool as he locked onto my face, the words landing square between my eyes. He smirked and nodded in Saana's direction. "Unless you have plans for that one."

I followed his line of sight and boiled. Stomping on his foot, I took off inside, through the main door and down the left side of the great hall. Gripping the hinges of the passageway door in one hand, I swung into the darkness and careened straight into Aeson. Growling, I shook my hands in the air, fingers bent like claws.

"All of you!" I roared.

He flung his palms open in surrender. "What have I done?"

Shuddering, I rolled my neck and crossed my arms. "Nothing. You have done nothing."

Standing at a distance, he raked a hand through his hair and bobbed his head towards the great hall. "I heard we are entertaining children for a few days."

"They're in the courtyard," I muttered. "I'm sorry. I should have asked you first."

Aeson shook his head. "No, you shouldn't have. Reeve might have my trust when it comes to accounts and rents, but you know you have mine when it comes to the people."

This angered me more. I whipped my head around, repeating the apology out of pure stubbornness and mild courtesy.

He sighed but he didn't refuse me a second time. "Do they have rooms?" His voice sunk into the tapestries as soon as it left his chest. I told him of Layla's offer, and he nodded, stepping forward and back. "What is wrong?"

"It is nothing."

"It is something. You're only happy when you are throwing your finest criticisms in every direction. I've been stood here for more than a moment and received *nothing*." He stepped forward again and kept the ground this time. "In fact, it's been nearly a month since I've had any of your typical malice. You are far overdue."

"And should you like these repayments in weekly installments or a grand sum?"

"Etta?" He stepped even closer.

I fisted both hands and pressed them into my sockets until a red haze grew beneath my lids. Then I dropped everything and shook my arms out. "I am fine, just restless. I feel useless."

"You assisted a mother in labor all morning, that's hardly useless," he said, cocking his head to one side. I wasn't interested in telling him what Garret said, and I was even less interested in seeing his reaction to it. In fact, the way he'd been acting the last few occasions we had been alone, I was positive I didn't want him to even hear of Garret's jest. When I offered no other remark, he stretched his neck and gave up.

"What did she name the baby?"

In spite of Garret and his absurd commentary, I grinned. "Grennly."

This made Aeson laugh, and the sound soothed my ears. Maybe I didn't hate Garret so much. "With luck, a close birthday is the only thing the boy will share. Hopefully he has better sense than his lordship."

My eyes rolled without a second thought. "Everyone has better sense than you."

He laughed again and before I could stop him, he reached out and pinched my chin too tightly, shaking it side to side until I pushed him off. "That's better," he said.

I thought we were in for another strange and silent moment but the doors in the great hall thumped open, echoing along the walls and into the passageway where we stood. A chorus of children clamored in with Prilla's voice barely maintaining above it.

"This way. This way. Do not touch that, young master. What's your name again?"

"That one is Arvis? I think," said Layla.

The patter of feet disappeared down the other hall, but two others lingered behind. Their voices reverberated over the tables.

I turned my head towards the sound of them when one voice came through raspy and recognizable.

"I'm sure I don't know you, sir," Saana said.

Neither Aeson nor I moved at first, turning only our necks to hear the other voice.

"But you've seen me, I'm sure. In the village. I was a friend of your father's."

My face contorted and I waved a hand at Aeson, mouthing to him, "Henrick?" To which Aeson shrugged and took a cautious step towards the entryway.

"Was?" Saana scoffed. "Are you implying he is both disappeared *and* dead?"

"No . . . no, no, no. 'Tis not what I mean at all, miss."

"What *did* you mean? I have a sister and brothers waiting for me to bid them goodbye and another sister and brother with my mother who needs me more than I need this odd association."

Aeson threw a grimace my way, mouthing his own quiet message. "She sounds like you."

I shrugged, stroking my hair.

Saana's footsteps tapped away, but they were followed by the heavier scuff of Henrick's work boots. The entryway door to the other hall never opened.

"Please, just look at me one more time. Surely you must've seen me speaking to your father outside the alehouse or by the troughs."

"I try not to pay attention to who my da deems acceptable company."

There was a grunt next, and one of them yelped. "Oww!?"

Aeson and I moved together, peeking out into the hall from our shadowed corridor as a table groaned. Its weight dragged over the stone floor while Henrick pulled Saana by the arms, begging her to look at him. She got one hand free and cuffed him on the ear. One lucky hit before Henrick grabbed her again.

Laying a hand on my waist, his fingertips clenched into my side and Aeson whispered, "I give you leave to scare the wits out of him."

But my eyes were already closed and my lips moving. The words were easy. Extending both arms before me, I grabbed every strand of magic, wind, and power that drifted by the front door and yanked. Hard.

Too hard. The front doors blew open and every candle in the hall went out. By the time the two youths could make sense of what happened, Aeson was across the room with Henrick's collar clutched in a fist. I followed at his right shoulder, sharing his disappointment but making sure I clapped three times and palmed the wind back out the door before the whole room froze.

Henrick held Saana's wrists while her muscles strained in the opposite direction. One shoulder of her cloak had slipped off. When she saw me, she slackened in relief.

"Tell me, Henrick. Are the forges done burning today?" Aeson projected his voice as he would if he were leading a proper banquet and not a quartet of hostility. Henrick at last found the wisdom to let Saana go. She came to my side and Aeson regarded us both, addressing me next. "Escort the young lady to her siblings, ensure she says her goodbyes. Then see her safely, and warmly, back to her home."

"I will." I took Saana and started to skirt the back wall of the room, but Aeson's hand found mine before I got too far.

"Come straight back to me," he ordered, glancing over his shoulder at Henrick. "We have work to do."

I blinked, agreed, and dragged Saana away before she had to see Henrick's lesson in chivalry. Once we were into the servants' quarters, I released Saana and asked, "Nothing worse occurred, right?"

"No. Of course not. Boys like him don't even know what to do with their own bodies, let alone ours."

I snorted and turned her into Layla's rooms. "I will wait here until you're ready to go."

Chapter Thirty Four

I STAYED WITH ELLARA and her three oldest children until all were comfortable and confident in their tasks. Keltin was to keep his mother and the baby warm, adjusting their pillows as needed. Saana was to watch her mother's bleeding and bring her food to eat and plenty to drink. Mello would do the same, only in service of her siblings. Ellara, I hoped, would stay in bed as much as possible so Grennly might pull her milk down and encourage her womb to return to normal.

I fetched Sparrow from his pen, then hesitated. Saana had ridden the piebald back down again. If they needed anything else from us, a horse was faster than trudging through the snows. Making yet another presumptuous decision, I left their shelter and stomped a path to the granary.

"The shepherds will have an extra animal for a few days' time," I explained to a wizened old man and his son in a room that smelled wet with hay. "You're to deliver extra grain, straw, and oats to them as soon as possible."

Leaving them with the last of my coins, I returned to Sparrow and we trotted back up the hill in the dark. Rounding the last curve before passing beneath the outer gate, I ran a hand down Sparrow's neck. It was thick and wooly with his winter coat. "I promise that's all for a few days. You may go back and sleep as long as you like."

I bent in my saddle and snuggled my face into his mane as it rose and fell with the rhythm of his gait. Glancing up, my brow furrowed. The courtyard was far too busy. There was no need for so many servants at that hour, especially in such weather. Torches were lit and carried back and forth and I sat up straight, trying to understand what they were shouting. Slipping out of my stirrups and to the ground, I grabbed the closest worker by their sleeve.

"What's all this?" I asked.

"One of those rascal children from the village has already gone missing. The young boy." He shook me off and stalked away, making a halfhearted attempt at looking under the wagons.

Snapping my fingers for a stable boy, I handed Sparrow off and rushed inside. Layla flew at me, pouring out apologies. "It's okay," I told her, taking her face in my hands. "Have you asked his brother? Where does he like to hide at home?"

"That's just it. He says when they play hide and discover, this brother is always the winner."

I sighed. "Of course he is. And what's this one's name?"

"Arlo. The younger one to Arvis."

"Let me lay my things down and I will help."

She nodded and rushed off to keep looking. Heaving another, much heavier sigh, I pulled myself up the stairs. Pushing my door open, the hair on my arms immediately tingled with magic. I would not need to help at all. There was more life in my rooms than there ought to have been.

Glancing towards the plants, I saw I was not alone in this knowledge. Those flowers and ferns and herbs that were not in total hibernation all craned their leaves towards something in the darkest corner. An intruder.

A small intruder, but an intruder, nonetheless.

Biting my smile into place, I took my time hanging up my cloak, emptying my bag, and stoking the fire in the very small hearth of my bedroom. I could've left and informed everyone to cease their search, but I didn't dare risk losing sight of the infiltrator.

Once everything was in its rightful place, I lifted the pail of water and began feeding the plants, some of which had the decency to turn back to me and stop ogling Arlo like he was some never seen creature.

"You know," I began as I got closer and closer to the trio of pots he lay behind, "I like to hide among my plants as well. They are good companions. They are gentle and peaceful and most of them are quite kind."

There was a hint of a whisper, but I couldn't discern it even with my ears turned his way.

"You'll have to be a little louder. I can't hear you over the chattering of the plants."

This brought his copper head straight up from behind the fronds. "Plants don't speak."

"Don't they?" I set my pail down. "Perhaps not the way you or I do, but I promise they communicate very effectively when they need to." I thought of Aeson's lip, realizing I hadn't offered to heal it.

Arlo raised his chin and set his mouth to a thoughtful pout. "I don't believe you."

"You don't have to." I shrugged. "Whether you believe it or not does not stop the world from existing the way it does. But trust me, you are missing out on something wonderful if you think nature cannot speak."

His round face folded next, considering what I'd said and trying to make it fit in his experience of the world thus far.

I bent closer to him and winked. "Do you want to see something disgusting?"

His eyes lit up and he dipped back behind the pots to crawl out under the bench. If I'd not been there, he might have stayed hidden for hours in that particular spot. Stifling a laugh, I offered my hand and brought him to the worktable where I had left the package from his mother. I would have to bless it and adorn it with herbs and petals before I went to sleep, but for that moment, it would serve a different purpose: redirection.

"Are you ready?" I asked Arlo, waiting for his square chin to nod with certainty before I unfolded the paper.

His nostrils flared and his lips curled, but he leaned forward all the same. "Which wretched Sister did you get that from? It's grotesque, it is."

I laughed from my belly, leaning all the way back in my chair to tilt my face to the ceiling. There were few people who could look at fresh afterbirth and see what I saw. Life. And magic. A healthy afterbirth was better than any spell. Few things in this world possessed the power a mother could create within her own body. Yet so many things were overstated in its place.

Arlo shimmied his way into my lap and planted his hands on either side of the paper, hanging his head over the bloody item with an unwavering fascination. "It looks like the slab da has butchered off a lamb flank. Where did it come from?"

"It came from your mother, actually. This is what grows beside a baby in her belly. It feeds and nourishes the infant until it's strong enough to be with us in this world."

Arlo looked between my face and the pile before him, studying the cord and its arteries where they spiraled into the greater creation. "We're just like the animals? On our insides?"

I hid a face from him. "To the discomfort and disappointment of many people, yes. There's nothing any more special about men and women that sets us above or apart from animals. We live and we die and we encompass all the same magic in between."

Arlo tried to scoot forward a little more and slipped. I caught him with both arms and locked my elbows to keep him steady right as the door kicked open.

"There you—" Aeson stopped and turned to shout down the stairs. "Prilla? He is here."

Prilla's voice billowed up the circular staircase. "The scamp. I suppose he's hungry too?"

Understanding that he was the center of attention, Arlo perked up and nodded his head. "Indeed. Can I have another biscuit? And that delicious yellow cheese they gave us at dinner?"

Hiding a curl of his lip, Aeson lolled his head back in the direction of Prilla and instructed her with Arlo's request. "A biscuit, if you would, Prilla. And that most delicious yellow cheese from dinner."

A few muffled curse words floated up the stairs before Aeson could close the door and join us at the desk. He looked at the parcel and then me and Arlo and decided against any comment. Instead, he dragged the little stool from the plants and came to sit beside us.

"You gave the castle a good fright, master Arlo."

The boy hung his head. "Are you going to send me home for disobeying?"

Aeson sat tall and scanned his eyes over the boy, but it was mocking in severity. "That depends. Are you like to be disobedient again tomorrow?"

"No, sir. No." Arlo was adamant for a minute, before his face fell. "Well, actually, your lordship sir . . . Perhaps it's best if you did send me home."

I glanced at Aeson in surprise but neither of us got the chance to ask anything because Prilla swept into the room with a fresh plate. She laid it before Arlo and squeezed his jaw firmly before giving him a pat on the head and muttering, "Sisters mischief."

When the three of us were alone again, Arlo sat back on my knees and picked up the block of cheese, forcing as much of it as he could into one bite. Pulling his tiny frame back against my chest, I rested my head on his, feeling the mechanical working of his jaw under my chin as he chewed.

"Arlo," I began, "I wasn't here when you disappeared, and I didn't hear the rules set forth for you. How have you disobeyed?"

His body went limp against mine and his handful of cheese fell to his lap. "We were told not to come in here."

"My rooms specifically?"

He set to chewing again and pointed to Aeson. "And yours. They said it was disrespectful to touch the rooms of his lord and dangerous to enter the chambers of the castle witch. They said you have an evil temper, and you'd roast our skin off if we touched anything."

Aeson pitched forward, sniggering and trying to cover his mouth. If I hadn't had a frightful boy in my arms, I might've kicked the stool right out from under him. Collecting himself, he cleared his face and looked at Arlo. "Then you must explain to us why you saw fit to hide in here."

Arlo wobbled in his seat, reaching for the biscuit and putting it right back. "I thought, if she's so scary, no one else would come in here either."

I shared a look with Aeson, both of us trying to follow the path Arlo was set on. Shaking my head and sitting up straighter, I asked the next question. "There's someone you didn't want to come in here. You were hiding from another person?"

He bounced his head up and down twice, and his body went rigid in my hands.

"I promise you are very safe, everywhere in the castle," Aeson reassured him, but Arlo shook his head stiffly. Looking up at me, Aeson drew another breath and tipped forward on the legs of the stool. "Who is here that scares you so?"

"The quiet man." Arlo pushed the plate away and pulled his knees up to his chest, unbalanced. I had no choice but to wrap my arms all the way around him and hold him tight so he wouldn't tumble off my lap. "I saw him. He *lives* here."

"Who is the quiet man?" I asked, using my cheek to sweep the hair back from his brow.

"He's the man that speaks to my da. They whisper in the pens at night. I've heard them. Da never knew I was there because I'm better at sneaking than the rest. But I know it was him."

I felt stupid for not considering that Saana might not have been the only one who noticed their father's strange comings and goings. While I rubbed my temple, Aeson pressed Arlo for a bit more information, if it was there to be had.

"What does the quiet man speak about, with your father?" he

asked.

His whole body lifted when he shrugged, tiny as he was. And he tossed his head as if the whole thing was made up after all. "He wants a body. Or he wants somebody. I couldn't tell, that's why he's the quiet man. And grown-ups never talk the right way."

Aeson chuckled lightly, pressing his mouth closed tight before continuing. "You're a very astute lad, Arlo. Us grown-ups are not always precise with our language, are we?"

I smirked and gave the body in my arms a little shake. "You're not in trouble for trying to hide in here, Arlo. But how do you know the quiet man is here? What does he look like?"

His face turned and he met my eyes directly with his mouth flattened as if the answer were in plain sight and Arlo was gravely disappointed to learn I was blind. "He was talking to Saana."

Chapter Thirty Five

I WAS HALFWAY DOWN THE HALL before Aeson caught up. He'd taken a responsible moment to give Arlo instructions before chasing after. Grabbing me however he could, he hefted my feet off the floor before they carried me any farther.

"We need to talk about this first. In case Arlo's suggestion held any appeal to you, you can't go barging away to roast his skin off."

"Roasting his skin off would be a kindness for that froggy heap." I wriggled but Aeson squeezed tighter until I could barely breathe. "All right. I'll listen. Put me down."

He relinquished, slowly, probably expecting me to dash off at the first chance. But I stood, smoothed my skirts and turned to him, scowling. "Where were you headed? Do you even know where he is?" he asked.

"To the courtyard. Surely someone has seen him in the last hour or so. If not, I suppose I will start roasting skins."

Aeson rubbed a hand over his face and speared the other one into the air, pointing to the third floor as if brandishing a sword.

"He is in my study with Garret. If you recall, you were supposed to come straight to me after delivering Saana to her mother."

"And I might have had I not rode into a castle wide game of hide and discover."

"I'm not arguing that. I understand. But consider that I was already prepared to interrogate the boy over his actions towards Saana. Now we have additional information, and I can't help but think that having a wind drag him from the third-floor windows might not give us the answers we need. Stop your temper where it lies. Here. In this hallway."

I hadn't considered defenestration until he suggested it, but I certainly liked the idea. Aeson was still scowling though, so I worked my jaw in a circular motion and eased the tension in my shoulders. After a heavy exhale, I gave a delicate flip of both palms to signify I was ready to cooperate.

With a stern look, he spun on his heel and led the way down the rest of the hall. "I swear," he said. "Sometimes, you are my least favorite witch."

"I am your only witch," I muttered. Then I stopped in my tracks. Something hot and uncomfortable spread across my entire body, and I wished more than anything for a sharp knife to scrape it off.

Aeson had stopped at the base of the stairs to turn side face in front of me. Cautiously he raised one finger. "But you are . . . mine?"

My scowl carved deeper into my brow, reaching the set of my chin. I glanced at the closest candle sconce, burning beautifully and precariously close to Aeson's hair. His eyes followed mine and before I could do anything he reached up and put it out with his whole palm.

I growled and pushed by him, stepping through the darkness alone. "This is a curious way to stop my temper."

The rest of the way felt clouded with spider webs and by the time I reached the study I was ready to roast my own skin off. I shoved the door open and left it for Aeson to appear when he wanted, bringing myself to the desk. Garret stood on the other side, and Henrick slouched in one of the chairs.

When Aeson swept in behind me, he bolted the door, and I was reminded of the last time we were locked in this room together. At that time, all there was to worry about was a failed seduction and a few peppermint leaves. Now we had a missing shepherd, a deviant smith apprentice, and still no idea how sweet water came to be on our lands or where it was.

Sitting comfortably, Aeson studied Henrick long and hard, giving the boy ample time to scoot around in his chair and begin to worry. I wouldn't have traded places with him for anything. Not with three very different temperaments posed before him like pillars of punishment.

It was Garret who started, turning his chin in Aeson's direction. "Henrick and I have been having a lively discussion while we waited for you, my lord. He has promised some compelling stories for you."

"Excellent. I haven't had a good story in a fair few months now."

Henrick didn't speak right away. His gaze slid from one of us to the other. Finally, he straightened in his chair and looked at Aeson. "The thing is my lord, there's no harm done by the way I see it."

"Tell your stories and we shall sort out if I see it the same." Aeson glared over the top of his fingers, tented before his face with elbows on the arms of his chair.

"What do you want with the girl?" I prompted. "What lack of harm did you intend for her?"

Something in his gaze softened and his mouth turned down. "She . . . Her father promised me . . . I wanted . . ."

"Her," Aeson finished for him and dipped his face lower, trying to look under Henrick's countenance to affirm his guess. "You wanted her for yourself?"

Henrick nodded and I muzzled a grunt. "You're all of eighteen, nineteen, Henrick. What need do you have of a wife?" I asked.

"I could have a wife," he bristled. "I could treat a lady well enough to keep her happy."

"Well enough does not involve forcing your hands upon her when she's already refused you twice," Aeson reprimanded.

My shoulder twitched, and despite the action at hand, I thought of all the times Aeson's hands had been on me in both private and public settings. The thought crept like a bark spider in my ear, scratching its way through and distorting every other sound. I'd never refused him.

Memories played over and over as if I was spinning in circles before a portrait. I blinked and pulled at my necklaces. No one was talking and I wasn't sure if Garret or Aeson had asked another question, but I cleared my throat and looked at Henrick. "You wanted a prize. And a pretty one at that. But what were you doing to earn it?" I asked.

Henrick looked quickly at Aeson and then down at his feet. Blowing a heap of air out from his chest, he mumbled, "He wanted to know the castle routines. What Lord Crennly does and when and how and where."

"You were spying on me? For the shepherd?"

Henrick nodded.

"All that in exchange for a girl who doesn't care to know you?" Garret asked.

"He promised me that he'd spoken to her." Henrick raised his voice at Garret, wailing his excuse like a lost calf.

I looked at Aeson who was already looking at me with the same line of confusion etched into his forehead. Garret asked the next logical question.

"I've seen you engage with half this household. You are not a shy young man. You didn't need her father to approach her. There is more to this agreement than you're letting on."

Henrick looked over each of our faces and swallowed. "It wasn't just a wife. He promised me livings as well. Said he had a homestead at the edge of Aevic Stow, but his wife didn't want to leave the village. He'd give it to us to take charge of."

I walked towards the window, flinging it open and letting the cool air in before the foolishness melted anyone else's mind. Henrick didn't seem malicious, but he was too trusting and impressionable if he had put his faith in a drug laden shepherd. Perhaps not a simple idiot, just a lovesick one. If that was the cost of infatuation, it was not worth it to my eyes.

"What lands? The shepherd has no holdings other than what you see in the village," Aeson explained, but I'd already crossed the room again and was pulling out the maps. The three of us circled the table and Henrick scuffled over like a hound with his tail between his legs. When Aeson weighed the corners down, he gestured across the spread. "Show me these lands you were promised."

Henrick eyed the paper for a moment, then pointed to one end. Garret, Aeson, and I all sighed and shook our heads.

Henrick's ears twitched and he looked around at us. "What? Are they truly not his to give?"

"They're not even *mine* to give." Aeson stuck his index finger to the page where Henrick had indicated. "Those are Gallo lands, not Crennly. I'm sorry, Henrick. The shepherd has lured you with false prizes of all kinds. I would've never condoned a marriage between half strangers as it is. And I could not give you those lands even if I had good reason to. As it stands, I've no reason to give you anything right now."

"What do you want with land?" I asked Henrick.

He shrugged. "Same as any man wants. A place of his own."

"What's wrong with your place here? You've not even finished your apprenticeship under Smithwik yet," said Garret.

Red shame coated Henricks expression, and he uttered something unintelligible at first, glancing between Aeson and me.

I smirked and flapped a hand at him. "I've already heard words from the shepherd. Speak your judgements freely, Henrick."

He repeated himself but avoided my face at all costs. "Shepherd says Lord Crennly is at the whims of your every idea, mum. He's a bastard who never deserved his station, and you're leading him to turmoil. The other lords will never let you steal the wealth out from under them. We'd all best find our own way before they do worse."

"And what is worse?" I asked.

"No," Aeson interrupted. "I've heard enough. Henrick, you are dismissed. I will think on your consequences. For now, you will return to your rooms and tomorrow you will work over those anvils with the most fantastic semblance of joy you can muster."

The lot of us startled at the shift of Aeson's attitude. Henrick dropped his chin, accepting his fate. He held his head as Garret walked him to the door though. Before Garret could turn back, Aeson dismissed him as well.

Alone in his study, like too many other times, I wrung my hands out and paced around the table towards Aeson. I had no idea what to say but I knew I was guilty. The shepherd had singled me out for some failing I didn't understand and Aeson continued to be the target. The thought made my blood boil. If people wanted to hate me, they were welcome to, but hurting someone who was good in place of myself was an injustice I couldn't accept.

"Tomorrow I will—"

"You can leave as well," he said. "I've had my fill of people today. I want to be alone."

I stood, unmoving, for longer than I should have given his request. But there was nothing in me. No lie I could conjure up, no excuse, no joke, or jest, or quip I could think of to stay in his presence. Nothing I could think of to keep him from stewing all night.

When I walked out and pulled the door tight behind me, a new thought tapped in my ears. It beat alongside each footstep on the stairs as I walked past the extinguished candle and all the way down the corridor to my rooms. It followed me into my sleeping chamber and under the blankets with my dress still on.

Of all times, Aeson had refused me.

Chapter Thirty Six

I WOKE WITH SHIVERS running the length of me even beneath the blankets and all my clothes. Something was wrong. I slipped out from under the wool and went to my main chamber shrouded in darkness. Snow had fallen again, gathering outside on the sill and in the corners. I pushed the panes open and closed my eyes to the weather. Most of the blizzard had come to rest but there was something else in the buzzing. Something fretful and erratic like a heart pumping too quickly.

Tugging my dress off, I threw it aside so nothing would mute my senses. Setting my hands on the stones, I kicked off my shoes next and breathed in long and slow. There was nothing in the castle save for one spot of worry, but I knew who that belonged to. Frowning, I shut the window to protect the plants and left my rooms with a handful of good herbs.

I pulled the storm's power with me and went from east to west, room to room. I laid my palms on every door and called the eyes of the Brothers to watch over everyone under our roof.

Wedging a sprig into each frame, I left every sleeping room with either rosemary for purification, lavender for serenity, or winter mint for clarity.

I wandered barefoot along the halls with only the moon to light the passageways. It felt good. It brought on an extra current of power. The threads of magic sang louder when no one else was awake to get in the way.

As I worked through the servants' quarters, I stifled a giggle. If the children saw me stalking around the castle at night, bedraggled, and muttering under my breath, they'd probably all beg to return home.

When nearly every door had listened to my spell, I made my way to the center tower and climbed the last set of stairs. But when I reached the top and set my palms on his door, I pulled them right back. The pops and bites I felt earlier were gone. As was he.

"I went to check on you." His voice came from the stairs. Spinning hard, I twisted my ankle and almost screeched. Covering a laugh, he hurried up the last few steps. I swatted at him, but he offered his support regardless. "Sorry."

"It's all right. I'm sure I've earned it somehow." I latched onto his arm with one hand and massaged my foot with the other. All refusals between us were gone in the silence of a snowed-in castle.

"I shouldn't have sent you away."

I shook my head and my hair tumbled off my shoulder, catching the moonlight and looking more silver than white. "You were within your rights."

"Was I?"

I jerked my head up. "What's that supposed to mean?"

"Only, I've never sent you off so brusquely. You did not deserve it."

Scoffing, I put my foot down and stood square to him. "I'm positive I deserved it. I'm sure we could sit right here and think of a dozen—two dozen—occasions just in the last year that I've earned your discourtesy."

He tried to hang a grin in one corner of his mouth, but it wouldn't stay. "It would seem mine isn't the only one you've attracted."

I pulled away, knotting my arms as tight as I could across my chest and biting my tongue. I fought the sting at the top of my cheeks, the ringing in my ears, and the prickle of my eyes.

"That wasn't meant to rake you through it again."

"I know." I turned away and took a few steps down the stairs, trying to escape back to my quarters.

He wouldn't have it. Trotting past me two steps lower, he stopped me with a hand on my middle. "You've been brooding for weeks. And it's not your everyday disenchantment. This is different. You storm at everything, every day, I swear it's how you breathe, but you're always centered within those rages." He gulped, moving his other hand to my waist as well and pressing his fingertips into my flesh like it might skewer me in place. "I can't find you in this. Whatever this is."

I thought of Layla's comment, of compasses, and stupid castle sayings and the way I had most definitely taken every obscure route from destination to destination just to avoid our center. The thought of our center was problematic at the very least. Catastrophic at the worst.

"I'll be better when this business with the shepherd is managed and gone."

"Promise?"

"Promise." I covered his hands with mine and squeezed,

hopefully reassuring him. "If the shepherd promised Henrick lands on Gallo's side of the border, then——"

"He's probably working with, or for, Lord Gallo," Aeson finished the thought. "I imagine Garret has arrived at the same conclusion."

I nodded and made to move past him, but he stopped me a second time.

"You missed a room." He narrowed his gaze. "Or is your lordship undeserving of your protection spells?"

I glanced over my shoulder at his door and rolled my eyes. I was out of herbs, so I planted my palms directly on him instead. He responded by gathering one more stair beneath him, making us chest to chest, and clasping his hands behind my back. Closing my eyes and parting my lips, I drew a long breath in beneath my ribs.

"Children's rest in winter storms; peace across these roofs and beds. Frozen crowns and plots on thorn; bring care and health for every head."

When I opened my eyes, he was closer still. So much so that I made out my shadow in the center of his eyes. My next words slipped. "You continue to look at me that way."

He gave a quick burst of air through his nose. It was a sliver of laughter creaking through a wall of restraint. "I thought you might ignore it forever."

Hanging my head, or rather hiding it, I asked, "How can you think of anything else right now? This, of all things?"

"I told you. There is more to think about, to consider, when it comes to the well-being of everyone here." He scooped the side of my face into his palm and buried his hand in my hair. "Everyone includes me."

"But it does not necessarily include *me*."

"How could it not? Did you hear me the first time? Half our successes here belong to you. And maybe some would like to call those whims, but I would call it love."

My mouth bittered, refusing to swallow the word.

"You might not like people very much Etta, but you dispense love to them as if they were yours to care for even though they are not. Not properly."

I let my hands fall lower on his chest, finding a seam and picking at it with my fingertips. Although I tried, there was nothing to take hold of and nothing to unravel. The arrangement and the stitching were as secure as they could possibly be.

"You are my favorite witch, Etta," he said.

My shoulders dropped, along with my expression. "I am not falling for that again."

He shook with laughter. "Well, you are, and it is not like you to be discouraged by the thoughts of someone who does not even deserve the privilege of your punishments."

He was right. It was not like me to worry over what the shepherd said. I drooped a little in his arms. "Perhaps all my storms have been directed the wrong way. They seem to be going inward instead of out."

"Come back to center. This place needs all of you, storms as well." His thumb found my scar, pressing it in small increments. "I suppose I never said you're welcome."

Rolling my eyes with a smile, I lifted his hand away and left on my tip toes. He let me, although I felt his gaze on my neck the whole way down the stairs.

Back in my rooms, I opened the window and laid my hands over the wall again. The worry within the castle was gone. But the air still sang with a frantic heartbeat. I shook my head and returned to my bed, shutting the door to my sleeping chamber with extra force. Pulling an extra blanket over me, I crawled beneath the wools and hid beneath the pillow.

Because there was another heart beating too fast. Mine.

Chapter Thirty Seven

WHEN I WOKE TO THE SUNLIGHT edging into my room, someone was pounding on my door. Again. As if the day before had not been long or tedious enough. I would've given almost anything for the castle to go back to normal.

When I wrenched the iron hinges into motion this time, it was Layla, white as a dove. "Garret is in the stables waiting for you. I'm to fetch Lord Crennly next. It's urgent."

I shook my head or wobbled it. Something to indicate I understood and would make haste. Layla disappeared and I went back to pull yesterday's dress over my shift and a robe over all that.

When I arrived in the alleyway of the stables, Garret was circled up with Smithwik, Riggs, and Prilla. As I joined them, I heard Prilla listing off items missing from the kitchen.

"Who has gone?" I asked.

Garret ran a hand back and forth through his hair. "Henrick," he said.

"What?" Aeson came up behind me looking at Garret, jaw dropped.

Gesturing to Prilla and the others, Garret explained that some broken pottery was the first thing noticed when the kitchen got started. Smithwik had found Henrick's bed empty when he went to wake him for the day. But a sweep through the stalls revealed that none of the other horses were missing excepting the one for Saana down in the shepherd's pens.

"That piebald is our best, save for yours, mine, and Lord Crennly's," Garret explained. "It appears Henrick felt stealing horses was too great an offense and opted for nothing, rather than one of our drafts."

"Do we have any idea where he might be going?" Aeson asked.

"They have dogs in Henrick's room right now, hopefully they can pick up a trail outside the castle walls. Any footprints have already been covered by the snowfall."

They continued talking but I walked back to the double doors on the side of the stables, stopping where the snow met the floor. It billowed about my toes like dust in a forgotten corner. But the only forgotten thing was Henrick.

I understood then what I felt from the blizzard. His panic. His hesitation. His thoughts of the castle. He was probably wondering if he should turn back. There was no way I could've known exactly what ensued beyond the walls. Fair magic couldn't do that. Even if I were capable of drawing in the entire winds of a snowstorm, it couldn't have told me precisely.

A hand came to rest on my shoulder, scaring me right out of my thoughts. It was Aeson, of course. His face was as haggard as mine felt. Neither of us had slept well and our fears for Henrick only added to the fatigue.

"I will go with Garret, and we will see if the dogs can pick up a scent outside the gate. What will you do?"

I looked forlornly in the direction of Sparrow's stall. He'd worked hard the day before, and I disliked the idea of taking him out again. I'd even promised him a few days' rest, but I felt little choice. "I will check the barrows. Maybe they have noticed something."

Before we parted, he wound his fingers into mine, clutching them for a moment before issuing a command. "Come straight back to me."

I couldn't reply. The look on his face was too bold. Too open and too honest. Giving him the barest nod of my chin, I backed away and left to gather my things.

After swiping some carrots from the kitchen, and slipping Sparrow an extra handful of grain, I guided him to the courtyard, touched the black alba for luck, and started with the southernmost barrow in the forest. He was asleep when I climbed up the branches and left a pile of food behind, but there was nothing in the nest. No scraps of cloth, no hair, and nothing that suggested Henrick had passed by, let alone the shepherd.

The next barrow was near the cliffs. He wasn't in his nest at all, but he chittered at me from the rocks above where I imagined he must have been licking water off an icicle. There was nothing in the crevice where he'd built up his patch of sticks and lined it with Prilla's cheesecloth. I searched the surrounding forest but found no footprints other than my own.

The third and fourth barrows had nothing to pass along either, but both were awake and happy to scurry across my shoulders as I lay their provisions down. With apprehension, I pointed Sparrow towards the last barrow, the leader at the knotwood tree.

Approaching it from the north, it was quiet when I tied Sparrow to the trunk and stood on the saddle to reach its lowest branch. Slipping on the bark more than once, I struggled to the top where he'd made his nest. Had it not been fresh after a blizzard, I might've been grateful he made his lookout so high. But frozen tree limbs are harder to hold.

Reaching the nest at last, I swung my leg over a sturdy bough and gaped. The barrow's nest was deserted, cheesecloth missing, and not even a tuft of fur where he might have slept. At the very center however was a sprig of leaves that didn't belong. I picked it up. It was a bit of willow, the length of my hand, and encased by frost.

I scrambled down the tree, keeping the last bundle of food with me, and untied Sparrow from within the saddle. Kicking him into a trot, we set off down the road and my apprehension was replaced by dread. I breathed as deep as I could, but the air was still, resting after last night. There was no wind to drag towards me. No way to hear if a voice waited for me at the willow, or which voice it might be.

Before I could discern between each wiry branch, I could tell someone had been there. The snowfall was uneven, having covered the tramped path of one or more people. I dismounted before I got too close and took my steps one by one, listening and sensing with everything I could. There was a life nearby, but I told myself it was the barrow, perched above, surely.

Parting the frozen strands with one hand, I slipped underneath the willow and found I was alone. There was no chattering squirrel to greet me. With a frown, I looked up, trying to understand why he would lead me here. A breeze finally stirred, coursing through the branches and blowing the top inch of snow past my skirts.

A clinking sound chimed from all above and around, pulling my eyes back to the branches. It was more than just ice creaking against itself. I grabbed the nearest bunch of knobby fingers hanging from above. Farther up, the thickness of the wood grew abnormally. Stretching towards it, my fingers closed around glass, and I yanked. A bit of frozen twine snapped easily, and I looked at what was in my hand. It was an amber vial, matching in color to the willows bark and small enough to fit in my palm. Pulling the stopper out, I sniffed nothing. Sweet water.

Reaching at other branches, I found five more in a matter of minutes. I thought of Garret's report, claiming the shepherd never lingered here. He didn't have to. One pass under the leaves to gather his sheep, and he could pocket two or three vials without anything looking amiss.

Glancing at the top of the tree trunk where it was wide and solid enough to serve as shelter, I was glad the barrow squirrel had not stayed. The effects of sweet water on a man were bad enough. I hated to think what a curious creature might experience under its influence.

Outside the white curtain of the branches there was a grunt, and horse hooves took off at a run. I ducked out to see Sparrow galloping towards the village with an empty saddle.

Chapter Thirty Eight

THAT SENSE OF LIFE prickled along my skin again, and I turned to see a lean figure covered in furs standing where I had left Sparrow. Pushing a hood off his face, the shepherd grinned at me, and I wanted to retch.

He approached, and I saw he'd lost more weight, chipped a few teeth, and more than likely, hadn't bathed in a long while. The rim of his lips was completely red now, and his tongue so covered in white he could've been a babe with thrush.

"You've been industrious this last season," I told him. "I hear you have holdings across the Gallo borders these days."

"Aye. So, you've caught him already. I knew he wouldn't be up for the challenge any longer than I needed."

"You were prepared to barter your own daughter just to gain the barest of insights on our daily lives."

"Bare? You think there's no value in what you do up there on your hill?" Sunken eyes roamed over my shape. "There is value. You might have the most, castle wife. It's time we sort out exactly what it is."

I shook my head and turned away. "You are being played just as you played Henrick. Gallo is not interested in rewarding you with anything. That's why he's been so generous with his gifts," I said, waving my arm at the willow tree's display, hanging heavy with plenty more vials, I was sure.

"You're so certain of your conclusions," he said, smacking his lips.

"It doesn't matter if I'm right or wrong. You've threatened the well-being of your family and the innocent life of another. You will face your consequences the way Aeson asks you to." I turned back with my arms folded. "Speaking of your family, you have a new son. Grennly."

He blinked at this, shifting his weight side to side. "Then I have another son to admire how I've tipped the scales in our favor. We will leave this whore driven land and gain status elsewhere."

"Is that really what this is about? Status?" I shut my eyes a moment and exhaled a hostile breath of air. The grand scale of a sad man's ego would never cease to amaze me. "Look at yourself, Shepherd. You will not live to see whatever false promises have been made to you. Your wife will not be able to claim anything from Gallo once that drink finishes you off."

"I will stop when I want, but you won't bugger me for trying to stay warm in this weather when I've been cast away from my own home."

I laughed, thrusting my hand out to show him the vials I still held. "You don't understand what this is, do you?"

Shepherd stepped closer, breathing in my face and spitting into the air. "When we get where we're going, it won't matter. You'll be made to heal me. My wife and family will join me, and you'll never see your righteous little bastard again."

"I'm going nowhere with you." I lifted my knee and pulled his belly into it, knocking the wind out of him and pushing him aside.

Stomping off through the snow to the road, I made it only a handful of steps before something looped around my neck and jerked me backwards. I fell flat, grappling at my collar and tightening my hands around his herding crook. He must've sunk it in the snowfall where I wouldn't see it, waiting for the right moment to put it to use.

I rolled to the side, unhooking my neck and getting a mouthful of snow. Pushing off the wet ground, I spat and looked up to see the other end of the staff flying through the air. It caught my right cheekbone and the end of my nose. Skin split open and my eyelid drooped as blood sprayed through the air, joining the snowflakes as they swirled about. Red ran hot over my chin and for a brief second, I spared a laugh. My face would be even with scars now.

I was ready for the next hit, knees ground into the packed snow, spine straight as he swung a second time. I caught the crook with both hands and twisted, cradling the hardened wood to my chest and letting my body follow the momentum. When his swing reached the apex, I kicked with my heels and pushed the arc farther, taking the weapon with me.

The move caught him off guard, and he fell with his own weight, trying to hold the only tool he had. Fighting for my balance, I set the tapered end in my palm and catapulted it away with as much force as I could.

Pulling my knife from my belt, I spun to see his feet catch on a boulder buried beneath the snow, giving him the traction to lunge forward. There wasn't enough time to turn the blade his way. I dodged instead, barely. He landed on the end of my cloak. As I tried to get my feet under me, the fabric pulled at my throat, crushing my windpipe until I slid the knife up and cut through the toggles.

The cloth broke loose but the shepherd was already standing with two hands on the heavy fabric, whirling it through the air and wrapping my torso inside. We fell together, hitting the ground like asparagus stalks snapped in the wind.

His arms linked around me, tightening the folds and rendering my knife hand useless. All I had left were words. He hadn't been smart enough to cover my mouth up.

I thought rapidly. I needed the spell to fit my needs specifically.

"Tethered, bound, and tied; make these fibers break abi—" Something hit my head straight on. Blinking, my vision wavered, but I could make out that Shepherd was shaking his head as well. He'd never head butted anyone before, clearly. I laughed again, and blood from my nose coated my teeth like oil.

"Shut that wretched mouth, you meddlesome bitch." He reached for a pile of snow and when his grip loosened, I rocked my whole body to one side and thrust him off. Tumbling back the other way, I finally found my feet and ran.

I needed more words and for that I needed time. If I could reach the willow and climb a few branches up, I'd have the high ground and a chance at another spell. A few more steps would have had me there but just as I crossed through the branches, something tore through my arm, flying past me and clinking against the icy drape of the willow. The curve of my shoulder stung hot and cold all at once. I paused behind the trunk to press my hand over it, fingers finding warm flesh and fresh blood.

Shepherd had taken a few spare seconds to find my knife. He'd missed though, and now it was ahead of me. I looked and leapt forward as he came around the trunk to do the same. Snow kicked up in another cloud as we scuffled blindly, each of us trying to find the cold metal on the frozen floor.

"Enough," he bellowed, giving up his search and diving my way. His tackle flattened me out and his nails scraped at the roots of my hair. Hooking arms and legs around me like a set of fetters, his chin ground into the back of my head until I couldn't move. His weight was too much in his crazed state and there was no room to maneuver between him and the ground.

I wriggled my elbows and kicked my ankles, but it wasn't enough. He had gained his bearings in the fight, pushing my face deeper and deeper into the snow drift and filling my mouth with it. Ironically, it would help stop all the bleeding, but it would also stop my words, and that's what he wanted. What good is a witch who can't cast a spell?

The exposed nerves beneath my eye screamed in pain and I started to cry, terrified the pressure would rip through the last layers of skin and press my bone to the snow. Tears burned and went cold as they left my lashes and met the icy powder, packing harder and harder against me. His weight crushed what little air I could find.

"Come straight back to me." That's what Aeson had said.

It was proving difficult. I had little breath for words, but I had intention. I could speak within the confines of my own mind. I just wasn't sure it would do any good.

Nevertheless, I closed my eyes tight and wriggled enough to get Shepherd's knobby joints from digging into me. I let my mind go dark. Thinking and recentering. Chomping a bite of snow before he shoved my head deeper, I swallowed and used the small divot to take one last pitiful breath. The willow tree was behind us, and I let my magic sense its footprint in the energy around me. In my head and my heart, I spoke to the tree, begging for wisdom and inspiration.

I needed to get away. I needed to be longer, taller. I needed to stretch and find purchase somewhere. I needed something to root and ground me. Even if all it did was give me the energy to live, I could lay here indefinitely like a tree until the shepherd moved on.

I pictured the roots, surely casting out below us in the cold earth. There was power in them, and if I could draw it up into myself, they could give me the strength to endure. I pictured the frozen branches, swinging listless with all their own powers stored away until spring. But I could feel them, the energy budding beneath each bump and bubble of bark. They would pop forth as soon as the sun revealed itself, ready to live and breathe again.

Behind me, Shepherd grunted but the sound was wrong. It was like the ache of a drawbridge with hinges that struggled to follow orders, weighed down by their own chains. A shout erupted from his chest and was just as quickly cut off with a *crack.*

The snag of his legs disappeared. His chin against my skull disappeared. When I looked back, he was gone from sight. I turned farther and squinted and saw nothing.

Pushing onto all fours, I took stock of my wounds and made sure nothing was bleeding beyond what I could survive and when I was sure I would be okay, I collapsed. Too tired to move, I stayed in the snow until the rhythm of my heart slowed and my tears ran dry. The ones that fell into my cheek stung like a Sister and I whimpered. I was alone and uncertain and so, so, tired.

The land was quiet.

I couldn't understand where the shepherd had run off to, or why. At last, I lifted myself from the ground and faced the willow tree, gasping when I saw the state of it. Broken. Split like a half-shucked corn cob. The bit closest to me was thawed through. There were green buds everywhere and icicles nowhere to be seen. The ground was brown and muddy and empty. Save for a body.

Shepherd's face had gone pale. His legs twisted one way and his neck the other. Surrounding him were tendrils of willow branches. They were limp and weakened from unnatural growth. Roots had emerged from the soil to rope around his lower body. Realizing what the tree had done, I doubled over and gagged, spilling nothing but red bile onto the ground. Tears sprung loose again, and I shuddered, resisting a scream.

Clutching my belly, I gathered myself up and took off, fleeing the sight. There was little life left in me. Running was a task I couldn't manage and within a handful of paces, I stumbled and gave in to walking.

Each step was another sob and another whimper and another lost breath as I replayed the event in my mind. I kept my head down so I wouldn't have to see the distance left to travel, but after a while I heard shouting.

I froze in my tracks, scared I had gone the wrong direction. If the shepherd had been waiting for accomplices, maybe they had come to investigate. The horses that came rushing upon me were recognizable, even with their winter coats.

"Ga—Garret?" The name sounded uneven in my voice. I'd forgotten my cheek was sliced open, swelling fast. I couldn't speak clearly.

"Brothers help you." His eyes went wide, and he turned in his saddle to shout. "My lord!?"

Aeson trotted up from behind and when he saw me, he practically fell from his saddle. Running the rest of the way on foot, he slid to a stop right as my knees buckled and I crumpled to the ground in his arms.

"Etta, Etta, Etta." His voice trembled, gurgling in his throat like he had no air to push from his chest. "Etta?"

His hands ran over me next, checking the other injuries and pushing my hair in place. He dragged the blood across my skin as he felt the cut in my cheek. I was vaguely aware of the guards and houndsmen that surrounded us but not one scrap of me cared what they might think watching their lord fall apart on my behalf. When he scooped my face up to meet his, he gulped and took the first full breath I'd felt in his chest since I'd collapsed.

"Was it him?"

"It was."

He shut his eyes for a long moment and pulled me tighter until I was tucked along the swoop of his neck. My unharmed cheek warmed instantly with his skin on mine. I sank deeper in his arms and as he pulled his cloak around to cover the rest of me, he whispered where no one else would hear, "I will kill him."

My eyelashes fluttered, shock settling in fast and pulling at me to sleep. But I licked my lips and did my best to shape the words correctly. "I think I already did that."

Chapter Thirty Nine

THE JOURNEY BACK TO THE CASTLE was like bobbing in a river current. Sometimes I was under and other times I was up. Aeson withdrew long enough to mount his horse and have the men hoist me in front of him. I was vaguely aware of Sparrow tethered to another horse, having been stopped by their party. Everything else came in glimpses.

Mostly it was dark, but now and then I seemed to rise to the surface and sunlight glared around me. I saw the end of the fence line in the fields, the well at the village center, the whitewashed stones of the outer wall, and finally, the distorted bodies of servants and staff swarming us in the courtyard.

"Layla." Aeson was stern. "Take her to her rooms immediately. Make her comfortable."

His touch disappeared, replaced by a more delicate hand. Her arm circled my waist, and my legs moved but I don't recall thinking about the direction I needed to go. I simply appeared before the foot of my bed a few minutes later.

I swayed as Layla undid what was left of my dress. There was little that wasn't torn, cut, or bloody. She stripped the sopping wet shift off my body and pulled a clean one over my head before seating me close to my pillows.

For a moment she disappeared, and I wasn't sure if she left the room or if I imagined it. Even when she returned with a pail of warm water, I couldn't place the sound of footsteps in my memory. She was hidden in waters as well, flashing in and out of my eyes. A fish after all.

As she wiped the blood off my arm and bandaged the cut, I sat unblinking. Silent. But when she lifted her hands to my cheek, I grabbed her. Drawing in a sharp breath, something finally floated close enough for me to grasp. "The tree. Someone must clean up the tree."

She nodded. "I'm sure Lord Crennly and the men will see to the area, Miss Etta."

"No." I shook my head. "Not the grounds. The tree. It's filled with vials. They're ... they're floating. They're all above. Someone must gather them and take them away before they are found."

Layla blinked, unsure of my meaning but trusting me all the same. She nodded and promised to deliver the message as soon as she left my side.

I went silent again, glancing out to the main room at my plants. When I was sure Layla's gaze was fixed elsewhere, I examined my hands. I had blisters bubbling along the center of one palm, a ripped nail, and broken skin but nothing to suggest anything was wrong.

"Is there anything I can bring from your shelves? A salve? An ointment?" Layla asked.

"It's this one," a voice said from my door. Aeson had crept

in, holding a jar in one hand. A blend of lavender, lemon oil, rosemary, and crushed carrot seed. I recognized it from my shelf. I knew it was my work, but I couldn't recall how it was made or how any of my medicines came by my hand.

Layla stood and dipped a quick curtsy but said nothing. Afterwards, I realized she didn't know how to address the situation any better than Aeson or I could. Either way, I was relieved when she took the jar from his hands and set to work on my cheek. The blood had clotted, and the blend would soothe the skin as it healed. It would've been better if a healer could close the wound and prevent a wide scar. But I was usually the healer. And I couldn't do anything.

While Layla worked, Aeson disappeared into the other room again. This time, I heard undoubtedly the sound of movement. Pots were turned and lifted and the benches creaked. He reappeared a minute later with arms full of greenery.

My mind came to life a little as he set them down around me. Lilies for love and comfort, geranium to settle my emotions, rosemary to remove the pain, and sage for expelling the wickedness that still lapped at the shores of my mind.

I hadn't given him any instruction, he just knew. Seven years of watching me work—he knew. It struck me deeply that while I had been so fixated, he had been fascinated. By me.

Clearing my mouth, the last taste of blood sliding down my throat, I spoke again. "I'll be all right, Layla. I need to speak to Aeson."

She left swiftly and Aeson knelt before me. I waited, avoiding his face and straining to hear the sound of my door clicking shut.

"Etta, I—"

"Something is wrong," I cut him off, turning my palms up

again and searching them one more time. "Something is . . . I've done something wrong."

"What you did," he exhaled in one quick blow. "It wasn't wrong."

"No. It was." I forced my eyes to find his. "I can't feel anything."

He searched my expression, one corner of his mouth twitching. "What?"

Covering my face, I breathed through the webs of my fingers and ran through my senses again. Although I tried to stop it, a teardrop slipped through and ran down the back of my hand to my arm. Swallowing, I reached out and laid my hands on him like I had in his stairwell. If nothing else, the feel of him, solid and steady, allayed the trembling. "I can't feel anything. I can . . . I can touch. I know that I am touching you."

His hands covered mine and his face came together, trying to grasp what I was circling around but too scared to approach. I pointed to the plants he'd brought in, and when the words left my lips, tears followed them. "I can't feel them. I can't. I promised you that I wouldn't, and I wasn't . . . But I . . ." Ripping my hands away, I buried my face again and sobbed.

"Your magic is gone," he said.

Hearing it aloud split me. I nodded over and over as the realization devoured me. I shook and I sputtered until his arms took me from the bed to his lap and cinched me so tight there was no room to shake. The quaking had nowhere to go but in. In where I was empty. My magic. My connection to Iya. My sense of the world around me and the one that fed me all my life had vanished.

"I'm sorry," I said. "I'm so, so sorry."

"What do you think you are apologizing for?" he asked, and I felt his voice against me more than I heard it.

"I didn't think. I didn't know that it would, that I could . . ." I wriggled my shoulders a little, asking him to release the grip he held around me. "I didn't mean to make it Fierce."

I hated how hard it was to speak. And it bothered me that Aeson was left to acknowledge things I was too frightened to whisper. He shifted me in his arms and pulled my knees to one side, so I was folded alongside him.

Bumping my forehead with his, his voice was another confession in the dark. "I dislike that it happened, but right now I dislike why it happened far more."

"You should be angry. You have always asked me to keep it away."

"Etta. If you think I only find value in you because of your magic, I'm sorry to tell you this, but you are an idiot."

I huffed, giving in to the silliness despite my heartbreak. He was being truthful and a part of me knew there was more to me than magic. I just didn't know what and I certainly didn't know where to look. A few more tears crept down my cheeks, and I wiped them off with steady hands, at last.

Aeson cleared his throat and loosened his hold on me even more. "You should rest."

My fingers hooked into his coat. "No," I blurted out, not wanting to be alone in such a strange, silent existence.

He scooped me up again but nudged my chin so I would see him clearly. "If you ask me to stay much longer, I'm afraid I might take a different sort of encouragement from it."

My hands retracted so fast that I was still looking at him when his face fell. I contemplated reaching for him again, but the damage was done. Hiding the next wave of tears, I crawled away to my bed. He seemed more than happy to avoid my expression since he had his own to hide. Nonetheless, he pulled the blankets over my shoulders before walking out, leaving me alone with the echo of nothing.

Chapter Forty

I CRIED FOR MOST OF THE AFTERNOON and the next day. Not heavy, exhaustive sounds, just dripping like a crack in a well. On the next morning Layla checked on me and brought me breakfast, although it hurt too much to eat even if I had wanted to. When she lingered in the other room, I called to her, "Did he tell you to make sure I stayed in bed?"

She shuffled her feet, together, apart, together again. "He did."

I sighed. "I have no wish to go anywhere. You do not need to nursemaid me."

Her eyes wavered and ultimately fell, skeptical, in my direction. "At least let me tend to your wounds before I leave."

Wiping my face dry, I sat up and did my best to collect myself while she worked on my arm first.

"Is there anything else I should bring you? Either now, or later on?" she asked, reaching to treat my face next.

"I don't think so."

She didn't speak for the rest of it, not until she'd put the salve away, fluffed my pillow and straightened the blankets over me. At the door, she looked over her shoulder, brow hooked above her eye. "If you get in trouble, I get in trouble. You promise you'll stay right here?"

"I promise. I wouldn't want you to feel slighted, Layla. I hate to think what you might do in retaliation."

Dipping her head low, she giggled on her way out. Once she was gone, I rolled until I was comfortable and shut my eyes again, trying to think of anything except magic. But if I thought of the fields, I thought of the crops and the seeds I had to finish spelling for Calise with magic. And if I thought of the kitchen and the work I might help with once I felt better, I thought of their gardens, then my gardens, filled with magic.

I flipped over and stuck my head under the pillow. Everything was tethered to magic. I didn't know how to view the world, or our lands, any other way. Squeezing a few more tears loose, I growled into my mattress and kicked at nothing.

"Ahem," said a voice from the door frame.

Popping up and tossing my pillow aside, I whirled around ready to shout at someone. But I bit my tongue at Arlo, fidgeting with the toggles of his vest and standing before Aeson.

"I'm sorry," Aeson said, glancing from me to the ruddy head of hair that stood before him. "Someone has been asking for you and, well, Reeve and I are on our way to . . . check on his mother and deliver a message to Saana."

They meant to inform them the shepherd was dead. I looked down at Arlo, then back up to Aeson, who shook his head. Arlo and his other brother and sister didn't know yet. If he did, I can't imagine he'd want to see me.

"I'm sorry m'lady. They said you were resting but I was wondering if you had anything else for me to examine?"

I wiped my eyes again. "You are an inquisitive young man, aren't you Arlo?"

He hung his head and puffed his cheeks. "Ma says I'm like to offend everyone in the village with my questions."

"Let them be offended," I told him automatically, easing my way to the edge of the bed.

"She's right," Aeson added. "You know who else offends everyone? Miss Etta."

"But you're so clever." Arlo's face crinkled and he shook his head.

Too tired to roll my eyes, I managed a smirk and pushed myself up. Aeson passed around Arlo immediately and helped me find my balance. He reached for a shawl and draped it around my shoulders, stepping behind me to tie the loose ends together. Craning his neck, he spoke past my ear to Arlo.

"How do you think she offends them?" he asked, slipping his hands to my waist and squeezing my sides. "Not everyone appreciates cleverness. Many find it insulting to their own minds."

I waved my hands at Arlo, ushering him to the main room, but he wasn't satisfied by Aeson's explanation. "Why should one person's knowledge be offensive to another?" he asked.

Without prompting, Aeson brought the lowest stool to my circle of plants and set it down, lowering me until I was sturdy upon it. I sighed and looked long at Arlo. "Because it makes others feel little," I said.

"That's a heap." He stuck out his chin and both Aeson and I had to laugh. I pointed him back to my rooms next and asked him to return the plants to their companions. When he was out of earshot, I looked up at Aeson.

"What will you tell them?" I asked. What I really wanted to know was, would they tell them it was me? My fault?

"We will put it as delicately as we can. Ellara is entitled to some recompense, so we shall deliver that as well."

I nodded. "And Henrick?"

Aeson looked away and that was all the answer I needed. Henrick had frozen to death.

"Was he that way when you found him?"

Looking to make sure Arlo was still busy in my sleeping chamber, he pulled at his mess of hair, shaking his head. "He passed during the night here in the castle."

Vitriol rose in my throat. "Could I have saved him?"

"Etta." Aeson looked at me, crouching to lay a hand on my leg.

"Please tell me." Tears fell without my permission.

He wiped them away, paying extra heed to the ones that tried to sink inside the cut of my cheek bone. Somehow, he knew that would sting too deep. "We could not warm him enough but, yes, you would have found a way."

Arlo came shuffling back in, two pots in hand, and I turned away, heaving a new breath and swallowing everything into my belly. Aeson instructed him where to place each one and sent him back for the others. Alone again, Aeson slipped his hands up to my hips, all but embracing me again.

"We've laid both him and the shepherd in the crypts until spring emerges." His thumb traced the joint of me, and I was grateful for the tenderness in his eyes, even if I could see the concern that hid behind it. He glanced towards Arlo again. "I'm sorry. I know this is awkward company."

I shook my head. "It is a welcome distraction."

His lips tightened, holding back his worries, no doubt. "I see you have already sent Layla away. Is there anything I should bring you from the village? Something from Emmaya's?"

"No." I pulled my shawl tighter. "I still don't feel much of anything, including hunger."

He gave my hair a tug and stood up, bowing to Arlo as the boy appeared with the last two pots. "I leave her in your hands."

Arlo puffed his chest and gave a little bow of his own. Once we were alone, he wrung his hands before him and looked everywhere except my face.

"Would you like to ask me something, Arlo?" I prompted.

"They said not to."

I smiled an honest smile, and it made the entire right side of my head throb. "They do not command me or my conversations."

He stepped a little closer and stared openly at my injury. "They said you had an accident."

"Mm." I cast my gaze around the room, thinking how best to answer his keen little mind without breaking his heart. "Aeson told you how I'm apt to offend people? I offended someone the other day and they hit me with a stick."

Arlo's eyebrows did a dance, and he wagged his head. "I'd never dare hit a witch. What if you turned me into a slug or something? And dropped me in a salt jar?"

I reached out and tweaked his nose. "I would never. Your mind is far too quick to be wasted as a slug."

He blew out a great breath from his tiny body. And then it was just he and I and a morning's worth of questions.

The boy was a quick study and within a few hours he had memorized a handful of plant names, the look of their leaves, and the concoctions I could make from them. As my energy waxed and waned, I managed to stand and make it to my shelves a couple times to pull down the dried herbs and explain those to him as well. When Prilla came to collect him so he might eat lunch with his siblings, he was perturbed but went, nonetheless.

In the door, Prilla eyed me. There was a question on her lips, but I held a hand up. "I want nothing."

She scowled. "Very well. But don't go starving yourself. That'll help no one, least of all you."

"Thank you, Prilla."

She left and I wandered back to bed, collapsing deeper into its comforts than I expected. I meant to close my eyes for only a few moments but when I opened them again, my lashes were heavy and stuck together with sleep. The sunlight on the wall had shifted and there was scratching at the foot of my bed.

Feeling with one hand, I patted along the blankets, which brought the noise to a halt. I had startled whatever was there. Something thin and wispy tickled my wrist. Whiskers. "I was wondering where you wandered off to," I muttered.

A copper brown face appeared and bopped my nose, turning his eyes into giant black orbs in a coat of velvet. His tiny paw pushed my face as he sniffed at my hairline, and I winced.

"I can only imagine how I must smell," I said, realizing he could probably detect the shepherd on my skin. He sat back and washed his paws, content with whatever my scent told him. "I've nothing to offer you, you know. Nothing to offer anyone."

He pulled his tail around him, grooming the wet snow off its fluff before settling against my chest and shutting his eyes.

I watched his belly for a moment as it rose and fell, setting a pattern against my skin. The heat of him was barely enough to warm the palm of a hand, but I knew if I kept him close, it would spread.

"Found you!" Arlo exclaimed, startling me and the barrow awake.

Footsteps rushed up behind him. Layla and Garret both. "I'm so sorry, Etta," Layla said. "He swore he would stay sat until all of dinner was over but the minute I turned away, he was gone."

Rubbing my face into the pillow I cleared my mouth and told her, "There is no harm done. He's welcome here."

"Better here, than under my feet," Garret grumbled, folding his arms and leaning against the archway of my door.

Layla punched his arm. "You hush. You've not even been the one to chase them around all day."

The barrow squirrel was wide awake and had gone to the foot of the bed to sit on the post, sniffing at Layla and Arlo.

"I suspect he remembers you both," I said.

"Is this the one you brought to the house and let us chase?" Arlo asked.

"It is. Although the chasing was not my idea and I am not sure he's up for it just now. Best keep him a secret from your brother and sister."

Arlo made the sign for five and one then offered both hands to the barrow. When the squirrel happily jumped aboard his arms, they disappeared into the other room. I heard Arlo teaching the barrow all the plants he'd learned that morning.

"How did it go in the village, do either of you know?"

"His lordship said that young Saana would be here the day after next to return the horse and collect the children. But neither she nor her mother were distraught at the news," Garret answered.

Layla nodded beside him. "I heard Reeve say they were quite stoic."

The relief that settled over me was dishonest. I was a thief. I had something I shouldn't. The acceptance of those who I had wronged most in the last two days. "And the tree, its branches?"

"Clear and empty. You have my word," Garret said.

I thanked them and asked Layla to bring me something easy to eat. When she left, so did Garret, and I joined Arlo on the floor with the barrow squirrel. He had found a jar of seeds and was hiding them one at a time in his fists, watching the barrow sniff it out.

Sitting cross-legged beside them, I smiled and watched through four more rounds. Eventually, Arlo put the lid back on the seeds and looked up at me. "I'm glad you're not crying any more, m'lady."

"Oh." I had hoped it went unnoticed. Clearly it hadn't. "I'm glad, too. I don't think I'm very good at crying. It feels unnatural."

He screwed his face up at me. "But I thought you were good at everything. And how can it be unnatural? I know you're a witch, but you're still a human, right? Or are witches different from us and the animals?"

I sat up straighter. "No, you are correct. I am still a human. Although sometimes I feel like I am something between human and animal. There is much that feels like an instinct, but I share the thoughts of people."

He crossed his legs and faced me, chin on his hands. "What's an instinct?"

"It's like a sense. Like touch, or sound, or sight. But it is deeper than that. It is an uninvited thought that drives your action. It tells the barrows to nest through winter, or your flock to eat themselves full during summer and fall." I watched his face frown in all sorts of directions and thought it better to redirect him again. "See that pail of water? Could you feed the plants for me?"

His expression brightened but the wheels of his mind turned it all over and over. There was so much he longed to understand and not enough answers to please him just yet. He finished his job easily and came back to stand before me. "So, you just need practice?"

I gave a laugh, regretfully, flinching at the ache of it. Everything hurt. "What is this wisdom you've sorted out?"

"If you are driven by instinct, like an animal, you must need practicing as a human. Humans cry. Kella cries every day." His eyes went wide. "It just doesn't make sense for crying to be unlike a human when it's part of being one."

He delivered this last bit with a jut of his chin as if concluding a very thorough study of the topic. I grinned at him because I didn't disagree. But getting my head and my heart to align had never been a talent of mine.

There was a knock at the door and Aeson stepped in. "I feel terrible for interrupting, but master Arlo must return to the servants' quarters to prepare for bed."

"Just a little bit longer," Arlo whined.

Aeson gave him a grim look. "I'll tell you a secret if you comply quickly."

He hopped right over and let Aeson whisper in his ear. They glanced back at me, but Aeson wagged a finger at Arlo, who offered a stone-faced expression before bidding me goodnight and running off.

"What was that about?" I asked.

"It is a secret. As I said."

Smiling at him, I shook my head and looked back to the plants. Their silence didn't feel as odd anymore, but I still wondered how other witches had ever borne it.

"Do you mind if I stay a moment?" His voice was still at the door, but when I agreed, he drew nearer. "I see your other friend found you as well."

The barrow ventured out from behind the plants to sniff at Aeson's boot. "You knew he was here?" I asked.

"He rode atop Meadow's head the whole way back from the shepherd's home."

"The shepherd's? That's where he was?"

Sliding to the floor next to me, Aeson nodded. "Asleep beside the fire."

My brow furrowed and I eyed the squirrel. "You are a curious creature indeed," I told him, although it was not lost on me that he had recognized Aeson and chose to follow. Meaning he could sense my presence on him. Once I was sure the hall was good and silent, I spoke up again. "There is more to what happened, Aeson."

He turned his body to face me, and I did the same.

"Shepherd revealed he planned to take me somewhere, and I'd be made to heal him once we had arrived," I said. "He did not betray a name. Not even Gallo's."

Aeson was quiet a minute before speaking exactly the words on my own mind. "It is hard to know now if I remain the target, or if it was always you."

Me.

I wanted it to be me.

I didn't need to touch the castle stones with magic to know what would happen if Aeson disappeared from these walls or these lands. He was our keystone. The valley people would suffer if he was taken away. If it were me, the Elder's alone would suffer. I hoped they had considered that. Then again, I hoped they hadn't.

Chapter Forty One

THE SECRET AESON HAD WHISPERED TO ARLO was that Smithwik had found and sanded two old sleds for the shepherd children to use on the back motte where the snowfall was untouched. I was grateful for the quiet in my rooms but a part of me was equally sad I couldn't see Arlo's face as he went flying down the hill for the first time.

The barrow had disappeared to terrorize the castle so in the peace of the day, I called for one of the better tubs and had Prilla order hot water for me. The room filled and fumed with heat misting off the water's surface. I bolted my door and climbed in.

My skin turned red instantly, but it was a true sensation, and I was determined to feel every moment of it. While I hung over the edge of the tub, I looked at my plants, wondering what my absence felt like to them. Reaching out brought no reaction, and I frowned at the windows above them, seeing the sun in a clear sky. We were hardly through winter and the thought, unfortunately, brought me back to magic.

I had no idea where I was. It had been only a few full days since casting Fierce magic without trying, and I didn't have any insight as to how long the fissure in me would last. I might've compared it to a vole in unexpected sunlight. My senses were gone. At least, my senses as a witch. But as Arlo had gently berated me, I was still human. I was just unfamiliar with using only those senses.

I was struck next by an even worse realization. Free magic was still available. The magic that could be used by anyone. The one I encouraged every person to utilize whenever they could. I would be a hypocrite if I refused Free magic out of arrogance.

Slipping beneath the bathtub's great swallow of water, I held my breath as long as possible, thinking under its weight, down where everything was distorted. My two greatest fears had been realized. I had accidentally killed someone with my magic, and another had died for the absence of it. Bubbles rose from my lips, but I stayed below, refusing to rejoin the world until I had no choice. When at last I sat up, it was with a breath of determination.

When the water had cooled too much to be soothing, I climbed out and ran my hands over my face and hair, wiping the rivulets away. Dressing slowly into my warmest overlay, I picked up the pail for watering.

One by one, I scooped the water from my bath and dribbled it into each pot. With every pour, I forced my eyes to rediscover the leaves. I caught different shades of green, swerves of yellow, and patches of rough stalk.

There was a time, when I was still learning the basics of Free and Fair, that I wondered at all the same details but as I acclimated to them, I took them for granted. Although I still tended to the plants and thanked them for their services, I didn't cherish them the way I had when I was just sprouting into my lessons.

"I hope you like this," I told them as I moved along the benches. "This water holds some less than savory memories. Ones that I don't need to carry with me, but you can make better use of. It may not taste good, but I suppose you can leave those parts for the bugs."

By the time I was done, half the water from my bath had been used and my head was as clear as my skin.

Chapter Forty Two

I FORCED MYSELF OUT OF BED shortly after the household stirred the next morning. Dressing comfortably, I tugged my apron down from its hook and brought my tallest stool to the worktable. There was plenty for me to do that didn't involve casting. Chopping, scraping, trimming, shredding.

When Layla came to check on me, I asked for a full breakfast and was rewarded by the relief on her face. I offered a painful smile and turned back to work. She returned shortly to slide a pile of food beneath my nose. I thanked her and picked at it as I went, restored with every bite.

Watering them again, it was easier to thank the plants than the previous day, but I still felt a kink in my spine at the absence of their replies. It might've been there, but I had no way of knowing for sure. Even that unnerved me, the recognition that I relied on their response. I didn't trust myself unless I was connected to Iya. Instead, I waited and depended on it to inform me if I was any good or not. If I was worth something or not.

Standing to stretch and turn about my rooms, I petted the largest leaves with my fingertips and spoke again. "I miss you," I said. "I'm trying not to. I'm trying to see what else I can do, or rather, *remember* what else I can do without you."

I kicked the tiny stool next to the nearest bench and sat. "It feels almost rude. It was one of your kin that saved me. But I guess it's better that—" I froze, reaching for the closest fern.

"It's not for me. It's for you." I understood at last. And had I not known for sure that my connection was broken, I would've thought the greenery rippled with applause. "It is for you, your roots, and your powers to rest. Not just mine."

I may have avoided hypocrisy, but it seemed I had not avoided selfishness. Iya would've made sure the earth was protected, not me. As I knew well, an entire caravan of witches casting together meant an entire caravan's worth of shattered connections. To keep us from being greedy and abusing the earth with our gifts. It protected our resources and gave us a reason to be patient with our spells. Unless, of course, we were being attacked from sunup to sundown.

I stood again and paced the room, alternating between a grimace and grin. Ignorance wasn't a feeling I was familiar with, but that seemed to be the tune I was dancing to. Stopping in front of my casting window at last, I pulled my arms to my chest and smiled at all the flowers around me. "I'm so sorry," I told them.

A knock came at the door, and I turned to see Saana push in. My stomach dropped and I angled myself away. I didn't want to guess what she was coming to tell me.

"Am I interrupting?" she asked.

I shook my head, glancing over my shoulder. "Not at all. Come in."

"I'm here to collect the children," she explained. I nodded, noting the height of the sun outside. Breakfast had long passed and, hopefully, Grennly was napping at home with Ellara, giving Saana this chance to come to the castle. Her face was flat for another moment and then it turned down. "I suppose you've heard about my da."

"Yes." I gulped.

"There are rumors that he was hiding something at the willow tree. Something Lord Crennly doesn't want on the lands."

Saana was too shrewd to lie to. "The rumors are correct," I said. "It is a drink. It's addictive and causes obsession and deliria and eventually death."

"You were there?" She lifted her head and looked down her nose at me. I knew what she was really asking and like so many other things that week, I wasn't keen to admit them. But I willed myself into facing her, patting the swollen flesh under my eye. She sucked in a breath and walked right to me, gaze glistening. "They said he attacked someone. I had hoped they were wrong."

I said nothing but spun towards my private rooms to retrieve the ointment for my cheek. It was overdue for a treatment, and it gave me a chance to hide my face from whatever might lurk in hers. She surprised me by crossing the room once more and swiping the jar from my hands.

"Sit," she said.

"Excuse me?"

She lifted both shoulders. "A maid downstairs told me that you are a bad listener. She said ordering you about without begging approval is the only way to hold ground with you. Sit."

I pursed my lips but followed her direction. The first thing I planned to do when my magic came back was give Layla a weeklong headache. Saana was curious at the ointment, asking what was in it and why each ingredient was important. Arlo was clearly not alone in his thirst for knowledge.

"Ma used to have bruises all over," she said, seemingly to no one since she didn't even look at me when she said it. "They've cleared up ever since da took off. I expect they won't come back any more than he will."

I closed my eyes and parted my lips, disliking the words that sifted to the tip of my tongue. "I'm meant to help the people of these lands, not remove them."

She went quiet, then motioned towards the windows. "You'd remove a weed if it was swallowing a life it didn't have rights to, wouldn't you?"

"A weed still has a use elsewhere."

"And maybe my da does too. You just don't know it or can't see it yet." She gave one last swipe along my cheek and sat back.

My eyes filled but did not spill, fortunately. "I see where Arlo gets his wisdom from."

She laughed, tossing her head to one side. "Arlo. It's not the questions that will bite him back one day, it's the demeanor that guides them."

"I wouldn't worry. He's found a steady protector in Aes— Lord Crennly. They enjoy the same mischief."

"Yes. His lordship was in the great hall entertaining them when I arrived. It's clear Arlo holds a distinguishment from the others." She rolled her eyes and shook her head. "It was kind of Lord Crennly to tend to them in such a way, considering how untended he looks himself."

I ignored the remark and put the jar back on my bedside table, returning to see her out the door. She didn't move though, so I gave her my best look of reproach and told her, "You're too clever to gloat, Saana. Temper yourself there. I have to."

She let a laugh slip before she caught herself and smuggled her grin away. "Good day, Miss Etta. I hope we see you at our home again. Ma would like it. She wants people to see Grennly. Maybe you can stop on your way to the tree."

"The tree?"

"Yes," she stammered. "Everyone, I mean, the village thought you'd be the one to fix it."

I grappled at her words but before I could ask, bootsteps echoed up the back stairs. Aeson caught sight of Saana first, then me. He faltered, looking between our faces. "I came to let young Saana know her siblings are aboard the cart and ready to return home," he said.

Saana looked between us and scurried down the stairs, leaving me to scowl at him in the shadows.

"What's wrong with the tree?"

Chapter Forty Three

"Nothing is wrong with the tree," he said, keeping his eyes from mine.

"What is she speaking of?"

Aeson flung his gaze down the stairwell. "She should not have spoken of anything."

I glowered with incredulity. "Whatever it is, you were aiming to keep it a secret from me?"

"No." His face whipped up to find me. "No. Not secret, just, not for your knowledge until you felt better."

What I wouldn't have given for a well-lit candle by his head. I ground my heel into the floor and stomped back into my room. Clicking the door shut behind us, he shifted from one foot to the other and pulled his hair into another raggedy mess.

Pacing across the room, I gave a great sigh and swallowed back as much annoyance as I could before looking at him. "I am well enough for this. Please."

He studied my face as if he might still find a hint of fatigue etched along my brow. But I was determined not to let him leave without hearing the news. "We have had a light snowfall since the incident, but that ground remains thawed, and the blooms keep growing. The other side of it is in a worse state, withering more each day."

Worry did indeed etch itself across my face. "The sickly side has roots intact?"

He nodded and hid something away in his expression.

"What else?"

"It is not anything I can be sure of." He came to my side, tugging on my hands. "I was not going to keep it a secret. Sisters know, nothing in this castle stays a secret to you. But I did not want you to plague yourself with worry."

I bit my lip, considering my realization from the morning that Iya made sure Fierce magic would not be abused and overused. I was forced to rest alongside the tree. But from Aeson's account, the tree was not resting. Additionally, he mentioned snowfall. I glanced outside and saw he was right, but I hadn't noticed and that kinked another knot in my neck. Exactly how much of my existence had I tethered to magic? If I still felt it, I would've acknowledged the snow but left with only my eyes, I hadn't even noticed.

"Your thoughts are busy," Aeson said, loosening his hands from mine to cup my face instead. He was so careful with the side that was wrecked I almost embraced him.

I gave in to fisting the sides of his shirt and frowning up at him. "Busy, but not clear. You asked me to return to my center and I am afraid it's not where I thought it was."

He frowned too. "I only said return, not rush. The tree will still be there for you to worry about when your connection comes alive. It is not so helpless."

Nodding, I let my head fall forward to his chest and he pulled me in, tightening his arms around all of me. "Will this give you the wrong encouragement?"

"No," he spoke into my hair. "Holding you when you're tired and frustrated is something I'm familiar with. When you come to me scared, that is entirely different."

"How so?" I didn't dare turn my head up to him.

"It brings me hope," he explained, and I felt the rise in his cheek as he smiled against my temple. Squeezing me tight for a moment more, he slackened and pulled on my hair next. I pushed him away halfheartedly. He laughed at first but adopted a strict expression. "Let us worry about the tree for now, Etta. I promise I will tell you if anything else goes amiss with it."

My eyes found a firm hold in his, and I dipped my chin.

With his departure, I finished the work on my table and cleaned all my tools. When everything was managed and there was nothing to keep my hands busy, I walked a straight line between the edge of my bed and the farthest wall in the main room, rubbing my arm. My thoughts wandered with me to an idea I shouldn't have entertained. I doubted if I was in any condition to execute it. After chewing my lip raw, I relented and bolted my door. Everyone wanted me to rest, so I would. Although they would disagree with my motivations in the morning.

Chapter Forty Four

IT WAS STILL DARK WHEN I OPENED MY EYES. Flat on my back, I took stock of my injuries then rolled out of bed for my warmest clothes and thickest boots. I shuddered as I pulled my wool cloak on. Repaired as it was, I did not enjoy the memory of when I had last worn it.

Out in the main chamber, I kissed my plants awake and asked them with Free magic to give me any spirit they could spare. Rolling my shoulders, I stood at my door and listened closely for anyone in the kitchen. I'd gotten lucky. No one was alert. No one was even warming the ovens.

Tiptoeing down the stairs, I slunk out the door and hugged the castle wall. The snow muffled my footsteps out the back gate. From there, I didn't worry; it was still black in the sky with only a hint of grey on the horizon. Although I may have relied on magic too much in the past, I allowed my eyes to do what they should that morning.

Once my sight adjusted, I made my way diagonally across

the white fields and behind the village to the main road. I was plenty warm, but my body protested as I scuffed up the pitch on the other side. It was easier than trudging through the fields. A smooth path was more forgiving to my knees than fighting the snow drifts that piled over the land.

When the willow tree came into view, I stopped completely. I hadn't prepared myself to see it. To remember it. Sunlight broke over the valley as I stood there wringing my hands beneath my wool covering. I'd never done anything with my magic that could be called cruel, and never as a means of desperate survival.

The sun rose higher still, shooting gold arrow tips across the snow, glinting everywhere. They kissed my crown first before falling to my boots. I forced myself the rest of the way, allowing a few tears to fall with my steps.

Aeson had not lied in his detail of it. The standing side of the tree, exposed to the ice and snow, was grey and dreary. More so than winter called for. On the opposite it seemed to be flourishing. Ripped and shredded to pieces yet sprouting with new branches. The tendrils that were weak and flat after I'd woken the tree were tender with fresh color and bark.

Without magic, I couldn't speak to it so I couldn't be sure, but I had a feeling in the bottom of my belly. I knew what Aeson had been hesitant to proclaim.

I'd woken the tree, yes, but only part of it. And I hadn't completed the spell because I hadn't realized I started one. The willow was still trying to do as I'd asked, growing and twining around whatever it could. But it was alone, and there was nothing for it to draw its power from except itself. One side struggled to complete its task while the other faded away.

As I dropped to the ground, I faded as well. Evidence of my

truest fears stood before me, and I had no immediate idea how to make amends for any of it.

My hands dug into the wet soil, and I sat with the wretched results of a magic I didn't understand because I only had one book and no one to teach me. There was no mother to consult or father who might've looked up from a spell book and said, "Ah, I have seen this before."

I would've even settled for a crotchety old mentor, bent over their cane and whipping my head with their necklaces. Anything that didn't leave me completely and resoundingly alone. My shoulders fell next, and my arms went limp. I pushed a hot gust of air out of my chest. The solitude of the land was deafening. A breeze whisked up around me, and with it, a wish. Something I'd never greatly desired before.

I wished I hadn't come alone.

It was a strange thought. I'd been alone so many times. Lost and stealing after the war? Not awful. Caught as a prize? Bearable. Dragged to a cold castle on a new land and put under a roof with people who wanted me dead? I had already survived worse. But everything felt less lonely after I fell under the pear trees.

I sputtered because Aeson wasn't there to tend to my wounds, literal or figurative. Both sides of that coin were molded by my own hand. Intent on being alone, I had left him behind. Rocking back, I pulled my knees to my chest and hugged them. Tears dripped slow and steady. It wasn't sadness that poured out with them. Just stupidity.

Stupid, fierce independence. The realizations fell like snowflakes upon me, building slowly but melting to my warmth and soaking me with the weight. I sat until my tears dried and my cloak was half drenched.

Pushing off the soft earth where winter surrounded a patch of unnatural spring, I wiped my hands and flicked the caked mud off my clothes. The back of my sleeve served to wipe my face clear and I shuffled, head down, back towards the road.

There was no use hiding so I stuck to the main track. The castle would be awake, and it was safe to presume Layla would soon notice I was gone, if she hadn't already.

I could barely put one foot in front of the other. My muscles resisted every stretch from back to front, and my toes pleaded to have something softer than a boot on. If ever I understood the inescapable drag that an ox must feel from a plough, it was then. Except a plough made way for something new. I was unsure what this debilitating flood of realizations would make way for.

The village came into view, windows gleaming in the sun, and the sound of a horse snorting in the cold air came up the road. My heart rattled in its cage. There was no way I could be that lucky, but my feet stopped and my breath with it. I stood, stupid once more, and watched him come into view.

Slipping off Meadowgrass before she had even stopped, he landed on his feet and crunched into the snow. Two armlengths away, he came to a standstill, reins left over Meadow's neck. Neither of us spoke at first, but his eyes scanned the length of me, and I knew he saw my defeat. I was glad for the chance to ride home, but it came with a sliver of guilt. Regret had barely hooked into my chest at the tree, and here he was to pry it loose.

"You left much earlier than I anticipated," he finally said.

I wiped a palm over my forehead. After he had caught me during his birthday, I should not have been surprised. "You knew I would sneak off."

"Of course. I'm only glad I tricked you into waiting for the morning," he said, a trace of a smile on his lips. "I wouldn't have been able to chase after yesterday."

I bobbed my head in understanding. That's why he placated me with a promise that if anything went wrong, he'd share it immediately. It was enough to keep me from running off in the twilight. My schemes might be deviant, but I wasn't willing to lose great amounts of sleep for them.

"You're right," I said. My eyes trained across the glossy white grounds. "The discovery you don't want to be sure of."

He exhaled, long and beaten. "It's still casting on its own, isn't it?"

"I believe so."

"You've always said—" He stepped closer, reaching for the wools draped over my shoulders, pulling me in. I let him. "You've always said nature will care for itself as long as we stay out of the way. But this isn't just nature, is it? This is you."

I nodded, hearing a crueler perspective in my head. It was my doing. My intention.

He pressed his forehead to mine, shadows of grief covering his face. "Which means only you can fix it, doesn't it?"

"It is a totem to the village. We can't let it die," I said. "It also means I have to write something equal. I will have to write something Fierce."

His gaze fixed far away in the distance and held. Whatever reservations and denials he had about Fierce magic, he would have to pack them away for this. There was no alternative. Grumbling, his hands found me through all our furs, bunching the folds of my skirt in his fists. "Should I let you sneak out again, when you come back, or can we ride together?"

I tilted away from our touch, then reached up to smooth

his hair all the same. "We should ride together. I'm going to need . . . help."

He didn't reply right away. Instead, he straightened in an icy breeze and wet his tongue to speak. "You're asking for help? *My* help?"

Dropping my hands and retreating a step, I cast my gaze away from him. "I'm not sure I want others seeing me in that state."

His breath fogged the air, forming and floating away as he set the plan in his mind. At last, he nodded. "Very well."

Chapter Forty Five

OFFERING HIS HAND, he dragged me to Meadowgrass. I glanced over my shoulder with a frown and my steps faltered. Aeson looked back. "What is it?"

"My knife is still there, under the snow. I meant to look for it."

Stopping beside Meadow, he considered this. "I will tell Garret to spread the word. If a villager finds it, they will return it," he said, pushing his cloak aside and fumbling at his belt. With it freed, he slipped his hands around me, snaking it across my back and tying it in front.

"I can't, Aeson."

"You can. And you will." He was resolute. "I will not explain to you how much I dislike the idea of you being unarmed. Especially when you don't have magic at your side."

I looked down at the belt, then up at him. It was too long to fit my waist correctly, but not quite long enough to wrap twice. He tied it to match the knot of my necklaces, making all my weapons the same. Something about that cheered me enough not to argue.

Reaching behind me again, he pulled the blade from its sheath and held it up. "You remember how to puncture the lung, right?"

I knew he wouldn't bring me home until I listened. Nodding, I took the blade from him and when he grabbed ahold of my collar, I swooped my hands up in between. Widening my forearms to break his grip, I dropped my arms next, hands behind his shoulder blades. This enabled me to twist our arms together and pull him in like a hug. Except my hands lay at his back with the knife pointed between his ribs.

Satisfied with my example, he smiled and took half a step back. "Then what?"

"Then you stumble." I pushed him a little bit as if he were truly off balance and gasping for breath. "And I slash."

I drew the blade through the air in front of his throat and his eyes tracked the motion. He took my wrist and pulled me in. "This blade is smaller than you're used to. You'll need to be closer."

Nodding, I grabbed his collar with my free hand and held the point flat against his skin. Knife to throat.

"You will have to push harder with this one too. With the tip so little, like," he continued, forcing my hand to create a hollow under his jaw. "And where's the line?"

"Ear." I spun the knife in my hand, so the hilt scraped over his neck. "To ear."

"Good," he breathed.

We stood still as the sun moved higher and melted the topmost layers of snow. It glistened, bright as the finest silver pots in the kitchen. From the village, shop doors thudded open and closed, echoing up the road. The people were awake and starting their days. It was a call to arms, disturbing our peace and mustering us in a direction neither wanted to go.

Slipping the knife from my hand and returning it to its hiding spot, Aeson broke the stalemate first. "Will the tree be okay until you are able to help?"

My brow stitched together, and I turned back in the direction of its splintered trunk. "It should, although, we should ask the village to help." I didn't dare look at him.

"Two pleas for help in one morning?"

"Quiet," I ordered, pulling my arms out from his. Done with our fighting lesson.

"I see you are beginning to feel like yourself again." He offered a hand. "Up you go. I'll ride second."

One hand on his shoulder for balance, he helped me into the saddle and waited for me to kick my left foot out of the stirrup. Using it for himself, he swung up behind me and gathered the reins with his right hand. Circling my waist with his left, he nudged Meadowgrass, and we turned towards the village.

I muttered to myself on the way, trying to form the best rhyme for anyone in town who was willing to help. Stopping outside the Bakers', Aeson dismounted and knocked on the door. Emmaya answered. Her face grew in surprise when he asked for a bit of paper and quill. Handing it to me in the saddle, Aeson explained our request as clear as he could while I jotted the couplet down.

Willow wards for witch's ease; take valley words, till life's appeased.

"You have to mean it." I looked at Emmaya. "Tell everyone who is willing to go, lay both hands on the bark and recite it word for word."

She smiled under sleep swollen eyes and promised she'd spread the message. I trusted her easily, knowing she'd do so without adding to whatever gossip was circulating. We passed by the shepherd's door, but there was no movement inside. If any family deserved a great length of rest, it was them. They may have welcomed a new life, but they'd lost one as well. At my hands.

Once we were out of earshot from anyone in the village, Aeson cleared his throat. "Do you think it will work?"

"It will if they want it to." I sighed, resting against him. He tipped his chin over my shoulder to adjust his reins and the action brushed his lips past my ear. If he hadn't been clinging to me so tightly, I might've fallen off. An itch crept down my spine much like a snake losing its first shed. It shivered from top to bottom. Gulping down a batch of cold air, I found his hand on my belly and grasped it tight before turning to look at him. I wanted an explanation, but I didn't want to persecute him either.

"You remain adamant on changing things between us."

A dozen or more hoof steps suctioned off the snow before he countered. "You remain adamant on proving me wrong."

"And both sides serve to incite the other."

There was no denial, he simply scanned my face and said nothing. Turning his attention back to the road, he kicked Meadowgrass on and held me firmly the rest of the way. My thoughts churned and my head ached through the distance.

Passing through the gates, he cleared his throat. "Do you need help back to your rooms?"

"No," I said automatically, rearranging our fingers, then, "Yes."

While the stable hands took over Meadowgrass, he held fast to my hand and led me past every castle worker it seemed. We moved through the front door, across the great hall, up the main stairwell and down to my rooms. Spinning me inside, he clicked the door shut and started again. "I am sorry. I know this sentiment angers you."

I rolled my shoulders, wanting nothing more than to collapse on my bed and be done with the morning. "It doesn't *anger* me. It worries me."

He didn't say anything back, but he studied my face as if the words were painted over my cheeks and he was hoping they'd color away. When the shade of my gaze stayed the same, he shook his head and stood at attention. "Do you need anything?"

I blinked, unsettled by the way he'd given up so suddenly, wishing he had argued. It wasn't like him to concede without one last affront. Aeson was the only one who ever truly challenged me, even if only for fun. Wiping my hands over my face, I pulled my arms tight like I always did, palms on elbows, and stared at the floor. "Would you bring me my book from the study?"

I caught the quick sweep of his head as he looked up at my request, hesitant but knowing it was the only way. When he disappeared at last, I found my bed and fell sideways onto the pillow, sleeping instantly with boots still on and my cloak only half unbuttoned.

When I woke in the afternoon, both items were removed and drying by the fire. I'd been covered with a blanket, and my bedside table held a plate of food, my book on Fierce magic, and my third necklace.

Chapter Forty Six

A WHOLE DAY PASSED before I dared to pick the red cord up from where he left it. I ran it through my hands over and over, arguing with myself. Carrying it to the main room with my book, I sat on the floor with the plants. My other necklaces slipped out of their knot easily but stayed twisted and committed to their shape. Laying the red one alongside them, I thought of the shepherd, and his head bent crookedly in the mud.

It wasn't what I wanted to use my magic for ever again, and I disliked that it happened because I had no control or understanding of Fierce. Using my fingertips, I smoothed the cords out together, re-tied the knot with three, and asked Iya to be forgiving of me. With Free and Fair, I felt competent enough to wear each necklace. But I would wear this one as a vow.

Shuddering, I pulled the book into my lap and opened it. There was sure to be healing powers I could use, but healing at the Fierce level meant the discomfort or sacrifice of another. A life for a life or health for health. If it was spring or autumn, I might've benefitted from fallen leaves or a sapling with enough life to be uprooted and given in pieces to the willow tree. I did not have that luxury.

After a few pages, I stood and turned about the room, grabbing a small piece of parchment from my desk. As ideas formed, I sat again and listed sacrifices I could offer in place of fresh wood or aged foliage.

Layla knocked and entered after a while, happy to collect my plate and offer me whatever I wanted from the kitchen. I shook my head as I bent over the book. Fixated as Aeson so often accused me.

"It was nice to see you left the room, Miss Etta. Even if it lacked sound judgement," Layla said, cocking her head to one side. "Although, I suppose that's the best sign of all."

"Thank you." I snuffed down a laugh.

She snuck off in the quiet and closed the door. Alone again, I stretched my feet out and laid back with the book on my belly. Maybe I could swallow it and absorb the lessons that way. If I knew how strong I would feel when my magic returned, I'd just feed the tree myself. But given the size of the willow, that might kill me.

I needed an offering. With the book upright on my chest, I skimmed a few more pages then let the binding fall over my face. I breathed in the dank old stitching and musty pages with both hands atop my abdomen. In a matter of minutes, the cold floor sent shivers across my skin. My thoughts went to Henrick slowly freezing in the warmth of the castle. Tortured with ample time to reflect on his mistakes before his life gave out.

When had he passed the point of no return in the fields? With no hope of finding a fire or suitable shelter and no hope of reversing the effects once the chill set in. Meanwhile, I had been standing with Aeson in the moonlight, exchanging stupid smiles.

Then there was the shepherd. If I had my thoughts set on anything else in those final moments with him, the willow might have consumed him all together.

An offering.

I lurched forward, book falling to the ground. Stumbling to my feet and out the door, I clamored down through the kitchen where I stopped short.

"Garret?" I exclaimed. He was sitting at the long worktable with a half-eaten cherry pie to his right and Layla in his lap stirring a batter smooth of lumps.

He glanced at me. "I heard his Lordship had to chase you down this last morning, in the cold. Is it trouble for me now?"

I waved him off. "His choices are his. It's not as if I asked him to chase me down."

The two of them eyed me with high drawn brows, then shared a glance before going back to their respective endeavors. "Get on with it," Garret said.

Knotting my hands together, I stepped closer so as not to be overheard. "Aeson said the shepherd and Henrick were laid to rest in the crypts to await spring."

"They were. They are."

"Could we unlay them?"

Garret set his fork down and looked straight at me. "You of all folks should know that messing with the peaceful dead brings nothing but bad intention."

"This is different. I think I can make this just as peaceful, if not more so."

"If I say no, I suppose you'll just have your way behind

everyone's back."

My eyes wandered the length of the kitchen wall. "Not right away."

He took up the fork again and twirled it in the air. "Just tell the lord. When you want them to haunt you, they will."

I shook my head, but he didn't notice because he was already back at the pie tin. Layla winked. Intentional and instigating. At the door, I stopped one more time where Prilla was stacking pans for the next morning. "I know we're well into the season and our stores are thin, but do you have anything left to butcher? I need to study the pieces."

She looked at me from the corner of her eye and didn't speak right away. "Does it need to be humanlike?"

"No." I covered my mouth to keep a snort from emerging. "Nothing quite that morose. I only need to refamiliarize myself with the feel of it, and maybe the sound."

"The sound?"

"Prilla, please?"

"Yes, yes. We have a few suckling pigs left and a fair dozen chickens."

"Thank you," I breathed. "You're wondrous."

I ran back upstairs and picked the book up again, along with the paper. There was still no indication of my magic coming back, but when it did, I wouldn't allow myself to fear it. Any of it.

Chapter Forty Seven

Four days later, Iya tickled my ear the way the moths liked to whisper in them at the early light of dawn. My eyes popped open at the sensation, and I threw the blankets off. In the main room, I flopped to the floor in front of my biggest fern.

Eyes pinched shut and hands tingling in my lap, I drew long breaths and felt it stretch along my skin. Waiting and waiting and waiting for the feeling to coat me completely, I didn't dare look at the fern until the last ache of power pinched between the webs of my fingers.

I cracked one lid open at last. The fern bounced happily in my direction. Some sort of messy, inane sob broke free in my chest and I doubled over, arms wrapped tight around my torso.

"I always have Free. I always have Free. I always have Free." I pressed my eyes closed again as I chanted. "I am good either way."

Shaking the excitement off, I gave myself over to looking at the plants. The exercise highlighted all the tiny details I'd noticed over the last ten or eleven days. I was determined never to forget them ever again.

I stood at the door for far too long, wondering who to tell and when. Part of me wanted to sprint along every corridor and scream it into every face I found. Another part wanted to retreat back into my room and curl up in a corner with the news clutched to my chest.

Aeson would want to know. He needed to know. But we'd barely spoken since he'd found me on the road and some other part of me was scared he'd be disappointed my magic returned at all. It would cement the fact that Fierce magic lived within my walls. Rubbing my neck, I turned from the door and patrolled the perimeter of my room. I heaved with every inhale, grumbling and staggering the exhales with no rhythm. Stopping at the window, I pinched the soft divots above my eyes with a stretch of my palm, thumb on one side and archer's finger on the other.

In the distance below was my garden. Branches poked through the snow as the sun melted a little extra off that morning. Winter was nowhere near finished, but this would sever the cold overlay of the land for a few days' time. The mornings might stay cool, but by the time the sun hit midday more snow would be melting than was falling at night.

It meant the ground would be softer, which I would need for my spell. Iya willing it worked at all. I returned to my sleeping chamber and pulled my boots on along with a shawl. The kitchen was alive and cooking as I walked through. No one noticed me in the hustle of it, of course. But for the first time, there was something about that fact that bothered me.

I shook it off and made my way to the garden gate, pausing

before I lifted the latch. The sensation was instant. It was in every bump of my spine, and a flutter of air under each hair on my neck. Blowing out a careful breath, I grinned. "Hi," I said to the little patch of ground that was all mine.

Birds chirped nearby at the sound of my voice. I swore there was even a tremor in the snow that clung to the shrubs and mounds of soil that lay beneath, waiting for their springtime seeds. I took my time walking along the circular little path, from one side to the next, reaching through my magic to find every root that slept underneath.

When my sense of it felt familiar again, I stepped out and shut the gate tight behind me. I was climbing the hill back to the side door thinking about the spell when movement caught my eye. Aeson stood in the archway. I stopped in my tracks and felt the edges of my boots soak through with snowmelt. Moments passed before he finally held up a fold of paper.

"I've had a letter," he said. "From Calise at Castle Bane."

Chapter Forty Eight

"What is it?" I asked.

"Lord Bane has passed. It was quite peaceful, and he was sure to name their unborn child as his heir without room for argument. She has comfortably taken over the household and inquires at the rest of our arrangement."

I nodded. Calise wanted to know when she could expect her supply of seeds, blessed and bewitched for planting. I could finish my work for her within a few days if I so wanted. But it also meant I'd have to work on my Fierce spell. I hadn't expected to confront Aeson about my magic so soon. No matter how much depended on it, it was a violation of the only unyielding request he'd ever made of me.

A breeze sped along the curve of the wall and spiraled out, billowing into my loose hair. I pulled my shawl tighter and shivered under its cold kiss. Aeson lifted a hand, pulling me the last few steps up to the doorway. I couldn't look at him, so I found his fingertips blindly and followed his pull until I was standing in front of him with my head down.

"What were you doing out here?" he asked.

I held my breath, shifting my weight from foot to foot. Before I found the courage to tell him, his hand snuck through the fold of my shawl and pulled out my necklaces. He hadn't seen them since he left the last one on my table. He hadn't seen me at all, in fact. Because for once, he'd been the one avoiding *me*.

Chewing into my bottom lip, I covered his hand with mine and touched the wall with my other. The ivy that held tight to the stones quivered, then found my wrist and curled around it the same way the tomato plants grew tight to their stakes in the heat of summer. I watched the rise and fall of his throat as he swallowed but avoided his eyes.

He clenched his jaw a long while before speaking. "You must finish the seed jars for Calise first. After that, we will see to the willow."

I nodded, rubbing my thumb over his hand as it gripped the knot of all three necklaces at once. Then I wilted. A moment prior, I'd felt renewed. Yet I had emptied again without clear reason.

"Etta?" His hand tangled into mine completely. Everything in me broke at the sound of his voice. It hushed through my ear like a spring current breaks the winter ice. I knew why he felt like magic to me.

It wasn't just a passing idea to change things between us. It was his intention.

And I needed to talk him out of it.

Unwinding myself from both him and the ivy, I stumbled back outside the castle walls to hide from the windows and everyone in them. He followed, of course, and I only managed a few snow laden strides before he pulled me around and pressed my back to the wall.

We did nothing except exchange breath for more than a few minutes. As it left me, it found him, only to return again when his chest fell. I looked at him unblinking for so long that tears fell without opposition. He wiped them clean before they ever kissed my chin.

I had been sure I would be cast out again after Old Jaeson died, rejected by a castle full of war wounded skeptics. Aeson turned up and offered me another chance. One with less strings attached. Be a good person. Have a good life. That was employment at his hands.

When I felt most out of place, he'd let me run free until I found it. Even if I'd been better at gratitude, there were not enough gracious words in the world for this position.

I tried to peel him away but made no progress. He shifted to me the way the ivy would for the sun, holding tough despite any attempt to cut him loose. My insides churned with unidentified grief. I'd lost nothing, but I was hollow all the same. "It's not worry," I sorted out. "It is something else."

Aeson nodded and cupped a hand to my cheek, tracing my first scar. The whole left side of me went numb. Every bit of skin his breath skittered across buzzed like bees. Like magic. "I know," he said.

I struggled to clear the sensation of him. "This intention of yours . . ." I shook my head, meeting his eyes. "It will take two targets and make them one."

He gave me a smile, shuddering as though an arrow had struck him. "My birth and elevation will always make me a target for something, Etta. You know that. But you are the eye and that is what you will not admit. Because it frightens you."

My brow came together in a scowl, unprompted. I didn't like Aeson being so far ahead of me in anything.

"If you would simply look a little harder," he continued, resting his temple against mine. "I am near positive it is the same for you."

The clouds shifted and I melted with the snow. I might've hit something in frustration but I had no room. Not with Aeson fitted against me.

He barely drew breath for his next question. "Have I spooked you away again?"

Shutting my eyes tight, I shook my head.

"I'm sorry nonetheless," he said. "I was determined to be patient and I have drenched you with my feelings."

"Your feelings are allowed." I glanced away. "I only wish I was not so confused by my own."

He ran his thumb along my scar again. Reaching the end, he rubbed up into the divot between my chin and bottom lip, pressing against the latter. "What *are* your feelings?" he asked.

I wasn't about to answer. I didn't wholly trust him not to hear one half and ignore the other. Instead, I slid my right hand up to find his heartbeat and I didn't need magic to understand what the rhythm revealed.

I wanted to give him what he was asking, but I couldn't escape my thoughts. In the last three seasons, Aeson had been the target of Calise and her father's attempted schemes. We'd uncovered two spies in our presence, a drink that would clear out the entire village if left unchecked, and I'd been attacked by the sole offender. An event that resulted in the shepherd's death and by extension, Henrick's.

Nothing good could come from Aeson's intentions. Nothing. It wasn't my place to argue his statement. Maybe I was the eye to his target. But I couldn't yet accept that he was the eye to mine.

Aeson was the lord of Castle Crennly, bastard or not. He had more than earned the respect and fealty of everyone in these walls. When he'd asked me to dedicate myself to the same people, I did. While that included him, it had never set him apart in my mind.

The war that brought us both here had taught me not to expect protection, let alone loyalty. Yet Aeson had taught me something entirely different and I had always relied on using one lesson to escape the other. This intention of his asked me to choose. Incessant skepticism or trusting devotion.

I set a growl free from my chest. Could I care for him differently than I cared for them? Did I already? I had to be sure, otherwise I'd risk hurting him in much worse a way.

My insides had not stopped swirling when he gave up on my reply and lay his hands on my waist. "Please, do not scold me for wanting you," he said. "I did not make you vicious and sweet any more than I made your eyes grey, but you have never denied me a place in your storms, and you cannot blame me for coming to love the rain." He paused to kiss my forehead, as innocently as ever. "But we will run out of time for this one day. *You* will run out of time."

Chapter Forty Nine

HE DIDN'T AVOID ME AFTER THAT, nor did he change his intentions. Each time he came to my rooms over the next few weeks, his voice was softer, his manners tempered, and his gaze wide. The only exception was the scant moments in which I mentioned my spell for the willow tree. He remained apprehensive but he did his best to hide it from me.

His efforts made it difficult not to dive in headfirst. If he took my hand to help me up from the floor, our fingers snagged like hair caught in a bird's nest. When he leaned over my shoulder to watch me study the scraps from the kitchen, I settled under his touch without pulling away. If he ran a hand over my head to keep the loose strands from my face, I leaned into his palm.

Mostly these moments were between us and behind a closed door. But the castle knew. My arm and my cheek healed and as I went back to my regular duties, tending winter fevers and healing chest infections, the servants noticed our behavior despite our attempts to hide it. I didn't need to touch the stones to know our energy had rippled out. If the walls were made of mud, not rock, I might've expected flowers to grow right out of the floor and down every hall.

One final evening, we crossed paths on the landing of the third floor after I'd been bent over the history books in his study. The two I'd kept in hand fell to the floor as we bumped into each other. I expected him to chide me for my deep concentration. Instead, he averted his eyes.

"What is it?" I asked.

He stepped away and messed with his hair. "The day was warm. Tomorrow should be the same."

I had noticed the same thing, but I didn't follow what he meant by the observation.

"We should see to the willow," he said. "And if the thaw holds, Garret and I will depart overmorrow for Castle Bane."

"Oh." I gulped. He was willing to see me through my Fierce magic, but he didn't want to be around for the aftermath. I chose not to argue. My spell was written as well as I could get it, and I'd practiced more than enough. It didn't seem fair to beg his witness over something neither of us were comfortable with yet.

"Tomorrow?"

"Before the dawn," I said. "I need the sunrise to be with me."

We bid goodnight and I walked the rest of the way to my rooms alone, wishing I had at least asked him to accompany me.

Chapter Fifty

I WAS AWAKE AND DRESSED before he even knocked on my door. Even that had been an odd development. For someone who used to kick my door in for any miniscule concern, he'd made a point of allowing me the choice of when and how quickly I opened my rooms to him.

His hair was pushed back, and he was already wearing a wool wrap to keep his shoulders warm. Thaw or not, winter remained strong in the morning and until the sun rose, we were at its mercy. With a bundle in my arms, I shut my door and followed him downstairs, out into the courtyard. When he left to rouse the stable hands, I called after him.

"We only need Meadowgrass," I said.

He turned, quizzically. "You're sure?"

I dipped my chin. "If it is anything like the first time, I won't be able to keep my seat on Sparrow. There's no point in saddling them both."

He considered this, then disappeared. When he returned, two

stable boys followed. One led Meadow and the other our piebald. As Meadow was tacked up, Aeson helped the other hand load the shepherd's body onto a cart for the piebald to pull.

"I'll ride second this time," I told him, standing back as he mounted and gave me the empty stirrup next. Snug behind him, I tucked my carry bag inside my cloak and cinched my arms around his torso, resting my head on his back. We crossed under the night torches mounted along the gate, and in the dark of the road it was easy to forget that we'd ever been different from that moment.

A lone witch and the bastard who kept her.

We cut around the backside of the village, acknowledged only by the snorts and murmurs of the household animals. The piebald and his cart trailed behind with the stable hand riding bareback. The last stretch of our journey was still, not even a gust of wind to bring in the sunrise.

At the willow's silhouette, I slid down and Aeson tied Meadowgrass to a fence post farther off. He helped remove the shepherd and place him before the tree, then he sent the stable boy home with the horse and cart. At last, we were alone with my Fierce magic upon us.

Neither of us had visited since the morning I snuck out, and I was relieved to see how it endured. Feeling the trunk with my hands, the weak side was not as dreary as it had been. The villagers must've held true to the spell I left with Emmaya. All in all, the ferocity with which each side had tried to compensate for the other had subsided.

It was still quite dark and my observations were grounded in the power I felt through my palms. When Aeson joined me, I pulled a regular candle stub from my bag and had him set the wick aflame.

As the light flickered over our faces, I watched him carefully. His eyes scanned the willow, nodding in approval. To my wonder, fear never joined his expression. Nor did anger or disappointment. Around us lay easily the worst thing I'd ever done, even if by accident, and he was looking on as if it was merely a broken wagon wheel. He surprised me further by reaching for my hand and squeezing with encouragement.

"I thought this plan upset you," I said.

"It did." He pulled me closer. "It still does. But denying you are a witch is about as helpful as denying I am low born. We will carry it no matter what, and someone will always look down upon us. Might as well give them something to look at."

"Yet you will leave and avoid looking yourself."

He grimaced and folded against me, tucking his nose into the pocket of air between my neck and my hair. "Please do not think of my distance as disappointment. As you put it, I'm not sure I want anyone seeing me in that state."

I tried to believe him but the smile I mustered felt more like a frown.

When he straightened, he cradled my face so closely that I stopped breathing for fear of what he might do. "Come on," he said, releasing me at last. "Time to see what you look like as a Fierce witch."

Shedding my cloak, I pulled the bag forward on my hip and unwrapped the other items. I had six candles and Grennly's afterbirth, pressed full of herbs and flowers. From the far too big for me belt at my waist, I felt for Aeson's knife and stepped forward, approaching the willow on its eastern face.

I laid the candles out in the shape of the six siblings. Inger and Aeo faced the impending sunrise, Iigus and Aelus went in the middle, and Iya and Aeden rested closest to the shepherd. Atop Shepherd's chest, I lay Grennly's parcel and made sure the father's palms rested over it. The knife served to open the back of my wrist and drip blood over the extra offering.

My extra candle sat a few paces in front, as a gateway. I could draw the power of the sun easy enough, but I needed the consent of the Innocents for the rest. Once I started my spell, the sun's power would move through the first candle and join the others. If each Brother and Sister allowed it, their candle would light.

Iya would be last. She was my singular superior and she could deny me if she so desired. I was, admittedly, skirting her demands for fresh sacrifice, but as I was hesitant to even cast this way, I hoped she would take pity on me for this blessing.

In the middle of the design, I spread my arms and shifted them forward and back in one last bit of practice. When I felt sure that my muscles would recall each sibling and candle in the right order, I kicked off my boots and tossed them aside. My toes retracted at the cool ground, but I needed it. The extra transference would help.

I gave the necklaces at my throat one quick pull and faced the horizon. Holding a palm above Aeo's candle, I began my spell right as sunlight peeped at the edges of the fields.

"Over steed and sky, the choice remiss; turn blue the eye with speed and bliss."

Twisting and twirling the power with my wrist, I jerked upward, snapped my fingers and watched the first flame pop to life. I exhaled and moved through the others with more confidence.

"Bring teeth to skin with paw spread wide; may flesh unpin the cowards hide.

Return to home in Maer's herd; soothe the bone, a song, no bird.

As seeds do sprout and sweetness eat; unsown the doubt to gift this meat."

In trembled sleep came lively wake; we pay the queens for honeys make."

Flames sizzled. Inger, Aeden, Iigus, and Aelus had all shared their power with me. Their candles burned brightly in agreement. I took a deep breath for Iya.

"Sisters, bridge, Alba bless; a kinship ridge to Willow's rest."

It might have been pleading but I reminded her that Grennly's afterbirth was offered without expectation. I wished to appease her needs for sacrifice without violence whilst also letting the father know his child as his body returned to the earth. They provided two offerings where Fierce only called for one.

Scooping from the elbows, I gathered the threads of power before me and bound them to my chest. I turned as the sun's belly lifted above the horizon line. Heat permeated my back. On my next exhale I pushed frontward and asked Iya a single word as my palm passed over her candle. "Please?"

At first there was nothing, and I held my palm flat, at the shepherd's vacant body. Eyes squeezed shut, I took another breath and asked once more. "Please?"

A crackle met my ears, crisp and sharp but slow to gain momentum. I slit one eyelid open and glanced down. Iya's candle was burning, calm and contained. Noticeably hesitant. Iya was skeptical often but stubborn always.

And Aeson pondered where I got it from.

Moving on, I swept my hands through the air, side to side, starting from the right. I repeated all my verses, conjuring the sense of bone and marrow and sinew and hair and nails and a dozen different layers of skin. Wordless and wicked, I pictured each string of flesh separating from the next, breaking down and losing its hold on the muscles and organs that lay cold inside the shepherd's ribcage.

I did six waves back and forth, one for each Innocent. Side to side and over again. I pulled the energy down to glimmers of nothing but faint, untethered power to be eaten up by the tree roots.

On the final sweep, I lay one wrist across the other and centered them above Iya's candle. I held them until the tingling along my neck and arms smoothed out. When it relaxed, I stepped out of the candle hex and approached the shepherd. Kneeling at his side, I pulled his arms tight to his chest to keep Grennly's afterbirth close to the heart. More blood dripped from my wrist, staining his bindings as I rolled his body away from me and bent his knees up. Shepherd was an infant again himself. Ready to rejoin the Innocents. I curled his back and tucked his head down so he was fetal once more.

With a hand on each end of his spine, I recited my spell to the Brothers and Sisters a third time. When I got to the end, I added my closing line. My book hadn't called for it, but it felt better to cast in good manners.

"Receive life and death, pains be well; take this breath, a witch unspelled."

Threads of power that were mine and mine alone stripped free of my veins. It crept from behind my ears, down the pulse of my throat, winding past the dimple of my elbow and out through my palms. In addition to what I'd drawn from the sunrise and the Innocents, everything else I possessed made its way down to the roots of the willow.

The ground rumbled like horses across a field. Dirt and stone crumbled loose. My hands were pulled fast to the shepherd in his linen wrappings. In front of me, the tree groaned, and the branches lashed about, whipping from side to side.

The tendrils that were called to life when I was fighting for mine recoiled to the trunk, twisting in a sinistrorse until the splintered half rose and crunched against itself as it righted its way to the sky. At the base, roots sifted aside the soft earth until a hole formed. Wooden fingers emerged, taking the body like prey in a web and pulling it to their depths below.

I stopped breathing and tears dripped for emotions I didn't own. While the last bits of my power emptied, sight and sound overcame me. Memories, from the shepherd.

At first, I was wrapped in a woman's arms. Her face loomed over mine as she smiled and my belly filled hot. Next, I was running along a fence, hiding behind posts and laughing as the same woman searched for me.

The scene changed. I was hiding under a table listening to a man bellow words like liar, cheat, whore, and bastard. In the next moment, I stood holding the same woman's hand over a fresh grave. When her hand released, I was alone in a field with sheep at my back and eyes caught on a girl in the distance. She had auburn hair and full lips. Ellara.

With a rumble at my palms, one last picture came through. Aeson when he first arrived. He was led through the village by Garret. The villagers surrounding me followed their path and the word *bastard* fell from everyone's tongue.

Chapter Fifty One

SHUDDERING, MY EYES FLEW OPEN, and I heaved the air into my lungs. The dirt that had opened for the shepherd had taken my hands as well, gripping me tightly. I pulled back with a yelp. Except I'd forgotten where I truly was. Scurrying backwards, disoriented, I lost my balance and thought I'd hit my head on the ground for sure. But Aeson looped his arms around me and stopped my collapse, although I jumped at the surprise of his touch.

"It's okay. You're done. It's all done," he said, grabbing my arms to stop me from flailing anymore.

Panting, I forced the bile and sloppy mess of tears back down my throat and gave my weight over. Adjusting me against him, he cradled me to one side just as the last bit of smokey light broke completely under bright yellow. The sun was alert and its heat caught us quickly, eliminating the last of the shadows we arrived with.

Strewn across his lap, I looked up at Aeson. His hair fell

forward to cocoon our faces together and after I caught my breath, I asked, "How is it?"

He looked up, and a sad sort of smile spread over his lips. "Relieved."

"Good." Filling my lungs, my chin trembled. I had to remember what a full breath felt like.

Aeson looked down at me again, tracing the contours of my face with an index finger. As it passed along my brow, his own twisted up.

"And, how am I?" I reached up to my cheek, wondering if maybe I'd split it open again in my focus to decompose the shepherd.

He pressed his lips to my forehead. "Still a witch."

"A Fierce one."

His mouth twitched, hiding a smile. "You look the same to me."

I breathed out, relieved by his attitude. We held each other's hands until I felt completely empty, then he sat me up. Leaving me to rest a bit longer, he thanked every candle flame on his own and blew them out one by one, leaving Iya for the last.

"Bless her, and bless you, First Witch."

With everything gathered, he slung my bag over his chest and offered both hands to help me stand. It wasn't until I was on my feet that I realized I was still barefoot. Winter was already reclaiming the patch of mud surrounding the willow and the frozen dirt jabbed like pebbles under my heel. Aeson spied my boots, but I pulled at his clothes and kept him close. "No. I'll fall over elsewise."

Dipping to one side, he lifted me with an arm at my back and the other beneath my legs, carrying me to Meadowgrass. Once he was sure I wouldn't topple off, he went back for my boots, and uttered one last blessing to the willow.

It looked funny now. The spindly branches had broken off and spiraled around the trunk as if the entire thing had swirled up from the ground. An odd bit of fresh wood stuck out here and there where the bark hadn't fit back together the same way.

Sitting behind me for the ride home, Aeson clung so tightly I nearly stopped breathing again. If I hadn't been sapped of energy, I might've complained. But if I'd been honest with myself, I savored how he held on as if I might disintegrate next.

We were halfway up the hill to the castle when he squeezed my whole body against his and told me to open my eyes. Blinking, I did as instructed and followed the direction he pointed. At the tree line there was movement in the ground shrubs. Shifting in the saddle, I squinted and saw the swish of a tail.

A pair of cherry foxes slunk between saplings, glancing at us over their shoulders and stopping beneath a heavy bough to pull our scent from the air.

"A pair of them. They bear good intention," he said.

"Mm." I closed my eyes again and nuzzled beneath his chin, pulling his arm even tighter across my belly.

We clopped the rest of the way uphill and into the courtyard, busy with more stable hands. Two of them appeared to help, one for the reins, and one to help Aeson ease me down after he'd dismounted.

"Can you walk?" he asked, hands clasped around my back. I said yes but wobbled like a goat kid come too soon. Laughing, he swooped me up again and walked through the front door, past the kitchen staff laying out breakfast for the household. I drew breath to argue but he shushed me immediately, making it all the way to my bedside with the door closed before setting me down.

The floor was comforting after the press of half frozen mud between my toes. Clutching Aeson's collar to keep steady, I rocked in time with his movements. He unbuttoned my cloak and stretched to hang it on the wall, adjusting my necklaces when they got pulled to one side. When it came to removing the burgundy kirtle I'd worn for the occasion, he spun me slowly, pausing with his fingertip's half tangled in the cords at my back.

His breath caught and I touched my chin to my shoulder. "It's okay." I attempted a jest. "I am not going to scold you."

Starting again with determination, he pulled the ties loose. "I know. It's just . . . everything about you feels familiar even when it is not."

As the chest piece fell, and the skirt followed, I pulled my hair to one side, fidgeting. "I know what you mean."

One hand crept around my hip, tugging me back around. Laying my palms against his chest, I could hardly mourn the absence of my magic. Everything was done now. The shepherd would be at peace. Grennly was growing and healthy and his afterbirth rested with his father. The willow had everything it needed to stop casting and heal itself.

There was nothing to separate either of us from our thoughts or curiosities. And looking at Aeson, I saw at least two dozen flit through his irises. "I wish I could change my mind," he said. "I should not have promised to leave tomorrow."

The thought amused me. "You *could* change your mind. And you could change it again," I said. "But that would make you a different man. I might not like that one as much."

He laughed, running his hands up my back and pulling my chest to his. "I wouldn't dare."

I glanced away for a second. A saccade between him and the window. "Likewise, I could never demand you stay, but . . ."

He swallowed. "I understand."

I tiptoed a hand up to twirl the ends of his hair. "Should you kiss me goodbye?"

"No. I shouldn't," he said, fixating on my mouth all the same. "I want all of you, not half of you. Not when the other half might still have reservations."

My eyelids fell shut, blocking out the sense of his conviction. Given the first time I used Fierce magic and the upheaval it caused, I wouldn't disagree. Although this time felt easier, it would be unwise to assume the pendulum of my heart had stopped swinging and found peace. "I'm sure you are right," I said, dropping my head to his sternum. "The castle will feast on the rumors while you're away. They'll say you've used your station to woo your castle witch."

"Now you're my castle witch?" He pinched my sides.

With the smallest laugh I would allow, I lowered my hands to wind them with his and looked out the window into the fields. "I've always been your castle witch."

He jerked me forward one last step, clasping all our hands and fingers together at my lower back. "You torturous little creature," he said, smiling like an idiot. "Do not ever be different from this, Etta. I'm far too attached to it."

My eyes rolled, but I let the creak of amusement grow at the corner of my lips. He was as bad as the stable hands that tottered after Saana. "I'm not sure unhindered triumph agrees with you," I said.

"Perhaps not, but it feels marvelous." He held his grin for another moment before dropping his gaze and forfeiting our games entirely. "You need sleep. And quiet."

I agreed reluctantly and settled against my pillows. When he made to leave, I grabbed his hand one last time and locked eyes with him. "Come straight back to me."

Grinning once more, he leaned down and kissed my forehead. "We will see which of us is faster. Me or your patron."

Chapter Fifty Two

IT WAS IYA. OF COURSE. Ten days later, I woke with the same itchy feeling in and around my ears. It oozed down my neck like water algae and joined the sensation in my chest. Together it spread over my arms, down my spine, along the back of my legs and under every finger and toenail.

Just like the first time, I paced in my room for a long while, still unsure who to mention it to first. Layla and Prilla had tended to me closely after Aeson left. But my relationship with Iya made little difference to them. I'd made sure to help them as soon as I was able, stirring and measuring whatever Prilla set before me. Drying anything she needed or blessing Free magic into it before storing it away.

Halfway through my severance, I even walked with Layla down to the village one day, to deliver some excess flour to Emmaya. It felt good to breathe fresh air and spring was prodding at winter's grip. But with my feelings about Aeson still as new as a sprout and Layla equally as unsure how to talk about Garret, the journey was silent and strange.

On that morning it returned, I eventually opened my door and crept down to the kitchen. Layla was the only one working at the long table. She looked up and slid a bowl of eggs over to whisk. As I joined her, she poured the sugar in and I gathered we were making a cake of some sort. Perhaps in preparation for the mens' return.

After blending all the wet ingredients in tandem, Layla took over again and I dropped to the bench. While she folded in the flour and a winter berry syrup, I tapped the nail of my index finger on the table to a melody that meant nothing.

"My magic is back this morning," I said in the end.

Smiling softly, she paused to look at me. "That's good."

"Mm." I stopped tapping and laid both hands on either side of the bench next. "I was hoping they would have returned first."

Her brow arched, and I watched her resist the smirk begging to curl her lip.

Heat rushed over me. One at a time every muscle ticked. Pushing my hair out of my face, I looked away and around and any direction I could that didn't risk Layla's wise cracked face. Stuffing several breaths back into my body, I nodded and stood up.

She grabbed my hand before I could leave, meeting my eyes. "The journey there takes five days in good weather. They left in the snow. We must be patient."

Chapter Fifty Three

I SPENT ANOTHER WEEK BEING PATIENT. Another week looking over Reeve's shoulders for news to explain the delay. But as the snow melted faster and faster, my heart thrummed quicker and quicker. They should have been home. He should have been home.

Hoping the pears might help, I wandered in and out of their trunks. Their buds were forming, pushing tentatively at the grey bark, asking if it was safe to emerge. There was just enough of winter remaining to make them cautious.

I stewed and replayed our first moment in my head for comfort, if it really was our first moment. Magic, or something like it, told me it wasn't.

A warmish breeze raced across my limbs and took the daydream away. Collecting myself, I blessed the pear trees the way I normally would. Then I walked to his spot by the stream and fell to the wet dirt.

"Is this punishment?" I asked aloud. I had stretched the

definition of a sacrificial spell when I offered an already dead body and an infant's afterbirth to the willow. And despite my justifications, I worried that Aeson was receiving the consequences of my actions.

However, if Iya had intended to disregard my spell as a proper sacrifice, there was no reason to have severed my magic. The thought eased some of my fears but not all. There were other reasons they could be late. A horse threw a shoe. A guard took ill. But those reasons still allowed letters to be sent and explanations to be shared.

To my right, something dull and green slid over a patch of snow and back onto the muddy stream bank. The garden snake made her way to the water for a drink, then slithered onto my hand for a moment. She changed course again and moved off towards whatever burrow she had claimed for hibernation.

In her absence I was immediately lonely and my concerns rang loud between my ears. I couldn't sit anymore without answers. Pushing up, I dusted my skirts free of mud and headed back towards the castle. A bath would do the trick I hoped. An entire tub of worry water was better than fretting all over the grounds by myself.

At the door in the wall, I hesitated. The last time I was there had been with Aeson and the memory burned. He knew what he wanted in that moment, and I didn't. If our separation was upsetting me even half as much as it was him, I could call myself a torturer as well as a witch. Perhaps stubbornness was not always worth it.

"There you are," a voice called. Reeve stood below the undercroft, facing me with a bundle of letters in hand.

"Finally," I breathed. "Have you gotten a message? Is there

news?"

Reeve took a quick breath and squared his chest before replying. "Guard Garret has returned with the others. They are in the great hall."

"And Lord Crennly. He is in the hall as well?"

Our castle keeper shifted his weight erratically, toe to heel, left to right. But he said nothing and that was enough.

Garret sat beaten on a chair near the head table. Layla was at his feet offering sips of water as often as he would take it. Filling the other chairs, only half the guards from their entourage remained. Before I could dare ask the question that plagued me, I surveyed their injuries and asked through a tight jaw, "Does anyone need immediate tending?"

Hair a mess, Garret shook his head. "We are mostly unharmed."

My eyes trailed over them. "And the others? Those who haven't returned?"

Wiping his mouth and the stubble around his chin, he nudged Layla's arm away and looked up at me. "I have no knowledge. I suspect they're just the same. It was a proper ambush."

"Were you on Gallo lands?" I had to ask.

Garret shook his head. "Country road, between boundaries. I suspect they wanted it that way to avoid accusation."

He was right. It would be the only way for another house to keep their name clear.

I hardened like stone before meeting his eyes. Inside, I crumbled. They set out with a dozen guards, a stable boy, and the two of them. Fifteen in all. Before me were six. The longer we stared at each other the more dejected Garret's expression became.

"You going to curse me, witch?" he asked.

Layla pulled his face to meet hers. "Etta would never blame you for this. You shouldn't, either."

I came out of my haze and used both hands to push my hair back. "Just tell me what happened," I said. As he began to explain, I carved a line up and down the rows of tables and chairs, turning back every few paces or so.

The trip to Calise's was uneventful. She was glad to see everyone and gave them comfortable rooms to rest as they delivered our supplies with my instructions. Even on departure, there seemed nothing to worry about and the first days went without issue. It was the fourth day that brought trouble. Garret knew someone was on the road behind them because the horses had turned their noses back more than once. But the travelers seemed to have turned off the track long before our party stopped to rest.

"We hadn't yet passed the mountains to reach Aevic Stow," Garret explained. "The strike was perfectly positioned between Gallo's land and at least three others. A handful more are within a day's ride. We didn't plan to stop long so we set no guard. A grave error on my part."

"Why were you rushing?"

"His lordship said he needed to get straight back home." Garret met my gaze for a definitive minute and turned away. "Some of the men, too many of them, left their weapons with the horses. They were easy targets."

My hands trembled at my belt, touching the knife Aeson insisted on giving me after I lost mine. He should've had something more to fight with. I should have argued like I wanted to. I should have ripped it off and tied it to his saddle. I should have done a lot of things.

Steadying my hands, and as much else of me as would cooperate, I turned back to Garret. "Who do you think it was? Thieves? Hired bandits? Will they ransom him?"

He shook his head. "They can't. They don't have him."

"What?" I stopped pacing and stood, stock still.

"Him there." Garret gestured at a guard on a makeshift stretcher with a brace on his leg. "Broke his ankle escaping with the young lord."

"Then where is he?"

"We don't know. We scattered into the woods, and they pursued whoever they could. This one crossed our path and said Lord Crennly and the others had to hide when another wave of men arrived to put chase on them. We didn't dare stay to track them ourselves, not without more weapons. We had no choice but to return home and resupply."

Fist to my mouth, I bit into my skin as hard as I could stand. "They will be tracked in snow or mud. Their footprints will be everywhere."

"Indeed, they will." Garret licked his lips at this, reaching for Layla's hand and clasping it tight before finding my eyes again. "I thought you deserved to know instead of wonder. And if anyone could find him, it would be you."

My arms went limp as I took him in. His disappointment. The idea that he'd failed at something he was solely responsible for. It whittled away at his features, and I understood the feeling completely.

Layla kissed his cheeks and turned to find me over her

shoulder. "He's right, you know," she said. "If you can't find one, find the other."

"Do not invoke that wretched statement," I threatened. I might've been ready to accept Aeson, but Aeson and I being accepted by everyone else was a different thing altogether. Behind me, a crowd had gathered near the door to the servants' hall.

Prilla was farthest into the room, Reeve at her shoulder. She smushed her lips up like a duck bill and glanced at the castle keeper. "Garret's done right, Miss Etta. If Lord Crennly had a wife, Garret would need report to her. But since he hasn't—"

"Do not finish that idea aloud," I said. "It's the most unfortunate claim any of you has ever made."

She shrugged. "I'm not saying I disagree with you. But the facts are the facts."

I stuck a finger in Reeve's direction. "He is in charge. Reports go to him."

But Reeve shook his head, slowly at first and then picking up speed. "Perhaps under normal circumstances, yes. But there's only one person here he would trust to this task."

Gaping, I took them all in. They looked on like ducklings eager to fall in line. Before I could tell them off again, Garret stood and walked to me. Scratches covered his face and a bruise purpled the flesh between his neck and collarbone. "I will go over every detail until we sort this out, and when you've decided what our plan is, I will do whatever you set before me."

The room went still when he bowed his head and laid his palm over his heart, signing for five and one. He had never sworn *to* me, only *at* me. I stared, slack jawed, and told myself not to burn the entire hall down.

My mouth was dry by the time I tried to speak. "Garret. You

miserable——" I couldn't finish. Pushing past the crowd filling the center row, I wiped my face with little success. If I made it to my rooms, I could fall apart in solitude. But I stopped when the front doors creaked open, Laken pulling at the handle. On the entry steps was a half dozen village boys. "What is this now?" I asked.

Laken shrugged as the boys made their way in and stomped their boots clean. Finally, one of them looked up and caught my gaze. "Sorry," he said. "The lot of us saw guard Garret returning with injured men. We didn't see Lord Crennly, though. Has something happened?"

"You are here to help?" I asked. He nodded and red brown hair shook loose from his cap. The rest of them nodded as well. The intention of the room pressed on me like an execution stone. It squeezed the air from my lungs and my shoulders drooped first, then hips, and knees. On the floor, I covered my face and allowed only the most fervent tears to stream down.

Garret had returned for my sake. Reeve had deferred to me. Prilla had agreed with them both. And the village boys, Aeson's summer charges, had shown up to help. It was quite the opposite of punishment from Iya, but it made me squirm all the same.

Someone touched my shoulder. Layla. "Up, my lady, what are our orders?"

I didn't obey right away, but I scrubbed my face clean of tears and looked to Garret. He was still in the threshold of the hall, expectant. The immediate ideas took root and I pointed at the empty hearth. "Laken, without burning yourself, light a fire and make better beds for the injured soldiers. Layla, get Garret in working order. Prilla, boil extra oat bran for the horses they brought back." I stood at last and sought Riggs out in the crowd. "You, feed the horses who have returned as well as you can until it is time for them to work. Reeve, you are to fetch Saana and Arlo Shepherd from the village immediately. And someone needs to get me a rotten map of every nook and cranny within five days' ride."

Chapter Fifty Four

I SET SAANA AND ARLO LOOSE IN MY WORKROOM to prep as many salves and remedies as we would need to heal the guards and stitch their wounds. Once they were comfortable with the tools, I left and found Garret in his rooms with Layla. I dropped the maps on the foot of his bed and cast my gaze wide.

"Show me where it happened."

With Layla's help and Garret instructing from his pillows, she and I laid them flat on the ground to make a larger display. We followed his story hour by hour. The attackers had gone without horses to keep their tracks light and easy to disguise but that meant they could hide their own footprints in those that Aeson and the others left behind. But they were not the ones hiding and thus, had nothing to fear.

"I know you're hoping to burn Lord Gallo's castle at the end of this, but I've met his men at the gathering. I've seen them fight and this wasn't them," he said. "This was crude, and unformed."

"Unless they truly wanted to disguise themselves." I wagged

my head in his direction. "It does not matter right now. What matters is that we find Aeson first, before anyone else."

It grated on me to admit, but it was true. The fact of it ate at my insides because if indeed it wasn't Lord Gallo, it meant this ploy came from someone else. And I was very tired of new players joining the board.

"How many men would we need to canvas the entire north woods of the valley mountains?" I asked.

"It's not the men, witch. It's the skillset. We need one sound tracker in each party, and a scout to watch for pursuers. If you can find ten guards like that in this household, you should be doing my job."

"Oh hush. I'm not yelling at you," I sighed. "I'm thinking."

"Well, think more modestly. We are a small holding. Half the reason either of you became a target for this treachery are the successes that started with *your* spells."

"*Garret!*" Layla exclaimed.

"You're saying this is my fault?" I whipped around to face him. "Would you rather everyone here still labored sunup to sundown in every field to fill our stores?"

He cranked his jaw around and mussed his hair up after Layla had so diligently combed it free of tangles and burrs. "No. Of course not," Garret agreed. "His lordship is kindhearted enough to attract anyone's jealousy."

I folded my arms and hung my head. "That he is."

"Surely it's just a spell you can cast," he stated.

"I told you. I'm thinking." I stamped one heel. "Theoretically, yes there is. But what if more of his group separated? What if I locate the wrong batch? There is only one of me, and I may need two spells. One to locate him and one for the others."

"Find *him* and we will track the rest if needed."

"And if he's since been caught or given himself up to save the others?"

"You can cast again."

I shook fists at him. "A fortnight later! Whoever we don't find could be dead by then."

"Make it a one-part spell."

"Oh, how novel. I hadn't considered that." I widened my gaze at him.

"*Enough, you two!*" Layla yelled. "You both miss him. Why not just say that? Why bicker like this? You're like a pair of goats smashing your heads together. It will solve nothing."

I tightened my arms across my chest and lifted my chin. "I'm sorry. To both of you."

"I as well," Garrett muttered, looking off to the window.

Kneeling to gather the maps up and return them to the study, I glanced between Garret and Layla. "We should get some rest as it is. This has been an awful set of days already and if they didn't want him alive, they would have attacked with more ferocity. They would have wanted a clean—" I cut off the words and stood up. At the door, I glanced back at them. Layla had sat down beside him, holding his hand and checking the ointment she'd smeared over his bruising. Jealousy ruptured in the depths of my belly, and I billowed out a gust of air, making my cheeks swell like a bloated water skin. "Layla is right," I said. "I just . . . miss him."

The tears that spilled over were hot and nearly scalded my skin. I pushed the door open and left before Garret could add anything. Up the stairs and halfway to the study, Layla caught up with me.

"Don't be angry with him," she begged. "You see, don't you?

He knows how this affects you. Both of you."

"I'm not angry with him any more than I'm angry with myself. If even one thing had been different, it might have ended better. But it might have ended worse," I reassured her, imagining if I hadn't tended the willow when I did. Or if Aeson had changed his mind like he suggested, choosing to wait until I could accompany him and teach Calise myself. Or had I whimpered and implored him to stay.

Everything could have been different if we ourselves were different. But we weren't and something told me the shadows surrounding us would have invited themselves into our valley with or without our permission.

The thought of Aeson or I seeing each other in duress was not one I needed to ponder. My accidental spell at the willow would be nothing compared to what I'd do if I saw him ambushed by hired crooks. Friends or otherwise, it was not a loss I would ever accept without a fight.

Layla nodded and shrunk beneath me. Reaching out, I dropped the maps and pulled her to me in what I hoped felt like a warm embrace, promising up and down that I held no resentment towards Garret. If anyone in the castle knew how easy it was to aggravate someone to the point of violence, it was me. And Aeson's method of leadership was sure to make him a target to any lord who valued profit over pride. We had always known that.

"I do wish you'd consider the words, Miss Etta," she said, stepping away. "If you can't find one, find the other."

I dropped my shoulders. "Layla."

"I mean it." She stiffened under my glare. "We don't just say it because we delight in pestering you. You are a match. You carry him everywhere you go as he does you. It's like a tether. If you look for him, you will find yourself and surely you can track that easy enough. If that's not magic, I don't know what is."

She left in a fury, as broken at Garret's demeanor as I was at Aeson's disappearance.

Gathering my wits for the hundredth time since the small cache of them returned, I delivered the maps to the study and made for my rooms. Saana and Arlo were hard at work though, and it made me feel in the way. I wandered the halls instead, worrying the necklaces at my throat for the rest of the afternoon and evening. If I were to cast yet more Fierce magic, I would need another to help me. Perhaps two others if I was going to consider Layla's idea.

I couldn't fathom how to follow her suggestion. I could barely articulate my real feelings for Aeson let alone write a spell that would weave us together whilst so far apart.

I was on the third-floor landing when the call to dinner sounded below. There was nothing that could possibly invite my appetite, so I stayed where I was until silence fell on the upper floors. Everyone was downstairs, eating as normally as they could, I hoped, so in my solitude, I climbed the final set of stairs and let myself into his rooms. The walls were heartbreakingly quiet. Lonely with his absence. His writing desk, over by the largest window, had a stack of empty papers on it. The quill had been laid on top. It must've been wet when he set it down, leaving the tiniest drop of ink to dry out and dome at the top of a page. His wardrobe chests lined the other wall, filled with Crennly blue and Mother Elma's favorite, stark red.

The smell of him attacked my senses the worst. Soap and clove and clean linen and something forest-y that was distinctly him. Fumbling my way to his bed, I took the boldest act I ever had in eight years behind these walls. I lifted the covers and crawled in, dirty feet and all.

Burrowing into his pillows, I pulled the blankets over my head and pressed my eyes shut, trying out a new phrase beneath its canopy.

"*Find the target, find the arrow. It's two and one that make the marrow.*"

Chapter Fifty Five

I WOKE TO THE DOOR SQUEALING ON ITS HINGES. Sitting up with a start, I wiped my eyes of sleep and found Laken at the foot of the bed. Her hair was singed on one side and shorter than it had been the day before. She called over her shoulder into the hallway, yelling to someone that she'd found me.

I didn't bother explaining myself when Reeve and Prilla paraded in next, and honestly, other than a brief glance at the bed itself, neither looked too surprised to see me there.

"What is it?"

Reeve stammered before Prilla took over. "Nothing." She smirked. "You only set the household in a frenzy when it appeared you were missing this morning as well."

"Oh." I lay a hand on my head. "I'm sorry. I should've thought."

Prilla curtsied, a bizarre action to my eyes. "Have you had any ideas, Miss?"

"Yes," Reeve spoke up finally. "I spoke to Garret already. He has set the farm boys to replacement posts, to have experienced men at the ready."

I sighed, running the edge of the blanket between my fingertips and scratching at the weave. "I'm not sure," I confessed, trying to hold the frayed pieces of a dream. "But bring me breakfast in the study, please. I need to look through my books."

Chapter Fifty Six

I WORKED FAST, flipping through pages and writing down the ideas as they came to me. The memory of casting before the willow tree was still fresh in my mind. The feel of it easy to conjure and easy to reimagine into something new. I had no way of knowing if Layla's idea would work but I'd come to believe there was something to it.

I shocked the seamstresses the next day when I dropped my purple dress at their feet with Aeson's blue coat next to it. "I need you to cut these into ribbons and braid them together into six different ropes."

They took the pile, wordlessly but wide eyed. I didn't stay long enough for them to ask any questions. Garret found me in the orchard after that. I was staring at our pear tree. His gait was precarious, still aching in his arms and legs from the fight and the hurried journey home. But his eyes were brighter, and it seemed Layla had stopped hovering around him every second.

"Are you trying to set it ablaze?" he asked.

I drew a long, sorrowful breath. "Yes, in fact."

He glanced at me out of the corner of his eye. "Truly?"

I dropped my head to one shoulder. "Not this exact moment. But it will need to be burned."

"Why this one?" Garret looked around the orchard.

Biting my lip, I gave the pear tree a long look. "This one belongs to us."

He didn't ask anything more, but he did turn the rest of the way to face me. "You've been hidden away in the study since yesterday. Have you worked it all out?"

"I hope so," I sighed. "We will have to wait a few more days for the full moon. Until then, I will make sure everyone and everything in the castle is set and comfortable before I am rendered useless again. And we will need his chair brought down from the study itself."

His apprehension was noticeable. "Why?"

I tweaked my neck. "It's the source of his power." *And that room is also ours.*

"Very well," he said.

"Will you be ready? If this works, you can't delay."

He signed for the Innocents again. "We'll ride the night if we need to."

Chapter Fifty Seven

THREE INSUFFERABLE DAYS LATER, I told Layla and Garret to rest through the afternoon as I would need them at nightfall. Then I called Riggs and Smithwik down to the orchard. When I showed them the tree, they exchanged a glance but set to work chopping it down to kindling and selecting six strong stakes from the bunch. With no one left to tend in the castle, I lingered nearby, apologizing to the other pear trees and swearing my plan would not be in vain.

One of the seamstresses emerged from the back door and came tiptoeing down the path to my side carrying a bundle of rope. Presenting it with a frown, she asked, "Will this do?"

I ran them through my hands. It was a tight weave, which would be difficult to burn but better overall. The longer they burned the longer I had to talk to him. "This is perfect."

The pale little seamstress dipped a curtsy. "Anything else m'lady, I mean, Miss Etta?"

Holding back a scowl, I straightened my stance. "No, thank you."

She rushed off, and I pulled the braided cloth to my chest. Eyes closed, I whispered to the Free magic surrounding me. "Please, work. Please."

As instructed, Garret and Layla met me at the outer wall after dinner was served and cleared. Behind Garret came two more guards carrying Aeson's seat from the study.

I had them set it atop the kindling where it best suited my spell and sent them off with one more set of orders. "One of you must find Saana. I know you know her." I gleaned a look across both their faces. "Send her to my side as soon as she's able. Do not delay her or I'll turn you into a sacrifice."

They scampered off while Garret and Layla chuckled behind their hands. Holding a fistful of witch grass, I pointed to the stakes in the ground. A stretch of rope was tied to each one. "Layla, when the moon is above the trees, you shall bind the cords to me one by one with each verse. Garret, when all six are tethered to me, wait for the blood to drip, then light the fire. Once it's well caught, you're to throw this bundle into the tallest flame."

"Whose blood will be dripping exactly?" He narrowed his eyes.

"Mine, of course."

"How is your blood going to find Lord Crennly?"

"I won't be looking for Aeson, not exactly." I glanced at Layla. "I'll be looking for me."

Layla took a turn being wary next. "And where will you be?"

Taking a long breath, I exhaled and looked towards Aeson's chair in the center of everything. "It's important you let the fire burn as long as possible. I don't care if my clothes are scorched. I'm not sure this will work at all but if it does . . ." I swallowed. "I'll need as much time as I can get."

"To do what?" Garret asked.

I shrugged. "To ask him where he is."

This appeased Layla. It was rooted in her idea after all. But Garret looked befuddled. He shook it off and voiced his next concern. "How will we know it's working?"

"We won't. Not until it's done." I cleared my throat with a tick. "I'll either be drained of my power or I won't. If I'm not, I'll have to devise a new plan, and find another chair."

Saana came up on us, striding easily as if being invited to a witch fire in the night was nothing new for her. "You requested me?"

I examined her face. It was ghostly and beautiful in the moonlight. Combined with her mind, she was bound to give someone a run of it, and I greatly looked forward to that day. Digging in my apron pocket, I handed her a bit of paper with my spell on it. "If the smoke takes me too strongly and I stop chanting, please finish the words."

She glanced over it and took a tight breath, determination soldering itself in the set of her jaw. "Free magic? Like we did for the willow?"

"Yes." I nodded, comforted that she'd helped the tree despite the circumstances. "If I fail but another takes up my request, Iya might still favor my spell."

She dipped her chin and took the paper from my hand reverently, unfolding it a step away and scanning the words as I turned back to the wood pile. The last silvery orb of winter finally broke over the treetops, transforming the orchard limbs into veins of moonstone. Garret approached, wringing his hands. "Are you sure about this? He'll never forgive me if I bring him home and you're not here."

"It wouldn't be the first time a witch was burned alive, would it?" I sneered at the makeshift bonfire, then looked at him steadily. "I'm ready for the lord of this castle to be back under its roof. Are you?"

He gave a quick jerk of his head and one last affirmation. I let my hair free and had Saana undo the back of my kirtle to remove it. I needed to be undone for this. Picking my way through the wood, I climbed up in Aeson's chair and sat cross-legged. Extending my left hand to Layla, she stepped up, and I offered her the palm blade from Aeson's belt. "See this line here?" I traced it with my pinky finger. Layla nodded and I gulped. "It's the love line. You will follow its curve on both palms and slash the back of my wrists for good measure."

Her eyes widened, revealing that even the bravest of women could fret. Setting her chin, she hardened her gaze at my open palm and told me, "When you are ready."

I glanced about one last time. The moon was waiting. Garret stood with a torch at the ready. Saana knelt in the grass a safe distance away to keep the paper from catching any flames. I thought it was my imagination, but even when I blinked I still saw five muddy red blobs on a nearby branch. Above them, an owl, and I presumed a whip of a garden snake was probably nearby as well. My intentions must've been stronger than I realized.

With a shaky breath, I looked back to Layla. "Ready."

She cut the back first, then flipped my hand over and slipped the knife along my skin as gently as she might cut an egg yolk. She trusted her eyes to follow the line I'd shown her. Next, she tied the first strand around me, laying the woven braid across the pool of blood and once it was secured, I began.

"Bluish boy or golden bear;

seek the joy of Valley Maer.

Pride unjust from ravage leech;

restore the trust whilst hope still sleeps.

In wallows tear, with gentle mew;

may bow heads spear embrace what's true.

Perhaps in shadow, a secret spoke;

for safety hallowed, the fire stoke.

Wretched lines, admit defeat;

these hearts divine make love complete.

Find the target. Find the arrow.

Two in one, what make the marrow."

We worked in tandem. One rope, one verse. When it was done, I shivered in the night air. I was conscious of how quickly my blood was spilling into the fibers I held. At last, a slow plip fell into the remains of the pear tree. I nodded at Garret and he set fire near each stake, following the same course Layla had. As he went, I recited the corresponding verses again. When the flames were steady, I gestured to Layla to toss the witch grass.

The smoke shifted from sooty black to greenish grey and when it encircled me, I drew my breath. It torched my eyes and flared in my memory. At first all I saw was wagon after wagon, burning to the ground. Bodies piled up in my vision, their necks and wrists slung with Cords of Iya. The strands charred black and burned through until one by one they fell from each witch.

That was a different time, though. And those were different choices, made by different men. I had stepped into this fire to find Aeson because he deserved it. Letting go was only one half of finding something new.

Chanting my spell, I addressed the Innocents one by one again, verse by verse with each exhale. I nearly choked on Iya's phrase and I wondered if that wasn't her attempt to test my intention. Heaving a gust of air in, the smoke reached my lungs, and the effects took hold. I was nearly there. I found Saana through the haze and shook my head up and down as rapidly as I could.

Through the pops and hisses of fire, her rasping voice took over, *"Two and one, what make the marrow. If words fall weak, and cast unspeak, let others quell, turn witch unspelled."*

I had the faintest sense of heat at my shoulders, and something ticked at the edges of my shift, the hem of which hung off the chair. Wafts of air flitted by and told me that some stray hairs were being burnt by the taller flames. I drew one more long breath and tilted my head back to find the moon. Fixating on it as the smoke worked through my senses, I asked, "Where am I?"

I faced the craggy wall of the forest cliff. Blinking to clear my sight, I took a shallow breath and found the air was clean. The world was silent and there was no breeze to swing through the branches.

"Why are we here?" I asked.

"How should I know?" Aeson replied.

I spun towards his voice, but there was nothing. In the corner of one eye, a shadow passed, and I spun again. Still nothing. Grumbling, I closed my eyes and reminded myself that I had limited time. He needed to reveal himself faster than this.

"Aeson?"

"Mm?"

Turning again, I spun all the way and ended up in my quarters near the window. The ferns bounced at my arrival. It wouldn't do. I had to ask more directly and risk revealing my plan. "Aeson. Where are you?"

"I'm right here," he said from behind. When I turned this time, the world whirled into his study. Leaning against the wall, he was looking into the darkened courtyard but turned when he sensed I was close. His smile was open, nothing hidden below anymore.

The sight of him made my whole body slacken but I was hesitant to reach out. I couldn't dare alarm him by revealing this wasn't a normal dream. "Tell me, are you safe?" I asked.

He jerked his head back, and beneath his reply I heard a grating thud like a log breaking in half as it turned to coal. "Of course, I'm safe. Come here." His hand reached for me.

I took it cautiously.

His mouth twitched and his black eyes scanned mine. "What's the matter, my witch?"

I didn't dare tell him I was in the middle of a bonfire hoping not to burn to death, all for the sake of speaking to him. "I'm well. But I need to find you."

Aeson barely heard me. His hands roamed my neck, my shoulders, my arms, and all the way to my fingers. "You're different this time," he said.

I sputtered. This time?

"You are so warm." He caressed my face.

If he could feel the heat around me, I was running out of time. "Aeson. You need to tell me where you are." I took his hand and lay it over my heart. "Not here, out there." Glancing at the window, an empty void outside of it, I looked back to him and hoped he would understand.

"Of course," he said. "I always miss you here."

"Come back. Tell me where you're hiding."

He frowned. "I am not the one hiding. You are."

I scoffed, feeling a scalding heat at my hip. "Yes. Yes, I am. I was. But I'm not now. You have to let me find you." I licked my lips. "You've never even kissed me."

"Whose failure is that? Not mine." He grinned triumphantly and I might've kissed him if I wasn't scared of waking him up. "I'm where I always am. In the rain." His nose brushed mine and his breath on my mouth was a completely different type of heat.

My brow furrowed. If rain was falling, my fire would be extinguished by now. "How can I find you in the storm?" I asked.

"They have found me already. I saw them."

My heart stopped.

"They will see to it. Trust me," he said, smiling.

I didn't understand his confidence, but right as I pushed the word "Who?" through my lips, something struck my middle and dragged me away.

Chapter Fifty Eight

I WAS FLUNG TO THE SIDE and my skin raised with bumps from the sudden cold. The light of the study was replaced by darkness. With a thud and a muffled grunt from the heap of leather that lay atop me, I hit solid ground and opened my eyes to silver painted treetops.

Hands grabbed at me, patting my clothes and wiping my hair with a wet cloth. As my lungs cleared of the witch grass, I cranked my jaw up and down. "Why did you take me away?" I pieced the question together.

Above me, Saana, Layla, and Garret exchanged a look. Offering his hand, Garret propped me back up to look at the fire. The back of Aeson's chair was gone as was the center of the seat. Logs crumbled into ash below it, and all that remained was three black posts. The last bit of chair legs.

Taking stock of myself, I began to cry. Wiping my face with the only part of my sleeve left, I folded up under half my shift. "I didn't . . . I needed more time. I couldn't understand him."

"Shh, shh." Layla pulled me close and swept the hair off my

neck. "Don't say that, Miss Etta. Garret wouldn't have pulled you out if it wasn't dire. I swear it. Give your mind a moment to quiet and we will make sense of everything together."

"Yes," came Saana's voice, touching my shoulder. "We can help you more."

I shook my head. "No, no, no, no, no."

Garret was less gentle. "What *did* you see? Was the young lord there? Did he speak to you as you'd hoped?"

"He spoke," I sobbed quietly. "It was riddles. He says he's in the rain, and they would find him."

"The rain will obscure their path, isn't that better for us?" Garret asked.

"We've had no rain." Layla looked up.

"*I know.*" I pulled myself tighter, smaller, pressing my knees into my sockets.

Saana cleared her throat and her voice pitched. "Do you think he meant them?"

My eyes flew open, and I scuffled back up, swinging my gaze about to follow her eyeline. Garret and Layla did the same. On the other side of the fire through the last little flames, four shining eyes watched us. They glowed yellow, nearly indiscernible behind the remnants of my fire. As the branches of heat licked lower, one of the foxes stood and reseated itself on the other side of its mate, blinking in our direction.

"Garret?" I breathed. "Rouse your men."

"You're sure."

I nodded. "Positive."

When he left, Layla took his place beneath me, holding me up while Saana wiped the soot from my face. I didn't dare take my eyes off the foxes, but they waited leisurely. Blinking long and slow and tapping the end of a tail occasionally.

The jangle of buckles and swords in sheaths rose, and Garret was there. The six guards at his back were all mounted. At their appearance, the cherry foxes stood and trotted away into the night. The white of their tails dropped into the black shadows. "Go," I ordered.

The men disappeared and I fell back into the grass, waiting for the slither of magic to finish its journey across my skin. I'd held on for so long that pain stretched over both arms, burning white hot. As if kissing me goodbye, blisters coated my palm, searing my cuts shut but stinging all the same. When I was sure my magic was gone, I croaked for help.

Layla and Saana helped me to my rooms, tending to my hands and washing my face again under the better light of stronger candles. Once they were sure I was comfortable, they shut the door tight and disappeared.

I managed a quick line of words asking for speed from any bit of Free magic that might listen. Whether it lingered near him or me, I knew it didn't matter.

SPRING

Chapter Fifty Nine

S LEEP HELD ME FOR DAYS. Countless days. It was not quite a punishment, but certainly a reprimand from Iya. Three Fierce spells back-to-back, all of which I had carefully avoided a greater sacrifice for, opting for different power sources instead. It seemed clear that my magic wouldn't return as fast as it had the first two times. I'd asked a lot from my patron of late, and I didn't expect anything in return other than Aeson.

Saana and Layla were there, naturally. They floated in and out of sight, obscured by the current of my sleep. I felt their care more than I witnessed it. Cool cloths to my head, water at my lips, and occasionally the shifting of my blankets.

It was late evening when my vision cracked open, clear and vigilant. There was no light to see by and I fumbled with one hand, reaching to my bedside table, hoping for a drink of some kind. Someone moved in my work room and swung the door open. Saana peered at me over a candle.

"You're awake," she said.

I paused at the statement. Clearly, I was awake. Why did she sound surprised?

Catching herself, she came closer and set the light down. "Sorry. Just, a bit of odd timing."

"I need water," I said, ignoring the strangeness. She left and came back and after guzzling an entire goblet, I wiped my mouth. "Should I have waited for a better time?"

Saana dipped her head away, crouching on the floor. "No," she said. "I think your timing is rather mystical." Her eyes gleamed. "He's barely just arrived, and his first order was *not* to wake you. Nor disturb you under any circumstances. Yet here you are."

I held my breath and replayed her words as the minutes dragged on. "Help me up."

Chapter Sixty

WITH A ROBE OVER MY SHOULDERS, I made it down the hall mostly on my own. Saana walked beside me just in case, and I had the wall to lean on. At the landing before his stairs, I sent her away. She went without argument but wore a disobedient grin.

I expected to tire halfway up the flight, but when I reached the top, I felt perfectly restored. My feet itched and I stood for far too long looking at them. Outside the tower window, fireflies danced. Shaking the curiosity off, I lay my hands on the door with sweaty palms. My heart hammered and reverberated all the way to my ears. Steeling myself, I pushed.

The squeal of the hinge went unnoticed in the chatter of the room. Aeson stood bare chested next to his writing desk. Layla was at his side, cleaning a wound on his lowest ribs. Garret stood at attention, facing away from the door and exchanging clipped words with Aeson. Prilla had laid a light dinner on another table and was trying to light a candle in between wiping her eyes.

Reeve stood farther away, a quill moving smoothly from left to right on his arm desk as he transcribed things from Garret and Aeson both.

"Oh." Prilla noticed me once she'd finally got the candle lit.

Everyone turned her way, then mine, and the chatter stopped.

"I'm sorry." I shook my head. "I didn't realize." What? What hadn't I realized? That I was not the only one who'd be anxious to see him? To check his wellbeing? To speak with him and ask which path we'd be setting ablaze for this awful attempt?

Layla recovered first and dropped into a curtsy. "My lady. You're here," she said, smartly. "I'll let you finish tending him." She held a cloth out and I had no choice but to move forward and trade places with her. The others gave their own little bows and curtsies as I crossed the room. Aeson's eyes flicked about, watching them all with fascination. I ignored it and gave Layla a wide berth as she joined Prilla a few steps away.

When I was close enough, Aeson used the drape of my robe to take my hand discreetly, squeezing so tight I couldn't tell which one of us was trembling. The pressure ignited the heat of my burns all over again, but I breathed through it. He was there. Standing in his own rooms. As he belonged. His gaze seared my neck, and I avoided it like the castle cats avoided the well. Afraid of falling. Still.

His wound wasn't deep, but it was long. A four-prong gash wrapping from back to front along the curve of his ribcage. I bent to inspect it more closely, and when I stood, I lifted his arm to rest on the knob of my shoulder. As calm as I could, I steadied one hand on his chest and washed the blood away with the other.

His abdomen rippled, flexing with tension that matched my own. We had never touched each other quite like this.

Garret prattled on about men and horses and guards and trails. All of it went unheard. A fingertip traced the curve of my neck, caressing the swoop of my ear. I nearly wept. "I told them not to wake you," he whispered.

"They didn't," I heaved, chancing to look at him at last. All his attention was on me. He didn't even pretend he was listening to Garret. It was so cavalier. The faintest little voice in my head told me to chide him for it. But my cheeks warmed like butter in summer sun, and I pressed my lips together, shaking my head again. "What is this from?" I asked, trying to focus.

"Some of their dogs didn't like me much."

I grit my teeth. "They set hounds on you?"

"They had a difficult time tracking us without them." He grinned, smug and jubilant.

"And where did you go?"

"A cavern we found behind a waterfall. Crisscrossed our trail for miles, doubled back, hiked the last bit through the riverbed and swam under the plunge to the undercut."

"You *were* in the rain." I laughed. "And you washed every bit of your scent away in the water."

He hummed like a little trumpet swell. "The foxes found us just fine."

The cloth nearly slipped out of my hand, and I pinched his side on accident, trying to close my fist around it again. Swallowing, I flicked my head to get some loose hairs from my face and fixed my eyes at the window. The moon waned outside.

"Have you always been able to do that?" he asked.

"I don't know."

"Would it work with anyone?"

I couldn't answer. Someone coughed behind us. Layla. She

stepped forward from her spot next to Prilla and I ignored the fact that we'd completely forgotten they were there. "With your permission, my lady, I'll take my leave now," she said. "Unless there is anything else you need this evening."

Rigid and annoyed, I turned no more than necessary and dismissed her.

"Me as well, my lady?" Prilla chimed next.

"Yes." I forced the words up and out of my chest. "You too, Prilla."

They both curtsied, but Layla wavered by the door. "Garret, would you escort me to the stables? The kitchen prepared extra mush for the horses you used. I must deliver it."

I rolled my eyes as Garret bowed to Aeson first, and then me. Last was Reeve, still flourishing the feather in his hand when the abrupt silence struck him. He looked up and around, stammering, "Oh. My apologies, Lord Crennly, Lady, Miss, erm. Castle witch." He bent over so suddenly he nearly dropped his arm desk, but he caught it in time and scurried out the door.

"I get lost in the countryside for a few days and you take hold of my castle," Aeson said.

I walked away to rinse the cloth in the basin, leaving his arm to flop down at his side. "It is just Layla, being cheeky," I said. "You're home now. They will forget this game in no time."

"I don't want them to."

I lolled my neck and scoffed at him over my shoulder. Wringing the water out, his blood with it, I folded the fabric with far too much attention and set it aside. Finally, I turned to lean against the table. In the intimacy of his room, I didn't know what to do with my hands. They knotted at my back, smoothed my hair, flicked a loose thread off my sleeve, then settled on bunching the sides of my robe in each fist.

He watched with half a smile before speaking again. "Are you going to greet me properly or just squirm about for the rest of the night?"

Heat swelled in my chest along with laughter and relief and a dozen other emotions I was not equipped to manage. "I've given you worse greetings."

"Dozens," he said, stepping closer. "It's all I've ever had from you."

My breath halted, snagged on the habit of always having a retort and at long last, having nothing. No words. None at all. Rocking forward, I gave my body to his and he caught me—prepared and waiting. With one arm around my back, he used the other to root his hand into my hair and pull my face to his, whispering against my mouth with one last semblance of formality.

"You promise not to hit me?" he asked.

"No."

"It is worth the risk," he chuckled.

The first touch was barely a peck of our lips. Something he could've done in the orchard all those years ago. His next kiss was braver, pulling at my mouth with his. What I imagine he would've done on the stairs if I hadn't barred the way. With his third kiss, I gave in to everything we should've done in the years between.

He tugged at every part of me. My hair, my clothes, my arms and legs. I did the same. If we winced, we apologized and found another place to lay our hands. In a matter of minutes, his mouth had mapped the curve of my jaw, down my neck, along my shoulder, and halfway up my arms, which were slung about his neck. My strength waned and my body begged to fold onto the floor, but my center begged to feel every strand of hair on his head.

I wanted him at my side. Not just to stand, but to be.

I ran my hands over him until I knew whatever was left to learn. I kissed his lips and found the bridge of his nose next, then his brow, his temple. Anything I'd memorized with my eyes, I memorized it again with my body pressed to his. He maneuvered my robe until it hung from my elbows. Caught. Just like me.

We kissed as if in the fire again. As if he were the flame, and me the ember. We were so eager and alive in it that I worried we might crumble like ash once we stopped.

His hands wandered where they wanted. I didn't stop him. One more sweep of his lips on mine and he paused for air. Neither of us crumbled, although I flinched when he lifted my hands. The burns that clung to my skin were well on their way to healing but still translucent. He kissed my palms, long and slow before searching my eyes.

"What's the matter?" The question warbled in my throat.

He led me to the chair at his writing desk, and I pulled the robe back over my shoulders as he strode across the room. I was relieved to be sitting, but he took far too long pulling a small wooden chest out of a much bigger one in the corner. Returning to kneel before me, he gulped too many times and furrowed his gaze.

"Aeson, what is it?" I scooted forward, cupping his face. "Why am I in your chair and why are you the one evading? Speaking of chairs, you need a new one for working."

Giving a burst of laughter, he nodded and swallowed again. "Yes, I was told as much. But this one is unburnt, and it's still mine to decide who sits in it." He smiled at last and pulled himself closer to me, steadying whatever was on his mind. Lifting the little chest from his lap to mine, he turned it, so the hook faced me. My fingers itched and I kept my eyes on his face as I slid the arm out of its hoop and propped the dark wooden lid on its hinges. When I finally looked down, my belly dropped.

"No," I said.

"Yes," he argued.

"No." I shook my head. "No, no, no. No, Aeson. No."

"Etta." He would appeal no matter what I said. "Look at this year. Look what has happened. We cannot do this separately any longer. This protects everyone. You and the people both. One target, perhaps, but a much stronger one."

Jaw agape, I looked at the silken pillow inside the chest. It cradled two silver cuff bracelets. Each of them emblazoned with the Crennly crest. One was wide and made with the circumference to fit a man's wrist. The other was narrower. It was hammered with more intricacy and made to fit a woman.

"Say something." Aeson pulled at my shift.

"We will be exactly as the shepherd accused us." I heard my voice, but I didn't feel it.

"Etta, we already have been. That is my point."

Nudging him out of the way, I set the chest on the table with the water basin. Then I paced in a squiggly circle, turning around and around until I was dizzy. Aeson stopped me with hands at my waist.

He exhaled. "I told you. You would run out of time one day. We are here. I'm sorry." He kissed my cheeks, pressing hard into the parts that weren't scarred. "If I could give you more time I would, but we have only this. This path."

I shook my head and pushed out of his arms, reaching for the door. "You are tired. I am more than tired. Let us rest and we will find another path."

He stepped around and blocked my way, lifting my hands with his like we were already binding ourselves to one another. "I am in love with you. And I will not be looking for another path." Letting his words settle, he studied my face before venturing on. "I know you don't want to hear that. But I have just spent days thinking I might not get to tell you, or worse, never see you wrestle and resist it." He let go of my hands to take my waist again, leaning to kiss the corner of my mouth. "If you won't reply, I will simply command it of you."

The heat of him got to me and I growled, eyes closed. "You have never commanded me."

"You're right," he said. "I like you better this way. But this answer I must have, Etta." He may have needed my answer, but he took the breath of my reply, kissing me again. Pushing the robe back over my shoulders, it slid down my back to the floor. He guided me to the edge of his bed, gathering more of my night shift in his hand. "Stay. Tonight, and every night. Please."

I resisted a remark that I was figuratively with him in the castle every night. We'd always been together. Even when we were apart, I now knew. But he was right. Apart wasn't going to work anymore. We needed to be stronger. Surrendering a little more, I gripped his hair with both hands and laid my temple with his.

"You said yourself, we need rest," he reasoned relentlessly.

"I can rest perfectly fine in my own bed," I told him.

"You will rest much better with me, I promise." He kissed me more.

"That seems doubtful."

He laughed as I smirked, and my resolve vanished at the sound. Then he swept my hair up and held my face to his and smiled just as he had in our dream. I had to give in. I would have gone mad otherwise.

Pulling me into bed, he tucked me beneath his chin and fit our bodies together. "None of this will seem so daunting in the morning, believe me," he said.

I inhaled his resolute belief and exhaled my uncertainties. The candles burned out on their own, and the food went forgotten. When the moonlight finished painting grey pillars across the floor and I was positive he'd fallen asleep, I kissed his collarbone and said, "I am in love with you too."

He pulled me tighter instantly. "You are a witch."

Last Chapter

TO MY HORROR, I woke to the sound of maids shuffling around in the room. Fluttering my lashes, I held my breath against the sounds of dishes clinking and drapes being pulled aside. Liquid was poured into a cup and a pitcher set down. All while Aeson slept at my back, scooped like a ladle with one arm across my middle. Unawares.

My pulse thrummed through every bone and muscle and joint and, moving slower than ever before, I rolled over and pinched him awake. He parted one eye and scowled for a second before looking over me beneath his covers and grinning instead.

I pinched him again and clenched my teeth, pointing above the blankets towards the noise. He tilted his head a little and listened. Then he shrugged. I grumbled and slipped lower, tapping a finger on his chest, too rattled to even appreciate what he looked like half naked. He was taut and muscled, as I might have imagined. I knew well that he hadn't had trouble swinging a sword in years.

When the maids finally left, I bolted upright, shoving off his bedcovers to escape. His arms found me across the folds, nonetheless. "Where are you going?"

"To my rooms, before anyone else—"

The door opened again, held by a sandy haired maid with her head turned towards the hall still. "Hush Rawley, I only forgot the—oh. I'm sorry my Lord. Lady. Lord Crennly."

Rawley, whoever she was, appeared next. She had short black hair and full cheeks. I loosely recalled them. They'd both seen me, seasons ago, for anklets of course. And here they saw me again. Frozen in place. Aeson's arms tangled around my body. Abed together.

I thawed, exhaling an icy breath. "Get. Out."

Aeson coughed behind me, but it sounded much more like a chuckle.

The sandy one glanced between me and the window table. Dashing across the room, she grabbed the goblet from last night and disappeared. "Sorry," she repeated, pushing her companion out the door and slamming it shut.

I dug my way out of the bed and swiped my robe off the floor. Yanking it over my back, I pulled my hair free and reached for the door handle. Aeson stopped me by laying a wide palm on the panels and leaning with all his weight. His chest shook, resisting amusement. If he didn't already have a wound on his body, I might've bitten him. Then again, he'd probably enjoy it. Worse, given the way his chest flexed with each wave of laughter, I might enjoy it too.

"You shouldn't have sent them off." He steadied his voice. "We could have asked for discretion. Now *everyone* will know by the time they reach the second floor. Although, I am sure Saana noticed you never returned last night."

I chewed my lip, eyes burning. "And what will they all think?"

"They will think that eight years of hostility has come to an end."

"You think this keeps you safe from hostility?" I snapped back into myself.

He pulled me in, leering. "Only for a little while, I hope." When I didn't respond, he frowned and used both hands to hold my face. "Etta, you are the most confident woman I've ever known. Why do you worry about this? Why can't you see they all love you as I do?"

I didn't reply. I wasn't blind. Only disbelieving.

"Don't think your lack of a true answer has gone unnoticed either."

Despite the gossip that surely burned on the other side of the door, I giggled. Aeson knew me far too well. Which meant he knew my answer, but he wasn't about to let me go without admitting it aloud. "Rest," I said. "Please."

His eyes narrowed and his arms locked at my back, carrying me over to the desk. Setting me down, he plucked the smaller of the two cuffs from the cushion and pressed it into my hand. "I will rest when you stop running."

It dawned on me the maids would have seen the pair of bracelets first and discovered me second. Which would guide them to only one conclusion. Mortified, I pinched my eyes shut and held the marriage bauble to my chest. "I need the morning to put this at peace in my mind."

"The morning." His voice was firm.

"I swear it." I opened my eyes again and looked at him, earnest. On my tip toes, I wrapped both arms around his neck and kissed him, hoping Free magic might assuage his worries. And mine. When I pulled back, he was wary, but he didn't stop me as I slipped out the door.

At first glance, I thought I was safely alone in my rooms. Then Arlo popped up from a cavern of ferns he'd made in the alcove. "Miss Etta," he exclaimed, grinning. "What are you doing over there?"

I drew a sharp breath and glanced at my robe. "I was outside. In the garden."

"Saana said you woke up, but she said not to bother you neither." He rolled his eyes, none the wiser, and scuffled forward on all fours to tilt his head up. "Look at this. It's about to fall out. Can you see?" His upper lip lifted in a doggish snarl, and he wiggled a tooth with his tongue.

"Yes, Arlo. I can see." I knelt beside him, leaving the door open.

"When it comes out, I want to carry it in my pocket like a token, but Saana says I can't."

"And where is Saana?" I asked, dragging in a long breath.

"Just down in the kitchen." He shrugged. "That angry kitchen woman asks her to help almost every morning."

"Prilla?" I chuckled lightly. "She can be a bit impatient, can't she?"

"Don't listen to him." Saana appeared in the hall. "He's upset because she's caught him stealing sweets from the pantry, thrice over."

I lowered my gaze at Arlo, but he held his nose to the air, guilt free. Saana stepped around us, laying a plate of bread and butter down. "Are you just returning, Miss Etta?"

Catching her eyes fast, I nodded. "Yes. From my walk in the garden."

Standing where Arlo couldn't see, she looked at my bedroom door, which was still hanging as she'd left it and then my clothes. "And how was the garden?"

"It was—it *is* fine," I said. For different reasons, the pair of them smirked at me and my shoulders fell. "It is happy and flourishing," I added. "And what have you two been filling your days with?"

Smiling, Saana answered, "Trying to serve in your place as best we can. We've stocked your shelves with the things we could identify for sure. And we've administered some remedies to the few that have asked."

"That's not all," Arlo blurted out, bulging his eyes. "Saana is learning how to fight."

I looked to her, and she shrugged, joining us on the floor. "I don't want to be unable if certain situations arise again," she explained. "The guards are more than happy to show me how to wield a knife."

"I'm sure they are," I said. It was my turn to smirk.

Laughing, she glanced at her brother before going on. "Some of them have asked how to pleat a skirt in exchange for the lessons they offer. But I'm afraid I don't make a very good sewing instructor." She winked wickedly.

Arlo sneered. "Why would anyone want lessons from you? You can't even boil the porridge right at home. Mello always has to do it."

Saana and I snorted with laughter. It felt good to smile. The spring held great promise to me but making sure the Shepherds had a comfortable life was quickly becoming a priority. Thinking of Aeson's proposal, I sighed and looked at the younger of my two companions. "Arlo?" I asked. "Which sweets are your favorite?"

He sat straight, eyes going a bit vacant. "Those cinnamon twists that she dips in chocolate."

"Mm." I leaned forward to whisper in his ear, "Go tell Prilla that I'm awake, and I'm craving two of them. She'll give you both and you can have one for yourself. I promise."

Scrambling out the door, he disappeared. Saana and I sat for another moment in silence. When I stood and made my way to the plants, she followed. "I found the spell you wrote for my da."

I paused in my reach for the water pail, unsure what to make of her discovery.

"You gave him a purpose after all," she said.

Smiling, I found her eyes. "You were smart to think of it before me."

"I didn't think of it. Leastways, not exactly that." Saana shook her head. "I had wondered, will the same thing need to be done for Henrick?"

My brow puckered. "You needn't fret about him."

"Could I try it?" she asked, coming to my side and practically pushing me onto my stool. She took over the watering but kept talking. "I know it would only be Free magic, but perhaps if I were the one to lay him to rest, his spirit might help us? To make amends."

"What help are you thinking of?"

"The earth around your pear tree, Miss Etta. Your fire burned deep."

Once more, her idea showed good intent. I'd burned away

one symbol of love. It was only right to replace it with another no matter how meager it was. Nodding at last, I said, "Speak to Garret. Tell him you have my permission. Then you'll have to rewrite the spell to suit Henrick."

"Of course." Her cheeks went rosy, inspired at the opportunity. She set the water bucket down and glanced at the door. Arlo hadn't returned yet. "Is there anything else you need?" she asked.

From outside, a muted applause from within the courtyard came through on a breeze. I smoothed my hair back. Reaching for the weight of metal in my pocket, I laid it in my lap for Saana to see. "Yes, in fact," I trembled. "I need to get ready."

Arlo never returned at all. Most likely, he'd found a stable hand to lead him around on a pony. Even more likely, he was wiggling his loose tooth a few inches from their eyeball.

Knowing better than to drag me through torment, Saana kept quiet company with me. She helped fill a tub to wash me in and treated my burns with the healing salve. My hair went up in a circlet at the back of my head and she pinned the tail down its center to mimic the winding slither of a snake. Happy with her work, she stood back and glanced at the silver cuff I'd been spinning in my hand all morning.

"Would you like me to fetch him for you?" she asked, adjusting the lay of my pale green kirtle at the shoulders.

"No," I said. "He'll know where to find me."

And he did. Of course. When I heard him coming, I stood up from the pocket of earth and hid my hands behind my back, spinning the new metal around one wrist. He approached with his arms folded and stopped a fair distance away, looking me over. "I've been told you burned your purple dress in the casting," he said. "You will need a new one."

"I burned your favorite coat as well."

"You mean *your* favorite coat."

I scrunched my face up and looked to the stream, but I didn't confess anything.

"Do you miss it?" he asked.

I found his worried eyes and offered a simple smile. "It gets easier each time."

He nodded, biting his bottom lip. "I agree." He watched my smile grow, then turned to dig at something in his coat pocket and reveal it with his left hand. "This fell from one of our ambushers before we fled. When you are ready, perhaps you could write another spell, to discover our foes."

It was a tiny brown vial. Identical to those I had found at the willow tree.

My grin played out before I could stop it. "And what shall we do when we discover them?"

He shrugged. "I was hoping the Lady Crennly would have an idea."

"They will come at us again. With more force, I'm sure."

Aeson beamed. "I expect them to. But they won't choose one or the other. It is *us*, right?"

Relenting, I dropped my hands out from behind my back. Clutching my right arm to my middle, I bent the left at the elbow and tapped my foot. Then I waited with my forearm straight up so he could see the silver crested cuff fitted to my wrist.

I highly doubt Old Jaeson imagined his wartime prize would be the woman to wear it, but I never imagined his illegitimate son would disassemble all the walls I had so carefully mortared.

Aeson's jaw ticked and mischief rose in his eyes. When he lifted his right hand, he was already wearing his. It would mirror my left when we stood side by side.

"Aeson," I simmered.

"What?" He grinned sheepishly, taking my hand and pulling me to his chest.

"Have you been wearing that all morning?"

He nodded. Vigorously.

"For everyone to see?"

Again, he nodded, filled to the brim with roguish confidence. I shook my head and pushed by him to the orchard. Gleeful, he trotted after and grasped my hand again before the remnants of our fire. "The Elder Lords wanted me married and so I shall be. My mother will be just as relieved."

I nearly blew away in the breeze. Looking to the fields, I knotted a finger through the loop of my necklaces. "Perhaps we should give this more time? A few seasons at least."

He shook his head twice. "Why would you keep this happiness from them?"

Even without Iya, I felt the energy coursing off Aeson in streams. Amusement yes, but pride also. Joy and relief and bliss and most of all, hope. I fended off a flutter in my chest, which stirred like bees in their hive. At ease and at home. He turned me and pressed our heads together, folding his fingers into mine but still careful not to disturb my injuries.

"Etaine," he started, ignoring an incredulous eye roll from

me. "Witch of Castle Crennly, please stand beside me. Make these people yours, properly and truly. They need you as their witch, and I need you as my wife. Give me this relief. If you swear to worry about our people and our love every day, I will swear to protect both."

I exhaled and pulled his mouth to mine in clear view of everything. Cold air lifted from the earth as the castle and the pear trees watched me give the last of my trust to him for safe keeping. When at last I pulled away, he refused.

"Say yes," he murmured. I shook my head and he repeated himself. "Say. Yes."

I held out a minute longer before yielding. "Yes." I bit the corner of his mouth. "Yes, Aeson. Yes."

We joined together with my hands in his hair and his cuff on my wrist. When at last we drew new breath, I held his face and swept a thumb over his lips, warmed pink from kissing.

"I still think we should give it a year."

ETTA AND AESON WILL CONTINUE
THEIR JOURNEY IN BOOK TWO

ACKNOWLEDGEMENTS

Peanut, you already have the dedication, but you deserve first billing here as well. Thank you for reading every ugly draft of everything that has ever left my head. This is nothing like what we planned but it feels better this way, don't you think?

To my husband, it's a good thing you and the kids like ramen because we'd all be really hungry without it. Thank you for tolerating me as I hog the kitchen table to draft, rewrite, and edit these stories into something tangible. For book two, please stop thinking your insight isn't helpful. You might not 'know' story, but you know people and that's the same thing.

Dexter, if you ever read this, just know that trusting your creativity is the most important part. I'm proud of whatever medium you choose. Tell the stories you want to tell.

Titus, Aeson's messy hair came straight from you, my love. You may be daddy's exact imprint but bringing you into this world is one of my proudest accomplishments. Follow your feelings, big guy.

Sebastian, everyone in this world is better upon meeting you. I don't understand your magic, but I know it's somewhere in these pages because you are honest and intentional with every fiber of your existence.

To my parents, I'm sorry I spent so much of my college fund on those other degrees. This is where I have always belonged. Your support in this new endeavor, however, is priceless — see what I did there? Dad, I know this business of creation isn't quite the numbers game you excel at, but your curiosity is important to me. Mom, thank you for taking my stories in stride. It's one thing to watch your child grow and express themselves, it's another to read their writing and see it as a separate entity. I've said it before and I'll say it again, I never knew how lucky I was until I heard other people talk about their mothers. What a gift you are.

Nicole, thank you for being my sister not just in spirit but in words. The memory of sitting on your living room carpet and talking through this book is one of many I never thought I could earn in this lifetime. I am stupidly blessed to have you so close and so understanding. You can tell me when it's over if the high was worth the pain.

To Shannon, my cold, wintery heart does not deserve you either. I sincerely believe there's a special place in writer heaven for the established authors who make themselves available to those of us just starting out and that means you. Thank you for manifesting me into your life and taking me seriously when I arrived. *flicks cheek*

Emmaline, my Tolkien white girl. Being called your colleague in anything is a freaking honor. I cannot believe I get to write alongside a mind like yours. Thank you for your critical eye and what it sees in my silly little stories. I hope I remain your Lewis through all our pages together.

My other betas, Stella, Erin, and Rebecca, I am begrudgingly grateful. All three of you pounded on the door to my email until I gave you a copy and that's the kind of insane fandom only people like Robert Pattinson get to experience. (He's the one from Twilight, Rebecca)

To the other Erin, thank you for taking me on as a client and reading my words. Aspects of this book are definitely much cleaner, courtesy of your industry experience. All I can say is the cliché. You made me a better writer. I'm sorry we disagree about the word "scoot" though.

Emerson. Holy shit. How did I get so lucky to find an artist like you!? You brought Etta and Aeson and their world to life so perfectly and never once batted an eye at my ideas. Thank you for putting up with all my tiny detail requests. You will do incredible things with your art. I just know it. But also, I'm keeping you on retainer.

For the multitude of weirdos I have met on Instagram, what a strange place to have found the people that understand me best. I love and appreciate you all for your many idiosyncrasies and quirks. You love Dog Vader, you peruse Meme Monday, and you're always so invested in Food Discourse. I hope you like this book. I know it might not be what you expected of me; I wish I could explain the romance, but I don't know how to without exposing the parts of me kept hidden for safety and sanity. You make it easier though, you do. Please stay with me on this ride.

ABOUT THE AUTHOR

Credit: Images by Rachel

Madeleine Elizabeth was raised in New England and spent her childhood barefoot in the trees with her favorite book of fairy tales and, later, all of Steinbeck's novellas. She attended college in Prescott, Arizona, and later at Southern New Hampshire University, where she received a bachelors in fiction. She remains in Arizona with her husband, three boys, a very spoiled Akita, and far too many British classics. When she's not writing she's baking something from the Great British Bake Off that no amateur should ever attempt. You can follow her writing updates on Instagram and Facebook.

www.ingramcontent.com/pod-product-compliance
Lightning Source LLC
Chambersburg PA
CBHW021404310726
48971CB00005B/1193